THE *Loyalties* WE BREAK

KATELYN TAYLOR

PLAYLIST

Trevor's Playlist
Best I Ever Had by Drake
Unforgettable by French Montana, Swae Lee
Believer by Imagine Dragons
All I Do Win by DJ Khaled
Not Afraid by Eminem
Gangsta's Paradise by Coolio, L.V.
See You Again by Wiz Khalifa, Charlie Puth
7 Years by Lukas Graham
Thunder by Imagine Dragons
Young, Wild & Free by Snoop Dogg, Wiz Khalifa & Bruno Mars
My House by Flo Rida

Erica's Playlist
Shut Up and Dance by WALK THE MOON
Cake By The Ocean by DNCE
Sugar by Maroon 5
Love Me Like You Do by Ellie Goulding
Shape of You by Ed Sheeran
She's Kinda Hot by 5 Seconds of Summer
Girls Like You by Maroon 5, Cardi B

Closer by The Chainsmokers, Halsey
Blank Space by Taylor Swift
Roar by Katy Perry
Pick Me Up by Gabby Barrett
Wake Me Up by Avicii

Sebastian's Playlist
Paralyzer by Finger Eleven
Last Resort by Papa Roach
Coming Undone by KORN
I Stand Alone by Godsmack
Down With The Sickness by Disturbed
Undead by Hollywood Undead
Dragula by Rob Zombie
Lift Me Up by Five Finger Death Punch, Rob Halford
In The End by Linkin Park
Remember The Name by Fort Minor, Styles of Beyond
Click Click Boom Saliva
Headstrong by Trapt

The Loyalties We Break

Written by Katelyn Taylor

Published by Katelyn Taylor

Cover art by Sammi Bee Designs

Formatted by Katelyn Taylor

The Loyalties We Break is a work of fiction. Names, characters, incidents, and places are used fictitiously. Any resemblance to real people or events is coincidental.

DEDICATION

To anyone who has ever been torn in two.
This one is for you.

PROLOGUE

ERICA

8 Years Ago

It's move in day. A day that has been planned for practically years but is only just now happening. My parents finally made the move to open their own law firm all the way across the country to a city called Grovebury, Oregon. A friend of theirs that they went to law school with lives out here and urged them that the market was just as booming but not nearly as competitive as it was in New York.

I made my displeasure known. What ten year old wants to leave behind all of their friends and everything that they have ever known to move to the other side of America? Not this one, that's for sure. Of course, my arguments fell on deaf ears. There is no winning arguments with them, they are literally professional arguers. One of these days I am going to finally win, maybe.

They promised that this was the best move for our family and for my future, but I don't buy that crap for a second. Kicking at the stray piece of bark in the driveway over to the perfectly manicured garden, I squint my eyes up and look over the mansion of a house we are moving into. Money seems to go a lot farther out here than in New York.

I hear the shrill but very authoritative tone of my mother ordering around the movers as if they were her personal assistants while my father barks into the phone to some unfortunate soul. I've been on the receiving end of his verbal lashings more times than I can count.

Don't get me wrong. They love me. They always make sure I have the best things, the nicest clothes, and the healthiest food. It isn't their fault. It's just the way they are. It's just in their nature. The only reason I notice it not being normal is from seeing the way my friends at school and their parents interacted. My mother used to call them tad poles while she constantly reminded me that Pembrooke's are sharks, they weren't even in the same league as us. I liked them all the same, but mother said one day that would change. Whatever.

As I make my way down our long driveway and out to the private cul-de-sac at the end, I suddenly hear several loud laughs and cheers. Curiously, my eyes follow the noise down the road a bit to see several boys maybe a few years older than me playing football. They look like they are having fun and playing football seems a lot better than standing around while the movers put our stuff away.

Making up my mind, I throw my shoulders back, lift my chin high and begin marching towards them. My mother always says that if you want to compete in a man's world, you have to prove you belong there. So, that is exactly what I do.

I have never actually played football, I'm not really sure how to even do it. I have only ever seen it on TV, but it didn't look too complicated. How hard could it be?

Five pairs of eyes all swing towards me when I am only a few feet away from them. They all look at me with blank stares, causing my stomach to clench for a moment in nerves. I can practically hear my mother's words in my ear. 'Don't show weakness, Erica. Never let them see you sweat.' Straightening my stance, I raise my chin a little higher before I look around at the group.

"I'm going to play," I say firmly, leaving no room for discussion.

As if they planned it, each boy bursts out into laughter at the same time. One boy even leans over like he can't breathe because he is laughing so hard.

"No. Why don't you go play with your barbies, little girl," one obnoxiously tall, dark-haired boy says.

The rest of the boys begin to laugh once again as my cheeks burn with embarrassment no matter how hard I try to push it away. Tucking a piece of my bright red hair behind my ear, I glance down at my shoes. Maybe this was a mistake. I'm not a shark, not like my parents. Maybe I should just go back inside.

"Shut it," a boy snaps as he walks from the house next to mine, making his way to the middle of the group.

He is wearing a red t-shirt and a pair of shorts with some tennis shoes. He has golden blond hair and the bluest eyes that I have ever seen. They look just like the ocean that my parents took me to yesterday when we first got to this coastal city.

The laughing stops almost immediately as he comes to stand only a foot away from me. I stand as still as possible, licking my lips nervously as he looks me over from head to toe.

"Have you played before?"

I want to be honest and tell him the truth. Something tells me he wouldn't laugh or tease me like the others obviously would. I don't want the boys to have more things to make fun of me for, though. So, I bite the inside of my cheek, nod my head, and roll my shoulders back again to look like I am way more confident than I actually am.

His eyes narrow on me for a moment before he nods at the boy with the ball. The ball is tossed at him, and he catches it easily. Turning back to me, the blond boy hands me the ball.

"Let's see what you got."

Crap.

Thinking about what all the players look like on the TV, I take a step back still facing the group before I pull my arm back and throw it as hard as I can. It doesn't spin perfectly like on the TV, but it does go pretty far. So far that the boy that told me to go play with my barbies can't even run fast enough to catch it.

The boys that were laughing at me all look at me with wide eyes and opened mouths while the blond boy turns to me with a wide smile that makes his eyes twinkle like shining stars. He reaches out, hooking my pinky with his as he pulls me over to the other guys.

"I'm Trevor, and you are definitely on my team, Little Red."

Chapter One

Erica

"I wish you would have just come down with me. I don't like you driving this far by yourself," Trevor's deep voice rumbles through my car speakers.

I roll my eyes as I cruise down the highway. "Trev, it's like a four hour drive. It isn't a big deal. Plus, you had to get back for football. I would have been bored on campus by myself."

He is so protective somedays. I swear, he worries more than my mother. Granted, she doesn't often worry herself with much outside of the courtroom but that is beside the point. Trevor Michaels has been my best friend since I was ten years old. We were practically attached at the hip from that first day on, apart from the last few years.

"I always worry about you, Little Red," Trevor says with a sigh like he doesn't enjoy his protective streak any more than I do.

I used to hate that nickname as a kid. I was so self-conscious of my bright red hair. It was just so different than everyone else I knew. Both of my parents were natural blondes, and I was just the odd redhead of the Pembrooke family.

"I know. Who needs an overbearing big brother when I have you?" I joke.

He lets out a strangled noise that sounds like a choke crossed with a laugh. I hear him mutter something along the lines about me having a smart mouth, but I don't hear it well enough to know for sure.

Though we are just friends now, it wasn't always like that. Trevor is your perfect All-American boy, always has been. He comes from a good family, has a huge heart and is the football superstar that every teenage guy wishes he could be.

He is devastatingly handsome with his blond hair, blue eyes and athletic build. Pair that with a smile that has girls throwing their panties at him during games (literally, that happened one time) and he is practically irresistible. I would have had to of been blind not notice how attractive my best friend had gotten over the years.

At the end of 8th grade, we had a formal dance at school and Jimmy Kowlitz had asked me to go with him. I was so excited and spent hours getting ready for my first official date, but the little weasel never showed up. He ended up deciding to skip the dance and *forgot* that he had a date that was waiting on him.

So, there I was sitting on the front porch all dolled up and devastated that I was being stood up. I sat there for hours until headlights blinded me before a familiar car pulled up. Trevor was two years older than me, so he was already driving. His car was practically a permanent fixture in our driveway despite him living just next door. His dad had bought him a Camaro for his 16th birthday, and Trevor treated it like it was his first born child.

Trevor got out of the car with a smile on his face that dropped as soon as he saw my tear-streaked cheeks. I told him about how I wasn't able to get a hold of Jimmy and how I felt too embarrassed to go back inside and tell my parents. He didn't say a word, just took my hand in his and walked me over to his car, opening my door for me before getting in and driving away. He took me to Moe's, a greasy little drive-in place with the best burgers and shakes in Grovebury.

We sat on the hood of his car and talked for a while and soon I had forgotten all about Jimmy Kowlitz or the 8th grade formal. Then when he took my hand and pulled me against his chest, something felt different. He locked his pinky with mine like we had done since we were kids and butterflies flew through my chest as his eyes locked onto mine before he leaned in and took my first kiss.

From that night on, we were closer than ever and the *It* couple for a few years. That is until a month before he was set to go to Brighton U in southern California. He got accepted to the university with one of the best football programs in the country. It was his dream and four long hours away from Grovebury and me.

He decided it was best that we go back to being just friends since he didn't want to do the whole long-distance thing. I was heartbroken at the time, and it almost tore us apart. I was upset that he didn't love me enough to try but I was also petrified that breaking up meant I would lose my best friend. He was my first everything, and I didn't want those memories to be tarnished with awkward hellos and ignored phone calls down the road.

It took a little while, but we were finally able to get back to being just Trevor and Erica. We texted and called occasionally and when he would come to town to visit his parents, we would hang out just like old times, minus the make out sessions in his car.

It was amazing how easy it ended up being for us to go back to just friends. I dated a few guys after him but nothing too serious while he mainly slept around campus. At least, that's what I hear.

That was two years ago, and now I am finally off to college at Brighton U myself. It is where both of my parents went to college, and it was always expected that I would go there too. It honestly wasn't my first choice, or my second, or my third. But going to school with Trevor makes it a little better and if it gets me out of my parent's house, I will take it.

Trevor seemed different this summer. Over the last few years while he has been at college we naturally drifted apart, but this summer he stuck to me like glue for the few weeks he was home before he had to go back for football practice. Where we would normally hangout here and there when he came back to town when he wasn't chasing girls around, we hung out every single day with not another woman in sight.

When he offered to drive me back to Brighton with him a couple of weeks ago, I almost considered it. But I would have had to crash with him since I wouldn't have been able to move into my dorm yet and I still hadn't even finished packing and definitely needed the extra time to get everything sorted.

I can't deny that a teeny tiny part of me held a torch for Trevor over the years. What we had was so strong, so unbreakable. I guess that's what happens when you date your childhood best friend. No one has ever come close in comparison. I gave up hope of us ever being together again a while ago, but the idea of what if has drifted through my mind a few times now that we are both on the same campus. Then again, it's probably for the best for us to stay just friends. I don't know if I could handle another heartbreak like before.

"So, when will you be here?" Trevor asks, shaking me out of my thoughts.

I peek at my GPS before smirking. "I will be there at 6:38PM, just like I told you five minutes ago."

He huffs impatiently. "Okay fine, I get it. I'm bugging you. I'll let you go on one condition."

"Hmm?"

"You have to come to a party tonight with me."

I sigh. "Trev, by the time I get unpacked I am going to want to just go to sleep. I have my first lecture at 7AM tomorrow."

"Well, that is your first mistake. Who willingly volunteers for a 7AM lecture?"

"Blame my mother. She said that if I didn't get into Professor Harper's Econ class she would just die of embarrassment. Apparently, he is a personal friend, and the class is very desirable. Anything to beef up my law school applications when the time comes."

He laughs lightly. "Ah, Mrs. Pembrook," he muses lightly, probably thankful that she isn't his mother.

I know the feeling.

"Well, just come by for a little at least, please," he practically begs in that tone he knows I can't say no to.

"I'll think about it."

"That isn't a no," he says triumphantly.

"It isn't a yes either," I argue.

"Yeah, yeah whatever. Okay, drive safe. Let me know if you need any help unpacking. I will text you the details for the party. You better be there."

"Okay I'm hanging up now. See you, Trev."

"See ya, Little Red."

I chuckle and shake my head as I hang up. He never takes no for an answer, I swear. If him and every other person in Grovebury, apart from his parents, weren't counting on him going into the NFL, I would suggest that he should be the one going to law school, not me.

The rest of the drive goes by pretty quick and soon I am pulling up to Brighton U. I have visited a couple of times and came to a few of Trevor's games, but it feels different now. This is my school for the next four years and as liberated and free as I should feel, it seems like just a different set of boxes to complete on the ever growing list my parents have created for me.

After a few trips to my car and up to my room, which is all the way up on the fourth floor, I finally have all of my stuff unpacked and neatly put away. I am a bit OCD and like everything to have a certain place or I literally can't function. The empty double bed across from mine and the blank half of the room makes me wonder if my roommate dropped out or is just getting in late.

Not three seconds later, a short girl with long brown hair comes bursting through the door, boxes piled so high that she can't even see where she is going. She is about to lose what looks like a lava lamp when I jump in and catch it.

"Ah! Thanks. That would have been a mess that I really don't feel like cleaning up," she says as she walks over to the empty bed and dumps all of her things on top of the mattress.

She turns to look at me with a bright smile and wide hazel eyes. "Hi! I'm Palmer. You're Erica, right?"

I nod and smile. "Yeah, nice to meet you."

"You too! And this is my boyfriend, Ethan," she says as a guy walks through the door, his arms filled with gauzy fabric, twinkle lights and god knows what else.

"Hey," he greets with a polite smile as he puts Palmer's things onto the bed before stealing a kiss that quickly turns heated. I feel slightly uncomfortable as they begin to ravage each other's faces like the world is ending and I finally turn away, fiddling with one of my textbooks before I hear a giggle from the other side of the room.

"Sorry. We are pretty affectionate. That makes some people weird. I would say we will work on it, but we've tried," she shrugs with an unapologetic smile that makes me chuckle at her honesty.

"Alright, well thanks for the warning. Just leave a sock on the door if you ever need alone time," I joke.

She laughs before pulling out a sparkly scarf. "Way ahead of you, girlfriend. Feel free to use it if you need some alone time this year too," she winks.

I nod. I'm not exactly a prude or anything, I mean, I have had sex. First with Trevor and then with my boyfriend Nick. That relationship only lasted a few months though and ended when I very embarrassingly had to go get an STD panel done since I found out that he was cheating on me with several other girls who had to get several rounds of antibiotics. Trevor about lost it when he found out. I had to do everything in my power to convince him not to drive all the way up to Grovebury and kick Nick's ass.

Thankfully, I had nothing but a bruised ego and a bad taste in my mouth from the idea of dating. But I'm in college now and I'm trying to put past experiences behind me and look forward to new ones. So, maybe I will be using the sparkly scarf in my future, that is what college is all about, right? Doing things you wouldn't normally? Discovering who you are? Sleeping with a ton of different people? Okay maybe that is just what I have seen on my favorite rom coms, but they can't be too off base.

In the 38 minutes that I have known her I will say this about Palmer, she is probably the most authentic person I have ever met. She is a little crazy but has a no bullshit attitude, which is refreshing since my life growing up was pretty much nothing but bullshit.

With her boyfriend's help, Palmer hung up the gauzy material and twinkle lights from the ceiling, with my permission of course, as well as a very cool tye dyed tapestry. All of her is vibrant and full of life. The best way to describe her style would be preppy boho. Is that a thing? When you look at my side of the room versus hers, it is almost laughable how plain and boring I seem to be in comparison. My mothers stern voice floats through my head.

Plain is appropriate. Plain is respectable.

Once everything is set up and put away, I turn to my dresser to pull out my pajamas. Palmer's eyebrows dip as she watches me.

"What are you doing?" She asks.

"Getting ready for bed. I have an early morning tomorrow."

"Ew, that sucks. But still, there are too many good parties happening to just sit inside. Come out with us!" She says with an excited gleam in her eyes.

I open my mouth to tell her that I am tired and that I just want to go to bed, but the puppy dog look she is giving me reminds me of Trevor and makes me feel guilty for wanting to blow him off. He seemed really excited to see me and it would be nice to hang out with him even if we did just see each other a few weeks ago. So, with a begrudging sigh and a nod I close my drawer and gesture towards the door.

Palmer claps her hands excitedly as she loops an arm through Ethan's before we are out the door. I feel a little underdressed to go to a party, but it isn't like they have a dress code. I'm not wearing anything bad. I have a pair of nicely fitted dark wash jeans and my favorite white t-shirt. I even slipped on my favorite pair of bright red high heels before we left. Palmer though is rocking a gorgeous black off the shoulder crop top with a pair of tight jean shorts and wedged sandals.

I told them that my friend invited me to a party, and when I showed them the address, Ethan's eyes widened in shock.

"Oh shit, we have to go! Those guys throw the best parties."

Ethan is a Junior this year, same as Trevor so I take his word for it, and we turn in the direction of the party. We pass a couple of other parties on our way, each looking crazier than the next. Then again, maybe this is just what normal parties look like.

I never partied much in high school. I couldn't risk putting a black mark on the good Pembrooke name. Internally rolling my eyes at myself, I shake my head as we walk through the slightly chilled night.

When we walk up the front steps and onto the wide front porch of a two-story home with the address Trevor sent me, I look up to the large door that is practically vibrating from the thumping music inside. This is it. New year, new start. Freshman year, here I come.

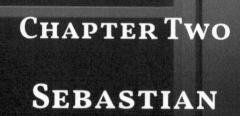

CHAPTER TWO

SEBASTIAN

I tip back my bottle to drain the last bit of beer before tossing it into the trash. I normally stick to water during football season, but it is the first party of the year, so I figured fuck it. Plus, my best friend and team quarterback, Trevor, is so wound up I feel like I have to get drunk just to handle his anxious babbling.

"She should be here by now," he huffs as he checks his phone for the 47th time tonight.

"Chill out. If you don't stop bouncing your knee, it's gonna fall off. You're fucking putting me on edge," I say as I pop the top off another beer and pass it to him.

He shakes his head dismissively and begins to type out yet another message. Ever since he got back to campus a few weeks ago, he has been going on and on about this girl from his hometown, Erica. I guess they used to date but split when he came to Brighton. Trevor has always been a ladies' man on campus, so it surprises me that he seems all twisted over this chick. Something in him changed this summer though, he seems, I don't know...different.

"I just miss her, man," he says with a sigh as he pushes away yet another drunk sorority girl that is currently rubbing herself against him.

Ah, the burden of being an up and coming superstar.

Trevor and I met in the spring before freshman year on a tour of training with the team, and we've been practically brothers ever since. I am a starting tight end for the Brighton Knights and was offered a fancy *free* college education to play football. I love the game. It is everything to me and is the only thing left in my life that I give a shit about, so when I got that offer letter I was floored.

Since I came to Brighton, I have had two goals. Get called up to the NFL and graduate. Though if I am being honest, I am less interested in the graduating part and more focused on the football part. I never planned to go to college when I was younger. Kids like me weren't the type. But if you want to go pro, then college is the best way to get seen. I know there is a huge possibility that I won't get drafted but losing isn't an option for me. When I want something, I go for it.

"You saw her like two weeks ago. If she comes, cool. If not, I'm sure there are plenty of other chicks that would be more than happy to warm your bed," I say as I gesture towards Cynthia Johnson, who is currently sauntering our way.

She is the captain of the cheerleading team, and has it driven into her head that her and Trevor belong together. They hooked up a few times freshman year and it was just enough to make the chick go crazy for him. Now it seems everywhere we are, there she is. If she wasn't so hot, I'm sure he would have gotten a restraining order by now.

"Hi Trevor," she purrs.

"Hey," he says absentmindedly, not taking his eyes off his phone.

She pouts a little at his lack of attention before screwing on a perfectly plastic smile.

"I was hoping you would be here. We haven't spent time together in *so* long."

"Uh-huh," he says, still not even looking at her.

Irritation flashes across her face before she huffs.

"Okay, well you know where to find me when you get lonely."

"Sure thing."

She walks away with a little extra shake in her step that has me rolling my eyes. She reeks of desperation and there couldn't be anything less appealing in my opinion. I don't know whether to laugh or feel sorry for her. She is hoping to lock Trevor down, but my man just isn't the type. At least I thought he wasn't until he started going on and on about this Erica girl.

Trevor blows out a breath and shakes his head.

"You know what, man, I'm just gonna call it a night. I'll catch her before class tomorrow."

I nod as he sulks off upstairs to his room. Trevor and I live together along with a few other guys on the team, Slater and Declan. Since Declan is the middle linebacker on the team everyone calls him Mike, or at least Slater started it and it kinda stuck. They are a year younger than us, but that shit doesn't matter. They are cool as hell.

Dorm rooms obviously suck and none of us have time for fraternity life when we are all working towards going pro, so when this place came available, we jumped all over it. It is a decent sized house with a big kitchen and a finished basement that is basically a decked-out man cave thanks to Trevor's black credit card.

Trevor comes from money, and it seems like whatever he wants his parents get him without hesitation. When I first met him, I thought he was going to be like any other stuck up preppy rich boy. I quickly found out that he was extremely down to earth and a genuinely good guy. He's more like my brother than my friend. I'd do fucking anything for the guy.

I am about to call it a night too when the front door opens. I casually look to the side to see who is coming in so late but pause when my eyes land on *her*. Who the *fuck* is that? She has to be new. I am sure of it because I definitely would have remembered seeing that face before. Her thick red hair cascades down to her mid back and perfectly frames her practically porcelain face. She has an adorable button nose accompanied with high cheek bones and full lips.

Her body is long and lush. She looks decently tall for a girl, probably around 5'8 or so. Her legs look like they go on for miles while her hips flare out just before tapering into a nice tight waist.

She looks around the room casually like she is trying to get her bearings in the crowded space, which gives me the perfect opportunity to properly check her out. When she turns her head to scan the room, I see that she has the brightest pair of aqua blue eyes that have ever existed. There is no way those are real. She has to be wearing contacts or something, they are practically glowing across the dimly lit room.

Her eyes make me feel like I am staring straight into the Caribbean Sea. She must feel the weight of my gaze because her eyes clash with mine and I swear all of the oxygen in the room gets sucked out in an instant.

It takes me by surprise when my heart practically leaps out of my chest before returning to its normal rhythm. *That was fucking weird.* Just as quickly as she looked towards me, she looks away with a tint of color filling in her soft cheeks. *Fucking adorable.*

I watch as another girl I haven't seen around grabs the beauty's hand before dragging her through the crowd. My eyes never leave her though, tracking her like a predator does its prey. That is exactly how I feel right now too. Like I am a hunter, and she is a baby deer that doesn't know where she is or what she has just gotten herself into. She won't know that I have her until it's too late.

It's no secret that I do well with the ladies. Being a football player alone is usually a turn on enough for most of the women around here. It doesn't hurt that I am not the worst looking guy around. I have longer brown hair that falls down to my shoulders and matching eyes that women seem to go nuts for. Most the time it is easiest to just keep it tied up but tonight I decided to leave it down.

I am a big guy at 6'6 and 240lbs, perfect size for a tight end. I am almost bordering on too tall for some girls which is why I have never really gone for the 5'0 spinners like some of my buddies. I don't want to have to break my damn back just to kiss the chick, which seems to always be the case.

Now I'm not exactly what you would call a love 'em and leave 'em kind of guy, mainly because that guy sounds like an asshole, and I'm definitely not one. I am however honest and upfront. I don't have time in my life for drama, bullshit and definitely no time for a relationship. If they want to have a good time and feel good for a night, then I am more than happy to oblige but that is all that I can offer. I have worked too hard to make it here and I can't let anything distract me from my goals.

I am definitely the quiet one out of my group of friends. I am the observer. I sit back and read people, watch the room and evaluate. I almost never approach women since they usually come to me anyways. I typically don't have to say more than 2 words to them before we are naked. Okay, maybe I am a bit of an asshole but show me a 21-year-old guy that isn't?

For the first time in a long fucking time though, I find myself trying to get a girl's attention instead of the other way around. She seems to be looking almost everywhere but towards me, like she is trying to avoid making eye contact with me. Either that or she is looking for someone in particular. If she is though, I don't think that she finds them since she shrugs her shoulders before her little friend drags her to the dance floor.

A shaggy dark-haired guy is trailing the girls, looping his arms around the tiny brunette's waist before grinding up against her. She tosses her head back and laughs before they start making out hard core in the middle of the room. The beauty looks a little uncomfortable at the display of affection and turns away from them, raising her arms up before she starts swaying her hips to the beat.

My eyes are zoned in on her perfect heart shaped ass and I can't help but imagine how good it would feel in my hands. I continue my blatant staring, hoping that she will get the hint and look my way or that she will just come over here already, but she doesn't.

Frustrated that her eyes seem to bounce right over me every time, I glance to the side and see that I am not the only one who is appreciating the view. A group of Alpha Sigma guys are staring at her like they are starved men, and she is a 5-course feast. A growl rumbles through my chest and before I can figure out where the fuck it came from, my legs are quickly crossing the room towards her.

Just as I step up behind her, I notice the president, George O'Connor, is walking towards her. From all of the times that I have been around the guy, I know one thing. He is a piece of shit. When he makes eye contact with me, he quickly turns away, shuffling back to his brothers with his head held high like he didn't just tuck tail and run. *Good fucking choice*.

Without hesitating, I rest one of my hands onto the beauty's soft waist, causing her to jump and spin around. She almost loses her balance before I reach my other hand out and grab her arm to steady her. Her large eyes look up at me with surprise, but no words come from her full lips.

"The vultures were about to swoop in," I say as I nod towards the guys that are still looking at her like she is a prime steak.

I don't know why but their leers grate me, which is so not my style. As soon as I get mine, I usually don't give a shit what the chick does after but something inside tells me that I wouldn't feel that way after I had her.

"Looks like you owe me one," I say with a hint of a smirk.

"One what?" She asks with a small smile playing at the corner of her mouth.

My smirk stretches as I move my hand from her arm down to her waist. "How about we start with a dance?"

She pauses like she is mulling something over before she gives me a shy nod and starts moving to the music again. I match her rhythm and make sure that I keep both of my hands on her at all times. Her body is fucking hypnotizing, and I have a hard time not getting lost in the way her soft curves move to the music.

We dance for a few songs and by the end of the third I am becoming increasingly impatient. I usually never have to wait this long before chicks are practically dry humping my leg and dragging me into the nearest bedroom. This girl though has kept a respectable distance the whole time, only brushing against me once or twice. Just enough to make me crave more. Why do I kind of like that she is teasing me? That she isn't falling at my feet. I don't do mind games or shit like that but fuck if I'm not into whatever the hell this girl is playing at tonight.

When she looks up at me, she smiles so wide that my heart does that weird leaping thing again. It sucks the breath out of me for a few seconds, and I have to physically shake my head to push the feeling away. This girl is fucking gorgeous, hands down the most beautiful woman I have ever seen, and that is saying a lot because we have some very pretty ladies at this school. But her? She blows them all out of the fucking water.

She turns around just as a guy is trying to squeeze by us, causing him to dump his entire cup of beer down the front of her shirt. She gasps in surprise before leaping back into my arms, which I instantly wrap around her.

"Oh shit. I am so sorry!" The guy says as his eyes flick from her to me.

I recognize him as one of the Freshman on the team this year. He is a third stringer and has been more like the team's whipping boy than anything else. His eyes round with recognition when he spots me and a hint of fear for how I will retaliate passes across his features. I am not really into all of that hazing bullshit though, so I flick my wrist in a move that shows him to just get lost, which he happily does.

"You okay?" I ask.

She looks up at me and her eyes blink quickly before she nods. "Yeah, don't think I can say the same for my shirt though."

I nod as I intertwine her fingers with mine and lead her through the crowd.

"Come on."

Being a big guy has its advantages. People have to get out of my way, they physically don't have much choice. When I make it down the hallway, I open up the laundry room before pulling her inside with me. I just threw some clothes into the dryer before the party started so I'm sure that I have something in here for her. No doubt it will fucking drown her slender frame, but it is better than wearing a beer-soaked shirt.

I scour through the pile of clothes until I find a Brighton U shirt that I got when I signed my commitment letter. It's probably my favorite shirt, but for some reason, I find myself handing it over to her instead of looking for another.

"Here, you can have this. It'll be big but you could tie it or something."

"Thank you," she says softly as her slim fingers brush against mine.

The touch sends that weird ass feeling in my chest and my stomach this time. What the hell is up with that? I stand there, staring down at her for several moments before I realize that she wants to get changed and I'm being a fucking creep just standing here watching her.

"Sorry. I'll give you some privacy," I say as I walk past her and reach for the doorknob.

"You don't have to go," she says, her voice huskier than it was earlier.

My hand flexes around the doorknob as my shoulders tighten. It's taking every ounce of willpower I possess not to slam her against the wall and take her how I have imagined over a dozen times since she first walked through the front door.

I hear the rustling of clothes and a wet thud that hits the ground before the movements stop. Slowly, I turn around, fucking shocked to see that she isn't wearing my Brighton t-shirt, but instead she is wearing nothing at all. Well, she still has her sexy little jeans on, but her bra and soaked shirt are in a pile at her feet.

My eyes lift from her discarded clothes as they make their way up her body until settling on her round perky breasts. Her nipples are hard and the lightest shade of pink that already has my mouth watering.

Without uttering a single word, a growl tears through my throat as I cross the room in two steps, burying my hand into the back of her hair before diving down to capture her lips. If she is surprised, she doesn't show it. Her mouth eagerly meets mine as her smooth lips brush against me, matching the passion that I am pouring into this kiss.

My other hand traces up the bare skin of her stomach before palming one of her breasts. When my thumb brushes across her hardened nipple, she shudders in my arms as she opens her mouth up for me, which I fully take advantage of by slipping my tongue inside.

Gently, my tongue strokes hers as I begin to explore her mouth. At first, I felt so desperate to kiss her that I thought I was going to lose it if I had to go one more second without, but now that I am, I feel like I want to take my time and enjoy this. The little noises that she makes when my hands brush against her velvety skin alone have me ready to cum in my pants like a fucking 12-year-old, which is both embarrassing and exciting.

Her hands reach out and brush against the cotton shirt that I'm wearing before slipping underneath to feel my rippled stomach. Another plus to being an athlete, you are always in shape. I pull at the back of my shirt with one hand and drop it into the growing pile of clothes.

She breaks the kiss as her eyes drop down to admire me while she drags her hands up and down my chest until she reaches the band where my boxers are peeking out of my jeans. When she looks at me her eyes are hooded and darkened with lust, which only makes my desire that much stronger.

Slowly, I reach down and flick the first button of her jeans open. When she doesn't push me away or show any sign of protest, I pull the zipper down until I am peeling the tight material off of her body, which holy fuck, is more incredible than I even imagined. Every inch of her is toned, smooth and fucking perfect.

I grab her by the back of her knees and lift her on top of the washing machine before I spread her legs open and step in between them. She lets out a surprised gasp as she nods her head in encouragement. I smirk slyly before my hand traces over the thin scrap of lace that is now the last piece of clothing left.

My fingers languidly move up and down against the fabric. I can already feel how ready she is for me. I pull the fabric to the side before easing one finger inside of her. She lets out a satisfied moan that makes my cock twitch in anticipation. *Fuck, she is so tight.*

I work her slowly before adding a second finger, which earns me another loud moan. I increase my movements as I imagine how good she is going to feel wrapped around me. Her hands dig into my shoulders as she throws her head back.

"Oh my gosh," she gasps breathily.

I work her faster until I am rubbing that golden spot that has her shattering apart in my arms. Once her body stops quaking, I tilt her chin up to look at me to see if she wants to continue. She answers by quickly undoing my belt, shoving my pants and boxers down before wrapping her slim hand around my cock. I hiss through clenched teeth as her silky smooth skin begins to slowly stroke me.

I tip my head back as a groan leaves my chest when she picks up speed. Clenching my teeth, I quickly pull the hair tie off my wrist, wrapping my hair up so it is out of the way before I reach into my back pocket and pull out a foil wrapper. I tear it open with my teeth before slowly rolling it on.

"Ready, baby?"

She nods desperately like she has suddenly lost the ability to speak. I smirk before pulling her face to me and crushing my lips against her as I yank her panties even farther to the side before I push inside her. She lets out a pained yelp that is muffled as my lips continue to move against hers. I already knew that she was tight as fuck and I'm definitely larger than average, so I was counting on it hurting, hence the distraction of the kiss. I still for a moment to allow her to adjust to me before I start slowly rocking my hips against hers.

Her legs wrap around my lower back which only draws me closer to her. I never break the kiss as I continue to bury myself inside of her. I don't think I could physically stop if I wanted to. With every thrust, her pussy clamps around me even tighter, practically fucking milking me. *Shit.*

I've fucked my fair share of women, most of who pleasured me just fine, but I have never felt anything like this before. I feel so desperate, so powerless. I feel like I'm fucking drowning in her but also finally getting what I need to truly live for the first time in my life, as fruity as shit as that sounds. It's exhilarating and fucking terrifying.

"Fuck, yeah," I grit through my teeth as she gyrates her hips against me. "Atta girl."

My hands reach down to cup her ass and slide her to me even more until we are completely plastered against each other. My thrusts are so rapid that the washing machine is physically shaking with her on top of it. Between that and her desperate moans, I'm sure we are making too much noise, and someone will probably come in here at any minute, but I'm too gone in her to give a shit right now.

I feel my balls start to tighten and I know that I don't have long before I lose it too soon in front of this fucking goddess. I move my hand down and brush my thumb across her clit a few times and that seems to be all that it takes for her. She shoots off like a rocket, gasping and shouting her pleasure while I bury my head into her neck and sink my teeth into her shoulder as I follow right behind her. The sweet smell of peaches surrounds me as I chase my release and I realize that I'd sell my fucking soul to stay buried in her right now.

I stay still for a few moments, placing gentle kisses on the hollow of her neck and inhaling her sweet smell one more time before I slowly pull back to look at her. She has an almost dazed look that is part surprised and part satisfied. *I know the fucking feeling.*

Without thinking twice, I lean down and brush my lips across hers, savoring the silky feel of her plump lips. She softly kisses me back as I lift my hands to cup her face and pull her in closer. Just as I am about to pull away, I start back up again. I just can't stop. I just need her closer, I need fucking more.

She doesn't seem to be too put out about it either as her tongue gently twirls around mine. A heavy knock suddenly comes from the door and we both jump before I stand protectively in front of her to block whoever is about to come in's view as I quickly stuff my still hard cock back into my pants. She grabs onto the back of me to hide better, and I don't miss the feeling that races up my back and across my body from her touch alone. Fuck, who the hell is this chick?

Slater peeks his head in before his eyes round.

"Shit, sorry man. I heard some noises and I thought someone was doing laundry or some shit. Uh, my bad," he laughs awkwardly before he pauses. "Hi, I'm Slater," he calls out to the girl clearly hiding behind me.

"Get the fuck out!" I bark.

"Shit yeah, yeah. Sorry!" He says as he scrambles out the door.

I sigh and curse under my breath before turning to look at my beautiful aqua eyed girl.

"Sorry about him," I grumble, pissed as all hell that the dumb fuck interrupted us.

She gives me an airy laugh and shrugs. "Could have been worse. He could have walked in 30 seconds earlier."

I let out an amused scoff as I nod before I grab her by the hips and slowly lower her to her feet. She looks up at me with a dreamy smile and for once I don't find it alarming. Normally, if a girl looks at you that way it's time to beat feet, and quick, before she tries to lock you down or some shit. Not her though. She just smiles before bending down and picking up her discarded clothes, quickly sliding back into them.

I take my shirt and slip it on as I stand back and watch her pull on my Brighton shirt and her jeans. She ties the shirt into a knot at the bottom so only an inch or so of her creamy skin is peeking out, the sight is sexy as fuck.

"Well, I should probably get going. Class and all tomorrow," she says almost awkwardly.

I find myself running through ideas in my head on how I can convince her to stay the night with me. But then I stop and mentally slap myself. *Stay the night?* That is against everything I fucking stand for. I have never stayed the night nor let a girl stay the night. It sends the wrong message and is no good for either party involved. So, why the hell do I feel almost desperate for this girl to stick around for the night?

She must take my silence as agreement because before I can say anything, she reaches up onto her toes, kisses my cheek and slips out the door. I stand there more than little stunned at the warring thoughts in my head. What the hell is going on with me? What the hell just happened? I mean, I know I just had by far the best sex of my life but what is all of this other shit bouncing around inside of me that seems to have come with it?

I shake my head and open the door, determined to chase after her even if I don't fully understand why I want to, but when I look around, she is gone. I search every room and even run outside but I don't see any sign of her anywhere. I don't even know her name. I don't know if she is staying at a dorm or a sorority or maybe off campus. I know nothing about this girl, but I sure as hell plan on finding out every fucking thing.

CHAPTER THREE

ERICA

I wake up the next morning deliciously sore in all the right places. So, I guess that wasn't a dream last night after all. As soon as I made it back to my dorm room, I crashed and fell into some of the best post orgasmic sleep of my life. I don't know what that guy's name was or if I will ever see him again, but I know one thing, I'm pretty sure he just ruined me for sex because I have never experienced anything like *that*.

From the moment that I stepped into the house, I felt like someone was watching me. It only took me a few moments to find the caramel-colored eyes that were drilling two holes into me. When our eyes locked, I swear it was like the whole room got quiet for a moment and we were the only two in there, which sounds totally crazy but true, nonetheless.

His brown hair was long, about down to his shoulders with a subtle wave to the texture. I never thought that long hair on guys was really attractive, until now. The curtain of thick hair only seemed to highlight his caramel swirl colored eyes. His jaw was sharp and strong, so sharp I wouldn't be surprised if he could cut glass with it. When my eyes traced over him, they kept going and going until my mouth damn near hit the ground. He was huge. Not just like a buff guy or anything but like a giant. He isn't just tall and lanky either, he was wide too like he worked out a lot or maybe he was a demi-god or something, either are very high possibilities.

Suffice it to say he was gorgeous, which is why I had to avert my eyes as quickly as possible. I never know how to act when guys give me heavy attention like he was. It makes me nervous, and I usually just freeze up.

When he approached me on the dance floor, I was a little stunned and when he spoke to me, goosebumps covered my entire body from his low tenor. My heart was beating like a jackrabbit from being so close to him and when his large hands spanned on either side of my waist, I had to suppress a shiver. There was something about him, something almost magnetic that drew me to him. I sank into his touch and hoped that he would never stop touching me.

Maybe that was what possessed me to strip half naked in front of the perfect stranger and basically offer myself up to him on a silver platter. What the hell was I thinking? That was so out of character for me I don't even know where to begin.

I sit up in bed and try to tame my crazy hair before I swing my legs off the edge and pad over to our bathroom. I was super thankful that the dorm rooms have their own private restrooms instead of shared bathrooms like normal campuses, but at the price tag for tuition here, it doesn't surprise me. Don't get me wrong, they are still pretty cramped and bare especially for most of the rich kids that go here, me included, but it could definitely be worse.

I pull the XXL t-shirt that the sexy stranger gave me off and shamelessly hold it up to my nose to smell the intoxicating combined smell of laundry and him just one more time before I hop into the shower.

Once I am out, I throw on a pair of light blue jeans, a white tank top and a grey cardigan. My hair is tamed into soft waves before I put on some foundation, mascara and a swipe of lipstick. I grab my bag and shove a few things inside of it before I am out the door and off to my first class.

I am so busy rifling through my bag when I open the door from my building that I don't even see the hard body that I walk straight into.

"Whoa, Little Red. I know that you are happy to see me and all, but you are gonna have to take me to dinner first," a familiar voice rumbles.

A wide smile stretches across my face as I leap into my best friend's arms.

"Trev!"

He takes a step back and wraps one of his arms around me, holding me tight to him while handing me the coffee that he has in his outstretched hand.

"Oh my gosh, I freaking love you," I moan as I kiss his cheek and cradle the Caramel Frappuccino like I am Gollum, and it is the Ring.

He laughs lightly as he runs a hand through his short light blond faux hawk. His blue eyes sparkle in the morning sun and I take the moment to appreciate him. It seems like he has grown even more since the last time I saw him, which can't be right because it has only been a few weeks. Still, though. Something is definitely different. I just can't quite place it.

Whatever the change is I find myself studying him closer than I have in years. His bright eyes flick over my face with a wide smile on his face and when they settle on my eyes butterflies suddenly swarm my chest. Wow. I haven't gotten butterflies from Trevor Michaels in years.

"Well, I figured if you were going to torture yourself with a 7AM lecture, then you at least need coffee to get you through it," he says, not making a move to set me down. I toss my head back and laugh as I slowly ease out of his arms before we start walking together.

"So true. If it were up to me, I would still be in bed. Where are you off to?"

"To walk you to your first class, duh," he says with a wink as he bumps his shoulder into mine.

"Wait. You don't have a class this morning? What are you doing out of bed *willingly*? Are you crazy or something?"

He laughs and shrugs. "I wanted to see you since you stood me up last night."

I cock my head to the side. "I didn't stand you up. You weren't there. I was at the party that you gave me the address to last night. I looked for you, but I couldn't find you."

He gives me a confused look as he ushers us past a couple who has stopped in the middle of the walkway to make-out.

"Really? I waited for you for a while. I decided to go to bed at like 10. I figured you weren't coming by then."

"Mhmm. And did you go to bed alone?" I tease as I waggle my eyebrows.

He rolls his eyes, irritation written plainly across his face.

"Yes." He pauses for a moment as his eyes crinkle in the corners. "Did you?"

My stomach flips at the reminder of last night. I always tease Trev about his exploits, but we never really talk about mine. Anytime I have mentioned a guy at all lately he gets all growly and protective. I definitely don't need him tearing apart campus trying to put the fear of God into whoever that guy was last night.

"Of course. And I gotta say, I am not loving the double bed situation."

I laugh as I bury my blushing face into my coffee cup. Technically, I am not lying. Did I go to bed alone? Yes. Did I go to bed without an orgasm? Absolutely not, but I don't need to share that bit with him.

He nods and what looks like relief washes over his face. Oh my gosh, is he seriously going to be trying to scare guys away from me? I guess I will have to remind him that he is just my best friend, not my keeper.

"Yeah, I lived in a dorm my freshman year too. Then me and the guys got into a house last year. California King for me now."

I scoff. "Like anyone actually needs a bed that big."

He shrugs and smiles as we stop outside of my class.

"Trevor!" A couple of girls call out before they rush over to us. Both of them are gorgeous, one blonde and one brunette. They are wearing tight clothes that looks way too expensive to be worn on a Monday to class but who am I to judge?

The blond bats her eyes seductively as she bites on her lower lip. "We just wanted to wish you luck for the game."

A charming yet a little irritated smirk crosses his face.

"Well, thank you ladies, but the game isn't until Saturday."

A look of embarrassment flashes across their faces before they go to play it off.

"Oh, yeah. We know. We are just super excited. You'll be amazing like usual," the brunette says before they both lean forward on their tip toes and kiss each side of his cheek before sending him little flirty waves and skirting off.

"I see you have been busy up here," I tease.

Trevor lets out a laugh before he shakes his head and runs a hand through his hair.

"I swear to god I've never seen those two before in my life."

"That's one of the many side effects of alcohol."

Trevor shakes his head and sighs, almost seeming a little irritated before he changes the subject.

"So, what is your last class of the day?"

I pull out my phone to look at my schedule. "Philosophy in Baynard Hall. Should be over by 1PM. Why?"

"I wanted to know if you wanted to hangout a bit before I head to practice," he says as he leans up against the wall casually.

"Sure, sounds good."

"Cool. Have a good first day," he says before bending down and pecking my cheek, his lips staying pressed against my cheek just a half of a second longer than normal.

I smile curiously as he pulls away but don't say anything. He gives me a wink before turning on his heel and heading back across campus.

Throughout the day I do my best to stay present, taking thorough notes and asking probing questions but honestly, I am already burned out. I am pre-law, and it definitely wasn't my choice. It is expected that I will work at my parent's firm once I graduate from law school. That has been the plan since I was practically in my mother's womb. It is their plan though, not mine.

When I had talked to my parents about me attending art school instead of Brighton, they practically had heart attacks. My mother was horrified that I would ever want to do anything other than practice law and my father thought that I was being senseless and impulsive.

Art is a fine hobby sweetheart, but I am afraid it is not a sustainable career path.

I don't care about having a sustainable career path though, I want to be happy every day. I want to do what I love. Even if that means waking up in a 500 square foot studio apartment above a Chinese restaurant just so that I can afford to paint every day, I don't care. I want to feel in charge of my own life, my own fate.

My parents have always had my whole life mapped out and the older that I get the more drawn I feel to take another road. When Trevor and I started dating our mothers had everything but our wedding colors picked out, and I was *16*. Unfortunately, my parents are very hardheaded like that, they think they know best about everything, and others should just go along with it.

I am taking all the core classes that a pre-law student should be this year, which I can already tell is going to be torture. What my parents don't know is that I snuck in an art class this semester. If I can't be an art major, I am at least going to get a few hours of it here and there, for nothing if not my sanity.

Once my last lecture finishes up, I file out of class with a large group of people when I see a familiar wide smile and sparkling blue eyes.

"What are you, my personal escort?" I tease as he comes up and hugs me tight before we start walking.

"Just wanted to be seen with the prettiest girl on campus," Trevor smirks.

I scoff and smack his rock-hard stomach. "Stop. You can't get me with that schmoozy bullshit, Trevor Anthony. I know all of your tricks."

He sighs dramatically and nods. "I know. Do you have any idea how hard it is on my ego that I can't make you swoon like I used to?"

"Well to be fair I was 14 and you were the first guy that ever really paid me any attention."

"Not the case anymore is it," he says with a hollow chuckle.

I cock my head slightly as I look up at him. His tone sounds equal parts disappointed and reminiscent which is not really like Trevor. He is one of those people who is always moving forward, always looking ahead, never backward.

Shrugging it off, we start walking down the courtyard as Trevor tells me all about how the team is looking this year and who they are playing Saturday. In a few short minutes, Trevor is leading us up to the house that the party was at last night.

"Wait, this is your house?" I ask with furrowed brows. I thought I was just meeting him at a frat house or something. He nods as we walk up the porch, rolling his right shoulder as he does.

"You been icing your shoulder?" I ask with a raised brow.

"Yes, mom," he says with an eye roll and a smile.

When Trevor was a junior in high school, he got sacked hard and ended up dislocating his shoulder. Thankfully it was the end of the season and with the best doctors and physical therapy money could buy, he was back on the field in the Spring, but it still gives him problems even if he won't admit it to anyone but me.

"Just saying. You don't want it to give out on you now. This is a big year for you."

"Yeah, it is," he says seriously as he looks down at me intently.

Trevor is eligible for the draft this year. We talked about it all summer. It's all he has ever wanted, and it is within reach. I just don't want to see him lose his chance. It would destroy him.

He shakes his head after a moment as if he is shaking himself out of his thoughts before he smiles and ushers us both inside. The place is a lot bigger than I remember. Probably because there aren't a hundred people crammed into the 1600sq ft space anymore.

"Oh, hey man. I didn't know you would be home. This is my friend from Grovebury, Erica. Erica, this is my best friend and our tight end, Sebastian Caldwell."

I smile as I step into the living room to meet his friend who is sitting on the couch and from the sound of it, watching some game film. However, my smile drops instantly when I see that the guy from last night, the one that fucked me until I could hardly see straight on top of the washing machine down the hall is Trevor's friend and roommate.

If I am surprised, he is absolutely shocked and he does a horrible job of hiding it. His fists are balled up on top of his thighs and his eyes are wide with what looks like horror. Ouch. Can't deny that isn't the look I was hoping to get from him if I ever saw him again. Not quite sure how to play this out, I decide to follow his lead. Since he is acting extremely shell shocked, I am going to assume that he would like me to pretend that we haven't met before.

"Hi, Sebastian. Nice to meet you."

He blinks a few times in silence, like his brain is trying to make sense of my words before he gives me a slow nod.

"You too."

An awkward silence stretches between us for way too long before Trevor laughs softly. "Don't worry about him. He doesn't say much. Most people usually just get a grunt so you should feel special," Trevor jokes.

I hold back a snort as I think about how familiar I am with his grunts.

"Do you want something to drink, Little Red?"

"You know-"

"Water," Trevor finishes and rolls his eyes like I am so pre-dictable before he winks and walks off to the kitchen.

I smile and shake my head before turning back to face Sebastian, who is still staring at me with a new hardened look. God. Even when he is seemingly pissed off, he is gorgeous. His long hair is tied up into a man bun, his candy-colored eyes reminding me of what it felt like to look into those eyes as I fell apart in his arms.

Shaking my head softly to cleat those thoughts away, I shuffle on my feet a little, unsure of what to say. His glare is practically setting me on fire and not in a good way. I have never had a one-night stand before, but I feel like it should be a little less...frigid?

"So, you are *the* Erica?"

His deep voice is even rougher than I remember and this time I don't suppress the shiver that runs down my spine at the sound of it. I hide it quickly as I pretend to rub my arms like I am cold, even if it is 75 degrees and sunny outside.

"Uh, the one and only. I mean there are probably at least a hundred Erica's on campus, but I am an Erica."

He lets out a frustrated huff and shakes his head in response. I take a tentative step closer as I soften my voice.

"Is everything okay? I mean, are you like mad at me or something?" I ask, completely confused to his cold attitude.

His eyes narrow as his jaw clenches before he shakes his head again. "No. Just forget last night ever happened. I don't need my best friend pissed at me over a piece of ass."

The words are harsh as they spill from his lips, and I know that I don't do a good job of hiding the hurt that spreads across my face. I mean damn, I wasn't expecting flowers and mixtapes, but I thought that if I ran into him again that he would be happy about it, or at least be able to look back on it as a good time.

Maybe it wasn't as great for him as it was for me.

Sebastian's face is a stoic mask that gives nothing away as he continues to stare me down like my very existence bothers him. I am so busy trying to discern what is going on underneath his handsome face that I don't hear Trevor come back into the room. He slings an arm around my shoulders as he hands me my water.

It doesn't escape my notice that Sebastian's eyes track the movement and stay locked in on where Trevor's arm is wrapped around me. Feeling uncomfortable under his scrutiny, I take a step out of Trevor's reach before lifting the water bottle to my lips.

Suddenly, Sebastian stands up and brushes past us, heading down the hall and up the stairs without so much as a word. Trevor's eyes follow him curiously before he shrugs.

"Is he always like that?" I ask.

"Sometimes. He isn't a social butterfly that's for sure. Want to watch some film?" He asks as he nods towards the TV.

I'm sure most girls wouldn't be interested in watching film, but I actually love it. Trevor and I would watch film almost every night growing up. We would make popcorn and watch game after game, commenting on players weaknesses and strengths and how Trev and his team could better prepare. Ever since we became friends, football became a big part of my life. At first, I took an interest because it was important to him but then I grew to genuinely love the game.

"Sure," I smile and nod as I take a seat on the couch and pretend to be into the film when really, my mind is racing with what went wrong from last night to now.

Clearly Sebastian didn't want Trevor to know that we hooked up, but did he really have to call me a piece of ass? It felt like more than that last night, then again maybe I was just being naïve. Maybe this is how things go in college, and I am just being sensitive. Deciding to move on and try to erase the memory of arguably one of the best nights of my life, I force a smile as I watch play after play flicker across the TV.

Chapter Four

Sebastian

Fuck. Fuck. Fuck. Are you kidding me? Are you fucking kidding me? I know I've done some fucked up shit in my life, but did I really do something to deserve this? I mean, the answer is definitely yes, but shit. My red-haired beauty, the girl who has been on my mind every damn second since last night, her name is Erica. *Trevor's* Erica, to be fucking specific. The girl who he is fucking gone for. Shit. Shit. Shit.

When I heard him and a feminine laugh come through the front door, I had a feeling that I was about to meet the infamous Erica. What I didn't see coming was that she would be the same girl that I fucked within an inch of my life on top of our washing machine last night while Trev was asleep upstairs probably dreaming about her.

Fuck.

As soon as I saw her glossy hair, I knew that it was her. For a moment, things didn't add up, and I was briefly excited. I thought that she had tracked me down like I had planned to do to her.

When I looked into her aqua eyes, just like last night, it was instantly hard to breathe. My eyes flicked down to her lips, and I remembered in that moment how good they tasted, how soft and fucking perfect they felt. She was even more beautiful than I remembered and all I wanted to do was tug her into my lap and have a repeat of last night. But then everything clicked into place as to why she was there. This is Erica, *his* Erica.

Fuck, shit.

When I told her that she was just a piece of ass, she looked so hurt and I instantly felt like an asshole. I didn't mean to hurt her or anything. I was just trying to get her to understand that she can never tell Trevor what happened. If I had known who she was, I never would have touched her. I mean, I still would have wanted her like crazy, but I would have never broken bro code like that. Trevor would cut my fucking balls off if he knew.

As soon as the bullshit lie slipped out, I instantly wanted to apologize. But I thought better of it. I need to keep her as far away from me as possible and being a standoffish dick sounds like the best way to achieve that.

When Trevor came back into the room and wrapped his arm around her like it was the most normal thing to do, I almost lost it. The familiar contact pissed me off and had me irrationally wanting to rip his arm out of its damn socket. I knew I had to put some distance between us and quick.

Trevor is my best friend, has been for over two years now and we have never even had an argument before. We know how the other works. We give space when we need it and call each other out on shit when we need that too. I feel like scum of the fucking earth right now knowing that I betrayed him, even if it was an accident. I feel even worse that I'm not totally sorry. Last night was probably one of the best nights of my fucking life.

I stay holed up in my room until the very last minute before I risk being late to practice, and I'm never late. I grab my stuff and blow out a deep breath before I put my game face on and head down the stairs. I see Trevor and Erica watching the film that I was studying as I get to the bottom of the stairs.

I step to the side just out of sight as I listen to her making really good observations about the holes in the opposing teams defense and how to exploit it in our game coming up. Her comments have me surprisingly impressed.

Girl knows a thing or two about football. Of fucking course, she does.

I see Trevor reaching out to drape his arm around Erica's shoulders and some ridiculous part of me doesn't like that one fucking bit.

"Trevor," I snap a little too forcefully.

He damn near jumps out of his skin and shoots me an irritated look. "Yeah?"

"We gotta get going, man. Practice starts in twenty."

"Shit. Yeah, okay. Sorry, we gotta go but come over anytime. If you need to get out of the dorm or whatever, just come over whether it is to get away or hangout. You know you are always welcome."

I want to interrupt and tell him that I would prefer that she doesn't come over, ever, but I don't know how to say that without sounding like a total asshole. It's not like I can explain to him that I don't want her over because I'm afraid of what I will do if I'm alone with her again.

Erica laughs lightly and shrugs.

"Well thanks Trev, but I don't want to cramp your style. I'm not just gonna barge into your house when you guys might have...company," she says suggestively with a waggle of her brows.

"Psh, what style? I'm not really into the whole sleeping around thing anymore and I can't even remember the last time big guy over here hooked up with anyone," Trevor says gesturing to me teasingly.

Erica looks at me and her blue eyes flare with what looks like mischief.

Don't you dare, troublemaker.

She seems to be able to read me like a fucking book because she doesn't say anything, but her face tells me that she thinks Trevor's comment is amusing. I mean, he isn't totally off base, though. During football season I usually don't mess around too much. Girls usually come with a lot of drama and expectations that I simply don't have the time or patience for, especially during the season.

Case in point.

"Alright. Well, we will see," Erica says before she reaches over to hug Trevor.

He wraps both of his arms around her and holds her close. The hug lasts several beats longer than a hug between just friends should last. Maybe Trev's feelings aren't completely one sided. At least it looks like I won't have to worry about her being a clinger. Why does that thought leave me with a slight twist in my gut.

Erica finally pulls away, giving Trev a sugary sweet smile before she walks towards me. For a moment, my heart kicks up in my chest and I think that she is going to hug me too, but at the last second, she veers to her right toward the door. When she opens it, she looks over her shoulder and gives me a cold smile that tells me she is definitely not over the shitty comment I made earlier.

"See you around, Sebastian."

I fucking hope not.

I don't say anything as I stare at her, watching each step she takes carefully until she shuts the door and is out of sight. I feel the tightness that had settled in my chest since she walked through the door loosen some when I know that she is finally a good distance away.

I look to the side to make sure that Trevor isn't watching me and thankfully he isn't. Unthankfully the reason he didn't catch me staring is because he was doing the same thing. Who fucking cares? I shake my head before I nod towards the door.

"Come on, man, let's go," I say.

He nods and runs upstairs to grab his stuff before we head off to practice.

Chapter Five

Trevor

"Fuck, isn't she gorgeous man? I told you. She is a fucking stunner," I say for probably the fifteenth time since we got to the stadium.

I know I haven't shut up about Erica since I came back from break and my roommates are probably sick and tired of me, but I don't really give a shit. I just can't get over it. It's like I am seeing her for the first time again. I feel like I am falling in love with her all over again. It only took one real look at her, knowing that she was going to be coming with me to Brighton once summer ended to know that I never stopped loving her.

"Mhmm," Seb says as he slips on his pads, only half listening to me.

I love my best friend, but he is a broody motherfucker. He doesn't talk much either, which isn't a huge deal since I am the more outgoing one. I am used to it, but a lot of people don't get him, not like I do.

"And she is cool," I go on, full well knowing he isn't really listening but don't care.

I have to tell someone what is running through my head, or I will fuck everything up and tell her. I thought about it long and hard this summer. I hurt her when I left for college, I know I did. I broke us and now it is up to me to fix us. I know Erica better than I know to see how great we can be together, remind her of how good we were together. It'll be some work, but she is worth it.

"She practically knows more about football than I do," I say. "Hell, she can probably throw a better spiral than me nine times out of ten."

"Well, that isn't too hard," Seb drawls dryly. I scoff before laughing as I nod. "She is just the best. I swear, biggest mistake of my life was breaking up with her, man."

"Why did you?" Seb asks as he walks over to the water fountain and starts filling up his bottle.

I sigh and shake my head as I run my hand through my hair and lean up against the lockers behind me.

"I was about to come to Brighton, and she was just starting her junior year of high school, four hours away. I didn't know if we could make the distance work and if I'm being honest, I was a little worried that I would do something stupid like cheat on her. So, I told her that I thought we were better off as friends."

Saying it out loud only solidifies in my mind what a fucking jackass I was. I remember the day that I broke us fucking vividly. I dreamt about it daily for my first few weeks at Brighton. I drove her out to Moe's; we got burgers and shakes and laid on the hood of my car as we talked.

"I'm going to miss you so much while you are gone. Thanksgiving can't come soon enough," she says with a smile, but I don't miss the sad gleam in her eye that makes my heart clench. Fuck. This is gonna be hard.

"Little Red, I-I've been thinking," I start before darting a look over to her.

Her smile instantly slips bit by bit until her face is transformed into a frown. I watch as her beautiful blue eyes are suddenly swallowed by a layer of unshed tears and fucking hate myself for being the reason behind those tears. *This is for both of us,* I remind myself. *It isn't forever, just for now.*

"It's just so far. I don't want the distance to get between our relationship or our friendship. And you are finishing up your last few years of high school. You should enjoy it. Go out, have fun without feeling like you are tied down with a boyfriend who can't see you more than a few times a year."

She winces as if my words pain her before she bites her bottom lip like she is trying to physically hold back her cries. It doesn't work, though. Her soft whimpers are almost not noticeable, almost.

"D-did I do something wrong?" She asks softly, her voice quaking slightly.

"Little Red, no," I say as I quickly slide across the hood and wrap her up in my arms.

She instantly tucks her head into the crook of my neck like she has done a thousand times over the years. I'm her safe space and if I'm being fucking honest, she is mine. But this is good. This is for the best. We both need to stand on our two feet for a little bit.

"You are perfect, more than I fucking deserve and we both know it," I say as she gives off a choked laugh as the first tear spills down her cheek.

I cup her face and swipe the tear away with my thumb as I stare down at her.

"This isn't over, we aren't over. This isn't forever, it's just for now. We need this."

She looks like she wants to disagree, but Erica rarely argues with people. She probably gets enough arguing at home with her parents, arguments that she never wins. So instead, she shrugs softly and hangs her head, nodding up and down just slightly.

I reach down and tilt her chin up to face me before I bring my lips to hers. Hoping that she understands what I am trying to explain.

That I want her to have time to just be her, that I want her to want me, not feel obligated to be with me and I want the same. I can't lie I have also had thoughts about what could happen at college. I've already heard some stories from some of the guys on the team when I went to check out the team. I would rather end this now, before I do something stupid that I could never take back.

This isn't forever, just for now.

"Well, looks like it worked. I mean, you guys seem to be good friends. I've never seen exes as chill with each other as you guys are," Sebastian says, shaking me out of easily one of the most painful days of my life.

I nod. "Yeah, but it bit me in the ass too. I think I accidently friend zoned myself, permanently. I think she held out hope that we would get back together for the first year or so but after that she just started seeing me as a friend. She makes little comments about how I need to stop acting like her big brother and shit like that. It's like she doesn't even remember that we used to date. I want to remind her how good we were, how great we can be together, but I don't want to spook her. Any advice?"

"I don't know man. I don't really know her. I guess just keep doing what you're doing. Be friends, spend time together and go with the flow."

I nod. That's what I thought too but now that she is here, right in front of me, looking like a fucking knockout on my campus, I can't help but want to swoop her up and claim her before some fucking asshole puts the moves on her. I'll have to put the word out that she is spoken for in case some fuckwad gets any ideas. I'm not saying I am top man on campus or anything but usually when I have shit to say, people listen, whether that is because of my family name or my skills on the field, doesn't matter.

"Hey, ladies!" Slater calls out to us as he and Mike jog over to catch up with Seb and I as we make our way out of the locker room.

"Sup, Slater, Mikey," I nod.

"So, Seb, sorry about walking in on you last night. Total accident bro," Slater says to Sebastian.

"Uh oh, did you walk in on him jerking it in his room last night," I tease as I shove Seb's shoulder.

"No, surprisingly," Slater snickers. "I heard some shit in our laundry room and I thought some punk was fucking with our stuff. Turns out that Seb here was fucking someone *on* our stuff."

My eyebrows shoot up at that. No shit? Good for him. He is such a fucking tight ass when it is football season. Hopefully he will loosen up a little, doubtful, but you never know.

"Bro, not on our clothes, right?" Mike whines.

Sebastian scoffs and roll his eyes. "Why the fuck would I want to have sex with someone on top of your clothes, Mikey? Your shit takes two washes just to be considered non-toxic."

Mikey shrugs as Slater cackles. "Sooo, who was she, man?"

He shrugs. "I don't know. Didn't catch her name."

"Yeah, boy!" Slater hoots as he jumps up and down, holding onto my shoulders. "That is the shit. Get off and get out, take notes, Trev. Then maybe you won't be going to bed all alone at the end of the night."

I roll my eyes and shake my head. I am all for getting some pussy, but Slater takes it to another level. It's practically a sport for him.

"Trust me. I did enough fucking around for the last two years. I'm ready to settle down a bit."

"The fuck?" Slater asks as he looks to Seb, probably to see if I'm joking but I couldn't be more serious.

"Who is the bitch that took your ball's, bro?" Slater scoffs.

I know he is joking but him just referring to Erica as a bitch sends my blood to a boil in an instant. Before he can even blink, I have him shoved up against the tunnel wall, my forearm against his throat. I'm not pushing hard but I fucking will if he disrespects my girl like that again.

Slater's eyes are wide and extremely confused while Mikey stands there in stunned silence, his eyes bouncing around us all. I get it, I'm not the hothead of our little group, that title definitely belongs to Seb and only after you push him past the point of no return. But this is Erica we are talking about so everything is different.

Seb steps to the side, gently pushing us apart as he backs me away a few steps. I let him push me for a few moments until the anger inside of me explodes.

"Don't ever fucking talk about Erica like that again or you'll be eating your teeth, Donohue!" I snarl.

"Easy," Seb warns in clipped tone. "He's just fucking around. He's never even met her, man. He didn't mean to offend. Right, Slater?"

Slaters eyes are wide as he nods.

"Yeah, sorry bro. I was just joking. I haven't met the chick but if you care that much about her, she must be pretty cool. Can't wait to meet her."

I roll Seb's hands off my chest before I storm out of the tunnel and onto the field. I can hear Mike and Slater whisper behind me while Seb stoically follows per usual. I don't give a fuck, though. Teammate or not, friend or not, no one will breathe a bad word about my girl, no one will harm a hair on her fucking head, or they will have me to deal with.

Chapter Six

Erica

A few days later, my phone buzzes in my bag as I step out of my English class. I grab it out and unlock it as I weave my way through the crowded hallway.

Mom: I know you are avoiding my calls.

Mom: Don't think that our conversation is over, Erica. We have put too much effort in for you to throw it all away.

I huff out an aggravated breath as I read her text messages. We got into yet another fight just before I came to Brighton, and I have been strategically dodging her calls ever since. Before I can type out what would probably be a smartass remark, a body comes flying into me out of nowhere.

"Whoa," I say as I stumble a few feet.

"Hey, chica!" Palmer says brightly.

"Hey, you know normally people just say hi instead of body slamming others," I tease

She rolls her eyes. "Whatever. You are the big football fan, I thought I was making you feel comfortable."

I let out a laugh and shake my head. "What are you up to?"

"Heading to grab some lunch. What about you?"

"I was gonna stop by the library-"

"Wrong," she interrupts. "You are going to come with!"

If I wasn't so hungry, I would probably be irritated with her, but I have been so focused on studying and getting ahead that I can't remember the last time I ate a warm meal. I roll my eyes with a smile and nod before following after her to the dining hall.

Palmer grabs a Caesar salad while I opt for pizza. We grab our trays and walk past the crowded tables as we look for a spot to sit. My eyes trail over the room until they stop on a large hand waving at us.

Trevor is smiling and waving enthusiastically as he motions for us to come to him. He is such a dork sometimes, but it is one of the many loveable things about him. He is so comfortable in his own skin and doesn't give a shit who sees him. I bump Palmer's arm and nod towards him before we start making our way to Trev. Palmer grabs my elbow as she leans in close to whisper in my ear.

"Uh, how do you know Trevor Michaels and why does he look so excited to see us?" She whispers hurriedly.

I give her a funny look as I lift an eyebrow. "How do *you* know Trevor?"

She scoffs. "Please, everyone at least knows *of* him. He is the star quarterback and looks like a damn Abercrombie model."

I laugh and shrug. She isn't wrong but it is still funny for me to hear. Sometimes I forget the way other people look at Trevor. To me, he is just my Trevor. To others he is a hot football god.

"We have been best friends practically our whole lives. He was the one that invited us to that party last weekend."

"What! How did I not know this? I thought you just heard about the party or something. Oh my god, this is epic," she says as she begins to practically bounce on her toes.

"Why?" I ask as we get closer to Trev.

"Because it is Trevor freaking Michaels. Just sitting with him at lunch is going to instantly upgrade our reputations."

I let out an airy laugh and shake my head. I really don't understand people that are so concerned with how others perceive them. I guess I have seen more than enough social ladder climbing to last me a lifetime to care anymore.

I am so distracted by Palmers rambling that I almost miss who happens to be sitting next to Trevor. *Sebastian.* I sigh to myself as I force my smile not to slip. I have been kind of dreading seeing him again. He was quite frankly a dick to me the last time that I saw him. I don't want to be that pathetic girl who got her feelings hurt because she thought she was more than a hook up, but damn it, I kind of am.

If he didn't look at me like I was something special that night and touch me like he never wanted to stop, I probably wouldn't have gotten ridiculous ideas in my head of anything past the night. But he did, so I did. Then his personality flipped like a switch.

I am sure he is the same smooth flirty guy with all of his conquests at first before he treats them like dirt. Silly me for expecting anything different, I guess. Consider my first life lesson from college learned.

My eyes dart over to see that Sebastian is watching me carefully. His face is fixed into a harsh scowl, and he looks seriously pissed about the prospect of me having lunch with them. Whatever. That is his problem, not mine. I am not going to cower in the corner and cry because he has decided he doesn't want to see me again. And he is sitting with my best friend anyways! I am allowed to sit there if I want. I guarantee if Trev found out the way that Sebastian treated me, he would lose his shit on him. He doesn't tolerate people disrespecting those that he cares about.

"Hey Trev," I greet as I set my tray down across from his, completely ignoring the gorgeous brooding asshole beside him.

Trevor stands up and leans over the table as he places a quick kiss onto my cheek before sitting back down. The featherlight brush of his lips sends a light fluttering feeling in my stomach. One I haven't found in years.

"Hey, Little Red. How are you?"

"Good. This is my roommate, Palmer. Palmer, this is Trevor."

Trevor gives her a polite smile and a nod while Sebastian continues to glare at me, not even sparing Palmer a glance. I make eye contact with him, and I watch as his eyes narrow slightly. Apparently, he noticed that I chose not to introduce him or really even acknowledge him for that matter. If he wants to ignore my existence, then two can play at that game.

"Nice to meet you," Trevor says to Palmer before he looks to Seb expectantly. He apparently realizes that Sebastian won't be joining in on the introductions. Trev rolls his eyes before hooking his thumb towards Sebastian. "The grump is Sebastian. Don't be intimidated. His growl is far worse than his bite."

"Don't be so sure," Sebastian rumbles lowly, never taking his eyes off of me.

A shiver runs down my spine as my thighs clench from the memory of that night. His bite *was* pretty damn good. He seems to know exactly what I'm thinking because his firm scowl softens a bit as the corner of his mouth twitches in what looks like amusement.

Asshole.

Palmer giggles before she shrugs. "Trust me, everyone on campus knows you guys. No introductions really needed."

Trevor gets a cocky smile as he leans over the table conspiringly. "Oh yeah? And what does everyone say about us?"

Palmer's cheeks redden as she shrugs. "I mean, everyone knows you guys are some of the best players on the football team. You are also known to be pretty popular with the ladies. My cousin Tamera hooked up with you a few times and likes to tell everyone who will listen all about it."

Trevor's playful smile falls and what looks like regret flashes across his face. I don't know why, but he has been getting almost embarrassed about his playboy reputation lately. Maybe he is finally starting to outgrow it, but the reaction is very unlike Trevor, so I decide to rib him a little to get him to lighten up.

"Oh, all the girls back in Grovebury were like that too. He even had a little fan club in high school. They would bake him cookies and make him posters on game days. Didn't Amelia Rodgers pretty much do all your history homework your sophomore year?"

Trev glances at me with a nonchalant shrug. "Most. She was a little crazy. When she found out we were dating she keyed her initials into my car," he says with a grimace.

"Wait, you two dated?" Palmer asks, her jaw practically unhinged as her eyes flick between Trevor and me.

I laugh awkwardly. Is it so hard to believe? I always felt like Trevor was out of my league, but he always made me feel like the most special girl in the world that I got used to it.

"Uh, yeah. Like forever ago."

"Two years," Trevor corrects.

I shoot him a sideways look but don't say anything. He shrugs again before he picks up a fry on his plate and pops it into his mouth.

"Anyways, we decided to just be friends," I say as I turn to Palmer.

I use the term *we* very loosely. To be honest, Trev kinda broke my heart. He didn't mean to, and he did it in the kindest way possible. At the time, I didn't really understand what I did or why he was doing it to us but eventually I got it. College is a whole other universe from high school. Pair that with being four hours away while Trev is the star QB. He wanted to spread his wings and live his life without anything tying him down.

It hurt but I couldn't blame him too much. I have grown a lot in the last two years. I didn't have my personal bodyguard constantly hovering over me, ready to make anything and everything better for me. It was good for me, both of us really, and I am just thankful that our friendship never suffered from it all. I would die if I lost Trev in my life.

"That's cool," Palmer says. "Ethan and I broke up for a little while a couple years ago too. The space was good for us."

I nod. "Sometimes you don't realize what you have until you lose it."

Sebastian makes some sort of grunt under his breath that has me cocking my head towards him.

"Something to share?" I bite out harsher than I normally would to, well, really anyone else.

I am already sick of his shit, and I have only been around him for less than two minutes. I want to snap at him and ask him where the hell the guy that I first met went and if he will be back anytime soon. Because this Sebastian Caldwell, I am definitely not interested in even sharing the same oxygen with. I just wish he hadn't given me one of the best nights of my life. I also wish I wasn't still so damn attracted to him.

Sebastian leans towards me, his eyes narrowed as his arms fold across his wide chest.

"It's just interesting that some people have to lose something to realize that it's good. If you can't see it for what it is, then you probably didn't deserve it in the first place."

His words instantly piss me off. I am always so calm and collected, I never had any other choice, but around him I feel out of control with my emotions. One moment I am drowning in ecstasy, the next I am hurt and feeling more broken than I should, and now I am ready to throttle his ass in the middle of the cafeteria. This man is severely messing with my head, and I am not okay.

"Yeah? And who are you to determine what someone does or doesn't deserve?" I ask as I lean over the table.

"I haven't lived a life of luxury unlike some, Princess. While you were fed from a golden spoon your whole life, others were forced to eat from a wooden one. It's usually the people that have had everything handed to them who take things for granted. People like that use and abuse those around them and then write a fat check to make things go away."

"Seb," Trevor snaps harshly.

My jaw tightens as I fight back the burning sensation that is building behind my eyes. Unfortunately, I am one of those obnoxious people that cry when they are angry. Then everyone thinks that you are sad when you are actually just so fucking mad, which only makes you cry even more. Fucking angry tears.

Without saying anything, I pick up my tray and stand up, keeping my eyes trained on Sebastian while I do so. I step to the side and dump my half-eaten food into the trash before I lean down to Sebastian, our faces so close that our noses almost brush. I have to fight like hell to keep my mind focused and resist getting drawn into his alluring eyes.

"You don't know a *thing* about me or my life," I say in the most even tone that I can muster as emotion quickly begins clogging my throat.

As I pull away, a lone tear drops, skating its way down my cheek. Sebastian's narrowed eyes soften as he relaxes back into his seat. He doesn't say anything as he watches me with what appears to be his signature impassive mask. Feeling that I have hit my max capacity for bullshit for the day, I turn on my heel and walk away without another word.

I hear Trevor and Palmer both call my name, but I keep walking. I don't want to talk about why some careless words hurt so bad. I don't want to explain that they hurt more than they should because of the person who is saying them. They wouldn't get it. I just want to push everything and anything about Sebastian Caldwell out of my mind.

CHAPTER SEVEN

SEBASTIAN

"Hike!"

Trevor shouts the word that causes the previous virtual silence on the field to splinter apart. I blow past the lineman in my way as my legs stretch out to gain as much yardage as possible. When I turn my head, I see that Trev is already looking at me, ready for me to give him the signal that I'm ready.

As soon as our eyes meet, he sends a bullet my way. I'm fucking fast for a guy my size but even this throw is a reach. My legs burn with the strain but when I feel that leather ball cradle into my hands and tuck against my chest all other thoughts fall away.

A few defensemen rush me and get fucking close, but my long strides have them beat and in no time, I'm crossing that white line.

Touchdown. Fuck, yeah.

My teammates clap my back enthusiastically as Slater practically jumps on top of me, whooping like a fucking monkey as he cheers.

"Fuck yeah, boy! That's how we dooooo! Whoop whoop!"

I smirk, shaking my head as I roll the crazy fuckers hands off my shoulders. I love football for a lot of reasons, but nothing beats bringing home a win for your team and when I hear that timer run out and signal the end of the game, I blow out a deep breath.

Another win for Brighton.

I may fuck up through life, but not on the field. On that green turf is where I fucking thrive, it's where I live.

After we all hit the showers and get the congratulatory speeches from the coaches, we are all ushered back onto the bus to head back to campus. We are up at Appleton State which is only about a four hour drive so I take advantage of the dark ride and try to get some much needed rest.

The rest of the week goes by in a blur of practice and classes. Things are good. Well, kinda. Trevor is still pretty pissed at me for being an ass to Erica the other day at lunch. I didn't actually mean to be. I'm a nice enough guy, usually. There is just something about Erica Pembrooke that gets under my fucking skin. She is a constant reminder of what a shitty friend I am and every time her name comes out of Trevor's mouth it becomes more and more clear that she isn't going away anytime soon.

I didn't know that she was going to take my words so personally, though. Not gonna lie, I felt like a piece of shit when I saw that tear slide down her face. For a split second, I had the urge to brush away that tear and make her show me that bright smile that causes my heart to do that weird stutter thing.

I quickly pushed that horrible idea down though and scolded myself for even letting it come to the surface in the first place. Maybe me being an ass was for the best. Maybe if she hates me, it will make it that much easier for me to stay away from her.

It's Sunday, which means rest day. I'm in my bed going over our playbook when a short knock comes from my door before Trevor barges in. I glance up to him before returning my eyes to the page.

"Please, come in," I drawl sarcastically.

Trevor scoffs as he reaches down to close the playbook before tossing it to the end of my bed. My eyes flick up to him and I give him an irritated glare.

"I was reading that."

"And now you aren't. Stop being a dick and come out with us. We are going to the Fall Festival, and you are coming too," he says as he crosses his arms with a look that brokers no arguments.

"Pass," I say as I reach for the playbook.

Trevor swipes it out of my reach before throwing it onto my desk across the room.

"It wasn't a question. It was a statement. Get your broody ass up and in the shower. You fucking smell."

I roll my eyes and stand up before rolling my shoulders out. Trevor nods seemingly satisfied as he turns to leave my room. He stops in the doorway and turns around quickly.

"Erica and her roommate are gonna meet us there. Try not to be a dick this time, yeah?"

I clench my jaw but give him a terse nod before brushing past him and shutting the bathroom door. His words piss me off even if they are valid. I don't want to cause issues between us by being cold towards Erica, but shit, the idea of being around her fucking turns my stomach.

In twenty minutes, I am showered, dressed and out the door with Trev. Mikey and Slater apparently already left and said that they would hook up with us later. The Fall Festival is a big thing at Brighton. The entire campus becomes one big fair. Vendors and shops set up stands, there are games and contests, the whole shebang.

It has never really been my thing, but I usually go with the guys for the beer and hot girls that traipse around in their 'country' clothes. They usually consist of shorts so tiny they'd make Daisy Duke blush and flannel shirts tied just under their tits. Maybe I can find someone to hook up with quick so that I can get away from Trev and Erica. They can go do their thing and I'll do mine.

Yeah, good plan.

Trevor and I are walking through the packed quad when a slim body launches into Trevor's arms. He seems momentarily taken back as he stumbles before catching the girl by the back of her thighs. The smell of peaches wafts through the air between us and I instantly know who is in his arms.

"Damn, Little Red. You hit harder than a lineman. You almost took me out," Trevor says as Erica pulls away and hops down with a big smile spread across her face.

"Like number 72 kept doing, yesterday? You weren't getting rid of the ball quick enough, and you deserved every one of those sacks."

Trevor scoffs with mock offence, though his cheesy grin tells me that he is anything but offended. He lights up like a damn Christmas tree anytime he is around her. It's fucking annoying.

"Always the critic," Trevor grumbles. "I liked it better when you blindly told me how amazing I was after every game."

Erica rolls her eyes and shoves him. "That was when you had a fragile teenage ego that I had to protect. You're a big boy now, you can handle some harsh truths."

Trevor and Erica laugh for a moment before Erica's eyes snag mine. Her smile becomes a little strained and her bright eyes dim just a hair. She looks less than thrilled to see me here and for some reason that shit kinda bothers me. It's stupid though. Her not enjoying being around me is a good thing because the feeling is mutual.

"Hey," she says softly as she watches me carefully.

Her silky smooth voice swirls around in my head for a moment, sending an unfamiliar feeling creeping into my stomach. Quickly, I shove that shit to the side and give her an unenthusiastic head nod. What looks like disappointment flashes across her face before she shakes it off and turns back to Trevor. I take the opportunity to let my gaze linger on her for a few moments longer than I intended and fuck if I'm not instantly pissed.

By definition, Erica isn't dressed provocatively. Unlike half of the women here today, she is wearing an appropriate length of jean shorts and her flannel is buttoned until just under her perky breasts where a white tank top hugs her curves perfectly. She is acceptably covered but seeing her creamy skin on display in any amount has my fingers twitching in anticipation to feel it again. I remember the way those thighs felt wrapped around me, I remember how her soft pink nipples practically melted into my mouth and I remember how her slim fingers felt as they traced over me.

I am so lost in thought as I rake my eyes up and down her body that I don't even realize that she has been talking to me until Trevor nudges me. My eyes flick up from her sliver of cleavage to her heated eyes. But instead of heated with lust, it looks an awful lot like contempt.

"Like what you see?" She sneers.

I school my features quickly and give an unimpressed shrug as I cross my arms across my chest.

"There are plenty of beautiful women out here dressing up like country sluts, you are just one of many, sweetheart."

My words are total horseshit, but she doesn't have to know that. Where others are desperately trying to be sexy by showing as much skin as they can paired with as much makeup as they can cake on to their face, Erica is just effortlessly beautiful. It radiates from her, and everyone knows it, everyone sees it. Even me. Unfortunately.

Hurt slams across her features before she shoves it away and raises her chin a little higher while she pushes her shoulders back a little farther. Most women would have probably crumbled, burst out into tears and ran away or told me to go to hell. Instead, Erica looks like a woman ready to go to battle. I wait for her jaded words, her harsh names or nasty insults. Instead, she just stares me down.

Trevor, however, does not stay silent. He roughly shoves me as his face colors to an angry shade of red.

"What the fuck! I can't believe you just said that. Stop being a prick for five fucking seconds and apologize!"

I take a small step back to get my balance before I square my shoulders towards Trevor. My jaw ticks as I look at him for a few moments, attempting to reign in my defensive anger that is beginning to rise. I glance out of the corner of my eye to see an impassive Erica watching us closely.

"Forget it, Trev. He isn't worth it," she says as she pulls on his arm gently. "Come on. I want a caramel apple."

Trevor nods, never taking his eyes off of me. "Yeah alright. Let's go," he says as he snakes an arm around Erica's shoulders before turning and walking in the opposite direction like the good little lap dog he seems to become when he is around her.

I stand in place for a few moments as an overwhelming feeling courses through my veins. It feels a lot like rage as I watch Trevor tighten his grip on Erica as he pulls her closer to his side. They look so natural together, like it is just the way things are supposed to be.

Well, if she didn't hate me before, I would say that I sealed the deal today.

The next day I stay late at practice. Anything to get just a little bit faster, a little bit better. Plus, Trevor is still pissed at me about yesterday. I expected him to come into my room and chew me out for yesterday, but instead he gave me the cold shoulder. Not like I didn't deserve it, I guess.

When I get to the house, I am beat and looking forward to taking a long hot shower and passing out in bed. Unfortunately, the thumping bass coming from inside tells me that won't be as easy as I was hoping.

I push the door open and see half of the team as well as the entire cheerleading squad pouring out of every room, all with drinks in their hands. College life, the party never stops.

I peek my head into the living room to see that Mikey and Trevor are playing Call of Duty on the couch with several girls sitting around them watching. I decide not to be a total anti-social prick and join them at least for a bit.

"Hey man, where you been?" Trev asks as I sit on the couch next to him.

"Practice. I stayed back to run some drills with Martinez."

Trevor nods as he continues to play. *I guess we are good now.* I notice that a girl has sidled up next to me and is practically sitting in my lap. I give her a questioning look and notice that she looks familiar. I think that I hooked up with her last year, what was her name? Brittney? Bethany?

"Hi Sebastian," she says shyly as she tucks a piece of her sleek hair behind her ear.

"Hey."

"How have you been?"

"Good. You?"

She smiles and leans in a little closer like she takes my one syllable responses as genuine interest.

"Really good. I lost five pounds over the summer and now I am a flyer! Isn't that amazing?"

"Sure," I nod as I turn my attention back to the TV.

I feel her hand lightly trail across my thigh before I glance out of the corner of my eye to see her giving me what looks to be a seductive smile. Unfortunately for the both of us, it does nothing for me.

I don't know what is wrong with me. She is pretty hot. With her long dark hair, full lips and curvy body, that if memory serves me right is pretty fucking banging, there isn't a guy on campus that would pass on the obvious good time she is offering. But for some reason, I'm not even a little interested.

It could be that she is coming off a little too easy, or maybe I am not interested in going after seconds. Or maybe it's because she doesn't have long vibrant red hair, bright aqua eyes and a smile that could knock a grown man on his ass.

Without saying a word, I push her hand off my leg and stand up before I head to my room. Figures the one girl that can hold my attention for longer than a night is the only one that I can't have. I should probably just take Bailey upstairs and screw Erica right out of my head once and for all. For some annoying as fuck reason though, I don't think that it would help.

Chapter Eight

Trevor

Me: Meet me at the stadium. I got us food.

Her reply comes in only seconds later.

Little red: Food? Say less.

I smile at her words as I tuck my phone into my pocket before sitting down on the turf of the field as I look around me. Sometimes I forget what a dream I am living right now. Being right here was all I could think about as a kid. Getting several hours away from my parents was only the cherry on top of the dream. Don't get me wrong, I love them, and they aren't nearly as hard on me as Erica's are on her, but they are definitely hard people to please and me hoping to one day become an NFL player is not something they approve of.

They are fine with me playing ball in college, they know I have to stay out of trouble and keep my grades up if I want to play so they were for it. But they have big plans for me after graduation, plans that don't include football. I can't fucking imagine a life like that.

For now, I am living the dream. I am an all-star quarterback for one of the top collegiate football teams in the country, I have the best teammates and the best friends a guy could get, and I finally have her. Not the way I want just yet, but I will. Erica Pembrooke is worth the fucking world, and I will do anything to get her back where she belongs, in my arms again.

I still hate myself for breaking her years ago, breaking us. I was stupid and ignorant. I wasn't sure if we could make the distance work. Of fucking course, we could have. When she is in the room, she is all I fucking see and when she is gone, she is all I think about. The excitement and unknown of college blinded that. I wanted to spread my wings, to experience everything to the fullest. The shine of it all wore off quicker than I could have thought, and I was left wishing that I hadn't thrown away the best thing that ever happened to me.

Once I pulled my head out of my ass, I went back home. I didn't tell anyone. I wanted it to be a surprise. When I showed up at her house, she was getting dropped off by that fuck boy Nick. He was sucking her face off like it was an Olympic sport, and it took everything in me not to rip his damn head off. But then she pulled away with a dazed smile and stars in her eyes as she looked up at him. I could see it all over her face that she wasn't thinking about me in that moment, she had moved on and I just couldn't bring myself to take that from her, even if I knew that I was the best person for her. That it was always us. I wanted her to come to that, not me put it there.

So, I got back in my car, drove back to campus and lost myself in some nameless girl that looked a hell of a lot like Erica. Fucked up, I know.

It's all different now, though. She doesn't have a boyfriend. She isn't hours away. She is unattached, here and mine. If she doesn't already know that yet she will, soon, just not tonight. The angel herself comes walking across the field, her bright hair in loose waves, her perfect face makeup-free as she smiles down at me while her long lean legs make their way closer and closer to me.

Not trying to hold back my smile, I stand up and close the space between us. Wrapping her up into my arms as I hold her as tight as possible. Her arms snake around mine as I bury my head into the crook of her neck. She fits so perfectly.

Erica is the one to pull away first, because if it was up to me, I would never stop touching her. She smiles at me wide, causing my heart to ball up in my chest at the sight. Shit, she is so gorgeous. She shoves me to the side playfully, probably trying to wipe off the goofy grin I have spread across my face. Good fucking luck, though. It's been a permanent fixture since this summer.

"So, where is the goods? Don't hold out on me, Trev. You know what I'm like when I get hangry."

I fake shudder as I walk over and hand her the strawberry milkshake and bag of burgers and fries.

"No need to threaten me. I make good on my promises."

Her eyes light up at the food as she practically takes my hands off to get a hold of it before sucking down the shake like it is the fountain of youth. She moans as the flavor hits her mouth while tilting her head back. My cock stiffens at the sound, and I have to shuffle my feet slightly to help hide the growing hard on that seems to come out whenever she is around these days.

"Shit. I've never been so jealous of a straw in my life, Little Red."

Her eyes widen for a moment before she swallows the drink and cackles out loud. Clearly not taking my words serious. That's okay, she doesn't have to know how true they are.

"You're too much, Trev!" She laughs as she shakes her head and plops down onto the ground.

I smirk as I do the same.

"Not the first time I have heard that," I wink.

"I'll bet. From what I hear you have been keeping the female population of Brighton pretty damn satisfied for the last two years," she teases.

My smirk drops instantly as my stomach twists. I know that some girls talk about who they have hooked up with, but have I

THE LOYALTIES WE BREAK

really developed that much of a reputation? Normally, I wouldn't care but I can't imagine me being known for sleeping with a ton of girls is anything close to a turn on for a girl, especially a girl like Erica. I don't want her to think she would ever have anything to worry about. That if she gave us a chance again, she would be my whole world, just like she was before.

"That isn't me anymore, Little Red. You know who I am, that isn't me," I say seriously.

Her teasing smile dims as she nods seriously.

"I know, Trev. I was just kidding. There is nothing wrong with having some fun. I haven't exactly been celibate myself over the years."

Anger burns through my veins at her words. I fucking hate that anyone else has ever touched her. I was her first and if I wouldn't have fucked things up, I probably would be her only. Fuck. I wish I could go back in time and kick my own ass. What the ever-loving fuck was I thinking?

"Yeah," I grit out between clenched teeth, trying and failing to lose the sharp bite in my words.

She cocks an eyebrow in question, but I just shake my head and reach for my burger. When she takes a bite of hers, she nods her head in appreciation as she talks over a mouthful of food. Only she could do that and still be cute as shit.

"Not bad. Not Moe's, but not bad."

"Free food is free food, lady," I say as I toss a fry at her face.

As an athlete, burgers and fries are not exactly in my daily regimen but for her, I decided to make an exception today. She has been kinda down lately, and I intend to find out why.

"So," I start as I finish the last of my burger. "You going to tell me what has been going on with you lately?"

Her back straightens slightly as she dusts her hands off and stands up, reaching for the football I brought with at her feet before walking backwards a bit.

"What do you mean?"

I roll my eyes and bag up our food before tossing it to the side as I stand up and start walking backwards. When we are a good enough distance away, Erica tosses the ball to me. I catch it effortlessly as I let out a short chuckle.

"You can throw a damn good spiral, Little Red but you're a shit liar."

She winces because she knows it's true. She could never get away with that shit, not with me. I can read her better than a playbook.

"I'm fine, Trev. It's just a lot," she says as I throw the ball to her.

"What is?"

"Everything. Life is different here, but it isn't. I'm living on my own, at a new school with new friends-"

"And old ones," I chime in, causing her to give me an eyeroll and a smile.

"And yet, it's all still the same. My parents control my life like they are puppeteers, and I am just here to keep the show rolling. Pre-law it's just...fucking hard."

I nod because I get that. "It'll be worth it in the end, Little Red. You have been working towards this your whole life."

"Maybe I'm realizing the future laid out in front of me isn't the one I want. Do you ever feel that way?" She asks as she tosses the ball back to me.

I shrug as it lands into my arms.

"I have the best of both worlds, I got football for now and halfway through my bachelor's."

"You don't need a bachelor's degree to play in the NFL, though," she points out.

I know where she is going with this. I'm being a hypocrite because as much as I would love to say screw it to my parents and chase the dreams, we both know the more likely scenario will be me giving up on my dreams to help run the family business. It's what my father has talked about ever since I was born. It's my legacy. Kinda like being a lawyer is hers.

"You'd make a great lawyer, Little Red. I know it's hard, but I also know you like keeping your family happy, as much as I do. Whatever you choose to do with life, you'll do great at."

She gives me a sad smile as she catches the ball and looks down at the ground.

"Yeah," she says, dejectedly.

I cross the space between us slowly and tilt her head up to face me. When those bright blue eyes look into mine my heart starts to pound as a million different memories flash through my mind. Then, a million potential memories begin. Ones where Erica and I move back home to help with our family businesses, ones where we move in together, build a life together. Where she has my ring on her finger and my baby in her stomach.

We could have it all, Little Red. Do you feel it?

Tentatively, I lean down slowly, giving her plenty of time to pull away. Her eyes flash with surprise but instead of her pushing me away like I half expected, the surprise leaves her eyes and interest takes over as she just barely lifts her chin in my direction. I don't waste another second, pressing my lips against hers as I begin to lose myself in her.

My tongue darts out and licks against the seam of her lips as she gently parts for me, allowing me full access. Stroking slowly, I brush against her tongue as my hands pull her head closer to me until we are practically smashed together. A needy whimper leaves her as I trail my tongue across hers again, our sweet kiss turning to something a lot more heated and a fuck ton better.

Pulling away from her lips I begin quickly kissing a line from her jaw down to her neck before pulling the strap of her top and bra to the side, freeing her full breast as my hand cups it. She lets out a heavy moan as she tilts her head back.

"Trev. We shouldn't be doing this here," she gasps.

Instead of answering her, I brush my thumb against the dusty rose pebbled nipple in my hand before I dive down and capture it in my mouth. Licking and sucking on her, I feel Erica's hand cup the back of my head, urging me on. My tongue flicks against her before I take her nipple between my teeth.

"Oh my god. Trev!" She whimpers.

Fuck. It feels like it's been forever since I have heard her say my name like that. I guess it has been. I want her in every fucking way possible I don't even know where to begin. I could fucking drown in Erica Pembrooke. Tearing my mouth away from her breast, I growl into her ear as I help lay her down onto the turf.

"I need to taste you, Little Red."

She makes an approving noise as she frantically nods her head. I make quick work of getting her leggings down before yanking her panties down and burying my face between her silky smooth thighs. Fuck. She still smells the same, she tastes the same. Like fucking liquid heaven.

Not being able to pace myself, I savagely devour her pussy, licking up every drop she has to offer me before I move to her clit, furiously flicking my tongue across as her legs begin to quake. I chuckle against her skin, causing her to let out another moan. She was always quick to get off when I went down on her and clearly that hasn't changed. My girl is more than ready to come and there isn't anything more I want than to have her taste explode on my tongue.

Slipping a finger inside her, I curl up until I am rubbing her g-spot as I continue to lick and suck on her clit.

"Trev! Oh fuck! Oh my god! I'm gonna...I'm gonna..."

I add another finger as I pick up my pace and shake my head from side to side rapidly, causing her body to quiver and shake as she shouts out my name for the whole empty stadium to hear. Her cum rushes against my tongue, and I don't waste a second as I lick and suck every inch of her release. Fuck. How I went two years without my mouth on her pussy, I'll never know.

Looking up, I see Erica staring down at me with a lazy smile. I shoot her a wink as I slowly sit up and palm my cock through my jeans. I'm so fucking hard I feel my balls are going to explode if I wait any longer. I have to be inside of her.

"Trevor," she says as she bites her lower lip.

"Yeah, Little Red?"

"Trevor," she says again.

"Yeah?" I nod.

Suddenly a hand lands on my shoulder, shoving me to the side until I stumble backwards. Blinking hard, I look around to see that I am standing, so is Erica, fully clothed. My brows furrow as I look down to the ground where I could have sworn, I was just feasting on Erica's delectable pussy.

"You okay, Trev? Looks like I lost you for a bit there," she says with a soft smile.

I blink hard as disappointment floods me as I nod and rub a hand over my face before giving her a tired smile.

"Yeah, I'm good, Little Red."

Erica nods as she hugs me tightly around the waist, leaning her head against my chest.

"Thanks for tonight, Trev. You are the best friend anyone could have, ever."

The word friend echoes in my mind and has my gut clenching with fear. Is that all she will ever see me as? Did I fuck up my chance as her seeing me as a man that would love and cherish and fuck her right given the chance?

Chapter Nine

Sebastian

For the next couple of weeks, my interactions with Erica are few and far between. We have been living and breathing football lately and traveling a ton for back to back away games. When we do have a free moment in our schedule, Trevor has reserved every second for Erica, thankfully for everyone involved. I am no longer invited along when they hangout.

It has been three weeks since that night together, and she probably occupies more of my thoughts than ever before. No matter how hard I try to forget her and that night, it doesn't work. The memories are burned into my brain. Seared into my skin.

When I do run into her either on campus or at the grocery store, I pretend that I don't even see her and when she is with Trevor and I have no choice but to acknowledge her, our interactions are practically glacial. Trevor has confronted me about why I am such a prick to her. I panicked for a moment before I gave him a nonchalant shrug and told him that she just rubs me the wrong way, which isn't a total lie. That wrong way just happens to feel really fucking good.

I have replayed nearly every encounter that I have had with Erica over the last three weeks in my head and have come to a conclusion, I'm a fucking asshole. As good as it is for me to keep my distance from her and keep up my cold front, I'm fucking sick of it. I know that she can't be mine, but we could at least be civil, maybe even friends one day.

Maybe if I keep feeding myself this bullshit, something will actually stick.

I don't know her that well but from what I do know she is nice when I'm not being an ass. She is also really cool, someone that I could genuinely enjoy being around, and that list is extremely fucking small. It doesn't hurt that she knows more about football than most the guys on the team. It's a fucking turn on to see a gorgeous girl genuinely interested in a game that is my whole fucking world. *As if she needed to be any hotter.*

On Thursday night, a panicked Trevor comes blazing down the stairs with a trash can in hand, hurriedly chucking all of the empty beer cans and garbage wrappers laying around the house. Most are thanks to Mikey and Slater, who are currently at a frat party, of course.

"Dude, what is with the speed demon cleaning? I thought you were going to that Alpha Sigma Party" I ask as I begin another set of curls in the living room.

"Erica is coming over! She will be here any fucking minute. The place is fucking trashed, I have to take a shower. Fuck! Who the hell leaves eggs sitting out all fucking day!" He shouts before dumping the half-eaten breakfast that Mikey made this morning into the trash.

My chest clenches and no matter how much I tell it to calm the fuck down it doesn't let up. Just the idea of seeing Erica in person has my body buzzing with anticipation. Fuck. I have got to get it together. I'm still wishing that this was all a fucked up dream and that when I wake up, I could go find my mystery girl from that night and her name wouldn't be Erica and my best friend wouldn't be nuts about her.

Unfortunately, this is not a dream, and my best friend is currently racing around, getting ready to spend the night hanging out with the girl that I can't get out of my head. The same girl he is hoping to convince to fall in love with him...again. How fucking twisted did my life get in three little weeks?

"Is everything okay?" I ask, instantly jumping to the conclusion that maybe something is wrong with Erica and that is why she is coming over. She hasn't been over since the day after the party. The one where I was a dick to her (Honestly, though. Who can keep track of all the times I was a dick to her at this point?). She obviously has been avoiding coming over so there has to be a reason why tonight is different.

"What? Yeah, everything is fine. Her roommate and her boyfriend are going at it, and they locked her out, so she doesn't have anywhere to go."

Trevor continues to ping pong all over the house like a mad man and I can't help but shake my head at his franticness. I get that he likes her, I mean who wouldn't, but he needs to chill the hell out. He turns into a flustered mess anytime he is around her, it's almost pathetic, honestly. Then again, maybe it's good if she sees him like this, it definitely increases my chances with her.

No. I scold myself. *You don't have a shot with her. She is your best friends ex. The same ex that he is still crazy about. You slept together once and that was one time too many. You can't have her.*

The more I tell myself that though, the more I fucking want her. Fucked up, I know.

"Trevor!" I bark.

He freezes mid-step at my harsh tone and looks up at me with wide eyes.

"Calm the fuck down and go take a shower. You smell like shit. I will finish picking up, okay?"

He nods and seems to visibly relax. "Thanks, man. Sorry. She has me all fucking twisted."

I let out a humorless laugh and nod. *I know the fucking feeling.* "Yeah. It's cool man. I got this."

Trevor jogs upstairs and I hear the water turn on shortly after. I move over to the couch and pick up a few stray pieces of clothes and carry them to the laundry bin before a soft knock comes from the door. My stomach dips for a moment before I tell myself to lock that shit down. She currently hates me and has every right to feel that way. At best, all we could ever be is friends. Friends don't get excited to see other friends, not like this. I slowly walk up to the door, forcing myself to breathe as I prepare myself to see her again.

Chapter Ten

Erica

I knock on the door before folding my arms across my chest. It's a little cold tonight, and I wasn't able to grab a jacket before I left. I wasn't able to grab anything but my phone, actually. One minute, I was sitting on my bed studying and the next, Palmer and Ethan busted though the door half naked and practically already screwing.

They stopped long enough for Palmer to hand me a twenty and tell me to go to the movies before she physically shoved me out the door and wedged a chair under so I couldn't get in. I mean she did warn me, but I thought she was at least mostly joking. The amount of times that I have seen Ethan naked in our dorm room just in the last week confirms that she was very much not joking.

It is Thursday and there are a ton of parties and different things going on around campus, but I am not really into any of that tonight, so I decided to take Trevor up on his offer. I told him that if he was busy, I could find something else to do but he immediately told me it was more than okay and to head right over so here I am, freezing my ass off while I wait for him to open the door.

I lift my hand to knock again but before I can, the door gets pulled away from me, causing me to stumble a few steps. A pair of large hands wrap around my waist, steadying me before I faceplant onto the floor. I look up to find a rich pair of caramel eyes that are watching me intently. We stand there for a few seconds silent, almost transfixed with each other.

"Hi," I rasp softly.

Sebastian blinks once as his fingers flex against my hips just for a moment before he pulls away quickly and steps inside.

"Hey."

I step through the door as he shuts it behind me before burying his hands into his pockets, watching me.

"Where is Trevor?" I ask after a few awkward seconds.

"Shower. He'll be out soon."

I nod as we stand in the entry way, not knowing what to say or what not to say. It's pretty crazy how the stars in my eyes faded so fast and all the warm fuzzy feelings that I was feeling for the man in front of me quickly turned into burning contempt. The guy has been officially branded a colossal jerk in my head and the worst part is that I know we will be having to put up with each other for a while at least for Trevor's sake. I'm just thankful that he has been scarce lately, guess the streak had to break eventually.

"Erica," his deep voice rumbles. I look up to him cautiously and watch as his stone like face, as always, gives nothing away. "Look, I'm sorry, for everything. Since that night, I've been an asshole and you don't deserve it. I just didn't realize that you were Trevor's ex and we...you know."

"Had sex?" I bite out as I cross my arms over my chest.

His eyes flick to the staircase like he is checking to make sure that we are still alone before he gives me a sharp nod.

"Anyways, I'm sorry. I don't want there to be bad blood between us."

His face is somber as he speaks and his eyes bore straight through me, like they are almost begging me to forgive him. It all seems a little too out of character for him, though. I narrow my eyes in suspicion.

"Did Trevor make you apologize or something?"

Sebastian's somber look begins to melt away as irritation seeps in.

"No. He didn't. I'm a grown ass man and don't need someone to tell me when I fucked up."

"Could have fooled me."

His nostrils flare as his eyes narrow.

"Whatever. I'm just trying to apologize but if you're gonna make it difficult then, just fucking forget it," he practically growls.

I let out an exasperated sigh and shake my head.

"Whatever. I'm sorry too. I know you're trying to make amends. I appreciate it. I don't want things to be weird between us either. Trevor is the most important person in my life, and I can tell that you mean a lot to him too, so I think that it's best if we just put everything behind us."

Sebastian's eyes flash with something that I can't quite name and he looks like he is about to say something before he thinks better of it and shakes his head.

"You're right. Truce?" He asks as he sticks out his hand.

I let a small smile slip as I nod and shake his hand. When I do, his frown lifts and what I would call an almost smile spreads across his face. Just like that, an almost smile transforms him from being a broody hot jerk to a melt worthy Greek God. Maybe it is good that he doesn't fully smile often, I don't think I could survive it.

It takes me a moment to notice that we are still holding hands. His thumb is softly stroking the back of my hand almost absent-mindedly. The feeling sends electricity zapping up my arm and I'm currently trying to think of plausible excuses that will get him to continue doing this all night. Just because nothing will ever happen between us again doesn't mean that I can't enjoy his touch, right?

Sebastian seems to notice his soft caress at the same time I do. His eyes glance down to where our hands are touching before his eyes flick up to meet mine. He opens his mouth to say something, but we are interrupted by Trevor's hurried voice.

"Hey! You're here! That was fast. Sorry, just had to pop in the shower."

He seems jittery and stressed which makes me instantly feel like shit because I know him way too well.

"Oh god, you had plans, didn't you? And then I asked to come over and you rushed around like a maniac to cancel your plans and try to clean the place up."

Trevor's eyes narrow as he glares at Sebastian who holds up his hands in surrender.

"I didn't say shit."

"No, he didn't. I just know you, dummy. We grew up together and you have the same panicked look on your face that you get every time you have to rush to do anything."

Trevor's anxiousness seems to slowly ease, and he nods sheepishly before laughing.

"Yeah. It's been a crazy week and the house was trashed. I was thinking we could watch a movie. Maybe order some Chinese?"

"Well, you know I can never turn down Sesame Chicken. Any good places around here, Sebastian?"

Sebastian seems completely taken by surprise that I would ask him his opinion and he freezes for a moment before looking over to Trevor and then back to me.

"Yeah, Bonsai Palace is pretty good, and they deliver. Best Sesame chicken I've ever had, and the portions are huge."

"Sweet. I'll call it in. What do you guys want?" I ask as I pull out my phone.

I glance up from my screen to see Sebastian and Trevor share some silent communication for a few moments before Sebastian turns to me.

"Nothing for me. I got some stuff to work on. You two enjoy."

I can't help but feel a pang of disappointment as I watch his retreating form head up the stairs. I know it's dumb and I should be happy that I get to spend time with my best friend who I came here to hang out with. I can't deny though, that the idea of spending time with the non-asshole version of Sebastian sends a thrill through me. Maybe now that he has decided to get over himself, we could-

No. Bad idea. I thought I already learned my lesson?

Turning to Trevor I smile. "Orange chicken?"

He gives me a lopsided grin and nods. "I'll look for a movie."

The Chinese food comes quick, and Sebastian was right, it's delicious. Trevor and I spend the night laughing and talking about our families, football and anything else that comes to mind. He has always been like my other half. Being around him is as easy as breathing.

When I blink my eyes open, I notice that the house is dark. I look to the TV receiver where it says that it is 2:03AM. Obviously, Trevor and I don't have the stamina for staying up all night long like we used to because he is passed out next to me with one of his arms flopped over his face. I notice that he has his other arm curled around me while my head is resting in his lap.

I don't even remember curling up into him. I remember we were watching the movie and then my eyes got heavy and...I guess that's it. It's almost like no time has passed. I'm right back to sophomore year, waking up in Trevor's arms after one of the hundreds of times that he spent the night at my house. There used to be nothing better than falling asleep in his arms. I have to admit it still feels strangely good. It feels comforting, like coming home.

I slowly ease out of Trevor's hold, doing my best not to wake him. When I stand up, I look down at him and smile before brushing back part of his hair that has begun to drape into his face. He really is handsome. I definitely see what all the girls go crazy for. Pair that with the amazing person that he is, and he is really a catch.

Ever since coming to Brighton he has been extremely affection-ate, always touching me in some way and spending practically all of his free time with me. Thoughts that I was sure had been long buried have been popping up lately. It isn't like he has out right said anything but tonight isn't the first time that I have wondered if he is wanting to give us a shot again.

Tonight, is the first night that I am seriously wondering if that is something that I want too. Just last year we agreed the breakup was good for us, that we needed it. I can't deny that the thought of trying again with Trevor has me equally excited and terrified. When you have so much history with someone how could it not be amazing, right? But we broke up for a reason, right? Was it all just because of Brighton? Or was there more to it? I don't know.

Since it is way too late/early to be thinking about something so serious I carefully pad my way into the kitchen to get a bottle of water. I open the fridge and see that it is practically brimming with old take-out containers and pizza boxes.

Nice to see these fine athletes are maintaining a healthy diet.

Just as I grab a bottle of water, a deep voice catches me by surprise from the entryway to the kitchen.

"Couldn't sleep?" Sebastian asks softly just above a whisper.

I let out a surprised yip as I turn around quickly and practically plaster myself against the fridge. It takes me a second for my eyes to adjust from the bright light of the fridge to the dark room but when they do, I find a sleep mussed Sebastian, his hair for once free and hanging at his shoulders. One of my biggest regrets about that night we spent together was that I didn't get a chance to run my fingers through his hair. It's all I can practically think about when I am around him.

"I didn't realize that we fell asleep," I whisper back. "I was just going to grab a water before I head back to my dorm."

"No," he says firmly.

My brows furrow in confusion. "No?"

He nods. "Yeah, no. You aren't going to walk across campus by yourself at 2AM. Just stay here."

I shrug. "Well, call me a snob but I would still prefer to sleep in a bed. Unless you know someone that is offering to share theirs?"

As soon as the words slip out, I instantly regret them. Seriously, Erica? Did we not just go over the fact that you need to keep things platonic with this man? Not try to jump into bed with him. It isn't like it worked out very well the last time, anyways. And there is Trevor to think about. You know, your best friend that you were just cuddling with not two minutes ago?

Sebastian's body stiffens slightly, and I don't think that he realizes that he licks his lips, but he definitely does, and it is one of the sexiest things that I have ever seen in my whole life. Quickly though, he shakes his head softly as if to shake his thoughts away before he clears his throat.

"I'm sure Trevor wouldn't mind if you used his bed."

Right. Trevor. My ex. My best friend. One of the best men that I have ever met in my life. The one I love and adore and could more than likely see myself ending up with again one day.

I nod softly and shut the fridge door, instantly plunging us into darkness. I only make it two steps before I jam my toe into the dining room table. I gasp in pain while trying to be quiet since I know that people are sleeping, but it hurts really fucking bad.

"Ow, ow, ow, owww," I whisper whine as I hold my foot with a pathetically pained face.

Sebastian is next to me in a flash and bends down to hold my foot in his hand. *Thank the lord I just recently got a pedicure.* He inspects my toe carefully, taking care not to accidently bump it before he gently lowers it to the ground.

"It isn't broken or anything, but that damn table has gotten me more times than I can count."

"You should have a night light in here. How are people supposed to get water at night without one?" I grumble as my tiny pinky toe continues to give me more pain than you would think a tiny appendage would be capable of.

"Good point. We'll have to get one," he says as he places his hand just over my lower back and slowly guides me up the stairs.

I don't miss the electricity that shoots through my body when his hand accidently brushes my thin top a few times. I think he feels it too because each time he touches me, his eyes flick down to mine almost questioningly.

"You should get one of those wax warmers that plug into the wall. Then it's a nightlight, and it smells great. The best ones are the ones that smell like sweets. Like maple drizzle or sugar cookie."

He looks almost offended for a moment and I rack my brain for what I could have said to offend him in my short and pointless ramble.

"Are you hinting that our house smells, Erica?"

I let out a surprised laugh that causes his face to twitch in amusement. It is seriously unfair that he can be so stoic and yet so sexy. It is even more unfair because he is off limits. So, no sex with the sexy as sin man for me.

"Well, it is a bachelor pad for four college football players. You take what you want from that information," I tease.

My joke earns me a rough chuckle as he nods his agreement. "Yeah, blame Mikey for that one. Dude needs to shower like twice after practice or a game and don't get me started on his laundry."

I snicker softly now that we are upstairs. I haven't met their other two roommates yet but if they are the same guys that have lived with Trevor since last year then I already know plenty about them. He mentioned the name Sebastian in the past but nothing too detailed beyond that they were tight. Now I wish he would have told me more.

Sebastian and I stop outside of a door and look at each other hesitantly for a moment before he clears his throat and speaks.

"So, this is Trev's room. Mine is right here," he says pointing to the door just to the right. "In case you need anything," he tacks on quickly.

Feeling bold, either from the darkness of the house or maybe just out of curiosity for how he will react, I take a few tentative steps towards him. His body goes rigid when my chest softly brushes against him, but he doesn't move. I lift my arms up and wind them around his neck so that I can hug him.

He stays frozen in place, seemingly unsure of what to do for a few moments. Disappointment sinks into my stomach and the sting of rejection seeps into my chest as I begin to pull away. Before I can fully, I feel his arms wrap around my lower back as he holds me against him. What sounds like a soft sigh comes from him as he leans down to rest his chin on top of my head.

We stand there for I don't know how long in the hallway, just holding each other. The innocent act alone has my heart fluttering and hoping that it doesn't ever end. Unfortunately, I know that it has to.

When I pull away, I notice that it takes him a few extra beats before he does the same. We stand only a few inches apart and my mind is racing with ideas of what else we could do in this dark house together but before I can get up any courage to actually speak those thoughts, he nods and clears his throat.

"Good night, Erica," he says, his voice almost strained.

"Night, Sebastian."

I open Trevor's bedroom door and look to my side where I notice that Sebastian is still standing in the same spot, his fists wrapped up into tight balls and his jaw clenched. He almost looks mad. *Is he mad that I hugged him?* No, he couldn't be. He hugged me back. Friends can hug. Are we friends now? I don't really know what all goes on in his head, so I decide to just shrug it off and give him one more smile before I close the door.

Trevor's room is a lot like it was in high school, messy and piled high with football stuff and books. My OCD would normally be freaking out, but at the moment, I couldn't care less. I step over all of his stuff and make my way to the California King bed he was bragging about.

The ridiculous thing takes up over half of his room and I can't help but laugh. What else is a college guy going to do in his bedroom that isn't on his bed though, right? *Oh, ew.* The thought of how many chicks have been fucked by him in this bed kind of grosses me out now that I think about it. I hope that he has at least changed the sheets from the last time he had someone over.

Since beggars can't be choosers, I strip down into my panties, tossing my bra and clothes to the side. If Trev wakes up and comes upstairs, it's not like it's anything he hasn't seen before. I slide into the bed and wrap the covers around me as I wait for a deep sleep that never really comes. Two pairs of eyes flash through my head consistently on a loop. Blue and brown, brown and blue. Ones that are soft and light the others hard and heavy. Total opposites but equally entrancing.

Chapter Eleven

Sebastian

I gave up on sleep a long time ago. How the fuck was I supposed to sleep when I knew that Erica was just on the other side of the wall, probably naked, in Trevor's bed. The thought both gets me rock fucking hard and pissed the hell off. She should have been in my bed last night.

No. You can't have her. She is Trevor's, not yours. She is too sweet for you anyways, too good. You knew it the moment you met her.

It took every ounce of my willpower not to toss her over my shoulder in the kitchen, carry her upstairs and worship her body all night long. Hell, her eyes were practically begging me to fuck her on that piece of shit dining room table. Okay maybe that was more than a little wishful thinking on my part, but she did seem to want me.

The way she plastered her tight body against mine under the guise of a goodnight hug told me everything that I needed to know. She hasn't forgotten about that night just like I haven't. And just like me, she wants a repeat. I wish it were that fucking simple.

I can't really tell if she knows that Trevor still has feelings for her or not. I embarrassingly watched them from the staircase last night for a little and noticed that while she was completely enthralled

At one point, he put his arm around her, and she gave him a funny look before she focused back on to the movie, letting his arm stay wrapped around her in the process. Now I don't know if that means she was just surprised but welcomed the affection or if she was thrown off by it. *I'm secretly hoping for the latter.*

How fucked up is it to hope that your best friend strikes out with who he describes as the perfect woman for him? I'd feel even worse about my fucked up thoughts if there wasn't this tiny dark voice inside my head that thinks she could be the perfect woman for *me* too.

When Erica asked me what I wanted from the Chinese restaurant and basically invited me to hang out with them, I got almost excited for a moment. But the murderous glare that Trev threw me made it clear that I wasn't welcome and that I needed to turn her down. I didn't want to, but I did because it was the right thing to do. I don't have much practice in doing the right thing in my life so I figured I should take the opportunity where I can.

A sweet girl like Erica will settle down with an upper crust guy like Trevor in the end, anyways. I know it and so does he. Trevor has all the right connections, a good family and more money than he knows what to do with. He can give her a life that guys like me never could so I know that any interference I provide will only be delaying the inevitable. Perfect girls like her don't end up with broken men like me. But damn if that stops me from wanting her.

I'm currently downstairs making a pot of coffee that I tell myself is just for me. Have I considered bringing up a cup to Erica if there is any left? Sure, you know, to be nice and help make up for being a total dick to her for the last couple of weeks.

As I wait for the coffee to finish up, I hear footsteps pad into the kitchen, and look over my shoulder to see a rumpled Trevor stumble in.

"Morning sleeping beauty," I jibe as I point to his messed up faux hawk.

"Fuck you, man," he says lightly as he grabs a water bottle from the fridge and takes a seat. "I guess Erica went home last night after we fell asleep. Man, it was fucking awesome. Not to sound like a chick or anything but having her in my arms when I fell asleep was probably the best feeling in the damn world. Didn't know I would miss something so simple."

"Well, you do sound like a chick," I joke before I add on, "But she didn't go home. She's in your room."

He perks up instantly and his eyes widen as he runs his hands through his hair. "Really? Why?"

I shrug. "I got up last night to get a drink and she was getting ready to leave. I told her it wasn't safe for her to wander around campus in the middle of the night and that you wouldn't mind her crashing in your bed."

"Fucking-a-right I wouldn't mind. You should have woken me up though, motherfucker!" He says as he hurries into the bathroom downstairs.

My smile is tight as I turn to pour the coffee into a couple of mugs. He's just lucky that I didn't fuck her like I wanted to. There is no way in hell I was going to wake him up so that he could have the opportunity to get all cuddly with her in his bed. The image of her curled up with him on the couch last night is enough to have me clenching my teeth so hard that I'm about to crack a molar.

Trevor comes in gargling mouthwash before he spits it into the sink.

"Can I take one of those for Erica?" He asks as he gestures to the two coffees that I just poured.

Biting back my immediate fuck no, I give him a short nod before I reach into the cabinet to grab another mug.

"Thanks, man," he says as he takes the mugs and hurries up the stairs.

Motherfucker.

Because I'm obviously a glutton for punishment, I sit at the dining room table and wait to see how long it takes them to come downstairs. To anyone else, it looks like I'm just enjoying my morning coffee, but in reality, I'm literally counting the minutes in my head.

Thankfully, it only takes them 2.5 minutes before they are both walking down the stairs and neither one is looking overly satisfied, which makes a comforting warmth spread through my chest. I know, I know. Fucked up.

"Morning," I say.

Erica's eyes almost instantly fall onto mine while she steps into the kitchen. It could just be my imagination, but I swear that her smile gets a little brighter when she looks at me and lifts her mug in the air.

"Good morning. Thanks for the coffee."

I nod as Trevor whines. "Hey, I'm the one that brought it to you."

She looks over at him with a no bullshit smile. "Yes, but I know that you didn't make it."

"How do you know that?" He says as he crosses his arms like a four year old.

Her light laugh fills the kitchen, the sweet sound wrapping around me causing my heart to spasm in my chest. Suddenly, all I want is to fucking bottle the noise so that I can listen to it on repeat. I'm so fucking greedy with this girl, all I want is more, more, more.

"Because when you make coffee, it tastes like straight up ass."

Trevor scoffs in offense, and I bark out a surprised laugh because she couldn't be more right. I don't know how but he always fucks up coffee. Hence why I'm usually the one to make it. Erica looks over to me, her eyes sparkling with delight at my amusement before she shoots me a sly wink that causes my stomach to dip. Shit. She is too sexy.

"Fuck you guys. Who needs to make their own coffee when there are like five carts on campus?"

Erica shrugs and smirks before she finishes her cup and rinses it out in the sink. I don't want to be so obvious as to turn around and watch her, so I watch out of my peripherals as she slightly bends over the deep sink to place the mug in before standing back up.

Trevor's eyes quickly snap to her face when she turns around and a guilty expression stretches across his face that she doesn't seem to catch, but I do.

"Well, thanks for letting me stay over last night, guys. I appreciate it. I probably would have been curled up in the hallway of my dorm if you didn't."

I hold in my derisive snort. Yeah, right. Erica could knock on any guy's door on the whole fucking campus, and he would offer her a place to sleep for the night, single or not. She is just that gorgeous. I'm slightly glad to hear that she doesn't know that, though, there is no way in fuck she will ever hear it from me either.

"Of course. I had a great night, come over anytime. What are you doing tonight?" Trevor asks a little too eagerly.

I shoot him a warning look to tamp it down and he seems to get the message because when he looks back to Erica, he fakes indifference, which he is really bad at by the way. What happened to the Trevor that I spent the last two years chasing women with? That guy was smooth and cool. One wink and a flirty one liner could pick up any woman anywhere. Now he is just a rambling idiot. Must be something about Erica that does that to a guy because I seem to always be doing dumb shit around her too.

"Well, since I got interrupted last night, I'm going to be catching up on some homework. What about you guys?"

"Oh, not much," Trevor answers for the both of us even though Erica's eyes are on me. "I could come by and help you if you wanted? I will bring pizza."

She shakes her head softly. "Sorry, but we tried the whole study buddy thing in high school, and we literally never got anything done."

Trevor's smile turns mischievous as he takes a step closer. "Oh yeah. I remember that. We were a little pre-occupied with things that were way more fun."

The insinuation in his words paired with his smile has me gripping my cup so fucking hard that it's about to shatter apart in my hands. I watch Erica closely and read her body language to his open flirtation. I breathe a sigh of relief when she takes a tiny step back and shakes her head.

"Yeah well at least we know that wouldn't be a problem this time. I know you suck at tutoring though, so I'm gonna pass," she laughs.

A hurt look flashes across Trev's face before he can mask it. I get what he was talking about before now. She really does have him firmly in the friendzone. Any other girl on campus would have fallen to her knees if Trevor suggested fooling around but not Erica. Why does his failure make me so damn happy? I am the shittiest friend in the world.

"Your loss," he teases with a strained smile. "Want me to walk you back to your room?"

She shakes her head. "I'm good. Thanks again," she says as she lifts up on her toes and kisses Trevor's cheek. Erica gives me a little wave and a smile before she is out the door.

The room is silent for a few seconds after the front door shuts until Trevor blows out a deep breath.

"Fuck, see what I mean? I feel like I'm a damn dog chasing after her. It fucking sucks."

I nod as I sip my coffee. "Yeah, maybe she just doesn't want to ruin your friendship."

"But that's the thing. She knows how great we were together. I swear if I hadn't been such a dumbass, we would still be together to this day. Hell, I'd probably have already put a ring on it by now."

My eyes flare at his casual mention of marrying Erica, and I try to quickly tamp down the unease that swirls inside of me at the thought. My extreme reactions to this chick should be enough to keep me as far away from her as possible, but it seems like it is just causing the opposite.

CHAPTER TWELVE

ERICA

Another week goes by that is filled with droning professors, too many assignments and little sleep in between. Today is Brighton's first home game and to Trevor and my disappointment, I had to bail on it. I am literally drowning in homework, so I opted to catch the game on the TV. Taking a sip of the iced coffee that Palmer brought me as an apology to keeping me up all night with Ethan.

When the game starts, I watch as our guys hold the line as WCU's offence tries to break through. Suddenly, I see a big guy with the number 36 scrawled across his back sack the quarterback hard. The poor guy goes down like a snapped stick, causing me to wince. The picture and stats of the Brighton linebacker flashes across the screen, and I recognize the name. Declan Daniels, 6'3, 250lbs. That's one of Trevor's roommates. Though, I haven't met him officially yet, I have heard of him.

Flicking my gaze back and forth between my latest assignment and the TV for the next forty five minutes or so, I pause and whip my head up when I hear the announcer speak.

"Trevor Michaels is looking for a place to dump the ball. He doesn't have a lot of options but, wait. Oh my god. Sebastian Caldwell just blew through three men, and he isn't stopping. Michaels sends the ball to Caldwell who catches it with ease. He is at the 40 yard line, the 30, oh. What a take down," he shouts as the camera slows down the footage to see a guy come from nearly nowhere and tackle Sebastian at the legs before tossing him over his shoulder and to the ground, which to do that to a guy the size of Sebastian Caldwell, is no easy feat.

My heart seizes in its chest as I watch the screen intently, waiting for Sebastian to get up but he doesn't move a muscle. Oh fuck. What seems like hours pass before I see a few guys run over and offer their hands out to him. Slowly, Sebastian's long arm reaches up to meet them and accepts the help to his feet. The crowd appropriately cheers for him as he stiffly walks off the field, never slouching over or stumbling as that bold number 89 stands out proudly across his back.

Blowing out a rough breath I shake my head before quickly turning the TV off. I'm never going to get any work done if I keep that game on. As much as I want to support Trevor, I have to put everything into my classes or feel the wrath of my mother. And if I'm honest, watching Sebastian Caldwell absolutely dominate throughout the game kinda pisses me off. Is it bad that part of me wanted him to be kinda bad? Then he would be a loser with an asshole attitude instead of a fucking beast with an attitude.

The only way I could get Trevor to agree to not flipping his shit with me missing the game was to agree to come to a party and celebrate their win. I was hesitant at first. It honestly seems like a bit of a disaster in the making. First because Sebastian will no doubt be there and things between us are...strange. Part of me wants him, the part of me that remembers how amazing that first night with him was. The other part of me wants to keep far away from him, the part that remembers what an ass he has been to me since that night together. Even though we called a truce and hopefully that means his dickish ways are behind us, it still isn't a good idea mainly because of one reason, Trevor.

Ever since I spent the night at his place, despite him being busy with football and me with classes, we don't go more than a few hours without at least texting. Every morning, he walks me to class with coffee in hand like the saint that he is. After classes and practice, he calls me every night and we just talk. I haven't felt so close to Trevor in so many years, and it all has me feeling confirmed in my original suspicion that Trevor wants more.

I still haven't been able to address my own feelings on the topic. I honestly don't know. On paper, Trevor and I make perfect sense. Our families get along, we are best friends, and we just get each other. If he would have showed an interest like this in me a few months ago, I probably would have been all over it. I love Trevor, but as bad as it sounds, I can't get his best friend out of my head. Ugh. This is a bad idea. I should just tell Trevor I'm not feeling well or something. I don't think I will be able to properly think with both of them in the same space at the same time.

Just as I pick up my phone to shoot off a bullshit excuse to Trevor, my dorm room door bangs open as Palmer and Ethan barge in, making out as clothing begins to fall to the ground.

"Ugh. Not again," I groan as I grab my phone and keys.

Palmer and Ethan don't even acknowledge me as they fall to Palmer's bed, now only their underwear on.

"You guys could at least wait until I leave the room," I call out as I stand from my bed and make my way for the door.

Still, they don't even grunt in acknowledgement as they continue their assault on each other. I roll my eyes and shake my head as I close the door and head down the hallway. Guess I'm going to that party after all.

Obviously, I didn't have time to change or anything so when I walk into the party, I get more than my fair share of disgusted looks from sorority girls that look like they are better dressed for Vegas than a college party. I am wearing a pair of black jeans and purple flowy shirt with a cinched waist with my white tennis shoes. Whatever.

To my mother's horror, I have never really been one of those girls who is completely obsessed with wearing the right outfit. My mother always says that how you present yourself determines how others will be expected to treat you, which I personally think is a load of shit, but whatever.

It doesn't take long for me to find Sebastian. I spot him almost instantly once I step further into the house. I see Sebastian sitting on a couch with another guy as girls are practically clambering to sit on their laps. As if he can feel my eyes on him, he turns to me immediately. When our eyes lock it almost takes my breath away for a second as I take in his black t-shirt that is wrapped like a second skin around his wide muscles and a pair of dark jeans that cling to his large thighs as his hair is tightly wrapped on top of his head.

He doesn't say anything. Doesn't even smile. He just stares at me, like he is as lost on how to handle me as I am with him. I consider going up to him and starting up a conversation. It has to be better than blatantly staring at him from across the room, right?

I go to take a step forward when a pair of arms band around my waist. I turn around to see Trevor smiling down at me.

"You made it! I thought for sure you were going to bail last minute."

I chuckle softly. "Would I really do that?"

"Yes, yes you would," he laughs. "But I'm glad that you didn't. Come on, let me get you a drink," Trevor smiles with his arm curled around my shoulders.

I peek a glance over my shoulder to see Sebastian watching us intently. I can't tell what that look on his face means, but it looks complicated. My view of him is quickly interrupted when a pretty blonde girl drops into his lap and wraps her arms around his neck like it is the most natural thing in the world.

What the hell? Does he have a girlfriend? Is that what this has all been about? He wasn't concerned about his relationship with Trevor. He was trying to save his own ass. Oh my god, I am such an idiot.

Turning back to Trev, I give him my best smile that I can muster and wrap my arm around his waist as he moves us through the crowded house. Yeah, a drink. A drink sounds good right now. Trev walks me through the house and into the kitchen where he pours each of us a beer.

I smile and nod as I listen to him tell me about his Econ professor's toupee when the smell of warm apple pie suddenly catches my attention. I glance around until my eyes land on a white plug-in light off to the side of the kitchen near the dining room table. Even though the lights are on, I can tell how much it probably helps when it's dark in here.

Did Sebastian buy that because of me?

Yeah, right. He clearly has a girlfriend. I'm nothing but a one time side piece to him.

Shaking it off, I accept the outstretched beer from Trev before tipping it back, chugging it and gesturing for another. Trevor gives me a wide-eyed look before he shakes his head and laughs, filling up my cup again before we head out to the dance floor.

After I don't know how many drinks and countless songs, I have practically forgotten all about Sebastian Caldwell and his shady ass. He wasn't even that great anyways, at least that is what I try to tell myself. The next song that thumps through the room is Shut Up and Dance by Walk The Moon and my mouth drops open as I turn to Trevor.

"Oh my god! This is our song!" I squeal as I toss back the rest of my beer before taking his cup and tossing his back too.

He groans as I take his hand in mine and start dragging him towards the makeshift dancefloor.

"No. I am not doing the dance with you. You can't make me," he laughs with a soft smile as we get to the middle of the room.

I spin around to face him, swaying a little until he wraps his arms around my waist to stabilize me. I giggle before sticking out my lower lip and batting my eyes. Usually, the puppy dog doesn't work on guys but with Trevor, it has always worked like a charm.

He groans again before is thumb reaches up to brush against my pouted lip.

"I'm gonna bite this damn lip off one day, I swear."

I give him a mischievous smile and a wink. "Don't make promises you can't keep, Trev."

His eyebrows raise in surprise, and he opens his mouth to say something, but I turn around and raise my hands up, starting off our perfectly choreographed dance that I made him learn when I was 13. I hear Trevor curse behind me before I see his arms go up to the side of me, mirroring my moves.

Ha! Got him.

We begin to move, every step flawlessly executed, if I do say so myself. Then again, my overinflated confidence at our dance skills probably has to do more with the overwhelming amount of alcohol in both of our systems but who cares, right?

Trevor grabs my waist and pulls me to where I am flush to him as we move our hips around. *Well, that is a new addition to the dance.* I don't pull away though, continuing every step as normal but only now, our bodies are pressed together.

Smiling, I look over my shoulder to see Trevor lazily smiling down at me. I can tell that he is just as gone as I am and we are no doubt going to be worshiping the porcelain throne in the morning, but for now, this is the most fun that I have had in I don't know how long.

Looking back away my eyes snag on a pair that seems to have been glued to me since we stepped on the dance floor. I turn fully to see Sebastian, staring at us with a clenched jaw, his hand flexed tightly around his girlfriend's waist. She is kissing up and down the length of his neck all while he has his eyes firmly placed on me. What a fucking asshole.

I don't know what comes over me. Maybe it is the alcohol, maybe it is the fact that I have been grinding against Trevor for the last few minutes or maybe it is the tiny little green monster that is raging inside of me at the sight of another girl in Sebastian's arms. Another girl tasting his skin.

Turning away from Sebastian, I look up to Trevor, wrap my arm around his neck and arch my neck to the side so that I have better access to him before I press my lips against his. Trevor stills only for a moment before his grip on me tightens as he pulls me to him closer.

One of his hands move from my waist up to my cheek to keep my head turned as he bends down further to deepen the kiss. I moan softly against his lips before his tongue darts out and flicks mine. I greet him happily as I slowly spin in his arms until we are facing each other. Trevor's teeth reach out and nibble at my bottom lip before pulling back, letting my slightly tender lip free.

His breathing is ragged, and I notice so is mine. He is looking down at me like I created earth itself, both of his hands holding my face like he doesn't want me to slip away. Not knowing what exactly has come over me, but also not wanting to question it, I lean up onto my toes and whisper in his ear.

"Take me to your room, Trev."

His pupils dilate and he nods wordlessly, intertwining our fingers before leading me through the crowded room and up the stairs. I don't look back. I know what is back there. I can feel it. I have felt his eyes on me since I came into this house and they haven't let up once, not even when his best friend's tongue was inside my mouth. It doesn't matter. Sebastian and I were clearly a mistake. But Trevor. Trevor is good, great even. He is the best man I know, and I would be lucky to be with him again.

It doesn't take long for us to make it up to his room. We continue holding hands as he opens the door. It is only when his bedroom door clicks shut, that the rubber band of our sexual tension seems to snap.

Trevor pounces on me, his lips crushing mine like he can't go another second without kissing me. My lips meet his eagerly. Trevor is an amazing kisser and everything about his kiss is warm, comforting, familiar, easy.

His hand goes up under my shirt, brushing against my bare skin. I shiver under the touch before his fingers peel the shirt off me, tossing it to the side as his kisses move down my neck. I arch into him, the familiar butterflies racing through my chest.

Trevor backs me up until I drop onto his bed. He wastes no time crawling on top of me, his hands tracing over me reverently, his touch is so soft and gentle its practically feather light. Moving one hand down to my jeans, he slowly unbuttons them before pushing them down my thighs. His hand cups over the top of my panties before he slips the fabric to the side and sinks inside of me. The feeling instantly feels familiar yet different all the same. I let out a satisfied groan as he slowly works me just how he knows I like. That's what is great about me and Trev, we have already gotten all the awkward fumblings out of the way. We know what the other likes.

My orgasm creeps up, my pussy throbbing with need as the familiar building feeling gets greater and greater as I shatter apart. When I do, I shout out my release but what I don't realize at the time is that somewhere along the way, I closed my eyes and that when I did, a pair of caramel brown eyes popped into my head. Dark, delicious and too fucking captivating.

When my body stops quaking, Trev slowly pulls his hand away as he looks down at me with a satisfied smile. It only takes one look of my face for him to know that something is up though. His brows furrow for a second as I try to think of a way to explain how I feel. That in this moment I feel unbelievably torn. That things feel so good and natural with Trev but that I can't get the memory of his best friend's touch out of my head even if he isn't mine and never could be. Trevor knows what I like but Sebastian seemed to know what I need. Maybe it's unfair to compare them. I was caught up in the moment with Sebastian. It was easy and fun and passionate which no doubt added to the high of it all. Still, I don't feel right going farther with Trevor until I get my head straight. I break the kiss and step away a few feet like his touch burns me.

"It's okay," Trev shushes softly as if he can hear the warring thoughts inside my head. I'm not sure he would be so comforting if he could. He wraps his arms around me and rests his cheek on top of my head as he speaks to me.

"We don't have to go any farther. Just stay, okay?"

I bite the inside of my cheek and nod. He reaches down to the end of the bed and grabs his sheet and comforter before pulling them over us. I snuggle into his side as his arm wraps around me so that I can rest my head on his chest. It only takes a few minutes before I feel Trevor's breath begin to steady into a rhythmic rise and fall until I know that he is passed out cold.

I try to close my eyes, but it just won't work. My mind is racing with so many things, all of which are instantly giving me a headache. I gotta get out of here. I can't think when I'm wrapped up in Trevor's bed, in his arms. He is my best friend, but he is also my greatest heartbreak. How could I think jumping into bed with him so casually would be the best thing for us? I need space to think.

Carefully peeling myself out of his hold, I tip toe out of bed and move to the door. Hopefully Palmer and Ethan are clothed and haven't locked me out by the time I get there. But at this point, I think I would rather sleep on the ground of my hallway than with Trevor. If I can't promise him all of me then I shouldn't give him even a sliver of hope for any of me. I have to figure my shit out before I ruin our friendship forever.

I don't feel nearly as buzzed as before, but it's still a struggle to get down the stairs. I let out a breath of relief when I make it to the bottom without completely eating shit. I take one more step to the door before a loud voice rumbles through the otherwise silent house.

"Where the fuck do you think you're going?"

I whip my head quickly to the kitchen to see a dark figure sitting at the table. My eyes take a minute to adjust to the darkness, though I don't need to see to know who it is. I'd know that voice anywhere.

"Home," I slur gently. Okay, maybe I'm not as sober as I think I am.

"Drunk, alone and at night? Are you out of your fucking mind!" He snarls before standing up, his chair scraping against the ground.

My eyes flick to the stairs before going back to an enraged looking Sebastian.

"Keep it down," I harshly whisper.

His scowl deepens as he crosses his arms across his chest.

"Oh, so Trev doesn't know that you are sneaking out? That seems to be your thing, huh? Fuck and run?"

I furrow my brows and shake my head. "We didn't sleep together."

Sebastian scoffs and shakes his head as he looks down at the ground, balling his fists tightly.

"We didn't," I say again. I don't know why I feel the need to defend myself to him, but I just do.

Sebastian's head lifts before he continues to stand there, staring at me. His jaw clenched and his eyes are practically on fire even in the dark room. His anger instantly bristles against something inside of me as I harden my features and cross my arms.

"What's it to you? Shouldn't you be with your *girlfriend*?" I snap.

He squints his eyes and shakes his head.

"What the fuck are you talking about?"

"Your girlfriend, the girl you clearly forgot to mention that night or every night since for that matter."

"Who?" Sebastian asks, clearly irritated and maybe even a little confused looking.

"Don't bullshit me! The girl that was in your lap all night! I saw you two. I watched her kiss your neck before I-" I pause midsentence, not wanting to utter the words on my mind.

Understanding seems to dawn across his face before he rolls his eyes at me.

"I don't have a girlfriend, Erica. Never have, actually."

My brows furrow. "Well, who was she then?"

Sebastian raises a brow and cocks his head to the side.

"What's it to you?"

I open my mouth to respond, but nothing comes to mind. I slowly close my mouth and stand there silent for a few moments before I shake my head.

"Whatever, I'm out of here," I say as I turn on my heel and take off for the front door.

I only stumble once which is pretty good, I think. I get the door open before I feel him right behind me. He plucks a jacket off the coat rack next to the door and drapes it around my shoulders. I look at him curiously, but he just gestures for me to start walking. Apparently, he is coming with.

I mumble a soft thanks, and he nods shortly. When we get to the stairs on the porch, he wraps his arm around my waist to help stabilize me. Just like every other time that he has ever touched me, an intense near electric feeling races through me. I close my eyes, letting him guide us, enjoying the feeling for just a little bit longer.

When we make it down to the bottom of the stairs, he steps away, and I instantly frown at the missing contact, but he doesn't seem to notice as he continues walking. Slowly, I trail next to him as we quietly walk towards my dorm. There are quite a bit of people milling about, going to different houses and dorms. You wouldn't think it is the middle of the night. A few of them try to get Sebastian's attention, but he doesn't give anyone more than a head nod.

"She is a cleat chaser," he says out of nowhere when we get to my dorm building.

I scan my key card to open the door and Sebastian holds it open, letting me go first before he follows behind.

"What do you mean?" I ask as we make our way into the elevator.

"She isn't my girl, she isn't anyone's. She wants anyone who is a football player, her choice changes every night. She's nothing but a groupie. A fucking annoying one at that."

"You didn't look too annoyed with her when she was perched on your lap, or when she was kissing you," I say as we step out of the elevator and walk down the hall to my room.

"Yeah. Well, I was a little busy being annoyed with something else," he says lowly.

Once we reach my door, I turn to face him, cocking my head to the side, waiting for him to elaborate. Of course, he doesn't, though. Instead, he just continues staring down at me with a complicated look on his face.

Carefully, he reaches out, his hand lifting up to my face before his thumb sweeps over my bottom lip several times. It doesn't feel like a cherishing touch. It feels like he is trying to achieve something. Like he is trying to wipe something away.

"You drive me crazy," he whispers, almost to himself.

I laugh hollowly and nod, savoring the feel of his thumb still brushing against my lip.

"I could say the same."

He gives me a barely there smirk before his hand drops to his side and he takes a step back.

"Take some ibuprofen and drink some water. You drank too much tonight."

I nod in agreement as I turn to my door, twisting the handle and thankfully, it turns with ease.

"Thanks for walking me," I mutter as I slide off his jacket to hand it back to him.

"Keep it," he shrugs before he turns on his heel and walks down the hall, never even sparing me a second glance.

CHAPTER THIRTEEN

SEBASTIAN

I only slept for a few hours before I decided to give up and head downstairs. I make some breakfast and start the pot of coffee that I know Trevor is going to definitely need. I haven't seen him drink that much since freshman year. I don't know if it was because he was trying to keep up with Erica last night or what, but they were both fucking trashed by the end of the night.

As soon as she stepped into the room, I knew it instantly. It was like I could feel that she was there. I found her almost immediately and she was already looking at me. There was so much to be said in her aqua eyes, I could practically hear it all from across the room. For a second it looked like she was even going to come over to me until fucking Trevor put his arms around her.

I watched as he held her close, and she smiled up at him like she was always meant to. It pissed me the fuck off. I was practically shaking. It took everything in me not to go all caveman and beat the living shit out of my best friend. That's why when Cynthia Johnson dropped into my lap and made herself right at home, I let her. I needed the distraction. I needed the buffer.

She apparently took me not shoving her to the ground as open invitation to bounce and grind her ass all over my dick. She thought I was hard for her, but she couldn't have been more wrong. There was only one girl that could apparently get me hard nowadays and that girl just so happens to be grinding with my best friend only a few feet away.

I did my best to block out Trevor and instead focus on Erica. I watched the way her hips moved and swayed to the beat. It was entrancing just like that first night all over again. I couldn't see anything but her.

I felt Cynthia's wet sloppy kisses trailing up and down my neck the whole time. The feeling was so gross that I literally cringed. I was just about to shove her away like I should have to begin with when Erica turned to me. Her eyes raked over Cynthia and me before she got a weird glint in her eye. Guilt rose in me for a moment, but I squashed that shit real quick. What the fuck did I have to be guilty for? Not a fucking thing, that's what.

Then Erica turned away from me to look up at Trevor. I didn't need to see more to know what was about to happen. I wanted to look away, I should have. But I didn't, I couldn't. Like watching a car accident, I watched as she rose up and pressed her lips to Trevor's. He happily deepened the kiss, his hands holding her tight as they began to make out right in fucking front me. I could feel every ounce of blood thrumming inside of my veins with undiluted rage at the sight. Rage and this weird ache feeling in my chest.

When they broke apart, I waited for her to look at me. I wanted to see regret in her eyes or...anything really. But she didn't look at me. She whispered something into his ear that he seemed to like before they turned and walked out of the party, hand and hand.

My eyes never left her. I was practically begging her to look at me. Just a glance. It was all I needed. But she didn't even spare me that. She happily marched out of that house to God knows where to do God knows what with him. Just like that, I felt like I was gonna be fucking sick.

Cynthia reached up to my jaw as she began to rub her lips against me, and I shoved her to the side. She stumbled a bit until she landed on her hands and knees on the ground. Normally, I would feel bad for potentially hurting her, but I am too fucking pissed to give a shit right now.

Standing up, I stormed into the kitchen, unscrewed the vodka bottle and lifted it to my lips, taking three healthy gulps before setting it down. The sharp burn that ran from my tongue to my chest was a welcome feeling. I would have taken any distraction that I could. Anything to stop me from chasing after them and tearing Trev apart piece by piece.

I took several deep breaths and closed my eyes tight, doing my best to calm myself but it didn't work. I had to get out of there. I stormed out of that living room like a fucking tornado and made my way to my room. I didn't want to think, I just wanted to move.

When I went upstairs for the night, I may have leaned against Trevor's door for half a second, fucking relived as all hell to notice that it was silent. There were no moans or heavy breathing that I could hear at least. It was just silent. I moved into the kitchen and sat at the table with my head in my fucking hands. I was losing my fucking mind and I didn't know how to get a grip on it.

Suddenly, the noise of footsteps coming down the stairs shook me out of my inner thoughts. I listened carefully, hearing them stumble a few times. The steps were too soft to be Trevor, they had to be hers.

When she stepped into sight, she looked overall put together. There was no doubt that she was drunk but she didn't look like she had just been fucked or at least not fucked properly. That didn't really do much to ease the growing tension in my shoulders, though. She kissed him, that much I knew. It's a sight that will probably haunt me for years to come.

I couldn't let her walk home alone. Even if she was sober and had the ability to be aware of her surroundings, it wasn't safe. I noticed that she forgot a jacket, fucking again, so I gave her mine to borrow. She looked good in it. So good, some unknown part of me wanted her to never take it off.

We walked quietly for a while until the words that had been on the tip of my tongue couldn't be squashed any longer. I had to tell her that Cynthia meant nothing, that she is nothing, not to me. Fuck if I know why. Like I said, I don't have shit to feel guilty about. She looked almost relieved by that information, though.

I was about to leave her at her dorm room, turn around and walk away so that I could put as much distance between us as possible. But when I looked down at her soft full lips, all I could think about was that I was no longer the last person to touch them. Trevor had kissed and bit at her lips, and I wanted to erase his touch from her body and her memory more than I wanted my next fucking breath.

Fuck. What the hell am I even doing at the house still? I have to get out of here. I can't be here when Trevor wakes up. He tells me everything and I can't. I just can't hear about their night and keep my shit together. Even though she assured they didn't fuck, I don't want to hear a single detail about anything else from him.

Running upstairs, I quickly grab my shit and practically run down the stairs and out of the house. Since today is a rest day and I wanted every excuse possible to keep my distance from Trevor, I decide to hit the weight room, hoping to burn off some of this extra energy that I still have buzzing inside of me.

I run through a full workout until my muscles tremble, but I still have this weird feeling bubbling inside of me that I just can't seem to shake. It usually spikes when I think about how close I was to Erica last night, how easy it would have been to kiss her, how bad I wanted to taste her lips again. It's an unwelcome feeling because it's like a thirst that can never be quenched, a hunger that will never be met. *She will never be yours.*

Once I'm covered in sweat and can barely move my legs, I decide to give it a rest for the night since it is nearly 8PM. I'm sure that I will be regretting this tomorrow during practice but for now, I'll take the distraction. I take a quick shower before I toss on a pair of grey sweats and one of my favorite Metallica shirts before I sling my gym bag over my shoulder and head across campus back to the house.

I'm lost in my own head when I faintly hear a familiar beat thumping in the distance. Not really sure why, but I decide to walk towards the noise. The closer I get to it the louder it becomes until I determine that it is coming from one of the art rooms.

I crack the door open to hear Seek and Destroy by Metallica pounding through the room. I look around and see a girl with her hair tied on top of her head angrily swiping her paintbrush against a canvas that has dark red, grey and white splattered across it.

It only takes me a moment to recognize that the girl is Erica. I didn't know she painted? And what is she doing here in the middle of the night blasting head banger music while she does it?

Based on her movements you would think that whatever she is working on is a messy disaster but when you look at the canvas it looks fucking good, like she has spent hours on it. It starts out heavy with color at the bottom and fades into almost pure white at the top. I'm sure they have a name for it but fuck if I know right now.

I'm the furthest thing from an artist, but my sister was one. An amazing one. It was the only thing she ever did for herself. I remember so many nights, waking up because I couldn't sleep, finding my sister painting in the corner of our tiny bedroom, seemingly lost in whatever she was working on. She had a sort of peaceful look on her face that seemed to almost calm me at the same time. You take the small amount of solace you can get when you come from where I did.

Erica hasn't noticed me yet and based on the thumping beat, I would say that she won't unless I make myself known. I can tell by her movements that she is pissed about something. I know I should probably just walk away and head home, but the idea of leaving her alone and upset bothers me. Not to mention, we are all the way across campus from the dorms and I don't feel right about letting her walk home in the dark. Again.

Slowly, I make my way around the room until I am right behind her. My hands twitch to reach out and grab her but I push the thought out of my head and settle for verbally getting her attention. I need to keep as much space between us as possible, for my own fucking good.

"Erica."

She doesn't hear me, as she continues to viciously attack her painting with her brush.

"Erica!" I bark.

She jumps before spinning around with wide eyes to look at me. Surprise flashes across her face before she grabs her phone and pauses the music.

"What are you doing here?" She asks almost breathlessly as she brushes some hair out of her face, smearing some red paint on her cheek in the process.

"I heard the music. Guess I was being nosey. Do you always play music that loud while you paint?"

She nods as she wipes her hands off on a rag. "The louder the better. It helps me get lost in the piece."

"I didn't know you painted."

"You never asked," she shrugs.

She seems alright, but when I look into her hypnotic eyes, I see that they are red and slightly swollen like she has been crying.

"Are you okay?" I ask tentatively.

She looks away from me and focuses on the supplies sitting on the counter next to her. "Yeah, why?"

"Because you look like you are three seconds away from crying," I say flatly.

Her face turns to look up at me and I watch as her jaw tightens with what looks like anger when a tear escapes, sliding down her face. Out of almost instinct, I reach my hand up to her cheek and brush it away with my thumb. I keep my hand on her face as I guide her to tilt her head up all the way until our eyes are fully locked.

"What's wrong?"

"Nothing," she huffs. "It's stupid. I'm not even sad, I'm pissed. I am just one of those obnoxious people that cry when they are really mad."

"What is it?" I probe again.

Why the fuck am I digging? I hate it when people dig at me. It drives me fucking batshit. Then again, this is Erica fucking Pembrooke. I need more. More information about her. More information about her past, especially with Trevor. More...just, more.

She looks at me warily for a moment before her shoulders slump and her face sinks into my hold, just a little bit. I slowly move my thumb across her cheek in a move that I hope is comforting. I know it feels that way for me. Touching her skin is like a balm that soothes something inside of me that I didn't know needed to be.

"It's just some stuff with my parents. It probably sounds like spoiled rich girl problems, but they have my whole life planned out for me and I'm starting to really realize that it's not the kind of life that I want to live."

"What do they have planned for you?" I ask carefully.

Erica lets out a hollow laugh as she shakes her head. "Literally everything. They practically picked my entire course load for the next four years and my major, pre-law, just like them. They are already talking about building up my application for when I apply to Harvard Law, just like them, and then when I graduate from there, I will start work at Pembrooke & Associates."

"Wow. Seems like a fast track to the high life."

She scoffs. "Yeah, I guess."

"What would you rather do?"

"If I could do anything?" She asks with a wistful look on her face. "I'd paint every single day. It's the best feeling in the world. When I have a paintbrush in my hand all my problems and worries melt away. Everything is just...perfect."

I smile softly as I watch her eyes sparkle with desire as she talks about her dream. Not a lot of people have that spark in them, that drive. It's fucking inspiring as shit and has me wanting to hear her talk about all of her dreams and desires all night long.

"You should do it then. Who cares what they want? This is your life, not theirs."

"Yeah, but my career of choice would most likely leave me living in a rundown shack eating out of trashcans," she laughs lightly with only a twinge of sadness underneath.

I shrug as I brush away another tear that has escaped past her eyelids and down her cheek.

"I think you should do it anyways. Happiness, true happiness is so rare. If we don't live for that, then what are we living for? What good is a comfortable life if it's an unhappy one?"

She cocks her head slightly, seeming to mull over my words before she nods.

"You aren't the dumb jock that you look," she says with a surprised face, though her eyes shine with mirth. After some of the shit I have said to her, I think I deserve worse. She pauses for a second, looking at her piece before glancing back at me.

"And you? What are your dreams?"

Her sea-colored eyes practically look into my soul as she gazes up to me. It feels like she already knows my every dream, fear and secret. I sure as hell hope that's not the case, but the way she looks at me makes me feel so...seen.

"Like any other guy on the team, I'd love to go pro. But if that doesn't work out it'll be nice to have a fancy college degree to open the right doors for me."

"Is that all you want out of life?" She asks.

I lick my lower lip slowly, thinking about another thing that I would love to have right now. Based on the look on her face, I can tell she knows exactly what I'm thinking, and she seems like she wants it almost as much as I do.

Slowly, I lean in until there are only a few inches separating us. She lets out a shuddered breath and just before I get the chance to feel her silky lips brush against mine, the door opens. I drop my hand from her cheek quickly and take a step back as I turn my head to see who is walking in.

"Hi, Professor Martinez," Erica greets as she looks at the person in the doorway

"Hi, Erica. Sorry to bother you, I need to close up now."

"Oh no problem. Thank you for letting me come in so late."

"No worries. I had some stuff to work on anyways."

The professor gives Erica an understanding smile as she begins to put back some supplies. I start grabbing some of the paints and brushes, putting them back where Erica does. Once we have cleaned everything up, Erica says goodbye before we make our way out the door.

As soon as we step outside, she instantly wraps her arms around her bare shoulders and shudders.

"Wow. It was way warmer when I came here earlier."

I nod as I hold my hand out to stop her from walking. I dig around into my gym bag and pull out my sweatshirt, smelling it quickly to make sure it doesn't reek like a gym bag.

"Arms up," I say.

She gives me a confused look but before she can say anything I'm pulling the sweatshirt over her head. When she pops her arms through the sleeves, my mouth twitches in amusement. The thing practically swallows her whole but at least she's warm. The hood is flipped up and I pull the drawstrings down to tighten it around her oval face. At this rate, I am going to lose my entire fucking closet to this girl. Fuck if I'm not mad about it, though.

We don't say anything as we walk back to her dorm, but silence has never really bothered me. I have always gotten shit for being the quiet guy in the group, but I think that if you don't have anything important to say then why waste your breath?

When we get to Erica's building, I cup her elbow and turn her to face me.

"Give me your phone," I say.

She furrows her brows at my command but doesn't protest as she hands it over to me. I take it and quickly put in my number before sending myself a text so that I have hers before I hand it back to her.

"It isn't safe for you to walk around campus at night by yourself. We've been over this. If you ever find yourself out at night call me and I'll walk you."

"But then who will protect you on your way back to your place?" She teases.

I smirk and look down at my 6'6 frame before glancing back to her. "I think I'll be fine. Plus, I'm not the drop dead gorgeous woman that any man would love to take advantage of."

Shit. Did I just say that out loud?

Her eyebrows raise in surprise as a satisfied smile spreads across her face. "You think that I'm drop dead gorgeous?"

Instead of denying it like a tool, I decide to go with the truth. "I think that you're the most beautiful woman that I've ever met."

She seems stunned into silence for a moment before her cheeks flare with a deep blush.

"Thank you," she whispers as she ducks her head.

I want nothing more than to grab her by the neck, pull her into me and crush my lips against hers right now. But I can't, I know I can't, and it's really shitty that I'm even contemplating it. So instead of kissing her or even touching her, I take a step back.

"Better get inside. I know Trev wouldn't like you out late. Maybe give him a call to let him know you are safe."

The words taste like vinegar in my mouth, but I push them out all the same with an air of indifference. A flash of what looks like disappointment passes across her face before she gives me a tight smile.

"Goodnight, Sebastian."

I stand there and watch her go through the front door before I turn to move. I wish she wasn't Trevor's ex, hell, I wish she wasn't Trevor's crush and I really fucking wish that she wasn't the first girl to make me feel something in well...ever.

Chapter Fourteen

Erica

I seriously do not understand Sebastian Caldwell. What kind of guy looks at a girl, tells her that she is the most beautiful woman he has ever seen, and then tells her to call his best friend? Seriously? Most of the time it seems like he barely tolerates me but then moments like that happen and I think that there is definitely something between us. I swear on my life that he was moments away from kissing me before Professor Martinez walked in. Maybe it's all just in my head, though.

I have known him for a month, and I just can't seem to shake him. He has been invading more and more of my thoughts which is both exciting and a little worrisome. I sleep in his shirt every single night and I haven't even washed it yet. Gross, I know, but I am afraid to lose the smell of him. Even if it is faint, it's still there. At least I have his sweatshirt now too along with his jacket.

Skillfully, I was able to dodge Trevor all day today. Normally he walks me to my first class of the day, but I left early this morning in order to avoid him. I'm not ready to talk about what happened the other night. I don't know what it means or what he thinks it means and then add Sebastian, annoying as hell, Caldwell into the

The next day, I'm able to dodge Trev again before and after my classes. Once I get back to my dorm, I dump my stuff off onto my desk before plopping onto my bed. I just had a frustratingly long conversation with my parents as they were practically breathing down my neck about 'staying on the path' like I am not already here and doing fucking everything they want and nothing that I do. I roll my eyes as I look up at the ceiling, Sebastian's words from yesterday playing in my head. If we don't live for happiness, then what are we living for?

My musings about my future are suddenly interrupted by a heavy knock that comes from my door and a thrill runs through me as my mind immediately jumps to Sebastian. I don't know why I would assume it would be him, I just do. I fluff my hair and straighten my shirt before I open the door with a smile. It only waivers for a nanosecond when I see that it isn't Sebastian, but Trevor.

"Hey Trev, what's up?"

His devastating smile widens as his blue eyes sparkle before he steps in for a hug giving me a kiss that lingers extremely close to the corner of my mouth. I wrap my arms around him before I step back so that he can come in.

"Well, my best friend is avoiding me, so I had to get creative," he says with a knowing look.

My smile wavers only for a moment as I go to sit on my bed. Instead of denying it like an ass, I decide to fess up.

"Look, Trev. I'm sorry. I-"

"Little Red, it's fine. I'm the one who should be sorry."

I pause and furrow my brows as he continues talking.

"We were drunk, we fooled around, and it freaked you out. Not going to lie that it kinda sucked waking up by myself the next morning, but I get it."

"You do?" I ask as I bite the inside of my cheek.

"Yeah. Can we talk?"

I give him a half smile, anxious as hell to hear what he has to say.

"Okay."

Trevor smiles as he laces his fingers through mine and walks over to my bed, sitting down at the edge before he brings his elbows to his knees and looks down at the ground for a moment. I know him all too well to know that he is collecting his thoughts. That gesture alone immediately sends my nerves misfiring. Did he find out about Sebastian and me? Is he mad? Does he hate us?

"Little Red, I'm just going to rip the band aid off. The other night was one of the best I have had in years."

I nod with a hesitant smile. "Well, you did come off a pretty big win."

Trev rolls his eyes and bats at the air like it was nothing.

"That doesn't matter. What made it such a great night was spending it with you."

My stomach drops and butterflies soar through my chest. Months ago, this is all that I wanted to hear. Even if I was over Trev and happy being his friend, I know I always held hope that we would one day find our way back to each other. But then Sebastian came in and muddled my brain, made everything blurry and unclear and then in the next moment he pulls away from me and makes it even worse. Fuck, when did my life become so dramatic?

"I have loved you from that first day you walked out into the cul-de-sac, Little Red. I've never stopped. Not for a moment. I'm so fucking sorry. I'm so sorry I fucked up. I'm so sorry I broke us, and I'll never forgive myself for the way I hurt you. I just-I want another shot. To do things right this time. It's always been you. Friends aren't enough anymore for me. I need my Little Red back."

My throat dries and my heart hammers inside my chest. My god. How long did I wish those words would spill from his lips? We never really addressed our breakup and how bad it hurt to lose him. We just gave each other space and picked up like friends who avoided a very large elephant in the room. I didn't realize how much I needed to hear his apology until now.

"Trev, I love you. I'll never not love you. But I...I can't lose you again. What if it doesn't work out between us again? I don't think we could come back from that. It was hard enough the first time. You threw us away to come party it up at college, which is fine, I get it, but how do I know that you won't do something like that down the road when another potentially straining opportunity comes between us?"

"I'll choose you," he promises quickly. "Every fucking time, Erica. I'll choose you. I'm not that dumb kid anymore. I have changed, grown and I have really thought about what I want my life to look like. Little Red, that life doesn't mean anything if I don't have you by my side to share it with."

My heart clenches in my chest. I want to believe him so bad. I want to give my best friend the world just like I know he wants to give it to me. But I just don't know if I can put my heart on the line like that. Not yet.

"This is a lot to process. I-I don't know what to say, Trev."

He nods for a second looking at his feet before he looks back up at me. He scoots closer, ending the distance between us before he cups my face and pulls my lips to meet his. The kiss isn't sloppy or slightly frantic like the other night thanks to our drunken haze. It is slow, languid, perfect. It sends those previous butterflies in my chest fluttering throughout my entire body. It makes my heart trip over itself just from the pure love and passion he is pouring into this kiss.

When he breaks away, he rests his forehead against mine as he closes his eyes.

"I know. I'm okay if you need time. I just couldn't go another moment without doing that. If you need space, that's okay. If you don't want labels, that's okay too." He pauses for a second, gritting his teeth before continuing. "If you want to spend some time with other guys, I won't hold it against you. It isn't fair that I got to live it up the last two years and then I expect you to not get the same experiences just because I realized what I was missing."

Trevor expels a ragged breath like the words were painful for him to even utter before he pulls away just a bit so that he can see me better. His hands are still cupping my face gently as his blue eyes search mine.

"I just had to tell you, and I've been thinking about kissing you ever since I woke up alone," he says on a self-deprecating laugh. "Seriously though, take whatever time you need. Just know that when you are ready, I'll be here."

I smile softly at that and nod before I lean forward and gently brush my lips against his. He practically sinks into my touch, but I pull away before it can go farther.

"Thank you, Trev. I appreciate it. I do love you, I just. My head is kind of a mess right now."

"What's new," he jokes lightly, though I see the flicker of disappointment in his eyes.

I'm relieved he isn't pushing me for an answer right this second. I don't know that I could give him one, honestly. Not twelve hours ago I was desperately hoping that his best friend would kiss me. Then again, the same best friend gave me the brush off and encouraged me to call Trev. He wants me, that much is obvious, but I don't think he will ever let himself have me. If I wasn't so disappointed, I would be impressed by his level of dedication for his and Trevor's friendship.

I don't know why I am even having a hard time with this? Sebastian was a one night stand, which I'll admit was incredible, but after that, everything between has been hard. He has been a prickly ass 70% of the time and the other 30% he is quiet and broody sending me too many mixed signals that just make my head hurt.

I'm over the mind games, though. Why would I ever fight for someone who wouldn't want to fight for me? Similarly, why wouldn't I fight for someone who is fighting for me? Trev is sitting here, fighting for me, for us. So maybe I should just say fuck it and dive in headfirst.

Chapter Fifteen

Trevor

"Enough heavy," I say with a slightly strained smile. "I came to kidnap you for dinner. Me and some of the guys from the team are meeting at Rocco's down the street. They have some of the best pizza. I swear it's gonna change your life."

Erica looks at me for a moment, indecision written across her face before she softly smiles at me and nods. I'm relieved that I haven't spooked her enough to where she doesn't want to hang out, but I can't say that I'm not a little disappointed, or a lot, that she didn't immediately agree to be mine. I'll give her time, though. Whatever she needs. I'll give her fucking everything because she deserves it, and more.

I stand up and hold my hand out for her to take and to my delight she does. Her fingers lace through mine as we make our way out of her room and to the elevator.

"Trev, do you eat anything that isn't deep fried, made of dough or soaked in sodium?" She laughs.

I furrow my brows. "No, what would be the point of that?"

She laughs before swatting at my stomach.

"It's completely unfair how guys can eat whatever they want and never gain a pound."

"Perks of being an athlete, Little Red," I say with a wink.

Letting out another laugh she tosses her head back slightly as she nods. Shit. She is fucking perfection. Even her laugh is practically melodic. It's a sound I took for granted when she lived just next door to me for years. It's a sound I missed more than I could even fathom when I was too far away to hear it except over a phone. Everything about Erica Pembrooke is addictive, and I know I'm not the only one that sees it.

I lead us over to where my black Porsche 911 is parked and open the door for Erica before shutting her door and walking around to my side. She always mercilessly teases me for driving what she calls a 'douche' car. I loved my Camaro growing up and I know she did too. We had some great times in that car but there was no way in hell I was going to turn down a graduation present from my parents like this beauty.

When I slide into the seat, I glance over to see Erica scrolling through her phone. She isn't looking at me but I'm sure as hell looking at her. How could I not? Everywhere she goes heads turn, even if she doesn't realize it.

My knuckles tighten around the steering wheel as mental images flash in my head from the years. Images of her 'boyfriends' at the time holding her, kissing her. Fuck, I wanted to destroy them just for breathing the same air as my Little Red. What the hell was I thinking telling her that I would be okay with her seeing other people until she decided about us? I most certainly would not be o-fucking-kay with it.

I know it was the right thing to say and that she appreciated it even if she never pursues anything with anyone else. The men on this campus better hope that she doesn't because if I see anyone so much as touch a single hair on her head, I will have no problem beating the shit out of every last one of them.

"How is the team doing? You guys ready for the game this Saturday?"

I shake my head out of the uncharacteristically violent thoughts in my head. She always did bring out a wildly possessive side of me. Forcing a smile that doesn't feel too forced after my eyes meet hers, I nod as I turn out onto the road.

"Doing good. Our defense is strong this year and they have me so we shouldn't have a problem," I wink.

Erica barks out a laugh as she shakes her head.

"Mhmm. And how is the rest of your offence? You know just in case you botch some throws."

I scoff at her because the very idea is completely ridiculous before my eyes flick from the road to her and I smirk.

"They're good. Seb is a solid tight end, and Slater, one of our roommates, is one of the best running backs in our division. He's got some wheels on him."

I nod. "Good. I can't wait to watch you whoop Cornwall's ass. I can't stand them."

"Does that have anything to do with the fact that Nick Jensen, your ex-boyfriend, is their star cornerback?" I ask with a raised brow.

She rolls her eyes and shakes her head. "No. We dated for like 2 seconds, and he was a total douche, as you remember."

My jaw ticks as I clench my teeth. Oh, I fucking remember. I remember the humiliation and pain he put my Little Red through. I also remember how good it felt to knock that little douche down a peg or two. He wasn't looking too well last time I saw him but he assured me he would never so much as look at Erica again so that was enough for me. Not that Erica knows any of this. I wanted to handle it on my own. See what I mean? She brings it out of me. I don't go around beating up dumb kids for cheating on their girlfriends. But for her? I'd do fucking anything.

It doesn't take long for us to get to Rocco's. The doors open with ease and the familiar smell of marinara, fresh baked dough and beer fill my nose, bringing with it more memories than I can count of the last few years. I see the guys immediately. Mainly because there are over twenty of them already here and you couldn't miss them if you tried. They are all built like brick fucking houses. When they see me, a few of them cheer, clearly already a few beers deep as a freshman rushes to pull up two seats for us.

As soon as we sit down, it's obvious that all eyes are glued to us, especially Slater. That guy is such a fucking flirt. If he wasn't staring at my girl with interest, I'd think it was funny but that's not the case. I kick his shin harder than probably necessary before I curl my arm around Erica's shoulders before addressing the rest of the table.

"Everyone, this is my best friend, Erica."

Erica smiles at them politely before Slater speaks up, flicking his eyes between Erica and me.

"Does Seb know?"

I cock a brow in question as I look at him. "Know what?"

Slater pauses for a moment before he shrugs and smiles. "That you have another best friend. You two have practically tied your dicks together. I am sure he won't like the competition."

I bark out a laugh before I flip him off and shake my head before turning to face Erica.

"And this douche bag is Slater. You haven't seen him at the house because he spends his free time banging as many sorority chicks as possible."

Erica chuckles and nods. "Nice, at least he is consistent."

Slaters snickers. "Hell yeah, that's a great way to put it. Why haven't I seen you around, baby? You seem like the type of girl that would definitely get my attention."

"Easy," I practically growl. Fucking flirt.

Slater's eyes are practically shining with mischief as he leans back onto the back two legs of his chair. He is just messing with her and as the unofficial jokester of the group, I guess he thinks it's his job, but when I look over at Erica and see a similar glint in her eye, I know he is in for it.

She smiles at him, letting her eyes rake over him from top to bottom in what I know to be feigned interest. I do my best to mask my smile but don't do a great job since Mikey sends me a questioning look. I just shake my head slightly at him before I turn back to face Erica. Licking her lips slowly, she stands up from her seat and puts her hands on top of the table, leaning over so that her face is only a few inches away from Slaters. Fuck. Even though I know that she is just messing with him, the sight still makes my blood boil.

Slater looks surprised for a moment until she gives him a slow seductive smile that would make a priest cum in his pants. Then the idiot grins wide like he just struck gold.

"It's a shame it took us this long to meet. You have a face that is hard to forget," she purrs.

She leans in a little closer until she is practically on top of the table as Slater lazily leans back into his seat with a dirty smirk across his stupid fucking face.

"Oh yeah, baby?"

All it takes is one little push of her finger to send him toppling over backwards as well as the tray filled with leftover food from the table behind him. He shouts in surprise as he busts his ass while the half-eaten food splatters across his face.

"Yeah, it's covered in barbecue. You should probably take care of that."

I can't hold it in any longer. I howl out a laugh as the rest of the guy's roar with amusement like we are at a comedy show. I look over to see Erica give Slater a challenging look, as if she is waiting to see how he will handle the public humiliation. She doesn't know it, but he is used to shit like this. He is constantly doing dumb shit to get girls attention and is probably the best at laughing at himself. Slater reaches over to Mikey's plate and snags a fry before wiping it across his sauce covered face and shrugs.

"Barbecue is my favorite."

Erica smiles and nods before she sits back into her seat while I am still chuckling.

"Oh my god. This is why I love you, that was fucking perfect."

She smiles up at me with so much adoration it nearly steals the breath out of my lungs before Mikey reaches across the table to shake her hand.

"I'm Declan but everyone calls me Mike. I live with these jack-asses and you, Miss Erica, have just become my new favorite person," he says with a slight southern drawl.

"Nice to meet you," she laughs.

A few moments later, a group of cheerleaders come sauntering up to our table. A few of them peel off from the pack and bounce their way over to their guys of the week laps while others sit and fawn over who they are hoping will be Mr. Next Week. I'd like to act irritated by the guys for feeding scraps to the scavengers, but I remember being a freshman and having beautiful girls throw themselves at me just for wearing a jersey. It was fun but I am definitely over it. Speaking of being over things, a seriously annoying blonde comes sashaying up to me before she slips right in between Erica and me, perching herself on to the edge of the table as she does.

"Hey baby," she coos as she runs her perfectly manicured fingers through my hair.

I instantly pull away and scoot back a few inches so that I'm out of her reach. This bitch is fucking nuts and if her dad wasn't golfing buddies with mine, I would have gotten her crazy ass a restraining order a long ass time ago.

"Hey," I clip out coolly, hoping she will get the hint that I'm not fucking interested, but of course, she never does.

"What are you doing later?"

"Just headed home," I draw unenthusiastically, wishing my dad didn't specifically ask me to be at least cordial with her when I told him about her over the summer.

"Can I come?" She giggles.

I let out a heavy sigh before I shoot Erica an apologetic look. I don't want her to think that Cynthia is anything to me. She is fucking nothing. It's even more clear when I can still taste Erica's lips on mine, when my arm is still wrapped around her body.

"No," I snap. If she causes issues between me and Erica, I don't give a fuck what my dad says, I'm getting the bitch locked up.

She pouts and reaches out to touch me again, but this time I pull away before she can, tugging Erica closer to me as I do.

"Come on. I'll do that thing you like," she sings as she gives Erica a triumphant smirk.

"Not interested, Cynthia," I practically snarl.

She huffs an aggravated breath before she slides off the table. "We both know you will be sooner or later."

I scoff because I'd rather eat broken glass then touch her psycho ass willingly again. Irritation slashes across her face before she snaps her fingers like the queen bitch she clearly is. As a unit, they all saunter out of the pizzeria, leaving behind a few mutters from some of the guys complaining that they got cock blocked. The table is unusually silent for a few moments before Erica chimes in.

"Well, isn't she just a peach."

Everyone busts up laughing and I shake my head as I lean over and kiss the top of her head as we dig into the pizza in front of us. She smiles up at me and winks before she digs into her food. I look across the table to see Slater looking at us with a weird look on his face. I get it. I'm not a one woman kind of guy, at least I haven't been for as long as these guys have known me. But that was because I knew there was only one woman out there that I wanted. Now that she is here, I'm shooting my shot and hoping like hell that she will be mine again, soon.

CHAPTER SIXTEEN

ERICA

Relieved isn't a close enough word to describe how I felt after Trev and I talked the other day. Part of me was thrilled at the thought of Trev wanting to be with me again but another admittedly larger part was terrified. So, when he wasn't in typical Trevor fashion, impatiently demanding a yes or no answer right then and there, relief was definitely the start of what I was feeling but then way too many complicated thoughts followed. Ones including a certain tight end.

When Trev mentioned he was going to eat with some of the guys from the team, I can't deny that my head immediately jumped to Sebastian, wondering if he would be there. When we got to the pizzeria and I noticed that he wasn't there, a small flutter of disappointment filled my chest before I squashed it like a bug.

All of the guys on the team were really nice and welcoming, and I finally got to meet Trevor's other roommates. But I think that might have just complicated things because as soon as Slater mentioned Sebastian's name with his eyes on me something clicked inside my head. He was the guy that walked in on us in the laundry room when we had just finished...yeah, shit.

If he was going to say something to Trevor, I'm sure he would have either then or within the last few days. If he did, I would know it because I have no doubt that Trev would rip my door down, demanding answers.

Obviously, Sebastian hasn't told Trevor and seems to be focused on making sure that he never finds out what happened between us. As much as it stung as first to be brushed under the rug like I am something disposable, I kinda get it. Trevor holds grudges and doesn't easily forgive. He would see what Sebastian and I did as an ultimate betrayal.

In our defense, neither of us knew who the other was at the time, and I didn't know that Trevor still had feelings for me. We were just two consenting adults with explosive sexual chemistry. Trev wouldn't hear any of that though. He would just focus on the fact that his best friend and I have slept together and then...I don't really know.

He wouldn't have much room to be furious, though. Clearly, he hasn't been as heartbroken and hung up on me as he claims if the bouncy blonde cheerleader practically straddling him the other day is anything to go off. I knew that he had a reputation, I've seen the girls throw him lustful looks like they have fucked a hundred times and if Cynthia's words are anything to go on, he has definitely fucked her. Why does that bother me so much? Ugh.

Shaking my head of the headache inducing thoughts building inside my head, I make my way from my last class of the day to my dorm when my phone starts to ring. I glance down and see my mother's name flashing across the screen, again. Fuck. Since our last fight I have been dodging her phone calls, pretty effectively I might add, but I know that if I keep this up for any longer there will be serious hell to pay. So, I bite the bullet and hit accept.

"Hello, Mother."

"Oh good, so you are alive," she snaps immediately.

I roll my eyes as I step into the elevator. "Yep. Sounds like you are still mad."

"Well, of course I'm mad, Erica! You already have your future mapped out for you perfectly and just when you start college, you

suddenly think that you know better than your father and me?
That you want to throw away all our hard work to fingerpaint like
a toddler!"

There are so many things wrong with her sentence that I don't
even know where to begin. I know that if I stand any chance in
making a reasonable case to her though, I have to use logic.

"I could make a sustainable career out of an art degree. I
wouldn't be limited to just being a painter, though that is my passion. An art degree can be translated over to music, film, fashion,
all of which are some of the largest grossing industries in the
world."

She lets out a condescending laugh, and I can practically hear
her shaking her head as I speak.

"Please don't treat me like I'm an imbecile that would actually
buy any of that shit. We both know that if you got an art degree
you would become one of those pathetic bottom feeders that has
to sell your work at flea markets for pennies on the dollar just to
eat scraps and live in a cardboard box. Is that the kind of life you
want for yourself?"

My teeth grit but instead of lashing out, I close my eyes and take
a calming breath. "Regardless, if that is how things turned out, it's
my life, right? I should be able to choose how I want to spend it,
and I definitely should be able to choose what degree I would like
to work towards."

"I beg to differ. Your father and I are paying for your education in
the intent of you becoming a partner at our firm. We are not paying
hundreds of thousands of dollars so that you can play around with
paint all day. This is an investment, dear. Nothing more."

The way she practically spits dear is anything but a form of an
endearment. Then again, Beverly Pembrooke doesn't use terms of
endearments. Ever. An investment? Are you fucking kidding me?

"What does Trevor say about all of this nonsense?" My mother asks when I don't respond.

"Trevor?" I echo. "I don't know I haven't really talked to him about it since probably high school."

"And why do you think that is? Are you worried that he'll judge you? Maybe not see you as long term material? You need a respectable career that can help support you and your family."

I blink and shake my head. What fucking planet is she on right now?

"What fucking family?! Last I checked I am single with no kids, mother. Besides, Trevor would support me no matter what I would want to do with my life. He always has."

"Erica, that's what men tell you but in reality, they want someone who is driven and put together. Someone who has a plan and knows how to execute it properly. I'm afraid starving artist is not a desirable career for a future wife."

Now I am laughing. Genuinely cracking up as my shoulders shake with amusement. She is joking right?

"Wife? Since when am I getting married? Have you sold me off or something?"

"Don't be ridiculous, Erica. All I'm saying is that there are handsome men out there that you would match with perfectly. Men like Trevor."

"Stop. That's enough. You are already telling me what I can and can't study in school. Now you are telling me who to date, potentially marry one day? Are you fucking with me?"

"Language! My god. Has just a few months away turned you into some ill-mannered delinquent?"

I bark out a surprised laugh as I step out of the elevator and down the hall.

"Delinquent? Because I want to paint? Was Van Gogh a delin-quent? How about Michelangelo when he painted the Sistine Chapel? What a drain on society, am I right?" I snark.

"Erica, do not think you can speak to me like that and get away with it. You and I both know-"

"You know what, I have to go," I bite out before I quickly hit end.

When I get to my room, I notice a sparkly pink scarf tied around the doorknob that seems to be permanently fucking attached by now. I let out a frustrated grunt and smack the wall before I slide down to the floor. I can't even retreat to my own space after that hellish conversation because my roommate is too busy getting her brains screwed out. Must be fucking nice.

I lift up my phone to see that my mother is already calling me again. Yeah, that's going to be a hard pass. I hit ignore and type out a text to the last person I probably should, but the only one that I want to right now.

CHAPTER SEVENTEEN

SEBASTIAN

Erica: Can I come over?

I have been staring at her text message for the last three minutes straight. She hasn't tried to text or call me since I gave her my number and neither have I. I don't know why I even thought it was a good idea to swap numbers. Since I got it, it has only left me hovering my thumb over her name more times than I'd care to admit.

I quickly type out a reply and hit send before I can second guess myself any longer.

Me: Trevor isn't here.
Everything okay?

I don't have to wait long before her text comes in.

Erica: I don't care. I just need somewhere to chill out for a little...Is it okay if I say no?

Me: Come over.

I wait for a few minutes to see if she will respond but it doesn't look like she is going to. I look around the room thankful that it's actually picked up for once before I go into my room and spray on some cologne, not for her or anything, just because I don't think I have today.

Trevor, Mikey and Slater went to some mixer thing over at the Kappa house. They tried to get me to come with, but I'm just not really into the party scene. Not unless I'm practically forced to go like the last few and look how well those worked out for me.

Just as I am coming down the stairs, a soft knock comes from the door and my heart practically trips over itself in anticipation. Seriously, what the hell is that shit? When I open the door, I see an exhausted looking Erica with unshed tears in her bright eyes. Her face isn't one of sadness though, it's anger, irritation and maybe a little bit of despair.

Before I can say anything or invite her in, she rushes forward and clamps her arms around my waist like a vice as she buries her head into my chest. I don't even hesitate to pull her closer to me as I wrap my arms around her shoulders. I feel her let out a big sigh and I take the opportunity to lean my head down to rest on top of hers as I subtly inhale. *Peaches.*

We stay like that for a few moments before she slowly pulls away and wipes at her face.

"Sorry," she whispers hoarsely.

I shake my head. "Don't. Come on," I say as I gently reach down and grab her hand to pull her inside.

I don't know if I did it or if she did but when the door closes, I notice that our fingers are laced together as I pull her through the house and into the living room. I also notice that I really don't want to let go. I'm trying to decide if it's okay for me to sit here and hold hands with the girl that my best friend is in love with or not. Unfortunately, I determine that it isn't, and I slowly pull my hand away, missing the feel of her soft skin instantly.

Since we sat down, she has yet to look at me, whereas I can't take my fucking eyes off her. I can tell that she definitely doesn't want to talk about whatever is bothering her, so I flick through the channels until I decide to just turn on sports center. I settle back into the couch like she isn't even here, and I think she appreciates it. I notice out of my peripherals that she tucks her legs up to her chest and eases back into a little ball.

We silently watch TV for almost two hours before she finally speaks.

"Where is everyone?"

I look over to her and try my best not to stare for too long before I turn back to the TV.

"Kappa mixer."

She nods. "Why aren't you with them?"

I shrug.

"You don't go out a lot, do you?"

I shrug again. Instead of getting frustrated with my silence, like many do, she just nods and accepts my non-verbal answer before she turns back to face the TV.

Another few minutes go by before I feel the couch shift slightly. I notice that she is sitting with her legs crossed as she leans towards me.

"I took your advice."

"What advice?"

"The going after what makes me happy advice. I talked with my mother a little more about switching my major to art."

I nod. "That's good. What did she say?"

She lets out a hollow laugh and shakes her head.

"It didn't go well. Basically, in my mother's mind if I don't become a lawyer, I will never make any money, I will live in a cardboard box, and no one will ever want to marry me. Can you believe that? I swear to god, she lives in the 19th century where it's crucial to be married off before you are 21 or die a haggard spinster. She is so contradictory, though! On one hand she wants me to be a proud feminist with a high-profile career, but on the other hand she wants me to be the picture-perfect wife for the picture perfect man."

"Do you not want to get married?" I ask, wondering myself why that is the piece of information I decided to focus on.

Erica shrugs. "I don't know. Maybe someday. I don't really care either way. You're supposed to get married because you can't imagine spending another moment away from that person, not because you want to look good in front of your country club friends or have live-in dick."

A surprised laugh escapes me at her words. I try to tamp it down, but she sees my obvious surprise and gives me a half of a grin before she starts laughing. We get into one of those stupid as hell laughing fits that makes you laugh because you're laughing. I don't even know why I can't keep it together right now, but I'm close to fucking tears right now and can't stop.

"Wow. Had no idea you were so eloquent," I say after the laughter subsides.

She lets out a soft giggle and shrugs her shoulders. The sweet smile she is giving me makes my heart lurch the way it seems to always do when she is near. I find myself smirking back at her, not saying a word as I get lost in her hypnotic eyes.

"What about you? You got any family problems that can take my mind off mine?" She asks with a soft laugh.

My relaxed smile falls away instantly, and I quickly turn away from her and focus back on the TV. A few heavy seconds pass by before Erica's small hand rests on my knee. I flick my eyes over to see a soft apologetic look on her face.

"I'm sorry. I didn't mean to upset you. I-"

"It's fine," I bite out a little too harshly causing her to wince at the sound before she begins to pull away.

I reach out and hold her hand in place, not wanting her to take it away. At least not for a few more seconds.

"I'm sorry," I grumble lowly. "I didn't mean to come across like that." I take a slight pause before I continue. "My-uh, my family died a while ago. I bounced around from home to home until I turned 18."

I don't know why I just said that. Trevor is the only other person in the world who knows that fact about me. Everyone else knows better than to ask me personal questions. I glance over to see a compassionate look on Erica's face. Normally when people look at me like that, it pisses me the hell off, but something about the way she is actually soothes me a little.

"You don't have anyone?" She practically whispers.

I give a quick shake of my head which causes her to bite the inside of her cheek before nodding. She seems to drop the topic just like that, and I am extremely fucking grateful for it. That is more than I was ever planning to share with her, and my throat is starting to tighten as the demons of my past begin to creep in.

Suddenly, I realize that I have been absentmindedly brushing my thumb back and forth against the back of her hand. When did I start doing that? And why didn't I notice? Why does everything feel so second nature with her? So easy?

"I'm sorry that your parents are giving you a hard time, but I'm glad you came over."

"You are?" She asks almost surprised.

I furrow my brows as I nod. "Yeah, why do you seem surprised?"

She shrugs. "Honestly, after that first night it kind of seemed like you always want to be as far away from me as possible. I didn't know if maybe you were only being nice to me because Trevor asked you to or something. I guess I don't really know how to read you. Most days I think that you actually kind of hate my fucking guts," she laughs but the sound is anything but happy.

I don't know what to say for a few moments because the idea of not wanting to be around her is unfathomable. True, I want to feel that way, but it's fucking impossible. I see her everywhere, in the halls, at the coffee stand, at the grocery store. All times I kept an eye on her but anytime I felt like she was about to notice me, I would turn away and pretend not to see her. I don't trust myself enough to be alone with her, which is part of what makes her being here so dangerous right now.

"That's not true."

"Which part?" She asks so quietly that it's practically a whisper.

I turn my head to look into her deep expressive eyes which dilate as I lean just a little closer. My hair falls against the couch next to me and Erica lifts her hand up, gently brushing a piece out of my face before slowly twisting her fingers through a few pieces.

"I'm kinda obsessed with your hair," she says softly with a small smile.

I smirk just a little before my eyes flick over her face, memorizing every faint freckle that is dusted across the bridge of her nose. You'd never see them if you weren't this close to her and unfortunately for me, this is only one of a few times that I have had the opportunity to be this close to her. She's fucking breathtaking.

"All of it."

Erica slowly eases towards me, her eyes darting down to my lips as my eyes do the same to hers. I should pull away. I should push her away. But when she looks at me like that, I'm fucking powerless. I want this girl more than any-fucking-thing and after weeks of me pushing everything and anything that has to do with her to the side, I want this, I fucking need it. Just before my lips can brush against hers, the front door bangs open with a loud crash. We spring apart like we were just caught doing something we shouldn't have, which granted, we were.

I look over to see Slater walk in with a raised eyebrow and a knowing smirk as his eyes bounce over Erica and me and how close we are sitting. Subtly, I put a little bit of distance between us as Slater turns his eyes on Erica.

"Hey girl, what are you doing here?"

She shrugs casually. "Just needed a place to hangout for a little. My roommate and her boyfriend are going at it like rabbits."

"Erica?" Trevor slurs loudly as he stumbles into the room with Mikey closely trailing him.

His eyes brighten when he sees her, but it doesn't totally remove the drunken haze that is currently clouding him. I look to Slater who just shrugs. Trevor used to party hard but tries to keep his nose pretty clean during the season, so I'm surprised that he is completely shit tagged on a Thursday night.

"Hey, Trev," she smiles softly, a look of adoration too plainly written across her face for my fucking liking.

He grins at her as he rushes over to the couch until he practically lands on top of her. My knee jerk reaction is to rip him off her, but I know that isn't really my place so instead, I ball my fists in my lap and bite my cheek until it bleeds as I watch him drunkenly gaze up at her.

"You're so fucking gorgeous," he says sloppily.

She laughs and brushes some of his matted down faux hawk off his face.

"And you're so fucking drunk. How much did you drink?"

He shrugs dramatically. "One or two-"

"Bottles," Slater fills in. "He drank an entire bottle of vodka to himself and at least three beers."

That makes me furrow my brows even more. Trev hates hard alcohol. What the hell is going on? Maybe I'd know if I wasn't being such a shitty friend lately. I haven't spent as much time with him as usual because Erica is always with him and things seem to just be easier when I keep my distance.

Trevor begins nuzzling his head into Erica's lap. She smiles at him as her fingers start running through his hair. She shifts slightly, probably to get more comfortable as he quickly follows, making sure that he never loses his contact with her. The intimate gesture of her caring for him when he is all fucked up burns a hole right through my chest. I don't give a fuck if I come across as a jealous asshole. Right now, that's exactly what I am.

"I think you need to go sleep it off, buddy," I say, attempting to come across as casual but the irritation in my tone is unmistakable.

Erica nods and forces a laugh. "Definitely."

"Only if you tuck me in," he says with what I think was supposed to be a charming smile.

Maybe it was fucking charming because Erica smiles at him before rolling her eyes. "Fine, come on. One foot in front of the other, Drunky."

Slowly, they make their way out of the room and up the stairs with Mikey following behind just in case. They look good together, even with Trev stumbling all over the place as Erica tries and fails to stabilize him. They fit. So, what the fuck am I doing?

Chapter Eighteen

Sebastian

S later walks over and slumps down onto the couch next to me before he turns.

"What's up with Trevor? He hasn't gotten drunk on the hard stuff in forever," I ask.

Slater shrugs. "I don't know man. He's been off all year. When we got to the mixer, he just started knocking them back and anytime a girl would even approach him he would damn near rip their heads off. He kept mumbling how he already has the perfect girl and that he won't fuck it up this time."

Anger simmers inside of me from hearing about Trevor referring to Erica as his girl. She isn't his fucking anything.

Isn't she, though?

If anyone has the right to say that Erica is theirs, shouldn't it be Trevor who she obviously cares about and was in a relationship with? Not me who was nothing more than a one-night stand on a fucking washing machine and is now barely an acquaintance.

Slater's obnoxious as fuck ringtone suddenly goes off for a second bere he answers it.

"Hey, Scar," he says before letting out a sigh and a laugh. "Yes, mom. I am home safe and sound." He pauses again, listening to who I know to be his best friend from back home before he laughs

After he hangs up, we sit in silence for a few moments before he finally speaks up.

"So, I take it Trevor doesn't know?" Slater asks after a few moments.

"Know what?"

"Bro, I walked in on you guys remember? She poked her head out from behind your back for a second. I didn't know who she was until her and Trev came to Rocco's the other day."

"Fuck," I hiss as I run a hand down the front of my face. "I didn't know who she was when we hooked up. If I would have known that she was the girl that he wouldn't shut up about I never would have even looked her way."

"Yeah, I call bullshit on that. You know who she is now, but you're definitely still looking her way."

I narrow my eyes as I glare at him. "It was a one-time thing."

"Uh huh. So, you two weren't about to jump each other when we came in?" He asks with a no bullshit eyebrow raise.

I grimace and throw my head back against the couch.

"I'm trying man, but she is..."

I trail off not knowing where to even begin to describe how deep Erica has wiggled her way under my skin in the short amount time that I have known her. Fuck knows how to make it stop. I have tried damn near everything, but nothing has worked. She has practically tattooed her name on my fucking soul.

Slaters eyes widen and his mouth drops, the gravity of this fucked up situation clearly just now registering with him.

"Oh shit. You actually like her, don't you?"

I clench my jaw for a few seconds, wanting to keep the information to myself but deciding that hiding all of this shit from my best friend is hard enough, I can't fucking handle bottling this shit up for much longer. I give him a short terse nod as I keep my eyes trained on the TV.

"Does she feel the same?"

I shrug. "I don't know. She sends out the vibes sometimes but then she is off jumping in Trev's arms in the next moment. Usually, that is after I shut her down or push her away. We get along really well when I'm not fucking things up and being a dick. I can't stop thinking about her, though, man. I just, can't."

Slater is quiet with this information for a few moments before he nods.

"Well, you know what you have to do then?"

I shake my head because no I don't know what the hell to do in this fucked position that I've found myself in.

"You gotta talk to Trev, and then you gotta lock that chick down because I swear the whole damn team fell in love with her the other day."

My fists ball up at the idea of any other guys looking her way. Trevor is bad enough. I don't need any more fuckers sniffing around her.

Before I can say anything, I hear the wooden steps creak and look over to see Erica striding down the stairs. I can't help but watch as her long toned legs stretch with each step while her soft red hair gently swishes across her back. When her sea-colored eyes lock with mine, I find myself smiling and when she smiles back, I know that I'm a fucking goner.

"Our boy okay?" Slater asks.

She nods. "Yeah, Mikey shoved some aspirin down his throat, and I left a bowl and a Gatorade by his bed since I have no doubt within a few hours he will be puking his guts out. He could never handle his liquor. You should have seen him at prom. While all the other guys were holding back their dates hair, I was the one consoling Trevor as we spent the entire afterparty in the bathroom of our hotel room."

I wince at the reminder that they used to date. It's just another blatant reminder that I have no right to think the things that I do and want the things that I want. I still do, though. I want it all. It makes me grateful to know that he got blitzed out of his mind that night because that hopefully means he was feeling too much like shit to leave the bathroom all night.

Such a fucked up thing to think.

Trevor is in love with her, he wants her, and I'm not sure if she wants him too. They are cut from the same cloth, from the same fucking section of the cloth. In the end I have almost no doubts that they'll end up together. I don't need to go fucking up everything just because I can't stop thinking about her. I have to push her away for fucking good. It's what's best for everyone. She deserves someone better than me, anyways.

"Anyways, I'm gonna try my luck at my dorm. Hopefully the fuckfest has ended," she jokes before walking to the door.

Despite my better judgment and the little pep talk that I just gave myself, I find that I'm grabbing a coat and walking towards her.

"I'll walk you," I say as I open the door for her.

"You don't have to," she says softly as her eyes flick over to Slater. I don't miss the worry in them before her gaze comes back to me.

I roll my eyes like her refusal is a waste of time because it fucking is. I gesture for her to go, and she shrugs slightly before waving to Slater. I turn to see him staring at me with a smug grin but what also looks like concern. I know he is probably worried that I am going to ruin everything, not just in the house but on the field. I have the same concerns myself yet here I am, walking her home alone. Again.

I try to tell myself that there are a hundred girls like her out there, that she is nothing special and that I'm getting hung up on a good lay and the forbidden fruit. But as soon as I think those things, I instantly know that they are all bullshit.

This isn't about a good lay or a pretty face. There is something else, something more. She has me wanting to peel back her layers to see what makes her tick. She has me sitting up all night and all day thinking about every encounter and every word shared between us as if I can dissect hidden meanings or intentions. To say I have become a little obsessed seems to be a huge fucking understatement.

We don't talk the whole way back to her dorm, and when we get outside the main doors, she stops and turns to face me.

"Well, thanks for walking me, again."

I put my hands into my pockets and nod. "Anytime."

"I had a good time tonight."

"Me too."

She smiles softly before she leans up onto her toes and places a featherlight kiss to my cheek. My skin instantly scorches from the contact and when she pulls away, I find myself letting out a small disappointed sigh.

Why does it have to be her?

Erica cocks her head questioningly, and I shake mine in response.

"Goodnight, Erica."

"Night, Seb."

I freeze in place as I watch her walk inside. I find myself standing there for several minutes, just in case she can't get into her dorm room and decides to walk around campus to find somewhere else to crash. When she doesn't come out, I assume that she made it inside before I turn around and walk back to the house.

Hearing her say my nickname fills me with equal amounts of happiness and guilt. Happiness because it's a familiarity that I love to hear come from her full rosy lips and guilt because Trev is the first one that started calling me that.

He's like a brother to me, and I can't help but feel like one way or another no matter how hard I try, I'm going to betray him. Fuck, I guess I already have. I'm going to have to decide what I'm willing to risk, potentially losing Trev from my life or wondering what could have happened with Erica, forever. Shit. I honestly don't know which is worse.

CHAPTER NINETEEN

ERICA

It's Saturday and the first home game that I've been able to attend this season. Since Ethan went home for the weekend to visit with his family, Palmer has decided to tag along with me. I'm wearing a Brighton U t-shirt that is white with crimson red accents, the school colors, and a pair of light wash blue jeans.

Palmer went for a more daring outfit of a Brighton crop top and white booty shorts with a pair of bright red heels. I tried to talk her out of it, but she insisted that she wanted to be ready for all of the parties that are going to kick off around campus right after the game.

"I feel like we haven't gotten to spend like any time together," Palmer whines as she loops her arm through mine while we walk through campus.

"Yeah, you and Ethan are pretty hot and heavy huh?"

She cackles and nods. "Yeah. Sorry. We have been apart for a few years except for summer and winter breaks. We are really soaking it up."

I shrug. "I get it. If I had a boyfriend that I was madly in love with, I'm sure I would be in the same boat."

"Why don't you? I mean, tell me to shut up if you don't want to talk about it but you are a total babe. How are you not with

"I don't know. I have never really been one of those girls that has been desperate to be with someone, you know? I'm happy just being me. I dated Trevor for a few years before he came here. I dated a few other guys after him for a bit but nothing really serious. I'm not interested in wasting my time with someone I don't see a future with just so I am not lonely, you know?"

"True. I dated a few duds before Ethan. I was a little wary at first, but I'm so glad that I gave us a chance. He is my whole world."

I nod and smile as we make our way through towards the stadium.

"So, you going to give me more details about you and Trevor or am I going to have to pull it out of you?"

My eyebrows raise at her brashness before I let out a surprised laugh.

"Not much to tell. You already know everything, Nosey."

Palmer rolls her eyes as we step around a group of people.

"Please. He is the school's resident playboy. He is never seen with a girl more than twice and tends to leave a string of broken hearts in his wake. Then here you are, his long-lost high school sweetheart, who he clearly still adores. What's your secret? How did you get him to commit?"

"Why are you so interested? Don't you have Ethan?" I ask with a teasing smile.

She bats at the air like that is irrelevant. "Of course, I do. But I'm a woman with two eyes, and I see how hot Trevor is. I'm allowed to look, just not touch."

I laugh at that as I shrug. "Well sorry to disappoint, but I don't have a secret. We were super close growing up and, I don't know, I guess it changed into more the older we got."

"Well, damn. I was hoping you had a strategic step by step guidelines that I could sell for a few grand to desperate hopefuls.

There isn't a girl at Brighton that wouldn't kill for a chance with Trevor Michaels."

A pang of something runs through my chest at her words. Not quite jealousy but something in that neighborhood. I still haven't decided how I feel about giving things a shot with Trevor again. As soon as I think that it could be really great, the best really, someone completely off-limits pops into my head and throws all of my mental progress into the fucking trash. Being with Seb would be so hard, so complicated and people around us would definitely be hurt. But for some obnoxious reason, the faint prospect dances in the back of my head, tantalizing me with the possibility of what could be.

We don't say anything more as we make our way to our seats. The stadium is absolutely packed with a sea of crimson red and white crammed in on the home side. The visitors side has a decent turn out of Cornwall students and families with orange and black dotting the stadium, but home field advantage is an advantage for a reason.

Palmer and I get settled into our seats for all of two seconds before she announces that she is going to get us food and drinks. Soon, music rumbles through the stadium as the Brighton Knights jog out of the tunnel. I get to my feet and start howling and whistling as the team captain heads over to the ref to do the coin toss.

Some of the guys begin warming up on the side lines and my eyes land on number 89 almost immediately with the last name Caldwell scrawled across the back. My heart flip flops when I see him briefly scan over the stadium seats just a little short of where I am, like he is looking for something or someone. I know that he can't see me or anything, but I like to think that he can feel it when I am around like I can him.

Yeah, keep dreaming, Erica.

We win the coin toss, and I watch as our team gets into position to receive. Cornwall starts the game off with a kick that lands around our 10-yard line when one of our guys easily catches it. He dodges a few Cornwall players that attempt to tackle him but doesn't make it too far before he is taken down at Cornwall's 40 yard line. The game keeps up a consistent theme of we get a few yards and then they take it right back.

Palmer shows up shortly after the game starts with nachos, popcorn and two beers.

"How did you manage to get your hands on these?" I ask as I take the outstretched cup from her hand.

"I batted my mink eyelashes at the guy and leaned over the counter, so he was too distracted with my cleavage to think about an ID."

I let out a surprised laugh before clinking our plastic cups together and taking the popcorn she hands me. When I look up, I watch as the center snaps the ball before Trev looks for someone to pass it to. He quickly throws it to Slater just before he is taken down. Slater catches the ball midair and takes off like a bat out of hell. Trev wasn't lying, he's got some serious wheels on him.

Slater makes it 30 yards before he is tackled. He instantly jumps up and beats on his chest like the pumped-up jock I know he is. I laugh and scream until my voice cracks. It happens at every game, and in my opinion if your voice is normal the next day, did you even go to a football game?

A few plays later, we finally get some points on the board and are sitting at 7-0 with a little over a minute until halftime. When the ball is snapped, Trev waits only a few seconds before he sees the hole that Seb has slipped through and throws a bullet to him. Seb catches it and tucks it close to him as he takes off like a rocket.

He passes the 30, the 20, the 10...touchdown! He graciously tosses the ball to the ref and begins jogging back to his team without even a hint of a celebration. You can tell that for Sebastian this isn't a game, this is just taking care of business.

His team doesn't see it that way though as several of the guys launch into his arms and bounce excitedly around him as the clock runs out and both teams make their way to the locker rooms. I'm smiling so big that I swear my face is about to crack. Trevor and Seb are two of those players that are just really in sync with each other. It's a magical thing to watch, and I just know that this is going to be a good game.

Cornwall comes back strong in the second half of the game until we are sitting tied 33-33. Their defense has been really solid and unfortunately ours has not been, despite Trev's boasting about how great they were this year. There is only a minute left in the fourth quarter, so this will be the last play unless we go into overtime.

We have possession of the ball, and as soon as it's snapped, Seb bursts through their D-line like it's nothing. One guy chases after him but Seb's long legs easily put distance between him and the defensive tackle's before turning around to face Trevor. I see the moment that Trevor decides to throw it to Seb. Trev angles his body just slightly and the ball spirals perfectly through the air and right into Seb's large hands.

He only gets about five yards before a big guy in orange and black rushes towards Seb from the front. For a moment, I'm worried he is about to get leveled, but surprising the hell out of me and every other person in the stadium, Seb keeps up his speed instead of trying to avoid the guy.

When the Cornwall player lowers himself for a tackle, Seb jumps straight over him like he is a damn track star and lands behind the guy, instantly picking up into a dead run. What the fuck?!

"Go! Go!" I shout like a crazy person as the crowd begins to roar.

His legs stretch out far and fast as he eats up the distance between him and the end zone. People trail after him, but he has such a significant gap that no one can catch him until...

"Touchdown!" The commentator booms through the speakers of the stadium.

People are screaming, leaping and even tossing their beers at each other. Not even wasting a second, the crowd begins to rush the field, the excitement palpable in the air. I don't even check to see if Palmer follows as I hurry towards the field.

I make it to the 50 yard line before a thick pair of arms picks me up from behind and twirls me around. I squeal and laugh before I'm set down and turn around to see Trevor's wide grin. I wrap my arms around him to properly hug him.

"You were great, Trev! I can't even believe it!"

"Believe it, Little Red!" He hoots as some of the other guys come over and jump on him and shout in celebration.

Trevor turns to say something to me, but Cynthia rushes over and jumps into his arms as she peppers his face with kisses. That pang spreads through my chest again as I watch Trevor attempt to pry her off him, irritation clearly written across his face. It bothers me to see her all over him, I won't lie. But it doesn't feel even close to how it did when I saw her all over Sebastian at the party the other week. Shit. I guess that answers some questions that I have been asking myself.

When I turn around, I see a pair of rich caramel eyes that are firmly fixed on me and like always everything else fades away. It instantly feels like it's just the two of us standing here, like we are the only ones in the world at this moment. Corny, but true.

We slowly make our way towards each other, and when we are only a few steps away, he stops and gives me a small smile. A real smile. Not a smirk or a twitch, but a smile that makes my heart seize up in my chest at the sight. His hair has been pulled out of his bun and is messy and perfect all at the same time. Damn, it really isn't even fair how good looking he is.

I decide to close the distance first and wrap my arms around him. His immediately band around me, and it feels like he holds me tighter than he ever has before, closer. I don't mind at all, so I close my eyes and allow my head to rest against his broad chest. When we eventually pull apart, I notice that he keeps his hands on my lower back so that I can't step too far away.

"Seb, you were incredible. People are going to be talking about that play for years to come!"

He looks almost embarrassed as he shrugs. "Thanks. We played a good game."

"You played a good game. I have seen your games in the past, but damn. That was just amazing!"

Seb smiles again a little wider this time which causes me to smile. All I want in this moment is for him to kiss me, and based on how many times I have seen his eyes flick down to my lips, I think he wants it too. I wish he would just do it already and put us both out of our misery.

Instead of kissing me though, he bends down to my ear so that I can hear him over the crowd.

"We're having a party at the house tonight. You coming?"

I pull back so that I can look up into his eyes. "Do you want me to come?"

He licks his lips slowly and nods while his thumbs absentmindedly brush the exposed skin on my hips. I give him a shy smile and nod.

"Then I'll be there."

Seb smiles again and gives me a wink before squeezing my hips and letting me go. I watch as he turns to head towards the tunnel, several people patting his back and congratulating him as he walks through the crowd. He gives polite head nods and acknowledgments but nothing more before continuing on his way.

When I look back for Trev, I see him shout at Cynthia before storming off towards the tunnel. The girl looks close to tears until her eyes land on mine, venom quickly replacing her tears. In the chaos of the field, I manage to find Palmer, and we decide to grab some dinner before heading over to the party. When we get settled in at our booth at the burger shack down the road, I look up to see Palmer giving me a secretive smile.

"What?" I ask with furrowed brows.

"I get it now."

"Get what?"

She rolls her eyes like I am being dense. "Why you aren't jumping at the chance of getting with Trevor Michaels. It's because you have a thing for his best friend."

My face flushes and I quickly look down at the menu in front of me, feigning confusion. "Who are you even talking about?"

"Wow, you're a really shitty liar. You should work on that. Sebastian Caldwell. You want him, and it's clear that he wants you too. I saw you two practically dry humping in the middle of the field."

My head snaps up. "We were not! I hugged him. There is nothing between us. He has hardly gotten within a few feet of me since..." I stop myself before I say too much but it is too late.

"You dirty slut! You already got with him, didn't you?" She squeals excitedly.

"Say it a little louder," I grumble as I look around to see if anyone is paying attention to us. Luckily no one is.

"How was it?" Palmer asks as she leans forward.

"I am not doing this with you," I scoff as I hold my menu up to cover my blushing face.

"That good, huh? So, I take it you haven't told your *best friend*?"

"Not worth mentioning," I shrug as the waitress comes over to take our order.

We order quickly and once she leaves Palmer picks up right where she left off.

"Okay, you obviously are in denial, but just so you know, if you want to keep it under wraps, don't hold onto each other like you are both afraid the other will slip away. You guys looked crazy about each other, and you were just hugging. The chemistry between you two is fire."

I give her a terse nod before looking out the window. I don't really know how to describe my relationship with Sebastian Caldwell, if you can even call it that. We had a one-night stand that he instantly regretted and then proceeded to treat me like shit for a while. Then he started being nicer to me while still maintaining his distance? All the while, I am sitting here wondering if I should be giving my relationship with my ex-boyfriend, his best friend a chance? Ugh. Why the hell is nothing in my life ever easy?

After Palmer and I finish dinner, we drive over to Trev and Sebastian's house. When we get inside, it reminds me of the first night that we came here. There are throngs of people filling up every room and loud music vibrating the walls. There is also this tangible energy thrumming through the room most likely due to everyone's excitement over todays win.

"I'm gonna go hangout with some of my friends. Do you want to come?" Palmer asks as she gestures towards a group of girls.

I shake my head and smile. "I'm good. I'll catch up with you later."

She shrugs and smiles before heading over to her friends. I start weaving through the crowd when someone shoves me from the side, sending me falling face first towards the floor. I close my eyes to prepare for an impact that doesn't come.

When I open them slowly, I see that I am being held up by two strong hands. When I crane my neck up to look at who saved me it shouldn't come as a surprise who it is.

"You okay?" Sebastian asks as he slowly lifts me up until I am standing again.

I swallow roughly and nod. "Yeah, wasn't expecting that."

"I'm sure you weren't expecting a drunk asshole to damn near knock you down," he spits out, his jaw clenched in anger.

"Easy, tiger," I tease as I place a calming hand on his chest.

I feel his muscles tense under my touch before they relax, and he nods, running a hand through his unusually free hair as he does. Before he can say anything, another pair of arms wrap around my waist and haul me into a rock-hard chest. I let out a surprised yelp before I smell the familiar cologne.

"Hi, Trevor," I say with a laugh and a shake of my head.

"Hey, Little Red," he says as he spins me around dramatically and dips me before bringing me back to standing. "Glad you made it."

I shrug. "You know me, I only hang out with winners."

Trevor winks before he lifts his hands into the air and shouts. "Go, Knights!"

The entire room breaks out with loud cheers and hollers in celebration. I laugh as he turns to look back at me.

"You guys did awesome today. I think it's gonna be one hell of a season."

"Fuck yeah, it is. But we need to get you some team gear," he says as he pulls on the bottom of my shirt. "Maybe next game you can wear one of my jerseys."

"Yeah, hook a girl up," I tease.

What sounds like a scoff comes from behind me. I turn around to see Sebastian leaning against the wall with his arms crossed and a scowl slashed across his face. Before I can ask him what his deal is Slater and some of the other guys grab Trevor.

"Come on, man. The Olympics are starting!" Slater shouts as he drags Trevor downstairs to the basement.

Trevor tries to pull me with him, but the guys take him away too fast. I wave and laugh before turning around to a surly looking Sebastian.

"Olympics?"

He grunts. "They set up a bunch of drinking games downstairs and have medals to give out to the winners."

"I take it you don't play?"

He shakes his head as he continues to stare at me intensely.

"What are you mad about now?" I sigh. Is this just a constant thing for him? I swear the guy looks like he is constipated at least twenty two hours a day.

His narrowed eyes soften slightly as he tilts his head. "I'm not mad."

"Bullshit."

Seb's mouth twitches for a moment. "What makes you say that?"

I take a step closer to him until my chest brushes against his. My head tilts back to make better eye contact with him as I give him a challenging look.

"Because I see you, Sebastian Caldwell."

His candy-colored eyes darken until they are practically black as his sharp jaw line tightens. Instead of acting like he doesn't know what I'm talking about or ignoring me like normal, he surprises me. One of his hands reaches out to grab mine, lacing our fingers together before he wordlessly starts pulling me through the house.

My stomach flips as he turns and starts up the stairs, not letting go of my hand for even a second. When we reach the top of the stairs, Sebastian opens the door to his room and pulls me inside before closing and locking it. I take a moment to look around the room and notice that it is the polar opposite of Trevor's room. He has a perfectly made futon, since a normal bed is probably too small for him, with a crisp black comforter. His books are all neatly stacked, and he has minimal knick knacks. Everything seems to have a place and the OCD freak in me fucking loves it.

When I turn around, I notice that Sebastian is watching me carefully with his back against the door. He slowly walks towards me, and I take a few steps back on instinct until my back is flush with the cool wall next to his bed. Sebastian's arms come up to either side of my head as he leans down so that he is eye level with me.

"You see me, huh? And what exactly do you see?" His gruff voice rumbles through the quiet room.

"Everything," I whisper softly.

I watch as the muscles in his arms flex at my words before looking back to his darkened eyes.

"Are you Trevor's girl, Erica? You two together?"

My heart thunders in my chest at his words. There is only one reason he would be asking me this, right? Does he want this as bad as I do? Does he need it as bad as I do?

Am I Trevor's girl? No, not in the way he is thinking. But are we in a weird limbo? Definitely. But didn't Trev tell me that he wanted this to be on my time, even if that meant exploring things with other people. Granted, I don't think he meant his best friend, but does it make me a shitty person if I overlook that part? Fuck. Of course, it does. But tell that to my stupid mouth that opens and tells him, "No. I'm not his."

Seb blows out a heavy breath, the muscles in his arms seeming to get tighter instead of looser.

"I don't want to fight this anymore. I can't," he says almost strained.

My blood begins thrumming in my veins as my stomach twists in anticipation.

"Then don't," I breathe.

As if all of his self-restraint has suddenly snapped, Sebastian lets out a short growl before his hands move to cup my face before his lips are on mine. The initial contact steals the breath right out of my lungs and a euphoric feeling that seems to resemble relief floods through me.

His lips crush against mine like he is trying to make up for all the almost kisses. He is kissing me like he has dreamed of it for too long. Maybe that's just me projecting but either way he is pouring fucking everything into this kiss.

I bury my fingers into the back of his hair, tightening my grip before I reach for his tie and pull, freeing his long strands until they fall like a curtain around us. Fuck. I have never been so turned on by hair in all my life. Sebastian's tongue swipes across the seam of my lips as he demands access. I open my mouth slightly, inviting him in which he gladly takes advantage of. The feeling sends a thrill through me as my head begins to spin. God. I never want this to end.

When I playfully nip at his bottom lip, he lets out a tortured groan before his hands slide down to my thighs, lifting me up into the air and carrying me across the room before laying me down onto his bed. I quickly grab the hem of my shirt and pull it up and over my head before tossing it to the ground. Seb does the same as he reaches down to unbutton my jeans. I wriggle free of them until I'm laying in just my bra and panties. His hands slowly rub up and down my body as if committing it to memory.

"You are so fucking beautiful, baby. I haven't been able to stop thinking about you since that first night."

"Me neither," I pant as I reach for his jeans. He gets the hint and makes quick work of removing them.

I reach behind my back and unhook my bra before tossing it to the ground.

"Fuck," Seb hisses as he reaches up to palm one of my breasts before he brings his mouth down over it, smoothly twirling his tongue around my nipple. "So sweet," he murmurs against my skin as he kisses his way up to my neck.

I arch my back which gives him the perfect leverage to slide my panties off my hips and down my thighs. I feel a thick calloused finger run along my damp slit. I whimper at the touch which causes a cocky smile to stretch across his lips.

"I know what you need, baby. Just relax and let me take care of you."

I nod my head frantically as he lowers his head and eases my legs apart. He places soft kisses on the inside of my right thigh, stopping just as he reaches the spot that I crave him most before he moves to my left thigh and does the same.

"Seb," I groan half in pleasure and half in frustration.

With my encouragement I suddenly feel his hot mouth wrap around my pussy. I gasp in surprise before I moan my approval. His tongue quickly works me over, sucking and lapping at me like I'm a 5-course feast. With every stroke of his tongue, it's as if lava floods my veins. My pussy begins to throb, and when his teeth gently nip at my clit, I shatter apart, shouting his name as I come so hard, I nearly black out.

"Wow," I pant, doing my best to catch my breath as Seb slowly rises from between my legs. "That was amazing."

"You act like we're finished," he smiles as he reaches over to the bedside table and tears open a foil packet before rolling it up and over his dick. Fuck. Did that thing get bigger since the last time?

I bite my lower lip as I watch him climb on top of me.

"Ready for me, baby girl?" Seb asks.

I nod and he quickly pushes into me with one deep thrust that has us both groaning. He stays still for a moment before he begins thrusting his hips in a perfect movement that rubs that spot that he seems to have fucking GPS'd.

"Again!" I beg as he quickly repeats the motion causing me to let out a loud moan. Fuck. Those thirst trap guys who 'dance' online don't have shit on Sebastian Caldwell.

"Keep those fucking baby blues on me. Eyes on me, Erica."

My eyes practically roll into the back of my head at his words, but I force myself to keep them focused on him. We find a perfect rhythm together before he leans back onto his heels, taking me with as his arms wrap around my lower back as he fucks me hard and fast midair. My eyes roll into the back of my head as my pussy begins clenching. I don't want it to end, but I can't help it. It's too much. My second orgasm crashes into me like a freight train. I scream his name again as I clamp down around him, causing his body to shake as he growls out his release. I can feel his dick pulse inside of me as he continues fucking me through his orgasm.

After a few moments, he slowly pulls out of me and stands up to walk over to the trashcan and takes care of the condom before slipping on a pair of boxers. I sit up and go to start putting my clothes on when Sebastian walks over to me, kneeling so that he is at eyelevel with me before taking my face into his hands and giving me a tender kiss.

"Stay," he whispers, his lips gently brushing against mine.

I smile softly and nod which earns me a swoon worthy grin before he pulls me in for another quick kiss. When we break apart, he lays down on the bed and lifts his arm up as he pulls me practically on top of him. I let out a soft laugh as I try to ease off of him.

"This can't be comfortable for you."

He grumbles before tightening his grip on me, holding me firmly in place.

"It's the best thing that I've ever fucking felt," he says seriously before he gives me dirty smirk. "Well, second best."

I roll my eyes and smack his chest before I rest my head against him. I feel him press a soft kiss to the top of my head before I let out a small sigh. I don't know what this means, if anything. Did we just become friends with benefits? Something more? Both concepts are too big for my brain to process tonight so instead, I fall asleep to him soothingly stroking my naked back.

CHAPTER TWENTY

SEBASTIAN

I wake up to some banging around coming from downstairs and the front door being slammed shut. My eyes spring open before I sit up and notice that I am in bed alone. I furrow my brows as I look around, as if Erica could hide in my hundred square foot bedroom. Was that her that just left? Why didn't she say goodbye? And why am I upset about it? This should be great, a dream really. We screwed and she let herself out before I woke up the next morning. If she was anyone else, I would feel relief but instead I feel a dull ache inside of my chest that I try to physically rub away, doesn't work though.

Last night was one of the best nights of my life, and it isn't just because of the sex, though that was fucking mind blowing. As strange as it seems, I think I liked falling asleep with her in my arms the most. I sat up for hours slowly rubbing her back and kissing her softly. I didn't want to close my eyes. I didn't want to wake up and it all be a dream, because I have dreamt of a night like that every day for over a month.

I wasn't sure exactly what I was going to say to her this morning, I don't know what this all means to her. Maybe it was just another hookup like the first time? Or maybe she really is into me like I'm into her. Fuck. I have never been an insecure guy but when it comes to Erica, I find myself questioning and second guessing

As I make my way downstairs to get a cup of coffee, I see sitting at the dining room table is the very reason that I have tried to hold back with Erica. Trevor. He looks like absolute shit with his head pressed against the table and a low groan coming from him. He probably has a monster hangover if he was up all night with the guys. And how fucking awful am I that while he was off hanging out with our friends, I was two floors up screwing his ex/crush. But he isn't the only one who wants her, and I am done standing on the sidelines.

"You look like shit," I say coolly as I shove my hair out of my face and pass him, making sure to mask my features in case guilt decides to shine through.

He grunts but doesn't say anything, doesn't even tell me to go fuck myself. My brows furrow as I start the coffee machine before walking over and sitting down at the table. Trevor's head is now in his hands, and he is shaking it. Instantly my heart races and I start to panic. Did he see Erica leave this morning? Does he know?

I'm trying to decide whether to ask for forgiveness or man up and admit that I'm not even a little bit sorry about last night, as much as it might hurt him to hear. I don't get a chance to decide which route to take though because when he looks up into my eyes, I don't see anger or betrayal. I see disgust and...regret?

"I fucked up," he rasps. I give him a look that tells him to go on which causes him to blow out a harsh breath and wipe a hand down his face. "I was pretty messed up last night. I don't even remember too much after the beer pong tournament. I do remember some though and when I woke up this morning..." He trails off and shakes his head.

"Spit it out," I snap a little too harshly. I'm anxious as fuck for his next words and am sick of him pussy footing around.

"I fucked Cynthia last night," he says as he looks down, his fists balled tightly on top of the table.

Relief washes through me that his sour mood has nothing to do with Erica or me, but it also feels like a warning of sorts. Like I need to think carefully before I even contemplate seeing her again without Trevor knowing. I can only imagine how utterly pissed and hurt he will be when he finds out, if she even wants to see me again. Her sneaking out the next morning doesn't exactly instill a ton of reassurance for us, if there even is an us.

"Well, that isn't too bad, man. I mean, you guys used to hookup freshman year. I know you have been trying to get her off your back but maybe now that she got what she wanted she will finally leave you alone."

Trevor shakes his head sharply. "I can't believe I did it. I don't remember having sex with her. I thought...it sounds stupid, but I thought it was Erica. I thought I was dreaming or something and apparently, I even called her Erica all night. She was pissed this morning when I was shocked that she was in my bed, and I kicked her the fuck out."

My jaw clenches and my nostrils flare at the thought that he fantasized about being with Erica. It's stupid and irrational to be pissed, but I am. She isn't mine, but I want her to be. I sure as fuck don't want her to be Trevor's and I know that one way or another all of this shit is going to blow up in my face.

"I don't know what I'm going to tell her," Trevor groans before thumping his head onto the dining room table.

"Who?" I ask suddenly confused.

"Erica," he says as he turns his head to look at me before slowly leaning back. "I have to tell her and hope to God that she forgives me."

"Nothing to forgive, man," I shrug, trying to appear nonchalant. "You two aren't together or anything. You didn't do anything wrong."

"Aren't we? I mean, we fooled around at the last party. We talked and I told her to take her time to decide what she wants. I made the stupid as fuck comment of saying I understood if she had to explore shit with other people but that doesn't mean that me fucking someone else is okay. The exact fucking opposite. FUCK!" He shouts as he yanks at his hair.

They fooled around after the last party? Why the fuck did I not know that? She said they didn't have sex. Which, I guess fooling around isn't, but I just assumed. Fuck. I cross my arms across my chest as I do my best to mask the pain of hearing that Erica may not be as much mine as I was hoping. It sounds like Trev has a part of her too.

"I just need to tell her what I did and come out with everything," he says as he shakes his head and leans back in his chair. "I know I told her that she could take her time, but I can't wait anymore, I have to have her. I've been going out of my mind sitting here, fucking terrified that someone else would come and catch her eye before I could convince her to give us a shot again. And then I go and fuck it all up. Again."

"What if she just wants to be friends?" I offer, doing my best to push down the panic building inside of me.

What if Trev gives her an ultimatum and she chooses to be with him, out of familiarity if anything? Hell, for all I know she could see Trevor as Mr. Right and I'm just Mr. Right now. Trevor looks at me for a moment like he is considering that possibility before he shakes his head.

"I can't be just friends with her, not anymore. It was easy for the last couple of years because I would only see her over breaks here and there. We mainly just texted but ever since this summer...shit man. It really woke me up."

"Yeah," I say as I stare off behind him before standing up and checking on the coffee.

"What are you doing today?" Trevor asks as he pulls out his phone and starts furiously typing.

I shrug. "Not much. Rest day so I am just going to take it easy. Those Cornwall guys were pretty fucking beefy."

A scoff comes from Trev as he taps away on his phone. "Coming from you. You are a fucking mammoth."

I shrug, not able to answer as Trevor's phone chimes. He reads it quickly before blowing out a breath.

"Okay. I'm gonna take Erica to Bastille tonight," he says as he stands up and runs his hand through his hair.

"Fancy," I murmur over my cup.

Trev shrugs. "I got some major fucking groveling to do, and she loves French food."

I nod before I pretend to busy myself with looking through the fridge for something to eat. Without saying anything else, I hear Trev turn and jog up the stairs before the shower turns on. I slam the fridge door shut a little too hard and lace my fingers across the back of my head.

Fuck, fuck, fuck. He asked her on a date, and she said yes. I wonder if she knows it's a date? I pull out my phone and hover over her name before I pause. What am I going to say? 'I know that you snuck out this morning, but I really like you. Please don't go out with Trevor even though you already said yes. Pick me.'

Yeah, fuck that.

With a rough sigh, I pocket my phone as I grip the edge of the counter tightly. She is a grown ass woman who can decide who she spends time with. I guess I just have to accept the fact that the person she may prefer to spend time with is my best fucking friend.

CHAPTER TWENTY-ONE

TREVOR

F uck, fuck, fuck. How the fuck did I let this shit happen? One
word, tequila. I already had a decent buzz on when Erica
showed up at the house. I couldn't wait to see her. After coming
off a win like that, there was nothing more that I wanted to do was
spend time with my girl because that is what Erica is, she's fucking
mine.

Then Slater and some of the guy's drug me down to the
Olympics. I tried to grab Erica but there were too many people
and I thought that I would help the guys get started and bow out
to go find her. One shot turned into two and then two to three.
Everything gets really fucking blurry after that.

I remember someone rubbing my back encouragingly as I
played beer pong, I remember soft lips pressing against my cheek
when I played shot roulette and then I remember kissing those lips
later. When we were in my bed, I remember catching the smell of
roses, which Erica hates. She always smells like fresh peaches. But
my eyelids were so fucking heavy, and when they stayed closed, I
could push the smell away and just like that it was Erica on top of
me...son of a fucking bitch.

I've been drinking more than I normally do lately. It's not really
like me, but I don't know what else to do. Erica is on my mind all
fucking day, every day. Our conversations play over in my mind
over and over. Why the fuck did I tell her I was okay with her

pursuing things with other guys if that is what she needs? Okay is the last fucking thing that I am, and it has been driving me slowly insane.

Ever since that day I have been going out of my mind, wondering if today would be the day that someone would grab her attention. If someone would be bold enough to ask her out and she would say yes. Fuck. I'd beat the fuck out of any asshole that even tried. I have the simultaneous urge to give her space and let her come to me because I am the only one that she wants and claim her for mine and tie her to my bed for the rest of our lives. Fuck. That second option is sounding better and better.

I've been trying to be patient with her, but it goes against every instinct in my fucking body. I have to have her. I can't be in this limbo any longer. I need to own up to the shit that happened last night and hope that we are strong enough to overcome it. We have to. She is my past, my present and my entire fucking future.

She agreed to have dinner with me, so now I have a few hours to figure how the hell I'm going to explain to the love of my life that I accidently slept with someone else when I should have been hanging out with her. Even if we are 'technically' not together, yet, I still feel fucking sick to my stomach. When we were together before, I never so much as looked twice at another woman and I sure as hell haven't been interested in a single fucking person since this summer. Longer if I'm being honest.

Fuck. This wasn't how shit was supposed to go down. I'm better than this, we are better than this. And of all people in the whole damn world, I had to sleep with Cynthia fucking Johnson? The bitch has been psycho for years and despite Seb's lackluster words of encouragement, I know that now that I fucked her, she is going to be even more persistent. I'm not sure if she is genuinely into me or if she just sees me as her meal ticket but either way I'm not fucking interested.

There is only one woman out there for me, and now I'm going to go get her.

Chapter Twenty-Two

Erica

"Hellooo slut," Palmer smirks as she leans up onto her elbows in her bed.

"What are you talking about?" I ask as I feel my face flush, while I step into our room.

"Oh, shut up. I saw you sneak upstairs with Sebastian Caldwell last night and the fact that you are just getting in now tells me everything I need to know."

I scoff as I walk over to my dresser and grab Sebastian's shirt before I sit down on my bed. "Whatever. We were just hanging out."

"Mhmm and did you hang out on his dick?"

My mouth drops at her boldness before she cackles. "Oh my gosh, you are too adorable when you get all embarrassed. Don't worry I'm not the gossipy type. Your business is yours, I just wanted to give you a little shit."

I nod as I try and fail to fight the smile that begins to spread across my face. "It was a good night," I say as I think about how amazing it felt to fall asleep in his arms. He held me so close like he didn't want an inch between us. I had never felt so intimate, so close to anyone before.

When I woke up early this morning, I thought it was probably best that I got out of there before other people started waking up. Last night solidified some things for me. I love Trevor, a part of me always will, but this pull I feel to Sebastian is too strong. I can't avoid it any longer and I don't want to, but I knew that if I wanted to salvage my relationship with Trev, then I needed to sit down and talk to him, not have him find me totally naked in the room next to his.

I thought about waking Seb up before I left, but he was practically snoring, and I knew that he needed today to let his body rest, especially after such an intense game yesterday. If I'm being honest, I was also a little nervous to have the awkward morning after thing with him. I don't think I would have been able to handle it if he looked at me with regret like the last time we hooked up. Call me a coward but I call it self-preservation. No one should have their heart crushed at 5AM on a Sunday.

Since it is only 5:30 in the morning, I decide to close my eyes for a little. I can deal with the impossible difficult situation I have found myself in later. When I close my eyes, the first thing that comes to mind is a pair of intense, guarded melt worthy caramel colored eyes.

A few hours later, I'm woken up to my phone buzzing. My eyes slowly lift open as my heart begins racing in anticipation. Is it Sebastian? Did he wake up and notice that I wasn't there? Does he want me to come back over? Or maybe he is telling me that it was a mistake. A little twinge of disappointment fills me when I see that it is just Trevor texting me.

Trev: Morning Little Red.

Trev: What are you doing today?

Trev: I was wondering if I could take you out to dinner?

My stomach dips a little at his words. I was hoping to stay in my little bliss filled bubble for at least a few more hours before reality settles in. I know that I have to talk to Trev, and I guess fate has decided that we will be having that conversation tonight. I'm not going to mention what happened between Seb and me, especially because for all I know that is the last time anything ever will happen between us. It didn't feel that way, though. Regardless, that information would just hurt Trev, and that is the last thing that I want to do.

Me: Morning. I didn't have anything planned. Sure, where were you thinking?

His reply is almost instant.

Trevor: Bastille, it's a great little French restaurant downtown. I think you'll like it.

Me: Alright, want me to come by around 6?

Trevor: I can pick you up!

Me: It's okay. It isn't far and then we can just leave from your place.

I know I'm totally pathetic, but if he picks me up, then I won't have an excuse to see Seb, even if it is only for a minute or two. I don't even know if he will be around or if he even wants to see me, but a girl can hope.

Trevor: Okay, whatever you want. See you then!

I toss my phone to the side and stretch out in bed before sitting up. I notice that Palmer isn't in the room anymore, she must have left while I was asleep. I decide to hop into the shower before slipping into some comfy clothes. I then drag out my bag and laptop and proceed to bury myself in the paper that I should have written for my Psych class yesterday but put off for the game.

The day goes by in a flash and before I realize it, I notice that it's already 5:15PM. I jump to my feet and rush over to my closet to pick something nice. I looked Bastille up, and it looks really nice. Usually, Trev and I stick to divey places since we get enough fancy restaurants that leave you hungry by the end of the night when we are with our parents. So, this place must be worth it if he is suggesting it. I slip into my blue Chanel dress that my parents bought me last Christmas and throw my hair into a braided bun before brushing on some makeup.

I'm out the door and heading over to Trevor & Seb's place in 30 minutes flat and find myself having to slow down as I'm practically skipping my way over there. Butterflies are flitting around in my stomach in anticipation of seeing Seb again after last night, I just hope that I'm not setting my expectations too high. I'm more than a little disappointed that I haven't heard from him all day, but I have never been that clingy girl and I refuse to be now, even if all I want to do is see him or at least hear from him.

When I get to their house, I step up the stairs and raise my hand to knock on the door. However, I don't even get to touch the door before it swings open, and my heart flip flops. Sebastian is standing in front of me, gripping the doorknob tightly as his mouth parts slightly. I watch as his eyes rake over me slowly from head to toe before they rise back up and settle on my face.

I smile shyly at him, but instead of smiling back he looks upset, angry even. We stand there for a few moments just staring at each other before I finally say something.

"Hi, Seb."

His jaw clenches as he reaches out and grabs my wrist, firmly tugging me inside and walking me through the house without a word. I don't fight him, but I do struggle to keep up with his long strides in my high heels. He quickly opens the bathroom door and yanks me inside after him before shutting the door.

I don't have a moment to say anything or even really think anything before his lips are on mine. I suck in a sharp breath before I melt into his hold. His body backs me against the door as his hands grip my hips so tight that I swear he is about to break me in two. Kissing him feels like the most natural thing in the world and I sigh softly when he pulls away and rests his forehead against mine.

"I'm not sorry for last night. I don't regret one second of it," he rumbles softly as his thumbs lightly move in circles.

"Me neither," I say breathlessly.

He nods before bending down and capturing my lips again. This time a lot less gently. His large hands quickly skate down to the hem of my dress before he hikes it up over my thighs before yanking on my panties so hard, they shred in two. I gasp as I pull away and watch as the black lace flutters to our feet.

When I go to ask him what he is doing, he is already lifting me up and pressing me against the door, more firmly this time as he reaches one hand between us and begins undoing his jeans.

"You on birth control?"

"What?" I blink as my heart begins racing.

"Birth control, baby. You covered?"

I nod.

"Fucked anyone but me since you last got checked out?"

I shake my head causing him to let out what sounds like an approving growl before he snaps his hips, shoving his bare dick inside me. I hiss at the sudden pain that stabs through me before my body slowly relaxes around him. When I'm as adjusted as I can get around his thick cock, I slowly wiggle my hips, silently begging him to move. Like always, he seems to get me without even having to speak. His thrusts start fast and hard, a lot like the first night between us.

"I don't like that you are going out with him," Seb practically snarls as his eyes bore into mine.

I'm not sure if he wants me to respond, but I physically can't right now, so I just watch him as he begins to mercilessly fuck me against the door.

"If I have to sit here all night, wondering what is going on at dinner then you have to suffer too."

"How," I gasp as he pushes deeper than ever, causing pleasure to spark behind my eyes.

"You're gonna be a good girl and sit at dinner with this sweet pussy full of my cum. I want it to run down your legs as you walk out of this house, and I don't want you to clean yourself up until you get home and make yourself come with your fingers, thinking of me and only me."

I groan at the image that he is painting. It's so dirty, fucking filthy. So why the hell am I so turned on at the thought of it.

"You gonna be a good girl, baby?" Seb asks as his pace quickens and his muscles strain.

I nod frantically, teetering on the edge of coming undone.

"Words," he commands lowly.

"Yes," I pant, my fingernails curling into his shoulders as I do.

"Good girl," he rumbles as his hand slips between us, rubbing my clit rapidly until I fall apart in his arms.

Sebastian follows right behind me, his dick twitching and pulsing as his warm cum coats my walls, claiming me, owning me. At least that is what it feels like right now. And fuck if I don't absolutely love it.

Slowly, he lowers me to my feet before rolling my dress back down my hips. He pins me into place with his eye, his calloused hands cupping my face tenderly as his thumb brushes against my cheek.

"You look absolutely stunning."

I smile softly and dip my head. Seb gently lifts my face until I'm eye to eye with him.

"Thank you. Any chance you want to come with us?" I ask hopefully.

Maybe Trevor and I can have our talk another night. I'd do just about anything to spend the night with him. A spark of something flickers in his eyes as a hint of a smile plays at the corner of his mouth.

"You want me to come?"

"Honestly? I wish it would just be you and me."

What looks like relief washes across his face as he gives me a sweet smile before stroking my cheek softly.

"We can make that happen another night."

"Yeah?"

He nods. "If you want."

"I'd love to."

Seb leans down and presses his lips against mine one more time before he pulls away, ducking his head down until his lips are pressed against the shell of my ear.

"Remember what you promised," he whispers before he pulls us away from the door, opens it and guides me to step out. Once I am in the hallway, I turn around to see that he closes the door behind me and stays inside of the bathroom.

My brows are furrowed but when I turn back around, I see Trevor bounding down the stairs. He is wearing a nice black suit with a white dress shirt, he decided to skip the tie which makes the look seem a little less formal but still very nice. His blue eyes light up as he smiles at me.

"Hey! I didn't hear you come in. You look gorgeous," he says as he walks up to me and scoops me into a big hug. He twirls me around for a moment before setting me down. I watch as his eyes flick to my lips for a moment before coming back up to my eyes.

Panic fills me for a moment. Are my lips as red and swollen as they feel? I didn't even have a chance to look over myself and make sure that I looked semi presentable. I know that my lipstick claims to be smudge proof, but there is no way that it is Sebastian Caldwell proof. On top of that, warmth begins to slowly run down my thigh, causing me to snap my legs together to hold it in. Shit. This would be a whole lot easier if I had some damn underwear on.

The bathroom door suddenly opens, a stoic Sebastian stepping out as he feigns surprise when his eyes meet mine.

"Oh, hey, Erica. You look nice."

I give him a nervous smile. I am a shit liar, everyone says so, and I can't deny that in the moment, getting fucked against the door felt so damn good but now that the lust haze has lifted, I feel guilty and kind of gross. What if Trev would have come down just a minute sooner? It doesn't help that my guilt only builds as I take a sidestep and can feel Sebastian's cum between my thighs once more.

"Thanks."

He seems to notice the tension in my eyes because his distant cool expressions shift for a second into concern before he quickly masks it.

"I just got to grab my keys and we can go," Trevor says as he heads into the living room.

I smile at him as he goes before I look at Seb. He reaches for my hand, but I pull away quickly.

"I'm fine. We just shouldn't have done that."

His face falls as he shakes his head. "Baby. It's-"

"Not now," I say with a shake of my head.

Seb reaches for my hand again but this time I take a healthy step back. I see hurt shutter across his face as he looks at me almost pleadingly. Before he can say anything though, Trevor walks into the room and settles his hand on my lower back. It doesn't escape my notice that Seb tracks the movement but still, he doesn't say anything.

"You ready?" Trevor asks.

I flick my eyes away from his and Seb's, opting to face the door as I nod.

"Yep."

Without another word we turn and walk out the door. Even though I never bothered to turn around I could practically feel Seb's eyes burrowing two holes into my back. It's not just on him. I was extremely consensual and all too willing. When I am just near Sebastian Caldwell, I seem to lose all sense of rationality. I get drunk on him, on who he is, on how he makes me feel, and I turn into a malleable mess, which sounds extremely dangerous for me.

The restaurant is just as nice as it looked online even down to a snooty maître d' with an accent. Trevor pulls out my chair for me and pushes it in when I sit down in the plush white seat.

"Thanks," I smile as he walks around to his side.

"Of course. I feel like we haven't gotten to spend tons of time together since this summer."

I laugh as I lay my napkin into my nap. "What are you talking about? We literally see each other every day. I don't know how I would start my days without the daily coffee."

Trevor winks as he picks up his menu and scans through it quickly. I don't even bother opening mine because I always order the same thing at every French restaurant I ever go to. Chicken braised in wine, lardons and mushrooms. *Yum*.

"Your 2007 Domaine Leflaive Bâtard-Montrachet, Mr. Michaels," our waiter says as he begins filling our glasses.

I raise an eyebrow at Trevor, who just winks before thanking the waiter.

"How'd you swindle them into not carding us. I know you are 21, but I most certainly am not," I say as I lift my glass.

"Never underestimate the power of the Michaels name, Miss Pembrooke."

I roll my eyes and scoff as Trevor raises his glass before smirking and taking a sip of his wine. We talk about how obnoxious our mothers have been lately, mine hounding me on school and his getting on him about giving up football and joining the family business. His dad is a real estate giant back home, and he feels the pressure to give up his dreams to follow in their footsteps kind of like I do with my family.

"Well at least you are able to chase your passion right now, and they can't say anything about it. Plus, *when* you get drafted, I think it will really put things into perspective for them that this isn't just a silly dream, this is within reach for you," I say as I take one more bite of my chicken before pushing my plate away.

"If I get drafted," he interjects.

I roll my eyes and toss my napkin at him. "Don't pretend to be modest with me, Trev. We both know that you are phenomenal. It's okay to say it out loud," I wink which makes him laugh.

"You always have been my biggest fan," he says as he reaches out to hold one of my hands.

My first instinct is to pull away, but I don't want to make things weird by making a big deal out of it, so I give him a smile that is only a little forced. His thumb strokes the back of my hand softly for a few moments as he seems to be thinking over something before he speaks again.

"Little Red, I need to tell you something. I don't want to keep secrets either."

My heart races in anticipation, but I do my best to school my features. He blows out a big breath and closes his eyes.

"Last night, I got fucked up. One thing led to another, and I blacked out." He pauses for a moment and fiddles with our hands before looking up at me, gripping my hand a little tighter in the process. "I woke up this morning and Cynthia was in my bed. I guess I slept with her, and I hate myself so fucking much for it. You have to believe me. I can't stand her. I didn't know what I was doing or who I was doing it with. I'm so fucking sorry, Little Red."

I'm silent for a few moments as I process his words. Something sours in my stomach, but I can't be sure if it is left over guilt from the bathroom, his news about last night or maybe it's the wine. Okay, it's definitely not the wine, it's fucking delicious.

A small part of me feels something. Again, I don't know if it is necessarily jealousy, maybe uneasiness? Or is it relief? I mean, I was worried about trusting my heart with Trevor again, and even though I know he would never willingly hurt me, shit happens. Would last night of still happened if I would have agreed last week to be with him again? Or was he just enjoying his freedom much like I was last night and this afternoon?

Obviously, he isn't as dedicated to being with me as he conveyed, and honestly, I have realized that neither am I with him. We worked once, and it was great. He will always be my best friend, but I don't think we are right for each other in the long run. If we were, we wouldn't have slept with two different people last night, right?

I look up to see his crystal blue eyes practically brimming with regret. I don't want that for him. He is a junior in college and the star quarterback of one of the best teams in the league, he should be enjoying his time here, not sitting here worrying if he is going to upset his ex-girlfriend. If we were meant to be, it would be easy, but it seems like things between us just aren't.

I squeeze his hand as I give him what I hope is a comforting smile.

"Trev, you don't owe me anything. It doesn't matter what I think."

"Of course, it does! Your opinion is the only one that does matter to me. She isn't who I want. It was a drunken stupid thing that should have never happened, and if I could take it back, I would."

I nod. "I believe you, but maybe it was for the best."

Hurt flashes across his face, and he leans back for a moment as if I slapped him.

"What do you mean?"

Swallowing over the giant lump that has practically blocked my throat, I soften my tone as much as I can.

"I've been thinking about what we talked about the other day. I think you are right. I need time in college to find myself, unattached, just like you did. I don't want anything to come in between us, but I also don't think that us getting back together is the best thing. I mean, we broke up for a reason in the first place, right?"

Trevor quickly shakes his head as his grip on my hand tightens, like he can physically feel me slipping away.

"That was the biggest mistake of my life, Little Red. I should have never let you go. I was an idiot and I have regretted it ever since."

"You say that now, but think about all the great times you have had, without me, since then. I think that we were exactly what we needed at the time, and you have continued to be what I need in my life since then."

"You are still everything I need. I love you Erica, with all of my heart. Please, give me another chance, give us another chance. I swear to god, I will never hurt you again. I'll never touch a drop of alcohol again. I'll do whatever it takes to get you back."

He pins me with a big set of puppy dog eyes as he waits for my response. I smile sadly and slowly extract my hand from his grip before I sit back into my chair.

"Trev, I love you too. I always will, but if I was really everything you want and need, do you really think there would be even a chance that you would sleep with someone else?"

"I was drunk!" He argues, disappointment and pain taking over his face.

I nod again. "I know, and I'm not mad at you. You have done nothing wrong. What I'm saying is that maybe you aren't as ready to settle down as you think, and that's okay. We are okay Trev. Just because we aren't dating doesn't mean anything has to change between us. We have been doing great for the last two years."

His face drops as he pulls his hand into his lap. He doesn't say anything for a moment as he looks away, seemingly mulling over my words. It breaks my heart to see the obvious pain painted across his face.

"What about the last few weeks. You have kissed me back. You feel something for me, I know you do."

I sigh and nod. "I did, I do. How could I not? You are you, but I think our story is over, romantically."

Trevor looks dejected as he stares at me for a moment before he leans back in his chair and looks across the room, seemingly stuck in his own head. I give him the space he needs as I sit there quietly. After a moment, he looks back to me, a hardened look across his face.

"Is there someone else?" He asks, a new steeliness coating over his words.

I hate that my first instinct is to lie. This is Trevor. I don't lie to him, ever. But there is no way I can tell him the truth. It will break him, and doing that to him will break me too. Fuck. What have I gotten myself into? Deciding to go with my gut and hating myself for doing so, I shake my head.

"No. I just think that we are better off as friends. I'm sorry."

His face seems to relax a bit, but the pain is still visible as he nods.

"Alright. Well, that settles it. I'm just going to have to make you fall in love with me all over again."

"Trevorrr," I warn with an exasperated sigh.

"Don't worry. I won't make a move until you ask me to. Ball is in your hands, Little Red."

"There is no ball, Trev. This isn't a game."

A challenging glint lights up his eyes as he smirks softly over his wine glass.

"We'll see."

The drive home is quiet and honestly a little awkward. I don't feel nearly as relieved as I was hoping to. As painful as the conversation was, I couldn't let him hold onto hope any longer, even if he refuses to give up. At least I finally told him how I feel. If he doesn't accept it, well, that's on him, I guess.

Trevor parks the car and jogs around to get my door.

"I can get my own door," I say with an awkward smile as he helps me out of the car.

"I don't think you are understanding the extent of my persistence, Little Red. Prepare yourself to be thoroughly wooed."

I roll my eyes and shove his shoulder as we walk to my dorm. "Trevor, please stop. You aren't going to be able to change my mind on this."

He scoffs and puts his hand across his chest in mock offense. "Are you saying that I'm not charming enough to make you fall for me?"

"Oh, you are charming enough alright. But it won't change my mind. We have had our time and now it's over."

We stop outside the doors of my dorm building when he reaches out and grabs one of my hands as he speaks.

"I know you think that, but I know that you are it for me, you always have been. And I'm willing to wait for as long as it takes for you to realize that too."

I sigh, getting a little irritated that he isn't listening to me. "Trevor, we are never going to be more than friends again. If you keep pushing me, we will lose even that and that would break my heart."

His cocky smile slips a bit as he pauses before nodding his head in understanding. "Just think about it, okay?"

"There is nothing to think about."

Trevor leans in and places a chaste kiss on my cheek that lasts a beat longer than appropriate before he whispers into my ear, "Please. I just...I love you so fucking much."

Before I can say anything, he pulls back and gives me a disappointed smile.

"Text me," he says before he turns and heads back to his car.

I stand there and watch him walk away until he is out of sight. Shaking my head, I turn around and yelp when a large, hooded figure is standing just a few feet away from me. It only takes me a second to recognize who it is.

"Seb?"

"Did you have a good dinner?" He asks stoically with his hands buried in his pockets.

"It was good. Do you like French food?"

He shrugs. "Never had it."

I nod as a heavy silence settles over us. After a minute or so, I point towards the door.

"Did you want to come up for a bit?"

To my surprise he nods immediately and butterflies race through me when his hand reaches out and touches my cheek in the exact spot that Trevor kissed, almost like he is trying to erase the touch.

We walk silently up to my room and when I open the door, I'm thankful to see on the dry erase board where Palmer and I leave notes to each other that it says she is staying the night at Ethan's. I keep the light off as I walk over and plug in our twinkle lights that hang from the ceiling and around the perimeter of the room. It gives off a soft pink glow through the gauzy fabric that is draped throughout the room, and it sets off a really intimate vibe.

I walk over to my dresser, and I pull out a pair of yoga shorts and Seb's shirt before I walk over to the bathroom and take off my dress and makeup. When I pull out my bun my hair falls into loose waves, and I look at myself in the mirror to make sure I still look decent before I leave.

When I step into the room, I see Seb sitting on my bed with his forearms resting on his knees as he takes in the room. As soon as he sees my feet walk in front of him, he turns to face me the blank look on his face making my heart race with anticipation. His gaze flicks over my outfit as he gives me a barely there smile.

"You kept it?" He asks.

I bite my cheek and nod. "It's my favorite."

"I've got tons more. You can have them all," he says sincerely.

I shrug as I sit down next to him and tuck my legs underneath me. "I like this one." I pause for a second before I speak again. "Trevor slept with Cynthia."

He nods. "I know. How do you feel about that?"

Blowing out a soft breath I shrug again.

"Weird, I guess. Weird because in any other time of my life, hearing that he slept with someone else when he had confessed feelings for me would hurt but I don't feel hurt. Trevor used to be my whole world. He was all I could see for as long as I could remember. Even when we went back to just friends, I held onto some of my old feelings for him. But then..."

"Then?" He hedges as he slowly licks his lips.

I nod. "I met you."

A conflicted look crosses his face as he winces.

"I don't want to be the reason that you two aren't together. I can't be. He's my best friend, Erica."

"I get that, and you aren't, but you did help me see clearly. If Trevor and I were meant to be together then do you think I would have happily slept with you the same night that he slept with someone else. There was only one person I wanted to be with that night, and he wasn't it. Deep down I think he feels the same, even if he doesn't realize it yet.

"So, he didn't take it well," Seb guesses.

"Well, he didn't really accept it at all. It was like talking to a wall."

"Of course, it was. He already let go of you once, he isn't going to make the same mistake again."

"I wish he would. I think it's for the best. Besides I..." I trail off as my eyes drift up to lock onto Seb's.

"Besides?" He says with a raised brow as I scoot towards him just a few inches.

"I like someone else," I whisper softly.

Seb licks his lips as he scoots towards me a little more this time. "Yeah?"

"Mhmm. But I don't really know where he stands."

His eyes flick down to my mouth as one of his hands lift to grip the back of my neck. "He is fucking crazy about you."

"Yeah?" I ask as he runs his nose along the length of mine.

Seb nods as he lifts my head a little higher. "Tell me you want this as bad as I do," he whispers against my lips.

"More," I breathe.

In the next moment he closes the distance between our lips and holds my face protectively in his hands, like he never wants to let go, and I hope he never does.

I wind my arms around his neck and pull him closer to me as he deepens the kiss. Slowly, I turn so that I am facing him before sliding my leg over his lap until I am straddling him. Seb grips my ass in his large hands and hauls me into him until our bodies are flush before he scoots back on the bed.

Our mouths battle for dominance as my hands roam across his solid chest before trailing lower. Piece after piece, our clothes hit the floor until there is nothing separating us. Seb leans up and grips the back of my neck before pulling my lips down to his. When he pulls away, he presses his forehead against mine tenderly.

"I wasn't planning on this. I wasn't even planning on approaching you. I just wanted to make sure that you got home safely."

I give him a small smirk as I pull back a little to look at him better.

"And by getting home safely, you meant you wanted to see if I was going to kiss Trevor at the end of the night or invite him upstairs?"

Seb scowls but gives me a sharp nod, which causes my smirk to grow wider.

"Well, it is a good thing you are the one naked in my bed then, huh?"

His scowl fades a little before nodding softer this time. His fingers reach out and dip inside my soaked pussy, pleasure flaring in his eyes as he pulls them out and looks down at his glistening fingers.

"You listened."

I bite my lip and nod softly. Bringing his fingers up to my mouth he begins to smear them across my lower lip softly.

"Open," he commands.

Immediately, my mouth parts, and my tongue darts out to meet his fingers as I suck on them, the tangy flavor of us mixed together spreading across my tongue. His eyes darken at the sight before I take his entire fingers down my throat, causing him to let out a pained groan.

Slowly, I pull away and lick my lips I lower myself down onto him and can't stop the sharp hiss that tumbles from my lips as I pause. Damn, I don't think I will ever get used to him. Even with his cum inside of me acting as lube, it's still nearly uncomfortable.

"Breathe, baby," he says lowly as his thumbs rub soothing circles against my skin. "Relax."

I close my eyes and let out a slow breath before lowering myself down the rest of the way until our bodies are flush.

"Shit," Seb curses with his eyes rolled into the back of his head. "You feel so fucking good, baby."

I smile before I start rolling my hips into him, which causes both of us to let out simultaneous groans.

"You're too beautiful, too perfect. Fuck."

I am too lost in the pleasure to respond as I shamelessly writhe on top of him. Our pace is near frantic at this point. I don't think we are capable of soft and slow sex. Every time we come together, it is like an explosion. We clash together like two unmoving forces destined for the same direction. It looks a lot like a rough fuck, but it feels like so much more.

Reaching down behind my back, I cup his balls as my hand begins gently massaging them. Seb groans in approval as he bucks up into me with a ferocity I haven't felt yet. I continue rubbing his balls as I thrust down onto him. My legs are starting to shake but that doesn't stop me. I continue my rhythm while Seb wraps his arms around me and slams up into me until he bottoms out. My mouth opens in pain, but with a few thrusts, his dick is rubbing against my g-spot I am coming hard. Following me instantly, Sebastian lets out a savage grunt as he empties himself inside of me, warmth flooding me for the second time in a handful of hours. *Thank god for the shot.*

I slump over on top of him and lay my head on his chest. My heart is racing so fast I feel like I am about to die from pleasure. After a few moments I speak.

"What does this mean?" I whisper against his damp skin as he strokes my back softly.

He stays silent for a moment before holding me a little tighter.

"It means you're mine, baby, and I'm keeping you."

CHAPTER TWENTY-THREE

SEBASTIAN

I tried to be a good guy. I did, I swear. But I couldn't handle one more minute of it. The look she gave me when I tried to play it cool with her in front of Trevor switched something inside of me. I was worried that I screwed up badly enough that she decided we weren't worth it. I wouldn't blame her if she did feel that way. I've been hot and cold since I met her, but not because I wanted to be.

I don't want to think about her every moment of the day. I don't want to dream about her every night. I don't want to have feelings for my best friend's ex, but I do, and I realized that whether I have her or not doesn't change the fact that I want her. So, I am a selfish fucking bastard because I am keeping her.

As soon as they left for dinner, I pretty much counted every single fucking minute that went by and when the clock clicked past two hours, I decided to go and wait for her at her dorm. I didn't know what I was going to say or if I was going to say anything at all, but I just had to see her. I had to see them together. I had to know if I had missed my shot or not.

I was too far away when Trevor was dropping her off to hear what they were saying but they didn't look overly affectionate. He did kiss her cheek which had me instantly filling with rage and wanting to beat his face into the pavement. I didn't and thankfully he left right after that.

It's a fucking relief to know that she doesn't hold any romantic feelings for Trevor anymore. I'm just hoping that he moves on from her. If I know my best friend as much as I think I do though, then I would say he is about as likely to give her up as I am, which is not a chance in hell.

I had to think about if being with Erica was worth jeopardizing my friendship with Trevor. In the end, I knew that I never had a choice. There is something about Erica that makes me feel completely powerless, like being away from her is like being away from air. When she isn't around me, it just doesn't feel right. Those are some scary as shit thoughts, but I'm just going to take it one moment at a time, starting with kissing this beautiful girl awake.

I lean down and kiss her temple before I move down to her cheek and over to the tip of her nose.

"Mmmm," she purrs with a small smile as her eyes flutter open.

"Morning, baby," I smile as I brush her hair out of her face.

"Good morning," she rasps softly.

"Fuck, you're gorgeous in the mornings," I say before I brush my lips across hers.

She snorts and rubs her hand down her face. "Yeah, right. I'm sure I look like a mess right now."

"You're perfect," I whisper as I run my fingers through her hair.

Erica smiles up at me before leaning forward into another kiss. I cup her face and pull her tighter to me as my hands begin to drift down her sides before reaching the band of her shorts. She breaks away and laughs lightly.

"Easy, tiger. I think we need to talk."

Shit. Nothing good ever started with that sentence. I try to calm my nerves and nod.

"Okay?"

She looks down at where her hand is resting on my chest and bites the inside of her cheek, seeming to think over what to say before she looks back up to me.

"I don't think that we should tell Trevor about us. Not yet at least."

I furrow my brows. I mean, I'm not exactly looking forward to that conversation, but I know it has to be done, sooner rather than later. Panic fills me that maybe she isn't over him as much as she convinced me last night. Tamping down my nerves, I school my features as I look at her.

"Why is that?"

"Because he practically begged me to be with him and then I rejected him. If I show up on his best friends arm the next day, it's like a slap in the face. I just think that we should be discreet for now until he gets over this thing, you know?"

I let out a short laugh that lacks any real amusement.

"Baby, if you think he is just going to simply get over you then you're fooling yourself. I don't think it's possible to get over you. Trust me."

She smiles sadly as she looks up at me. "I hope he does. I don't want to lose my best friend and I don't want either of us to feel like a dirty little secret but..."

"I get it. And I'm good with it, for a little. I know he will never be happy about it, but I think we should wait until the season is over at least."

Erica nods. "Maybe we can still see each other once in a while, though?" She asks shyly. "I mean, I know you have football and all but after if you aren't too tired and-"

I silence her with a kiss. She fights me for a second before her arm loops around my neck and pulls me down to her. I slip my tongue past her lips and slowly move my tongue against hers. I swear I could kiss this girl forever and never get sick of it.

When I pull away, she looks up at me dazed as I brush my thumb across her swollen lip.

"Yes. Even if I have to curl up into a ball to be in your damn midget bed, it's worth it."

Her eyes get wide and so does her smile. I lean in to kiss her again when the door bangs open. A bouncy brunette known as Erica's roommate comes in, her eyes widening when she sees us lying in bed. Thank god, we have the blankets over us still otherwise she would have gotten more than she bargained for.

"Shit, sorry! I didn't know you had company. I just need my bag and to get changed," she says as she turns around to face the hallway.

Erica chuckles as she leans up, keeping the blanket against her chest. "You're good, Palmer. I have to get ready for class anyways."

I groan and bury my head into her neck as I start kissing across her collarbone. She giggles and squirms, brushing up against my morning wood, which only makes me more desperate to keep her in bed with me. But sadly, she gestures for me to get up. I sigh before reaching down to pick up my boxers and quickly slide into them and my pants. I'm reaching for my shirt when Palmer turns around. She doesn't hide that she clearly checks me out when she smiles and whistles.

"Damn girl, you're gonna kick that out of bed for class? Your mama didn't raise you right."

I let out a snort of amusement as I pull on my shirt and sweatshirt before tying up my hair. When I look over, I see that Erica has wrapped a towel around herself and is standing in the doorway of her bathroom. I reach over and grab the edge of her towel while I pull her towards me. She yelps in surprise as she clings to the fabric.

"Seb! Stop!" She laughs.

I chuckle before swatting her ass and grabbing the back of her neck, pulling her into me. My mouth crushes against hers and she lets out a small whimper as she parts her lips for me. Breathing heavy, I pull away and hover my lips just over hers as I tangle my fingers into her long hair.

"I'll see you tonight, baby girl."

"Okay," she smiles before I steal one more kiss.

I turn around to walk out the door as I pass Palmer. I nod my head in greeting while she gives me a mischievous smirk. Well, looks like Erica and I are not off to a great start with the whole keeping things on the down low. But her roommate of all people was bound to find out if I'm gonna be coming over, and since her coming by the house isn't really possible, it looks like I'll be over a lot.

The day passes by in a blur. I get the weirdest looks for the first part of the day, and I couldn't figure out why until Slater asked me why I was smiling. I didn't even realize that I was walking around campus with a cheesy ass grin on my face like a fucking idiot. Just the thought of being able to see Erica again tonight, to hold her and kiss her and fuck her tight pussy until we pass out has me practically vibrating with excitement.

For the first time in my entire life, I can't wait for football to be over. It's all that is left between me going and seeing my girl. *My girl.* That shit feels good. As I'm getting changed into my uniform, I see myself in the locker room mirror and here I am again, grinning like the luckiest bastard alive. I fucking feel like it too. She's like a damn dream. I never thought a woman could get me twisted up like this but her...she's just something else, something special.

A mopey Trevor comes into the locker room and grabs his stuff, slowly pulling on his practice uniform. He looks upset and like he has a million thoughts running through his head. I already know who is responsible for his sour mood, but I'm not supposed to, so like an asshole, I play dumb.

"You good, man?"

Trevor lets out a humorless laugh and shakes his head. "Fucking great, except for the fact that I told Erica that I just want to be with her, and she basically told me no fucking thanks."

He clenches his fist and punches the metal locker as hard as he can. I instantly reach out and grab his arm before he can do it again.

"Easy, man. Easy. Don't fuck up your throwing hand."

Trev sighs and tosses his head back. "Maybe I should have waited a little longer, given her more time. She didn't respond to any of my texts all day, and I waited over twenty minutes this morning to walk her to class like I always do but she didn't show. So, either she skipped, which isn't likely, or she left early in order to avoid me."

I run a hand through my hair and turn back to my locker so that I can finish getting ready.

"Maybe she just needs some space. You know how it can be, the tighter you try to hold on to someone the more desperate they are to be free. It's human nature."

He nods. "Yeah, maybe. You know I told her about the whole Cynthia thing, she didn't even seem that bothered by it. I'd flip the fuck out if she told me she had fucked someone else, together or not."

I swallow as I mess with my gear, doing everything I can not to look him in the eye. Fuck. Guilt tastes like shit.

Trevor sighs. "I think she is going to take a lot more convincing than I was originally thinking."

"Convincing?" I question as I keep my head ducked down so that he can't see the pissed off expression that crosses my face.

"Yeah, I mean, I knew it wasn't going to be easy, but she seems really adamant that we stay just friends. I'll just have to wine and dine the shit out of her. Prove how devoted I am to her."

"Why are you so hung up on her?" I bite out before I have the chance to cool my tone down. "I mean, I know that you care about her and stuff, but if she doesn't want to be with you, what can you do, right? There isn't another girl on campus who wouldn't love to be with you. Why get stuck on the one that doesn't seem interested?"

Trevor's forehead wrinkles as he looks at me like he doesn't understand my words before he shakes his head.

"Because man, she isn't just a girl, she is *the* girl. I love her, my family loves her, and her family loves me. Our lives fit together perfectly. We are good for each other. She isn't just a girl that I am into for now. I am gonna marry her someday. Fuck. I'd give anything for a time machine right now. If I could go back to two years ago before I ruined us none of this would be happening right now."

My nostrils flare at his words and I am fighting like hell to keep my temper in check, but he is talking about *my* girl like she belongs to him and it's fucking bullshit. Granted, he doesn't know that she is mine, but would that stop him? Hell fucking no. Is he always going to see her as his?

I nod pushing down my raging thoughts. "Well don't stress about it, man. Just give her some space and see how it goes."

"Yeah, maybe you're right," he says as he shuts his locker door.

I close mine too and we make our way out of the locker room and towards the field when he looks at me.

"By the way, where were you last night? Find someone to hook up with?"

"Yeah," I shrug nonchalantly.

"Nice. Who?"

I shrug. "I think she was a freshman. I haven't seen her around until this year."

Trevor nods. "Good for you, man. You have been acting like a damn monk this year. I know football is your life, but it doesn't hurt to have a little fun."

I roll my eyes and jog onto the field to start my warmup. I hate lying to Trev and though I technically didn't, I know that every word I say and every time I play dumb is only going to make my betrayal that much worse. I wish I could stop. I really wish I could.

CHAPTER TWENTY-FOUR

ERICA

I have been dodging Trevor for a little over a week now. He made it clear he wants more and doesn't expect to take no for an answer. That wouldn't be as big of a deal to me if I wasn't also sleeping/casually dating his best friend. Now I understand a little better why Sebastian kept me at such arm's length before. This thing we have ourselves in is messy.

True to his word, Seb has spent the night every single day for the last week. Even when he got back to campus at one in the morning from their away game on Saturday, he came right to my dorm room and crawled into bed next to me. I tell myself that we are keeping things casual in my head, but things feel so much deeper than that. I have this connection with him that I have never felt with anyone else before, even Trevor. I can talk to Seb unlike I can with anyone else in the world. I know that I'm falling for him way too quick, but I don't think I can help it.

I'm leaving my last class of the day on Monday when I slam into a hard body that seems to come out of nowhere.

"Ow," I groan as I step back and shake my head.

"Shit. Sorry. I thought you saw me. Are you okay?" Trevor asks.

I look up at him and the first thing I feel is guilt. Guilt because I have been avoiding him like the plague. Guilt because what Seb and I are doing will no doubt kill him when he finds out. Guilt because I can see in the way he is looking at me that Seb is right, he is definitely not giving up anytime soon.

"I'm fine. You surprised me. How are you?" I ask with a forced smile.

"I'd be a lot better if you weren't avoiding me, again," he says with a playful smile, but I see the hurt in his eyes.

My plastic smile cracks on the edges before it drops all together.

"I'm sorry, Trev. I just needed a little bit of space."

He nods. "I get that. I even understand if you decide in the end that you don't want to give us another shot. I just don't want to lose you from my life completely. You are everything to me, Erica."

I give him a sad smile and shake my head.

"I don't want to lose you either. I'm sorry about avoiding you. Are we okay?"

Trev gives me a lop-sided grin before nodding and pulling me into a hug.

"Always, Little Red," he says as he kisses the top of my head.

I wrap my arms around his waist to hug him back and am thankful that when I pull away, so does he.

"So, if you are talking to me now, does that mean you'll start hanging out with me too?" Trev asks as we start walking towards the dorms.

I laugh. "Sure. When?"

"Tonight?"

My eyes narrow in suspicion for a moment.

"Don't worry. I'm not trying to trick you in to going on a date with me. Some of the guys are getting together at the bowling alley in town after practice. Pizza, beer, bowling, it'll be funnn," he sings with a smile.

I relax a little when I hear that other people will be there. I'm glad that he's understanding that I need a buffer between us for a little while at least.

"Sounds like a lot of fun. I don't think I have bowled since Suzie Castello's sweet 16 birthday party."

"Oh, I remember that party. Sweet indeed," he says with a waggle of his eyebrows.

I let out a surprised laugh and smack his arm. "Gross, Trev!"

"What? We weren't together yet, and it was her birthday," he says as he shrugs like there was nothing that he could do about it.

"Once a manwhore, always a manwhore," I tease.

His smile gets tight, and the humor that was glittering in his blue eyes disappears. We don't say anything else until we get to my dorm.

"Well, I gotta get some stuff done before practice. I'll pick you up around 7ish?" Trev asks.

I nod before I step up to hug him. "Sounds good. See you then."

When I get up to my dorm room, I shut the door just as my phone starts to ring. I pull it out and instantly smile when I see who it is.

"Hey, handsome."

"Hey, baby," Seb's deep voice rumbles through the phone. "What's up?"

"Not much. Just watching some film. How about you?"

"Well, I just ran into Trevor."

He is silent for a moment.

"What did he say?"

"Basically, that he doesn't want to lose me in his life just because I don't want to be with him. I'm going with him and some of the guys tonight for bowling after practice."

The line is dead silent again. I wait for five awkward seconds before I speak again.

"Seb?"

"What time are you guys going?" He asks, his voice a lot colder than it was before.

"Trev said around 7ish. Will you come?"

"You can count on it, baby."

I smile as I settle onto my bed. I hear some voices in the background of the phone before Seb speaks again.

"I gotta go. I'll see you soon."

"Bye."

He hangs up quickly and then I am left with six hours to kill and three assignments that have been weighing on my shoulders. I crack open my books and get to work. I have to practically tape my eyes open just to stay awake but push through anyways.

I wish my parents would realize how much happier I would be if I was pursuing a degree that I actually wanted. I wish they could see that if I live the life that they have planned for me, I will never be happy, not truly happy. It seems like now isn't the right time to fight it, though. My mother has been digging her heels in on this pretty firmly and I know it's better to let things settle for a bit before I reapproach the topic.

Around 6, I start getting ready. I throw some loose curls into my hair before I slip on a fitted black shirt with lace short sleeves and a pair of dark jeans. I just finish applying my bright red lipstick when a knock comes from my door.

I open the door to a smiling Trevor. He is leaned up against the door jamb casually, wearing a dark blue polo that only makes his bright eyes that much brighter. Trevor's style is basically a really rich jock, always has been. I'm sure if he wasn't born into money then he would probably dress similarly to Seb, but he was, and the boy can't stay away from Ralph Lauren for the life of him.

His eyes instantly flick down to my lips before they come up to my eyes. Unease seeps into my stomach, and I instantly wonder if maybe we should have kept some more distance for a little longer. I'm not sure if us hanging out is going to make things easier or harder.

"You look beautiful, as always," he says as he leans in to kiss my cheek briefly.

I smile politely and nod. "Thanks."

He places his hand at the small of my back as I lock my door and we head towards the elevator. Once we make it to Trev's Porsche, a surprised smile spreads across my face as I see a very large passenger in the very small backseat, the bun on top of his head is practically crammed against the top of the roof as he hunches down, clearly uncomfortable. Seb doesn't smile as he glances our way, but I can see his eyes flash with what looks like excitement before he turns back to face forward, a blank look on his face. He's a damn good actor. I'll give him that. If the NFL doesn't pick him up, then he should really consider Hollywood.

"Hey, Seb," I say as casually as I can manage.

He gives me a head nod but doesn't say anything as Trev holds the door open for me. I slide into my seat while Trev walks around and fires up the car. I notice the tension in Trev's shoulders as he drives, and I casually glance in the rearview mirror to see similar tension in Seb's. Even with the top down, the energy is thick, and I find myself fidgeting awkwardly.

When we get to the bowling alley, Trevor hustles around to my side and opens the door for me. I thank him as I step out and linger near the car while Seb unfolds his large body from the back seat. Trev places his hand on my lower back as he steps to the left of me and walks us to the front door.

Seb follows closely beside me on my right and a few times our hands graze each other in what I know is a deliberate move. My eyes flick over to him briefly, and I notice that he is watching Trev and I out of the corner of his eye. I give him a small smile before I face forward again as we head inside.

"Baby doll!" Slater shouts as he rushes up to us and scoops me into his arms.

He twirls me around a couple of times as I squeal before he sets me back onto my feet. He gives me a mischievous wink before slinging his arm around my shoulder. When I look behind us, I see two equally pissed off expressions and four balled up fists. I guess Trevor and Sebastian don't think that Slater is as amusing as I do.

"Slater, do you always have to be such a dick? Erica doesn't want you feeling her up every time you're around her," Trev says with an irritated huff.

"That isn't what she was telling me last night in bed," Slater jokes before bending down and planting a slobbery kiss onto my cheek.

Before I can say anything, he takes off running as Trevor chases after him. I shake my head and laugh when I look up to a very unamused Sebastian. I roll my eyes and shove his shoulder.

"Oh, come on. You know who I was with last night, you have no reason to be pissy."

Seb grunts but doesn't say anything else as he gestures for us to head over to get our shoes. When we have our shoes in hand, we walk over to the other guys and slip them on before grabbing our balls and starting the game. Slater and Trev join us a few minutes later, Slater with a shit eating grin and Trev with a childish pout.

We split up into different lanes because there are way too many of us. Trev, me, Seb, Slater and Mikey are all on one lane together, and currently, everyone is kicking ass...except me. When I throw my fifth consecutive gutter ball, I let out an aggravated huff and stomp back to the ball retrieval.

Trev lets out a soft laugh as he hops up from his seat.

"You always were a sore loser. Do you want help?"

"I'm fine," I snap a little too harshly over a friendly game of bowling.

He rolls his eyes at me before picking up my ball and walking me out to the lane.

"I can do it myself, Trev," I grumble.

He ignores me though as his hands reach down to my hips to angel me appropriately. I notice that his touch lasts a beat longer than necessary and I glance up at him.

"Trevor," I warn softly.

Trev gives me a lopsided grin and a little wink. "Just helping you out, Little Red."

His hands move up to my arms as he hands me my ball. He gently holds my arm as he helps me draw back and swing forward. When I release the ball, it sails down the middle of the lane at an easy coast until it knocks down all of the pins.

"Oh my god! I did it! I did it! I got a strike!" I shout as I jump into Trev's arms.

He lets out a whoop as he catches me and spins me around. After a few moments, he lets me down and my celebratory smile fades when I look over and see the anger in Seb's eyes. I walk over to the seats, feeling Seb's scrutiny the entire way. I grab my purse from my seat before I look at the guys.

"I'm gonna use the bathroom. Be right back."

They all say okay and nod as I turn on my heel and walk away as quickly as I can. When I get to the bathroom, I go to the mirror to touch up my lipstick. I don't actually need to go to the bathroom. I just needed to get away for a minute. Did I do something wrong? Can Trev and I not even be friends without getting underneath Seb's skin? I mean, I know that Trev having feelings for me probably makes Seb feel uncomfortable, but I didn't do anything wrong, right?

After one more bright red swipe across my lips, I cap the lipstick and put it into my bag when I hear a knock on the door.

"One second," I shout as I sling my purse onto my shoulder.

I unlock the door and open it up, surprised when a large body plows into me and backs me up against the bathroom wall. Before I can do anything other than gasp, Seb has locked the door and crushes his mouth against mine. I immediately melt into him and move my lips against his eagerly. His tongue harshly ravishes mine as his hands grip my hips almost punishingly.

When he pulls away, his breath is ragged and his voice low.

"I don't like seeing other men touching my woman, Erica. Especially when I can't do a fucking thing about it."

"We are friends, Seb. Sometimes friends hug, it's not a big deal. You're just being sensitive."

"Yeah," he barks. "I am being *sensitive* because the guy that is hugging and rubbing all up on you is the same guy that is trying to steal you from me. He can't have you! You. Are. Mine."

I place a hand on his chest and can feel his erratic heartbeat jack hammering through his soft Henley.

"I know," I say softly. "No one is going to take me, okay? The only person that could get me away from you is you."

His breathing is heavy as he watches me intensely. "Say it. Say you're mine."

I tilt my head a little higher so that I can look deeper into his eyes. Swirling in his light brown eyes is something like desperation. Like if he hears those words from me all our problems will go away. I don't know about all of that, but I have no problem admitting what is undoubtedly true.

"I'm yours."

Seb dives in for another kiss that is even more frantic than the first. His hands run across my body, palming my breasts to my hips and then cupping my ass.

"Bend over, baby. Show me how much you are mine," he demands.

My eyes widen as I glance around. "Now?"

His jaw clenched. "Now."

I hesitate for a second and apparently it is a second too long because in the next, Seb is spinning me around, flicking the buttons of my jeans down and pulling them down to my knees before he bends me over the counter.

"Hold on, baby. I don't have the time or patience to be fucking gentle."

Seb quickly pulls his cock out of his pants before slamming into me. The sudden intrusion has my back arching and my mouth opening on a silent scream. Seb slips a hand over my mouth to make sure I stay quiet as his other strokes my back gently as he bends down to whisper into my ear.

"There's my good girl," he growls. "You like having my cock buried inside you, don't you?"

"Mhmm," I moan against his fingers as Seb fucks me with a ferocity that I have never felt before.

It's as if he is trying to get as deep as possible, like he is trying to leave his mark on me. The whole thing is so barbaric and caveman like and fuck if I am not soaking his cock as he does.

Taking his hand away from my back, he slips his hand around until his thumb reaches my clit, quickly rubbing tight circles as he leans down to whisper into my ear.

"Look up, baby. Look at me."

I do as he says, glancing up to find him watching me with a hungry gaze through the mirror.

"There you are," he says as he picks up his speed, practically pounding into my cervix as he does.

"Say you're mine when you come, baby," he growls. "Say my name when you drench my cock with that sweet pussy."

His words are my undoing as I fall apart, my body shaking and convulsing as I moan out his name. His hand is still over my mouth, so it comes out muffled, but I think he was able to hear just fine because he follows right behind me, hot cum spurting inside of me as his cock jerks and pulses until his thrusts stop altogether. His head is resting against my shoulder as he is capturing his ragged breath.

When Seb pulls out of me, I feel his cum slowly start to leak out of me and he makes no effort to step back so that he can grab something or I can. Instead, he just stands in the way, staring down at the cum that is now running down my thighs. He licks his lips hungrily, like he is just getting started with me and despite the fact that heat pools low in my stomach at the thought of that, I remember that everyone is waiting for us, and we are in a bowling alley, in the bathroom. Kinda gross but definitely worth it.

"Seb," I say on a half of a laugh.

His eyes snap up to mine in the mirror like he is coming out of trance before he shakes his head and grabs a few paper towels, making quick work of cleaning me up before he spins me around and crushes his lips to mine. He nips at my bottom lip harshly before pulling away and rubbing his thumb across it to ease the pain.

"I like this color," he whispers hoarsely.

"I'll wear it every day for you."

His lips twitch in what I know to be the start of a smile. I kiss his cheek softly before he pulls away as I pull up my panties and jeans.

"Go before I say to hell with this fucking night and spend the rest of our time here buried inside you."

I suddenly have the desperate urge to stay in this bathroom for as long as we can. It's like he can read my mind because his eyes darken with desire as he swats my ass and sends me on my way with a wink. I giggle as I hustle out the door and over to the guys.

Chapter Twenty-Five

Sebastian

Wiping at my mouth to get rid of the last bit of Erica's bright red lipstick, I stand at the bar top as I wait for the pitcher of beer I ordered for the table. It was my half ass excuse to leave and follow Erica. Of course, the guys were more than willing to agree to me buying them beer.

I couldn't take it any longer. The car ride here was tense as fuck for all sorts of different reasons. For Trev, probably because I decided to tag along seemingly out of the blue and asked if I could ride with him. He looked like he wanted to tell me no but then begrudgingly nodded his head.

The ride was awkward for me because I had to do my best to conceal my excitement when I saw how beautiful my girl looked tonight, even if I couldn't kiss her or touch her like I wanted. Hell, I could barely acknowledge her existence without tipping Trev off. I'm sure Erica felt the thick tension also which made it a fucking awesome 20-minute silent drive.

A meaty hand claps down on my shoulder, and I look to the side to see Slater hop up on a bar stool.

"What's up, big boy?" He asks.

"Just waiting for our beer. What are you doing?"

"Oh, I volunteered to come look for you. Trev was bitching about you taking so long. We didn't know what you were up to," he says with a nonchalant tone but a knowing grin.

I grumble to myself before I look over to him. "Don't say a fucking word."

He throws his hands up in surrender. "Hey now. No need to get hostile. I didn't say anything. Just wanted to let you know that if you think you're fooling anyone, you aren't."

"What do you mean?" I ask coolly.

"I mean, the fact that your eyes haven't left Erica the entire time that we have been here isn't doing you any favors at keeping your little crush on the down low, bro. Or the fact that when Trevor touched her, you looked two seconds away from murdering his ass-"

"I was!" I snap before I tilt my head to the ceiling and shake it.

When I look back down to Slater, he is giving me a wide toothed fucking grin.

"So, I take it that you guys have finally given in?"

"She's mine," I say simply as if that takes care of everything. I fucking wish it was that simple.

Slater nods. "Well, that's cool and all, except your best friend thinks that she is his. You got yourself into a mighty sticky situation there, man."

"I know. She is the last girl that I should have fallen for, but the only one that I could. She is something special and I'm not going to fuck up my chances with her like Trevor did. He had her and he let her go, I won't make that mistake."

Slater looks at me for a second before he tilts his head to the side.

"Do you love her?"

His question is like a 240lb linebacker tackle. Love? Shit, I haven't even thought about that. I have never been in love before. Honestly, with the way I grew up, I was so sure that there was no such thing outside of movies. I have always been cynical like that. Everyone has a motive, and you are always just a means to an end, except Erica isn't like that. She doesn't make me feel that way, not even close.

Love. Shit, I don't know.

I don't know how to answer that, so I don't. I shrug as the bartender hands me five frosted beer glasses and a pitcher of beer. I throw down some cash and Slater reaches over to help me carry it all.

"Alright, well Trev does. He is crazy about her. If you're really into her, then cool, I'm happy for you. But don't fuck up your friendship with him if she isn't the real deal for you."

I nod because I get where he is coming from. If the roles were reversed, I would be thinking the same thing and probably offering the same advice. Granted, if I had never met Erica, my advice would more likely resemble, 'No chick is worth a friendship. Ditch her and move on to the next.' But Erica has changed fucking everything.

When we are only about 20ft away from the table Slater stops us and wipes at my cheek. I smack his hand away and scowl at him.

"The fuck?"

"Sorry, man. I don't know what you have been told, but red is not your color."

He smirks at me as he walks over and passes out the glasses to everyone. I quickly wipe at my face just in case he missed any of Erica's lipstick. I got it off my mouth, but I guess I didn't think about the little peck she gave me on my cheek.

When I settle into my seat, I notice that Erica and Trev are talking about some memory they had in high school and laughing their heads off. They don't even notice me as I sit down next to them, and I'm not proud to admit that I feel jealous as fuck because of it. Even if they are friends, I don't like Erica's attention being on any other man besides me. Call me an asshole, call me possessive,

I don't give a shit. That is my woman laughing with the man that is trying to steal her.

"You want a beer, Erica?" I ask, casually interrupting their story.

She turns to face me and gives me a soft smile and a nod. "Thanks."

Trevor gives me a little irritated smile before he reaches for the pitcher and pours himself a glass. The rest of the night goes by good enough. When Trev would get up to bowl, Erica would drop her hand between us and graze her slender fingers against my thigh. The touch would send electricity shooting through my body and all it did was make me crave more of her.

After Trevor dropped her off at her dorm, we drove back to our place where I told him I promised to meet up with the chick I am seeing (not a lie) and headed off to see Erica. Even though it irritated me like hell to see Trev openly flirt with her and touch her like he had the fucking right, at the end of the night, it was my chest that she fell asleep on and that felt pretty damn good.

A few weeks go by, and my life is completely consumed by Erica. We spend every moment that we possibly can together and when we can't, then we are texting or talking on the phone. She is like the sweetest drug, and I'm a damn junkie. She has been at every home game and even drove for a couple of our closer away games.

I can't deny that the whole love thing has been rattling around in my brain since Slater asked. Is this what love is? Feeling desperate just to be around the other person like they are the blood in your veins? Or is it just lust?

I have my fair experience with lust, but I don't think that is what this is. I think trying to pass what we have off as lust just cheapens it, because we are so much more than that. Although I don't know what it is exactly, I know that it is raw, deep and real as hell.

When I get home after an extended workout with the offensive coach, I hear laughter and jokes coming from the living room. I poke my head in and nearly swallow my tongue when I see Erica all dolled up in a one shoulder green dress.

It fits her body like a glove and makes her normally vibrant red hair practically fire engine red. She is wearing that red lipstick that I love so much just like she has every day since the bowling alley. Every time I see it, I can't help but imagine all the places that she has left smears of it since that night.

Unfortunately, my excited mood quickly shifts into irritation when I notice that she isn't the only one who is dressed up. Trevor is wearing a navy suit with a white button up and a pair of dress shoes. Mikey and Slater are playing some video game while Trevor and Erica are standing in the entry way, looking like they are getting ready to head out. Why didn't she tell me that her and Trevor were going somewhere? Shouldn't that be something that a boyfriend should know?

As if she can feel the weight of my gaze, she turns around fully to look at me. She gives me a weak smile that doesn't do much to ease my nerves. My brows dip for a moment before I school my features and step into the room. Trevor looks over at me and nods.

"Hey, man, where were you?"

"Just working on some stuff with Martinez. Where you guys off to?"

Trevor smiles as he hooks his arm around Erica's waist. I notice that her body instantly stiffens at the contact before she gently pries herself out of his grip. Trevor doesn't really seem to notice though as he speaks.

"Taking my girl for a hot date on the town," he says with a sly smirk.

"And by hot date, he means that our parents are both in town for your home game this weekend, and they want to have dinner tonight," Erica interjects quickly as she shoots Trevor an irritated look.

He shrugs seemingly unbothered by her putting him in his place. Meanwhile, I'm standing over here doing my best not to break every bone in my best friend's face. My fists are balled so tight that a few of my knuckle's pop but the only person who seems to notice my near murderous rage is Erica, who shoots me an apologetic look.

"Cool," I say sharper than I meant to.

Trevor's brows furrow and he cocks his head slightly at me for moment before he shakes his head and looks back at Erica, giving her a cheesy smile that pisses me the fuck off.

"So, Erica, you got a man or something? We haven't seen you around much lately," Slater calls out as he keeps his eyes glued to the screen.

I curse his fat fucking mouth in my head and make a mental note to kick the shit out of him later. Erica's eyes shoot over to Slater, and she does a terrible job of hiding the panic that flashes across her face. Trevor lets out a little laugh before it dies in his throat as he looks over at Erica.

"Wait, do you?" He asks.

She shrugs in a way that doesn't even look a little nonchalant.

"It's super casual."

I suppress the scoff that gets lodged in my throat at her lame attempt to downplay what we have.

We are anything but fucking casual.

Trevor frowns as he crosses his arms against his chest. "Who is he?"

Erica rolls her eyes and shakes her head. "No, Trev."

"No, what?"

"No, I'm not doing this with you. I'm allowed to have a social life just like you are."

"Yeah, but-" he breaks off and shakes his head before he takes a deep breath. "I'll be right back. Then we can go."

Erica nods softly as Trevor's heavy footsteps thump up the stairs. As soon as he is out of sight, I grab Erica by the elbow and walk her into the kitchen and around the corner. Slater already knows about us, and I'm sure he has already told Mikey, they are close like that, so I don't really care if they see me sneaking off with her. I just need to clear something up.

"Why didn't you tell me you were going out with Trevor?" I ask as I back her up against the wall.

"It wasn't really planned or anything. My mother called me a little over an hour ago to tell me we were all going to dinner. You were at practice. I wasn't trying to hide it or anything."

My jaw ticks in irritation before I nod because I know she wouldn't do that. She is the most genuine person that I have ever met, and I know that she cares about me, probably not as much as I do about her, though.

"Okay. Second issue, you know that we are not even close to fucking casual, right?"

Her eyes flare for a moment before she gives me a shy smile and looks down to the ground. I slip my hand underneath her jaw and tilt her head up to face me.

"Oh, well, I was hoping. I didn't want to assume though-"

"Assume away, baby. Let me make it perfectly clear that we are as serious as a heart attack. I told you that you were mine and I fucking meant it."

I hear the shutting of a door upstairs and let out a sigh before I bend down and quickly capture her lips between mine. She leans into me and begins to weave her arms around me when I take a small step back.

"Text me when you're back from dinner. I'll come over and then we can talk more."

She bites her lower lip in a way that instantly sends the blood rushing to my cock before she nods. I give her a small smile and swat her ass as I shoo her back into the hallway. I'm not thrilled that she is going out with Trevor, the fact that their parents will be there only provides me a little bit of relief.

I know that I can't keep this up for much longer. It kills me to pretend like she is nothing to me when really, she is fucking everything. We have to tell Trevor soon before he finds out in a shitty way that will make him hate us both forever.

I'm gonna tell him.

Soon.

CHAPTER TWENTY-SIX

ERICA

My heart is still beating wildly in my chest in anticipation for tonight. I'm practically counting down the minutes until I can see him again. To say that I would rather be anywhere but here is an understatement. I stab my mixed green and fig salad a little too aggressively as Trev and my parents schmooze the hell out of each other.

Trev kicks my foot gently causing me to glance over to him. He gives me an exaggerated eye roll as he gestures to our parents, which causes me to let out an amused snort. His usual playful smirk peeks out before he gives me a wink. The ride over was a little awkward. He tried to find out who I was seeing but I shut him down before he could get more than two words out.

I don't know what possessed Slater to say that today. I don't know if he knows that Sebastian and I are together now or if he just suspects something or maybe he is just too damn nosey for all of our own good. Regardless, it complicated things greatly because now Trevor has it in his head that the only reason that we are not together is because of some mystery guy.

"Aw look at them, Bev," Trevor's mom, Shannon, coos as she smiles at Trevor and me.

My mother has a satisfied smirk on her perfectly painted lips as she reaches for her glass of Chard.

"We always said they would find their way back to each other."

"Wait, what?" I ask at the same time that Trevor groans, "Mom."

"You two. You are just adorable. Trevor has practically had stars in his eyes all night. Your mother and I knew from the first day you all moved into the neighborhood that you and Trevor would end up together."

I let out a sharp laugh that probably sounds a little meaner than intended. "We are not together."

Trevor's playful smirk vanishes, and a disappointed frown takes its place. I instantly feel bad that I hurt his feelings, and I glance up to see that his parents are both wearing matching pouts while my mother is staring daggers at me with thin lips while my father is too enthralled in his glass of scotch to know that there is any tension at the table to begin with.

"Oh, I just assumed..." Shannon trails off.

"We are friends, mom," Trevor says with a stiff smile.

"You two have always been friends, sweetie. I just thought that after being at school together and spending so much time together-"

"She is seeing someone," Trevor interjects bitterly before his mother gets too far down the rabbit hole.

I send him a wide-eyed look, because why the hell would he spill the beans about something like that in front of both of our parents when he doesn't even have all of the facts. He purposefully doesn't look at me, keeping his eyes firmly trained on his plate.

"Oh?" My mother asks as she raises an eyebrow towards me. "You haven't mentioned anyone, Erica."

"Nothing to tell, Mother."

She narrows her eyes slightly as she silently waits for me to give her more information. It is the same look that she gives people on the stand to make them sweat, but I grew up with it, and I have skin like concrete. I learned from the best.

After thirty seconds of a silent stare down, my mother huffs before she turns to Shannon and begins talking about the Christmas benefit that they are co-hosting this year. Trevor risks a glance towards me, and I let him know with my eyes exactly how irritated I am with him for inserting my mother into my business.

He knows how overbearing and opinionated she is. That means the only reason he would have done that is to get her to pick apart whoever I am dating until I broke up with him just to get my mother off my back. That was a shitty thing to do, and it makes me look at him a little differently.

I keep my head down and tune the rest of the night out and don't focus back in until I notice that Trevor is parking outside of my dorm. He puts the car into park before he turns to face me.

"Little Red," he starts.

"Don't. That was really shitty of you, Trev, and you know it. I thought you were my friend but you sure as hell didn't act like it tonight."

"I'm sorry. I knew my mom was going to keep digging at it and I just wanted her to stop. Besides, it's true, right?"

"It doesn't matter," I huff.

"It does to me," he says softly, his sapphire blue eyes shining in the moonlight. "Look, Little Red. You are my oldest and closest friend. I care about you, and I want you to be happy. Even if that happiness isn't with me. So, I just hope that he treats you right, whoever he is. Make sure to tell him that if he makes you shed even a single tear, I'll beat him into a bloody pulp."

I crack a half smile before nodding. I lean over and wrap my arms around his shoulders and hug him for a few moments before I pull away.

"Thank you, Trev. I appreciate it."

He gives me a sad smile and nods. I give him a little wave before getting out of the car and heading up to my dorm room. I'm glad that he seems to finally understand that we aren't going to have anything more than friendship. I just can't give my heart to him, not when it has already chosen someone else.

As I open my bedroom door, I let out a startled gasp when I see Seb sprawled out across my bed, scrolling on his phone.

"How did you get in here?" I ask with my hand over my racing heart.

He looks up at me and tosses his phone to the side.

"Palmer let me in before she went to her boyfriend's. How was dinner?"

I wince slightly before I shake my head. "Could have been better."

Seb stays quiet as he seems to be trying to read me. You would think having his heavy gaze would make me uncomfortable, but I understand that it's just how he processes things. He is an observer. He retains almost everything that is said to him or around him and he processes all of it before he responds, if he even thinks that a response is necessary. For growing up with parents that could fill a hot air balloon with useless chatter, it's refreshing.

"And Trevor? How was he?"

I roll my eyes as I cross the room and swing my legs over to straddle him. "Babe. You don't have to be jealous."

His brows furrow as his large hands rest on my hips. "Of course, I do. My girlfriend went out to a nice dinner with another guy. I'm not just jealous. I'm pissed the fuck off! We haven't even been able to go out on a real date because our whole fucking relationship is one big secret."

I see the irritation in his eyes but also what looks like disappointment. I know that we agreed to keep things to ourselves until the season was over in case Trevor lost his shit, but after our talk tonight, I think things might be okay. Well, as good as they will ever get at least.

"Do you want to go on a date?" I ask, trying but failing to conceal my smile.

His scowl softens slightly as he drags my body closer to his until our chests are flush.

"I want everything with you. I want to take you on a date and spoil the shit out of you. I want to hold your hand in public and walk you to class. I have the most beautiful, incredible woman in my arms, and I want everyone to know that she is mine."

My small smirk breaks out into a wide toothed grin before I lean in and peck his lips.

"Okay. Let's do it."

"What about Trevor?"

"We had a talk tonight. He says he wants me to be happy. You make me happy, Seb."

He smiles softly and kisses the tip of my nose. When he pulls away, he opens his mouth like he is about to say something before shaking his head and letting out a soft sigh.

"Baby. I think we need to talk."

"Uh oh," I say playfully though nerves instantly seep into my veins.

I slowly climb off of him and lay down onto my bed. He lays down next to me and wraps his arm around me before pulling me into him. I have to crane my neck up to look at him from this angle, but I will never complain about being in his arms.

Seb brushes some hair off of my forehead before his long fingers run slowly down the side of my face.

"You're so beautiful," he whispers almost to himself.

I smile and lean into his touch. "Thank you. You're extremely handsome."

A serious look plays across his face as his eyes search mine for a few heavy moments before he speaks again.

"I care about you, Erica, a lot. More than someone like me probably has a right to."

"Someone like you?" I ask as my brows dip.

His fingers still as he seems to be thinking of what to say next.

"There is a lot you don't know about me," he says cryptically. "I have done things that I'm not proud of."

"We all have," I say as I reach out to rest my hand on top of his chest.

Seb shakes his head as he shuts his eyes for a second. He opens his mouth but then shuts it. After a few seconds, he tries again, but the same thing happens.

"Hey," I say softly, which causes him to slowly ease his eyes open. "You don't have to tell me about it. Just know that I'm always here. I don't think that there is anything that you could say that is going to scare me away. I'm kinda crazy about you," I say with a small smile.

Seb wets his lips before he takes a deep breath. "I'm in love with you, Erica."

My breath hitches as my heart skips out of rhythm. He loves me? I know that I have been falling for him since the first night that I met him, but we have only been officially together for a little over month. I didn't expect to feel this way about him so fast, nor did I expect him to feel the same.

"I love you too," I whisper softly.

In the next moment, Seb crushes his lips against mine. I angle my head up towards him as his hand wraps around my jaw. His lips move across mine fervently like he couldn't stop if he tried, like he needs to just to breathe.

I know the feeling.

Seb's hands run down my sides until they discover my zipper. He slides it down quickly and eases the material off my skin as I wiggle out of it. I'm still wearing my high heels and when I reach to unclasp them, he growls before nipping my lower lip.

"Leave them on."

I run my tongue along my lips before nodding. Seb makes quick work of removing my bra and panties while I strip off his pants and shirt.

"I'm sorry, baby. I can't wait any longer. I have to have you," he pants before driving inside of me.

I let out a sharp gasp before my body relaxes and a satisfied moan slips from my lips. Seb doesn't let up once. His mouth never leaves my skin as his hands trace over my curves as if committing them to memory.

My back arches when he drives into that sweet spot and he reaches down to lift my right thigh, curling it around him until the tip of my heel digs into his back. The position is incredibly deep and completely amazing. He grunts in appreciation as he continues his relentless pursuit.

I curl my other leg around him as his hands reach down to cup my ass. He practically picks me up off the mattress and bounces me against him until we are both shouting and cursing out our orgasms. We stay still for a few moments before he pulls away and goes to the bathroom. He comes back with a warm washcloth and begins to slowly clean me.

I watch him with a content smile before he places a tender kiss to the inside of each thigh. He tosses the washcloth into my laundry hamper before sliding on his boxers, in case Palmer bursts in, before crawling under the covers with me.

My head settles against his chest, and I let out a soft sigh as I close my eyes. I feel like we just took a huge step in our relationship tonight. It wasn't just him telling me that he loves me, it wasn't just words. I felt the sincerity in the words he spoke. It was like he was baring his soul to me, giving himself to me fully. I fall asleep with a smile on my face and happiness in my heart.

CHAPTER TWENTY-SEVEN

SEBASTIAN

I t feels like a 10-ton weight has been lifted off my chest. The words were so close to slipping out so many times before. I didn't want to go there, to open myself up like that without her knowing the truth about me and my past. But when I tried to tell her, I froze. The words died on my tongue as I gazed into her aqua eyes, and I couldn't stomach the thought of saying anything to make her think any differently of me. Selfish, I know.

I know that I need to tell her eventually, I don't like this shit between us, even if it is in the past. For now, though, I'm going to soak up the fact that my dream girl is mine and she is in love with me. I haven't wanted to push things, and to be honest, I wasn't sure when it would feel like the right time to announce our relationship to the world, but I know that sooner is better because I don't feel right about sneaking around with her. She is a woman that deserves to be shown off and worshipped.

After a very good night together, I left her this morning with the promise of the best date of her life tonight. I told her to get all dolled up and that I would pick her up at 7. Do I want to take her on a fancy date because it's eating me up that she got all dressed up to go out with Trevor and her parents last night? Maybe. Do I feel like it will make me feel more worthy of her if I can give her

I headed home, knowing that I have a very uncomfortable and potentially dangerous talk to have. I told her that I'm going to tell Trevor today. I just want to get it over with. She wanted to come with, but I told her that it was best if I do it on my own, just in case he flips out like I'm sure he will.

When I get to the house, I look around everywhere but the only person I can find is Slater.

"Hey, man, Trev around?"

Slater leans back against the counter with a beer in his hand. "He had to get to class early for some assignment."

I nod feeling both frustrated and relieved that I most likely won't get to talk to him before our date tonight. There is no way I'm going to talk to him about it right before practice, and I think that it will take too long to talk about after practice without missing our date, and there is no way in hell I'm missing that.

"Everything cool?" Slater asks.

I give him a hesitant smile. "I don't know yet. I'll let you know. I'm going to tell him about Erica and me."

Slater's eyebrows shoot up but instead of his trademark smirk or inappropriate comment, he just looks a little uneasy.

"Yeah? So, you guys are serious?"

I nod as I bury my hands into my pockets. "We don't want to keep sneaking around. The longer we keep it up the more we are going to hurt him, and I'm honestly sick of not being able to touch my girl in public."

"Are you prepared for the outcome? The day before a game?"

I shrug. "Fuck, I don't know. Will there ever be a good time? Any advice?"

Slater lets out a humorless laugh and shakes his head. "Don't fall for your best friend's ex."

A little late for that.

I didn't see Trev all day except for in the locker room before practice. I could hardly even look at him, I tried to play it off like I was just focused on the game tomorrow. The guilt is really starting to weigh on me, and I just want to come clean already, but I guess it'll have to wait until later. I have a hot date with an even hotter girl.

After practice, I shower and change, deciding to leave my hair down because I know how much Erica likes to play with it, before I hop into my car and drive around campus to park in front of Erica's dorm. I drive a 2010 Tahoe that I picked up for a couple grand when I moved out here my freshman year. It isn't fancy like Trevor's Porsche, but it's clean and runs good, so it's good enough for me. It's the nicest thing that I've ever owned, and I'm not ashamed to admit it.

Someone lets me into the dorm, so I am able to make it up to Erica's room and pick her up properly. When I knock on the door, it opens a half of a second later, all the air getting ripped out of my lungs with it. She looks even more gorgeous than last night. Her dress is tight and hugs her body in the best way. It's black lace with a low neckline that has me rethinking the whole dinner idea entirely.

Would it really be so bad if we just ordered in and spent the night wrapped up in the sheets? *No.* That is what we have been doing for the last month and I want more. At least my head does, my cock on the other hand thinks a night in bed isn't such a bad idea.

I shift slightly to try to conceal my instant hard on as my eyes trace over her porcelain face as I step inside and shut the door. Erica's hair is done up in large curls that I want to run my fingers through while her lush lips are painted that blood red I like so much while her eyelashes seem to go on for miles. Her aqua eyes sparkle as they look up to me, and I'm in total awe that someone like her is mine.

"I take it your silence means you approve?" She asks teasingly.

Without saying a word, I hook my arm around her lower back and crush her body against mine before capturing her lips. She lets out a surprised gasp before she melts into me. My hands dive into her thick curls, and I hold her as close as I possibly can. It's never close enough with Erica, though. I always need more.

Erica steps so that she is on either side of my thigh. As if she can't help it, she presses her hips against me and begins rubbing her pussy against my thigh like she is dry humping a fucking pole. My start of a hard on has now escalated to a raging fucking boner that is begging for attention. Her leg brushes against my cock, and she moans into our kiss as she reaches her hand down and begins stroking me through my pants. Fuckkk.

When we break apart, she bites her lower lip as she bats her eyes at me.

"That seems kinda painful, babe. I don't know if we can go to dinner with you like that."

"I'm fine," I rasp hoarsely as I do my best to clear my throat.

A mischievous look takes over Erica's face before she slowly lowers down until she is on her knees. Before I can try to stop her, which let's be honest, I don't really try that hard, she unzips my pants and pulls them down slightly until she frees my cock. Her silky hand wraps around me before she pumps a few times and kisses the head.

I let out a shuttering breath as I close my eyes and hit my head against the door. Suddenly, her warm tongue licks from head to base, lazily drawing lines all over as her hand cups up to cradle my balls. Fuck. Fuck. Fuck.

Erica lets out a soft chuckle before she looks up at me, gives me a sultry wink and sinks my cock down her throat.

"Holy fuck!" I bark as my hips involuntarily jerk, shoving my cock even farther down her slim throat.

She gags as her throat constricts, tightening around me even more before she pulls back for a moment before she takes a deep breath and shoves me to the back of her throat again. Fucking hell. Who is this goddess on her knees for me?

Her head moves in a steady rhythm as she bobs and sucks on my cock until I can't take it any longer. I bury my hands into her fiery locks, wrapping it tightly in my fists as I begin to fuck her throat without mercy. The sounds of her gags and the feel of her mouth on me is enough to send me over the edge as I spill my cum down her delicate little throat. She swallows every single drop like a good girl before licking her lips slowly and standing up.

I slowly lift my thumb to my mouth and wet it before gently wiping away the smeared red on her face. Her eyes watch me carefully as a sly smile spreads across her face as my fingers trace over her jawline.

"Fuck, baby," I rasp.

She shoots me a wink before she reaches for her purse and goes to pull the door open. I quickly tuck myself away before I grab her and haul her against me, bending my head down so that my hair falls to each side of us, almost sheltering us in our own little space.

"Do you think I'm gonna let you suck my cock like a little slut and not doing something about it?"

She lets out a throaty laugh as she turns her head to look up at me.

"Do something about it after dinner, this little slut is starving."

A rough chuckle escapes me before I capture her lips one more time and nod. We step out the door, and I take a step back so that Erica can lock her door. As soon as she has, I am right back to her, my arm slung around her shoulder possessively. We walk together through the common room where a group of cheerleaders are currently sitting.

All of their mouths go slack jawed as they watch us, and I know that us being together will probably be common knowledge come tomorrow morning. Hopefully I'll have a chance to talk to Trev before that happens.

I take Erica to an extremely expensive Italian restaurant downtown. The place is dimly lit which only gives it a more sophisticated vibe, with white tablecloths and large candles in the center of the table. Growing up there is no way I would have come within a hundred yards of a place like this. But this is Erica's world and I want to do whatever it takes to fit into that.

"Wow this place is fancy," Erica says as she opens her menu.

"Only the best for you," I say sincerely.

She smiles before leaning over the table a little. "You're sweet, but can I be honest? I'd honestly prefer a divey pub over places like this any day of the week."

I let out a surprised chuckle as I nod. "Fuck, me too. Next time."

"Deal," she snickers as our waiter comes over.

His eyes linger on Erica's neckline longer than I would prefer, which causes a near feral growl to rip through my throat. I must look as intimidating as I feel because the waiter visibly pales when he looks at me before turning back to Erica, keeping his eyes firmly above neck level from then on.

Once we order, Erica lets out a suppressed laugh. "Did you seriously just growl at our waiter?"

"He was staring at your tits like they were his to look at!"

An amused smirk spreads across her face as her eyes twinkle with a mischievous glint.

"If they aren't his, then whose are they?"

"Mine," I rumble lowly. "You are mine. Every inch of you belongs to me, and I have no problem with making that known to every man that comes within thirty feet of you."

She gives me a challenging look for a minute before she nods happily and leans back into her chair, seemingly satisfied with my answer.

The food was really good, and the night was mainly filled with Erica telling me stories about growing up. It seems like a charmed life from the outside, but I see the tension that settles in the corners of her eyes when she talks about it all. Like she has trained herself to smile even when that is the last thing she wants to do.

"You know you don't have to do that," I say.

"Do what?"

"Act like you love your life and wouldn't have it any other way."

Her fake smile becomes a little tighter as if she is trying to convince me even more.

"I have a good life. I have been very fortunate with all the right doors opened for me, the right connections and financial stability. What more could someone ask for?"

"Happiness."

Her smile slowly falls until she gives me a look of agreement and nods her head. I can tell that she doesn't want to talk about it anymore so instead, I flag down the waiter with the wandering eyes and pay the check. I tell Erica about the time Slater crawled into bed with Mikey, thinking that he was in his room and his hookup of the night was in bed.

"No!" She gasps.

I smirk as I nod, hovering my hand at her lower back as we make our way to my car.

"Yeah. They say nothing happened, but Trev and I are not so convinced. It was dark, and they were pretty drunk," I say with a shrug.

Erica bursts out into hysterical laughter as she scoots into her seat. It's fucking contagious. I really could bottle it and sell that shit. Anyone and everyone would kill to have it.

And it's all mine.

Once we start driving, instead of taking a left to head back to campus, I hook a right to get onto the freeway. Erica looks over to me with a cocked brow.

"We aren't going home?"

I shake my head. "I promised you the best date of your life. I think that requires more than dinner, baby."

She shakes her head with a smile. "The company makes it the best date of my life."

I smirk before leaning over and quickly pecking her lips. She lets out a content sigh as she settles back into her seat while she spouts out random guesses as to where we are going. All of which are wrong.

Twenty minutes later, I find some street parking and shut my car down before getting out and going to open her door. She gives me a grateful smile as I take her hand in mine.

"Now are you going to tell me where we are?" She asks as we walk down the dark sidewalk before crossing the street.

"See for yourself," I say as I gesture to the sign sitting outside of the building we are entering.

"Alexandra Campo?" She gasps as she looks at me with wide eyes.

I smile and nod as I hold the door open for her. When she first started hanging around with Trevor, I overheard her talking about her role model, Alexandra Campo. She is an artist from around their hometown who made it big about ten years ago. Apparently, Erica has been studying her work ever since high school.

When we step into the room, Erica lets out an audible gasp as her eyes dart around. The lights are dim with some edgy pop song playing in the background. The main lighting in the room is directed towards the dozens of pieces that are on display around the gallery. Dozens of nicely dressed men and women mill around the room with champagne glasses in their hands as they use wide hand gestures as they talk about the different pieces.

I stand back and smile softly as Erica's head ping pongs all around before she practically rips my arm out of its socket and begins to rush over to each painting. For two hours, she rambles on animatedly about the attention to detail and composition of each piece and how they differ. If I'm being honest, they all just look like a bunch of different colors to me, but I would gladly learn about anything that makes her this happy.

"I love this one. Though there could have been a little bit better usage of the negative space to be more impactful," Erica says as we look at one of the last ones.

There are a crowd of people around us also admiring the art when a voice comes from the back.

"How so?"

Erica and I both glance but can't tell who asked the question as everyone stares at her expectantly.

"Well, it isn't a popular opinion, but I believe that less is more in most cases. The piece has fantastic texture and vibrancy, but it's almost overpowering the subject matter. Instead of feeling the message deeply, I find it being drowned out by the overcompensation to strive for something that could have been organically achieved."

I don't even know what all that really meant, honestly, but she looked beautiful saying it.

A person steps through the group to stand face to face with Erica and based on the gasp that escapes her, I can tell this isn't good.

"Ms. Campo," Erica stutters with wide eyes. "I-I am sorry. I-"

The middle-aged woman smirks before she shakes her head. "No, you aren't. And that's okay. I couldn't agree more. I wasn't too happy with this piece, but a few close friends in the community said that it needed more when I wanted to leave it as is. I should have trusted my instincts."

"It's still remarkable," Erica adds on.

"Thank you. What's your name?"

"Erica Pembrooke."

"I take it you're an artist?" She asks.

"Oh, not rea-"

"Yes, she is. An amazing one," I interject.

Erica shoots me a wide-eyed look, but I just smile down at her. Ms. Campo looks at me and smiles before looking back to Erica.

"Do you have a portfolio?"

"I-uh. Not on me, no."

"Well, of course not. But at home. Could you send it to me?"

"You want to see my work?" Erica asks, seemingly confused.

Ms. Campo lets out a haughty laugh as she places her hand over her chest.

"Yes. With an eye like yours, I'm interested to see what you create."

Erica nods wordlessly, obviously star struck. Ms. Campo smiles before pulling out a business card and handing it to her.

"Send me your portfolio. I'll be in touch from there."

"In touch?" Erica echoes.

I place my hands on her shoulders and give the woman a polite smile.

"Thank you. She will."

"Enjoy," she smiles before walking off towards another group of people.

Erica still hasn't moved in her spot, and I squeeze her shoulders to shake her out of her stupor. She turns around to look up at me.

"Did that just happen?" She whispers.

I smile. "Yes, it did, baby. Do you have a portfolio?"

She nods as I gently stroke her cheek and lean down to kiss her. When I pull back, her eyes flutter open as she smiles at me.

"Guess you have an email to send then, huh?"

A wide grin splits across her face that makes my heart stall. Fuck, I love this girl.

On our way back to campus, it doesn't escape my notice that she keeps sending me heated glances as her slim fingers lazily draw lines along my tensed thigh. My cock has been permanently hard since I first picked her up, but it's becoming damn near painful at this point.

I whip into the first available parking spot before turning the car off and sprinting around to her side. She is only able to unbuckle her seat belt before I scoop her up and toss her over my shoulder.

"Seb!" She giggles. "Put me down!"

I swat her ass as I jog up to her building. "Keep that wiggly little ass covered, baby."

"What if I don't?" She asks as she continues to wiggle in my arms.

I reach back and smack her again. "I'll spank your ass red if even one other man sees what's mine."

"Promises, promises," she mutters which leads me to grin and let out a rough chuckle.

I drop her to her feet when we get outside of her building only so she can unlock it. She huffs as she digs through her clutch.

"Caveman."

I push against her until she is flush with the glass door while her ass is plastered over my raging hard on.

"You got no idea, baby," I whisper into her ear before nipping at her lobe.

She lets out a breathy moan before she turns around to face me. I don't waste anytime wrapping my arms around her and devouring her silky lips. I feel her delicate hands run down my chest and across my abs when I hear the worst possible thing.

"Are you fucking kidding me?"

Erica and I break apart like we have been shot. When I turn around, I see an extremely pissed Trevor standing only five feet away from us with a bag of Chinese takeout in his hand.

Shit.

"Trev-" I start.

"Are you FUCKING kidding me!" He shouts as he cuts me off.

"Calm down," I say as I tuck Erica behind me a bit, just in case this gets ugly.

"Calm down? Calm down! Oh, I'm fucking calm. About as calm as a guy can be when he finds out that his best fucking friend has been screwing the girl he's in love with behind his back!"

"It isn't like that," I say with a shake of my head.

"Isn't like what? You saying that you haven't screwed her?" He spits angrily.

I stay silent because I know that no matter what I say, it won't help. Plus, I'm more than done with all of the lying and bullshit. A disgusted laugh leaves Trevor as he shakes his head.

"I can't fucking believe you! You were my best friend. I told you EVERYTHING! I told you how much I wanted her, how much I love her, and you do this to me?"

"Trevor," Erica says softly as she steps to the side so that he can see her fully.

I watch as his eyes flare with hurt and anger as he takes in her disheveled appearance. His eyes are blazing like the pits of hell when he turns to me, winds back his arm and decks me right across the face. I stumble a few steps before I get my balance. But before I can fully stand straight, he plows into me and tackles me to the pavement.

He gets a few more good hits in before I toss one back. I don't want to hurt him. I don't want to fight at all, but he is practically rabid right now and I know that there is no reasoning with him when he is like this. Fuck, honestly, I've never seen him like this.

"Trevor!" Erica screams as I see her making her way over to us to pull him off me.

"Get back!" I bark at her as I swing and pop Trevor in the eye.

He curses and leans back slightly, which gives me the opportunity to peel myself away from him. I jump to my feet as he does the same. I feel blood running down my face from where he punched me in the nose as he cradles his eye.

"You are the biggest piece of shit I have ever met. You are fucking dead to me," he sneers before spitting a glob of blood at my feet.

He gives Erica a disgusted look before shaking his head violently and storming off towards the parking lot. When I know that he won't turn back and try to hit me again, I turn to see that Erica is shaking and silently crying. These aren't angry tears this time though, these are real.

The sound of Trevor's Porsche rips through the otherwise silent night air, he piss-raps the engine before he takes off like a bat out of hell from the parking lot. Erica and I both watch him go as he practically drifts out of the parking lot. He didn't look before he pulled out though because not a half of a second later a box truck going way too fucking fast plows right into the car.

The world stops spinning for a moment, everything suddenly turning into slow motion. I hear the sharp sound of metal on metal crunching anything in its path. I hear the loud blaring of horns. I watch as Trevor's Porsche rolls over once, twice, three times before landing on its lid. I don't realize that I am moving towards the wreck until I am tugging at the passenger door, desperate to get my best friend free but the fucking thing won't budge, and his door is completely caved in.

Quickly, I drop to the ground to look through the shattered-out passenger window and see Trev laying against the roof. No fucking seatbelt. His head is bleeding more than it should, at least I think, all I know is there is a fuck of a lot of blood, and he won't open his goddamn eyes.

"Trevor! Open your eyes! Are you okay? Trev!"

"Oh my god!" Erica screams as she gets down next to me. "Someone HELP!"

I glance up to see the box truck driver stepping out of his rig which looks like it got into a simple fender bender. He is already on the phone, wide panicked eyes flicking down to Trevor's car and over to me. I don't know much about first aid, but I know in an accident as bad as this one you can't move them. So instead, we sit and wait for the ambulance. Despite my protest, Erica practically climbs into the car and holds Trev's limp hand, begging him to wake up in between broken sobs. The sound shatters something that was broken a long time ago inside me. This can't be happening. I can't lose my best friend. Not like this.

But it is fucking happening. And a tiny voice keeps replaying the same mantra in my head.

Your fault.

Chapter Twenty-Eight

Erica

The sharp metallic smell of blood invaded my nostrils hours ago and it hasn't left since. I've never seen that much blood in my life. The only thing close to that was when the cook cut his hand open at my father's birthday party a few years ago. I couldn't believe how much blood poured out of his hand from one cut. But that was nothing in comparison.

Sebastian said that the ambulance was to us within minutes, but it felt like hours. My heart was cracked when Trevor looked up at me with all of the disappointment and heartache that he did when he saw me in Sebastian's arms. It was fucking obliterated when I climbed over broken glass to see my best friend in the world lifeless and bleeding out in his demolished car.

I held Trevor's hand the entire time that we waited and only let go because Sebastian physically extracted me so that the paramedics could get him out. That only lasted a minute at most before I broke free of his hold and flew into the ambulance with Trevor. Everything from there was one giant blur. Sirens wailing through the night, doctors rushing and shouting things that I didn't quite understand and the cold sterile smell of a hospital waiting room.

Sebastian called Trevor's parents, and they were at the hospital only a few minutes after I got there, my parents in tow. We waited for so long to hear anything and with every passing minute, a cold like I had never felt before began to seep in.

This is all your fault, you selfish little girl.

My mother's voice plays over inside my head like the personal demon it is. From what I gather, Sebastian didn't tell them why Trevor was driving erratically or why he didn't have his seatbelt on. If so, I'm sure my mother would have uttered the words that are on a loop in my head by now. But no, it's just me and my poisonous thoughts, slowly weakening me by the second.

As soon as the doctor called out Trevor's name, I nearly tackled him, rattling off question after question. His mouth was moving a lot but the only words I heard was medically induced coma. I collapsed, literally. I wish I were kidding, but I quite literally fell to the floor and curled up into a ball. Not Trevor. Not my best friend, my sidekick, my other half.

This is all your fault.

Strong arms lifted me up and carried me over to the seating area. I stayed hidden in my little ball, not relaxing for a second despite Sebastian's attempt. His large hand rubbed soothing circles on my back as his voice whispered things to me that I couldn't quite hear. It was like white noise had flooded my brain and the only thing I could hear was that fucking voice.

Your fault. Your fault. Your fault.

I don't know how long I stay like that. Hours, days maybe. I know at some point Sebastian fell asleep for a bit because I could hear his breathing even out before it returned to normal when he woke up. Not me, though. I couldn't if I tried.

"Erica," Shannon's shaky voice called from a foot or so away from me.

I peeled my head out of my safe cocoon as I looked up at her. The normally perfectly put together woman was a mess. With puffy eyes, mascara streaks down her face and a blotchy nose, the woman looked like the picture of heart break. I know that I probably don't look much better but for some reason seeing someone who has been nothing but smiles since I met her broken like this, it squeezes on my already battered heart.

"Do you want to come to his room?"

I nearly bolt out of Sebastian's arms.

"He's awake?" I rush.

A pained look crosses her face as she shakes her head.

"No. Not yet. But the doctor said that family could sit in his room until he does. The swelling is still there so they are going to keep him under for at least another day and then go from there."

Goosebumps race across my skin, I don't know if it's because I have been inside this tundra of a waiting room in nothing but a dress for an unknown amount of hours or from the news that Trevor is really hurt that bad. Either way, they are there, and I don't know if the chill will ever go away.

"You are as close as it gets to family, sweetheart. You are his girl," she says with a sad smile and a half gasp half laugh. "That's what he always calls you, did you know that?"

I swallow over the lump in my throat and shake my head softly. Shannon nods.

"Anytime we speak on the phone, he tells me about how his girl is doing. Or during the summer when he practically spent every moment with you, he would tell us that he was going to see his girl. He loves you so much, Erica. He would want you in there, waiting for him to wake up."

I nod because I couldn't speak if I tried, not with the way my raw throat is constricting by the second. I thought I ran out of tears hours ago but the familiar burn in my eyes and chest tell a different story. Shannon brings me into her arms and squeezes me tightly before escorting me down the hallway, Trevor's dad, Jonathan, walking sullenly behind us.

Glancing over my shoulder I see my own parents with distraught looks on their faces, though they still look perfectly polished worry and fear definitely plays heavy in their eyes, which I can honestly say is a first for them. My eyes move over to the silent mountain of a man that has somehow folded his body into a tiny hospital chair. His eyes are solely trained on me and the weight of them nearly sends me toppling over. There is so much pain, so much fear, so much regret.

I wonder if I'm one of those regrets.

Your fault.

When I step into the room that Shannon guides me into, I suck in a sharp breath. I don't know what I was expecting but it sure as hell wasn't what lays in front of me. Trevor Michaels. A man larger than life. The guy who always persevered, never gave up, annoyingly so. His sparkling blue eyes are closed, his flawlessly tanned skin bruised and marred. There are several machines that he is hooked up to with wires everywhere. My rock, my best friend is lying unconscious and broken in a hospital bed.

My eyes flick over and widen in horror. His right arm is in a cast from wrist to elbow. *His throwing arm.* No. Oh my god. *No.* What have I done?

"His arm is completely snapped in two," Shannon says shakily. "His shoulder was dislocated, but they set it when he came in. It's the swelling they are worried about. He lost so much blood. They say he is lucky to be alive, but it doesn't feel like he is lucky."

Her voice trails off as she begins to sob. Jonathan quickly gathers her up into his arms as she breaks down in her husband's arms. Slowly, I make my way over to the chair next to his bed before bringing it closer until I am right next to him. Reaching out, I carefully take his hand in mine before leaning down and kissing the back of it. I don't raise my head as I clutch his hand tightly like I am the one that is slowly slipping away as I proceed to cry until the sun comes up.

CHAPTER TWENTY-NINE

SEBASTIAN

E rica didn't come back from Trevor's room all night. I dozed for a few hours when we first got there and again after I knew she wouldn't be coming back out. Her parents left shortly after her and the Michaels went to his room, not sparing me so much as a second glance as they did. To be fair, they don't know my relationship with their daughter, but even if they did, I have a strong feeling they wouldn't like it.

The look that her mother gave me when I scooped Erica off the floor and pulled her into my lap was one of confusion and a hint of disapproval. I held her stare head on for several seconds before she broke the eye contact and turned to talk to her husband. I've heard enough about the woman from Erica to not hold too high of an opinion for her myself. But Erica is my whole fucking world, my future, so it looks like this won't be the last interaction I have with the Pembrooke's.

I called coach and let him know what happened. He told me that they understood if I needed to stay at the hospital and sit this game out, but I could tell in his voice that he didn't mean it. They were already down their star quarterback for the game and now potentially a tight end. As if college football was more important than my best friends fucking life.

When it was the morning, I snuck down the hall to check on Erica, but I found her head tucked against Trevor's side fast asleep.

his parents also asleep on the couch in the corner of the room. I know she didn't sleep all night and so I decided to let her sleep. As much as I wanted to stay here for Trev and her, I decided to go to the game. It wasn't going to help anyone with me hovering, and I needed to get some fucking aggression out.

When I got to the locker room, Slater and Mikey swarmed me instantly.

"We heard! How is he?" Slater asks with wide panicked eyes.

I shake my head.

"Not great. They put him in a coma. His right arm is broken, and the rest of his body is fucked up like-"

"Like he got hit by a truck?" Slater asks, his usual humor nowhere to be found in his words.

I grit my jaw and nod sharply.

"Fuck," Mikey curses as he shakes his head.

"Do you know what happened? All we heard was it was a car accident."

My stomach turns, ready to reject the cheap coffee from the hospital and the single piece of toast I was able to keep down this morning. I know what happened. I went after Erica Pembrooke, that's what happened. I put my relationship with her ahead of my friendship with Trev. I had every opportunity to come clean, to own up and try to explain to him how I feel about her, but I didn't. I took the cowards way out every chance I could and now I don't know if he will ever wake up again. The worst fucking part of it all? I can't regret it. How I handled things, most definitely. But regret being with Erica? Not a fucking chance.

I blow out a breath and shake my head. "He found out about Erica and me. We got in a fight. He got in his car and..."

"Jesus," Slater curses as he wipes a hand over his mouth. I swallow and nod, not willing to elaborate any more.

"Are you sure you are up to play, man?" Slater asks warily.

Not really, if I'm being honest, but I couldn't stand to sit in that hospital waiting room any longer. Too many bad fucking memories. Plus, it's not like I am needed and to be honest, I don't know if I'm really wanted there either, at least right now. Mr. and Mrs. Michaels like me. They have never looked down their nose at me and basically treat me like a second son but right now all their focus is on their real son and once they find out that it's my fault he is in that bed in the first place. I'm not sure if Erica has even realized I left or not. I have checked my phone nearly every ten minutes, but it remains silent.

Warmups go by in a blur and before I know it the ball is snapped, and I am bulldozing past the defense man across from me before I turned to signal the second string QB. We are lucky that our second string is solid. The kid is a freshman, but he's good. He sends a perfect spiral to me that I catch easily as I turn and start running as fast as my legs will let me. I'm taken down after twenty yards and the next play starts out.

The next time we have the ball, the QB sends it to Slater, who gets us some more yards but is quickly taken down. Stilliard U is a solid team and a tough one to beat on a good day and based on the looks on all my teammates faces, clearly feeling the hole left in us, it's a pretty bad fucking day.

I tried to stay in the game, but my head and my heart just wasn't in it. They were back at Brighton General Hospital. Worrying about the two most important people in my life, one hurting physically and the other emotionally, and it's all on me.

The game ended 7-27. Coach reamed all of our asses, but not one man on the team seemed to give a shit. It's just a fucking game. Some of us may go on to play professionally but 90% won't. A fact the coaches lose sight of a fuck ton.

When we get to the locker room, the first thing that I do is check my phone for an update of some sort. A text, a phone call, anything. But it's blank. I guess no news is good news, but I overheard the doctors say they would try to wake him up once the swelling had gone down, so that doesn't give me too much reassurance.

CHAPTER THIRTY

ERICA

P eeling my eyes open, the first thing I register is the sharp pain stabbing in the back of my neck. Slowly leaning up, I slouch back into a rock-hard chair and groan as I try to stretch my neck. I blink a few times to clear the sleep from my eyes, and when I do, I look down to see Trevor laying perfectly still in the same position he was when I dozed off earlier.

Oh, Trev.

I hear murmured voices coming from just outside the room and decide to investigate.

"He's stable. We are going to do another scan, and if the swelling has gone down, we will wean the meds off. Then it will just be up to him to wake up."

"Thank God," Jonathan, breathes as he rubs Shannon's back.

"You said there could be neurological damage. What kind?"

"That's hard to say. We won't know anything for sure until Trevor wakes up so that is our first and foremost priority."

"He's going to be okay, though, right?" I ask, chiming in as I come to stand in front of the doctor.

All eyes turn to me, but I am only focused on the man in a white coat who looks to be in his early fifties. He gives me a practiced kind smile as he speaks.

"We won't know until he wakes up and we run some tests on him, but that is our goal, yes."

I don't know why I don't feel as relieved as Trev's parents look. Some knot inside my chest won't unease, though. I know that doctors have to be careful about their words. Even when they are positive about something they have to hold their tongue until it is a one hundred percent certainty. Still, something just doesn't sit right with me.

My stomach begins to twist in pain. Food is the last thing that I want to think about right now, but I know I need to eat at least something, or at the very least get some coffee.

"I'm going to go look for some coffee. Do you want anything?" I ask Shannon and Jonathan.

Jonathan smiles and shakes his head. "We're okay, sweetheart. Thank you, though."

I nod as I glance back at Trev's room once more before I start down the hallway and follow the signs to the cafeteria. When I pass by the waiting room, I look out to see that my parents have left, no surprise there, but so has Sebastian. It doesn't surprise me, sitting in a waiting room all night and day isn't anyone's way of spending the day. I have my phone on me, but unfortunately, it's dead. I could probably scrounge up a charger, but I don't know if I want to. What if Sebastian is thinking the same thing that I am, that this is all my fault?

I'm the one that proposed us holding off on telling Trevor. I'm so stupid. We should have just gotten it out there from the beginning, or maybe I shouldn't have pursued Sebastian in the first place. No. I can't think like that. I don't regret being with Sebastian, but I do hate that our love has cost such a high price.

When I get to the cafeteria, I practically fall to my knees when I find that they have an actual espresso cart in the corner and not some gross machine. I order a Venti black coffee since I know I'll need every last drop of it and a banana before I head back up to Trevor's room.

The next few hours go by at a snail's pace. They did another scan on him and were happy to announce that the swelling had gone down significantly, and they were going to take him off the sedatives so that he could wake up. Well, that was nearly eight hours ago, and now I am a panicky mess. The doctors say that it could take a day or two for him to fully wake up but I don't care. Eight hours is too long. I know it.

"Erica, why don't you go home. Get some rest, sweetie?" Shannon says with a sad smile. "We are headed back to our hotel room to do the same. They will call us when he wakes up, because he will. Soon."

I shake my head. "You guys go, but I want to be here when he wakes up. I don't want him to be all alone."

She gives me a soft smile as she cups my cheek.

"My baby is so lucky to have you. I couldn't ask for a better match for him."

It's on the tip of my tongue to correct her, to remind her that we are not together but it seems ill timed and inappropriate right now, so instead I give her a tight smile before her and Jonathan make their way out of the room as I sit back down into my claimed seat right next to Trevor's left side.

Not a few seconds later, a heavy knock sounds from the door and I look up to see Sebastian in the doorway. He is wearing a pair of black sweats and a black t-shirt and his hair looks freshly showered. Oh, yeah. The game against Stilliard was today. Sebastian and I were talking about it just last night, not even twenty four hours ago. My god, this has to be the longest twenty four hours of my life.

He doesn't say anything for a few moments, he just flicks his eyes back and forth between Trevor and me. I don't say anything either because what is there to say? I can read the pain and regret splashed across his face like an open book. The guilt is practically pouring off his broad shoulders. We fucked up.

Swallowing roughly, he takes a step inside and holds up a bag of mine that should be back at my dorm.

"I had Palmer put some stuff together for you. I figured you wanted to get out of that and into something more comfortable. There is also some bathroom stuff in there."

When I don't make a move to take it from him, he nods almost to himself before setting it down on the couch next to the bed and buries his hands in his pockets.

His intense caramel coated eyes stare me down once again, as if he is peeling back every layer of myself for his analysis. I let him see everything, the bone crushing pain I feel in every inch of my body, the guilt, the fear. It's all there plainly written across my face. I can fucking feel it.

Wordlessly, he holds his arms open, patiently waiting for me to come to him when and if I need to. It's something that cracks my resolve, and I break down into harsh ugly sobs as I get up from my chair and race over to him. Seb catches me midair before clutching me to his chest like he will never let me go. Fuck, I hope he doesn't. I hope we are stronger than all of this. I hope we can make it out the other side.

"I missed you so fucking much, baby. I didn't want to leave, but I didn't want to hover, and I just needed to move. I needed to do something."

I nod into his chest as I cry harder. There is something about being cradled in this man's arms that makes me feel safe, protected, whole. Well, about as whole as I can feel when my chest feels like it's been broken to pieces. He has a way of taking all my broken pieces and making them fit a little bit better.

Seb pulls back just a bit before cupping my face with one of his hands and pressing his lips against mine. My body practically melts into his touch as his tongue flicks out and strokes gently against mine. The tightness that hasn't left my chest for hours slowly eases as Seb continues worshiping my mouth like he will never get the chance again.

"I love you so fucking much, Erica," he says as he pulls away slightly, pressing his forehead against mine as he closes his eyes like he is speaking from his soul. "You are everything to me."

"Everything?" I gasp softly.

His eyes open as he looks at me, the truth spelled out right before me.

"Everything."

I can't help but press my lips to his. We stand there wrapped up in each other for way too long before I finally slip out of his arms and land on my feet. Seb doesn't let me go that easy though, giving me one more quick kiss before speaking.

"Go get changed and then come back. I want to hold my girl."

I smile up at him before I nod and grab the bag he brought before I slip into the bathroom inside Trevor's room. I grab the pair of leggings, t-shirt and oversized sweatshirt that Seb brought and slip them on before I come back out. When I do, I see Seb staring down at Trevor with furrowed brows and a pained look across his face.

Quietly, I slip up beside him and take his hand, squeezing it softly as he looks down at me. His eyes are a little glossy which makes my heart clench. I hate that he is feeling the same pain that I am right now.

"We are going to be okay, right? We can make it through this?" I ask vulnerably.

He cradles my face gently as he nods.

"I can do fucking anything with you by my side, baby."

I smile before I respond but stop short when a noise that steals the breath from my lungs freezes the entire room in place. A soft groaning sound comes from the bed behind us. I whip my head around faster than you would think would be humanly possible. Trevor's left hand flexes just slightly but it is enough to send me flying across the room and over to my chair.

"Trev! Oh my god! Are you awake? Can you hear me?"

He makes another soft groan before his eyes slowly flutter open. It looks like it takes him a few minutes to clear the fog before he can fully take in the room around him. His eyes land on me also instantly, a soft smile touching his lips as his thumb faintly brushes against my hand that is white knuckling the sheets next to him. Holy shit. I never thought I would get to see that smile again. Relief washes over me like a long-awaited rain, slowly healing the wide cracked wounds that have been growing by the second.

"Hey, Little Red," his hoarse voice croaks.

"I'm so glad that you're okay. I was so worried."

His smile gets slightly confused as his eyes flick around the room, landing on Sebastian in the corner. To my surprise, there is no hostility in his gaze. No anger of any kind. Sebastian is watching him warily, concern and relief warring for dominance against his handsome face.

"Seb? What are you doing here? Wait. Where am I?" He asks, his head moving around slightly to take in more of the room before he winces.

"Don't move," I urge as I lean over him and hold his neck still, as if I could stop him from getting hurt with my hold alone. "You are in the hospital. You were in an accident."

"Shit, really? Were you with me?" He asks as his eyes move over me as if he is looking for any sign of injury.

I shake my head. "I wasn't in the car with you."

Because you were trying to drive away from me.

"Thank fuck. C'mere Little Red," he says as his left hand reaches up behind my head and pushes me until my lips are on his.

I tense immediately before I spring backwards just as Sebastian crosses the room and yanks me out of his grip, a look of fury on his face.

"What the fuck?" Seb practically snarls.

Trev blinks for a moment as his eyes flick between us.

"What? I can't kiss my girlfriend after I found out I was in a car accident?"

His girlfriend?

"Your girlfriend?" Seb asks with a raised brow, voicing my own thoughts.

Instead of answering his question, Trev's eyes flick over to me, that same adoring smile appearing again as he reaches his pinky out to link with mine. We haven't done that in years. It sends a strange pang through me as a million memories flash before my eyes. Slowly, I take a few measured steps until I am within reaching distance of Trev. He hooks our pinkies as he smiles up at me sweetly before turning to face Seb.

"Yeah. Erica, this is Sebastian, he is a freshman this year too. He's a tight end. Seb, this is Erica, my girlfriend."

Freshman? This year? Girlfriend?

What. The. Fuck.

CHAPTER THIRTY-ONE

SEBASTIAN

W hat. The. Fuck.

My eyes find Erica's immediately, the confusion and horror that is no doubt spread across my face pours off hers. What the fuck does he mean that Erica is his girlfriend? And that I'm a freshman this year, too?

A nurse walks in with her head down, looking over a chart when she looks up at us with a smile, pausing as she notices Trevor awake though looking a bit confused. Fuck, we all are.

"Oh good! You're awake. Mr. Michaels, do you know where you are?"

His eyes flick from me to Erica and back to the nurse.

"Uh, the hospital. My girlfriend said that there was an accident."

I fucking flinch at his casual tone. His girlfriend. If he wasn't laid up in a bed after a near death experience and he wasn't very clearly confused, I'd beat the piss out of him. The nurse casts Erica and I a slightly disapproving look. She was on shift when we first came in and no doubt saw Erica and me close. I can only imagine what she is thinking right now, I'm sure she has seen worse, though.

"That's right. Let me go grab the doctor and we will go over everything with you, okay?"

Trev nods softly before he looks up to Erica, still holding her fucking pinky as he smiles up at her like she is his goddamn sun

"Baby, can you call my parents? I'm sure they will shit a brick when they hear about this."

Baby. What the ever loving fuck is going on?

"Mr. Michaels! It's good to meet you. You had us worried for a minute there. I'm Dr. Chandler and I'll be-"

I cut him off, asking a question that has been bouncing around in my head over the last few minutes.

"Trev, man. What year is it?"

The doctor throws me a slightly irritated glare, but I could give a fuck. I watch him intently as he looks at me with a raised brow like I'm the one who has lost their mind.

"2015. Why?"

The room goes unearthly still. We all seem to freeze in place simultaneously before we start sharing nervous glances, not one person wanting to correct him. Soon, Dr. Chandler clears his throat as he turns to the nurse.

"Becky, can you please take Mr. Michaels vitals. I want to get him in for another scan just to make sure everything is progressing well. If I could have you two step out for a minute," he says as he looks at Erica and me.

We both nod as I turn to follow the doctor. Erica does too but not before Trevor pulls Erica towards him for a kiss. She narrowly turns her head, having his lips land on her cheek instead but the action is still enough to send my blood boiling. What the FUCK is going on?

When we get out to the hallway the doctor turns to face us as soon as the door has shut.

"What has he said since he woke up?"

Erica's panicked eyes find mine before they flick back to the doctor.

"Uhm. He introduced Sebastian to me like we have never met and then made comments about him being a freshman in college and...and that I was his girlfriend. We broke up two years ago. He is a junior in college. What's going on?"

I reach over and tuck Erica into my side, rubbing her arm comfortingly even if I am freaking the fuck out myself. I won't let her see it.

I glance behind me to look through the window into Trev's room. He is getting his blood pressure taken by nurse Becky, but his eyes are firmly on Erica and me, a confused furrow of his brows sitting firmly on his face. I grimace as I face forward. What a fucking cluster fuck.

"I'm not sure. Brain injuries are complicated, unpredictable. We'll take him in for another scan and see if we can see what happened. Most of the time, without serious indication of brain damage the memories come back eventually."

"And if they don't?" I ask.

The doctor gives me a sympathetic shrug as he shakes his head.

"Let's just get the scan done for now and go from there. In the meantime, try not to put any stress on him. We don't know anything for sure until we have all the facts."

Erica and I glance at each other, both seeming to read between the lines simultaneously. He doesn't have to say the words out loud. We all know what that means and I'm not sure how I'm going to fucking survive it.

CHAPTER THIRTY-TWO

ERICA

S wallowing over the grapefruit sized lump that has been permanently stuck in my throat since Trevor woke up, I blow out a ragged breath as I push through the door. I called Shannon and Jonathan after Trev went for his scan. Shannon burst into tears over the phone when I told her that he was awake but then fell speechless when I mentioned his missing memories.

Two years.

They said it would be an hour or two before the doctor would be in to go over the scans, and I have been pacing the hospital like a crazy woman, avoiding room 722 like the plague as I do. When I went to call Trev's parents, Sebastian took off for a walk so I think he is taking the space he needs too. How can Trevor be missing the last two years of his life? Two freaking years.

And it's all your fault.

Bile turns in my stomach, ready to come up at any moment. How am I supposed to look him in the eye and tell him that the reason he is in this position is because of me? Because of something I did. Because of my deceit and lies. Shit.

Screwing on a plastic smile, I step into the room as my eyes instantly fall on Trev. He is sitting upright, cradling his broken arm with a frown marred across his face. As far as I know, no one has corrected him about the year or anything else really so he is probably thinking about how he may never play college ball. Little does he know he was pulled in for the first game of his freshman year in the second quarter. With the first snap he got, he found the perfect gap and sent a bullet over thirty five yards that landed safely into the arms of a wide receiver who took the ball all the way to the end zone.

I was in the crowd for that game. Even though I was still heartbroken over our breakup, I wouldn't have missed that moment for anything. The jumbotron lit up with Trevor's face, and though you couldn't see much through his helmet and mouth guard, I saw it all. Pride. Happiness. Fulfillment. The fact that, that very special memory, along with countless others, is now gone shatters my heart to pieces.

He must feel my eyes on him because his head swivels and his frown falls away before he smiles. It's that heartwarming, toe curling smile that he used to give me when we were dating. *Because he thinks we still are.*

"Hey, Little Red. I was beginning to think you ran out on me," he teases.

I force myself to chuckle even if laughing is the last thing that I want to do right now.

"Just wanted to give you some privacy with your family," I shrug.

He cocks a disbelieving eyebrow as he shakes his head.

"My family? Baby, you are just as much my family as my parents. Get your sexy little ass over here and kiss all my boo-boos better," he smirks as he licks his lips salaciously.

"Trevor Anthony!" Shannon scolds as she covers her mouth and shakes her head disapprovingly, though she can't hide her smile well enough behind it.

Trev rolls his eyes with a slight smile as he shoots me a wink. He mouths to me, "Later."

I do my best to keep my smile in place, but every word mentioned, every familiar look cracks my heart wider and wider. I'm sure by the end of today there will be nothing left of the bruised and battered organ laying inside my chest.

Feeling awkward as hell, I shuffle towards him but stop when I'm at the end of the bed. Trev shoots me a confused look before he pats the bed next to him. My eyes flick over to Shannon and Jonathan who are both wearing matching smiles with pain filled eyes. Nodding to myself slightly, I step forward and perch myself onto the edge of the bed. Trev reaches his hand out to lace his fingers with mine as he squeezes it firmly.

"I'm okay, Little Red. You don't have to worry. I'm not going anywhere."

A choked sob slips out of my throat as I smile and shake my head at him. He is the farthest thing from okay. Leaning forward, I place a soft kiss against his cheek before pulling away and cupping his face.

"I was so worried about you."

He leans into my touch and gives me a warm smile.

"I know but as long as I have my family and you by my side, then nothing else matters."

Something inside of me twists at his words. I can't tell if it's a good feeling or a bad feeling. Maybe both. My mouth opens to say something, what I'm not too sure when a heavy knock comes from the doorway before a large set of shoulders barely slips through as he crosses the room, his eyes subtly flicking between Trevor and me. I pull back gently, a feeling of shame washing over me when Sebastian's eyes hold mine before he comes to stand at the foot of Trevor's bed.

"How you feeling, man?"

Trevor shrugs softly. "I'm alive. I appreciate you sticking around, means a lot."

"Of course."

Seb puts his hands in his pockets and nods, a mask of indifference on his face with only peeks of concern shining through.

"Coach is gonna be pissed," Trevor laughs sardonically as he gestures to his obliterated throwing arm. "Doc said I may never play ball again. I was really looking forward to being a Knight."

"You already are one, broken arm or not," Seb says.

A small smile touches Trevor's mouth as he nods before bringing up our still interlaced fingers and kissing the back of my hand. The way his eyes sparkle as they look over at me, the smile that matches it and the soft press of his lips against my skin sends a spark inside my lower stomach. It quickly fizzles, though when I realize that I'm sitting here holding hands with my ex-boyfriend, who still thinks that he is my boyfriend, while my now boyfriend, who is his best friend watches. What a fucking shit show.

My eyes flick over to see Sebastian watching us intently, his jaw clenched so tight I'm surprised he hasn't broken a tooth yet. I want to go to him and kiss him, to take his hand and reassure him that I am still his girl, but Trevor just needs me right now, he needs Sebastian too. Though, if he doesn't even remember his freshman year then the only memories that he likely has of Sebastian is of the days that he toured the campus and a few clinics the team did the summer before his freshman year.

The tension in the room begins to grow until it is nearly stifling. I don't know if everyone else can feel it or if it is just me, but I can't fucking breathe. I am just about to excuse myself from the room just so that I can catch my breath when Dr. Chandler walks in, a folder in his hand and the same nurse from before in tow. He smiles at everyone politely before he grabs one of the swivel stool chairs and scoots it towards the end of Trevor's bed before he speaks.

"We just got back your scans, and we didn't find any sign of long lasting damage or impact from the accident."

Though his words would normally be celebratory, the heavy tone he pairs it with has them falling flat and even Trevor picks up on it.

"Okay, that's good, right?"

Dr. Chandler meets eyes with each of us before turning back to Trevor and softening his voice.

"Trevor, what is the last thing you remember before the accident?"

Trevor's brows furrow and he sits there in silence for several moments before he answers.

"Erica and I went for Burgers and Shakes. We went to Clifton point that overlooks Grovebury and we..." he trails off for a moment before making eye contact with his parents and then me, tossing me a sly smirk and wink before facing the doctor. "Spent some time together," he censors not so subtly, causing me to cringe as I peek a glance up to Sebastian, who looks like he is ready to vibrate out of his body.

"After that, I was driving us home and then...nothing."

"Nothing after that? What day was that?" Dr. Chandler asks.

"I'm not really sure. It was on Saturday, right, baby?"

Trev asks me as I swallow roughly and nod. It's weird that I know what day he is talking about. I can see it vividly in my head, practically feel it. Trev had just come home that Friday from Brighton for the last clinic before he had to head to campus full time. That was the last full week we had together, and he took me out in his Camaro and promised he would love me forever. Little did I know he would break that promise not a week later. Then again, maybe he never did. He broke up with me sure but stopped loving me? I don't really think so, anymore.

"What month?" Dr. Chandler questions.

Trev looks at him funny but answers.

"August."

The doctor nods. "And the year."

Now Trevor looks at him like he is insane. "2015. Is this part of the neurological exam or something? I can also tell you my full name and what color panties my girlfriend was wearing last night."

"Trevor!" I scold on a surprised gasp as I lower my gaze, knowing better than to meet anyone's eyes in the room right now. He laughs lightly in response and squeezes my hand as Dr. Chandler continues.

"Trevor, sometimes when the brain is compromised in an injury, it can cause issues, specifically with short term memory. Though your scans are clear, I think we need to get a neuro consult done immediately."

Trevor nods, picking up on the serious note in his tone. His eyes move from his parents and then to Sebastian before landing on me.

"What's going on?" He asks, a slight tremble of panic in his tone.

"Sweetie," Shannon says softly, her voice breaking off with a gentle sob.

"It's 2017, Trev," I say gently, tired of everyone beating around the bush.

We all watch him closely as he looks at me, his eyes narrowed like he is waiting for the punch line of a joke. I fucking wish I was joking.

"What? What are you talking about? It's 2015. I just graduated and am about to start school at Brighton."

"No, man," Sebastian cuts in gently, only sympathy pouring through his words. "You already started your freshman year at Brighton, and your sophomore and your junior. We are juniors right now, and it's November 2017."

Trevor is staring at Sebastian like his words don't even make sense, like maybe Seb is speaking some kind of foreign language.

Then I see as it all clicks for him, panic floods his gorgeous blue eyes along with fear as he whips his head over to the doctor.

"I-I lost my memories? Two fucking years of them!" He near shouts with wide eyes.

I set my other hand on top of our clasped hands and rub gently.

"I'm so sorry, Trev," I say as tears begin to cloud my eyes.

"Baby, please don't cry. You know I can't take it when you cry," he says before he pauses for a moment and lowers his voice slightly, though not low enough. "Wait. Is that why you have been so distant. Did we...are we not together?"

The pain in his voice guts me. I am literally bleeding out in the middle of this room, and there is not a person in this hospital that can stop the flow. He watches me as if what I have to say next will determine everything. I do my best to give him a smile, but I know it looks more like a pained grimace as a tear runs down my cheek and I shake my head. Trevor's eyes begin to water as he leans his head back against his pillow and stares at the ceiling, seemingly taking in all of this information.

"What can be done?" Shannon asks.

"Well, I'm not neuro so I can't say for sure. There have been studies that show regular, non-strenuous exercise can actually stimulate the growth of new brain cells and improve memory and cognition. We could get you into some physical therapy since you will need it for your arm anyways. Other than that, routine is key. Getting back into your old routine is vital, sleeping in your bed, going to your classes, spending time with your friends. All that and just time, though I don't want to get your hopes up. There isn't too much that is certain when it comes to the brain. It is a very unpredictable thing."

Shannon's face falls, and I watch as Seb closes his eyes like the words devastate him as much as Trev. When Trevor brings his head back up to face the room, he nods at Dr. Chandler.

"Whatever you think, let's do it." Trevor pauses before he faces me, speaking to the room but never taking his eyes off me. "Can we talk? Alone?"

My heart thunders inside my chest as my stomach flips and definitely not in a good way. I send a panicked look to everyone in the room, hoping that someone will send me a life preserver, but they all watch on awkwardly, clearly feeling unsure as to how to proceed.

"Of course," Dr. Chandler says. "Keep in mind what I spoke with you about earlier. It's important that Trevor remains as stress free as possible until he gets back into a normal routine."

Shannon and Jonathan make their way out of the room along with Dr. Chandler and the nurse, leaving only Sebastian there, standing at the foot of the bed, though I don't think Trevor even notices because he is only looking at me as he speaks.

"What happened to us, Little Red?" Trevor asks, a hollowed note carrying in his words.

I shake my head softly as I give him a gentle smile.

"I don't think we should go into this, Trev. You heard the doctor, I don't think we should get into anything heavy, not today, at least."

Trevor, being the stubborn man that he is, doesn't accept this, though. He shakes his head at me as he speaks.

"No. I have to know. I just, I don't get it. The last thing I remember is us making love, me promising you that I would never stop loving you. Promising myself that I was going to marry you one day. When did we break up? Who broke up with who? How did it happen? Why? What the fuck is going on!" He rambles, each word becoming more and more panicked as he pulls his hand out of my grasp and runs his fingers through his hair.

"It doesn't matter. It's in the past, Trev."

"Not mine! It's my present or future. Fuck, I don't know. Where the fuck are we? Are we in Grovebury or Brighton?"

"Brighton," Sebastian chimes in. "You got hit by an oncoming truck just outside the dorms."

"Sebastian," I hiss, sending daggers at him as I do but he just ignores me as he watches Trev, no doubt looking for any spark of memory from that night, but his eyes just look confused and panicked.

"Fuck. When was this again?"

"Two days ago," I rasp before clearing my throat.

Trevor nods almost to himself. "Where do I live?"

"In a house just outside of campus, with me and Slater and Mikey. You don't remember them, do you?"

Trevor slowly shakes his head with his brows furrowed like he is desperately looking for the missing pieces in his mind but coming up short.

Sebastian gives him a sad nod and shrug. "We are all friends, best friends."

Trevor nods as if that piece of information is the first part that makes sense to him. He blinks slowly a few times as if the weight of the day is crushing down on him.

"That's enough for today. Let's let you get some rest," I say.

I go to stand up when Trevor grasps onto me for dear life, panic heavy in his eyes as he shakes his head.

"Don't go. Please, I just...I know you say we aren't together anymore, but I fucking feel it, right here," he says as he gestures towards his chest. "Can you just stay until I fall asleep at least, I," he pauses for a second as he flicks his eyes around almost nervously as he lowers his voice. "I don't want to be alone right now."

Pain flows through me once again as I nod softly.

"Of course, Trev."

He smiles gently at me before settling back into his pillow, still holding my hand as he closes his eyes. I glance to my side to see Sebastian staring down at our linked hands stoically for several seconds before he looks up at me, a heavy look passing between us before he turns on his heel and walks out the door.

Chapter Thirty-Three

Trevor

Two years. Two fucking years. Gone, just like that. One accident, one mistake that has changed my whole fucking life. Well, maybe not just the accident. Something had to have happened between Little Red and me, though I can't figure what the fuck it could have been. I mean, I have been feeling uneasy about being so far away from her for so long and sure I had the brief thought about us taking a break until she came to Brighton with me but then I was gone for a week and missed her so fucking bad I knew I couldn't do it.

On Friday before the team was heading back home for the last week of summer before move-in day, some of the guys decided to hit an off-campus party. I was going to skip it, but some of the other guys talked me into it, convinced me that it was a good bonding opportunity and a chance for the upperclassmen to see us as equals and not some walk on freshmen. It was fun to hang out with the guys and there were some gorgeous girls there, seriously fucking gorgeous.

One of the girls, Cindy or something like that, was all over me. We danced for a few songs, and it was a good time until she tried to kiss me. It was like a bucket of water had been dumped over my head and shook me from whatever haze the cheap beer and hope to impress had over me. I shook out of the girls hold and drove all the way home.

When I got into Grovebury at the early hours of the morning, I snuck over to Erica's house and into her bed. As soon as my arms wrapped around her, I knew that I was home. Just the smell of her set me at ease and I knew that I was so fucking stupid for even dancing with another woman. Little Red was all I would ever need. So maybe I wasn't all she would ever need. Did she break up with me? Because I was going away? Or did I do something? Did she? Fuck, no. She'd never do anything to hurt me or us. Neither would I but something had to have happened, and I'm going to find out what and fucking fix it.

Losing football is a huge heartbreaker. I love the game and I have been looking forward to playing college ball my whole life, but in the back of my head I always knew my family wouldn't be happy with me playing professionally. My dad wants me to take over the business one day so I guess I figured I would enjoy playing for as long as I could before I had to start work with my dad. But losing Erica? Un-fucking-acceptable.

The doctor seems adamant that no one gives me too much information at once, they don't want to stress me out, send me into a mental break down, like being trapped in this hospital bed isn't doing that very fucking thing. It's been three days since I woke up and found out that my world tipped on its axis. I haven't gotten virtually anything else out of anyone other than what Sebastian and Erica told me that day. But I'm getting discharged today and much to my parents' irritation, I am choosing to listen to the doctor to go back to Brighton. I want to go and see my bed and my classes and my girl. Because she is my girl. Erica Pembrooke has been mine since I first set eyes on her, and no one and nothing is going to get in the way of that.

Chapter Thirty-Four

Sebastian

I park the car and blow out a breath as my hands practically strangle my steering wheel. How the fuck did shit get so twisted so fast? How the fuck did all of this happen? I knew that when Trevor found out about Erica and me it wasn't going to be pretty, but did I know that he would drive away in such a rage he would forget his seatbelt, get hit by a truck and hit his head so fucking hard that he forgot the last two years of his life? Fuck no.

When Trevor woke up, I could have collapsed with relief but as soon as he looked up at Erica with stars in his eyes, more vivid and bright than even I had seen before, I knew something was wrong. Then when I saw her looking at him with a new level of adoration that I most definitely had not seen before, I thought I was going to be sick. My fucking gut twisted, and my chest clenched painfully tight as they clung to each other like they were long lost lovers. I guess they are. So, where the hell does that leave me?

I haven't been by the hospital over the last few days though I know Erica hasn't left his side longer than a few minutes at a time. I would have been there, but I had football and classes and honestly, I didn't feel needed or wanted. Being in a room with those two is like being in the audience at a movie, like you aren't even in the same reality as them. And it fucking hurts.

Erica and I talked a little after Trevor fell asleep when we told him about his memory. She was able to find a charger and we texted for a while. She apologized if her being there for Trevor hurt me and of course I lied and assured her that I understood, which I do, but the lie was that it didn't bother me. It really did. A fucking lot. She promised to call me soon so that we could talk more, but that was three days ago, and my phone has been fucking silent until this morning. They got word that Trev was getting discharged and that he wanted to go home to the house. *Glad I'm useful for something, I guess.*

Blowing out a rough breath I open my door and slam it shut, doing my best to lose the tension in my shoulders but not succeeding. I know this is a delicate situation, I know that we can't stress him out, it's our fucking fault he is in this position in the first place. Still, though. I can't stand him looking at my girlfriend, touching my girlfriend like she is his, like she belongs to him. Haven't we been through this shit? I claimed her, she agreed. She is fucking mine, and my patience is about run out and we haven't even gotten back to campus yet. If she wasn't my fucking world, I would throw in the towel and say she wasn't worth it, but she is. She is worth fucking everything.

I make my way through the hospital and pause outside Trevor's room before I blow out a deep breath and roll out my shoulders as I step inside. When I do, I find Trevor standing just in front of a wheelchair with Erica holding him up around his waist as she helps him into it. They are both laughing about something as Trevor eases into the chair.

"I can't wait for Nurse Erica's undivided attention for the next six to eight weeks," Trevor smirks.

Erica rolls her eyes and shakes her head as she steps behind the wheelchair.

"I will so ditch you if you refer to me as Nurse Erica. Seriously, Trev. That's just ick."

He leans his head back so that he can see her better as he laughs and gives her a wink. Gritting my jaw in irritation I do my best to push down the anger inside of me as I step inside further.

"Heard some bum needed a ride."

Trevor looks over and sees me, a happy yet guarded smile on his face. It's a tiny reminder that I know him, but he doesn't know me, not really. It surprises me how much it bothers me that he doesn't remember our friendship, or at least the majority of it.

Erica smiles at me and the sight instantly melts away some of the tension that I have been carrying inside my chest for the last few days. It's one full of happiness, excitement and what looks like love. Her eyes practically shine from across the room as she looks at me, her glossy red hair falling softly over her shoulders. Fuck. I love this woman.

"Thanks, man. You didn't have to do that. I could have found a ride to the place."

I roll my eyes. "Bro, we're best friends, it's whatever."

Trev's unfamiliarity seems to ease for a minute as he gives me a grateful smile and a nod. I'm sure he is tripping the fuck out. I can't imagine losing several years of my life, even if some of them are better off forgotten in the past, at least it's my choice to push that stuff away. Trev got them ripped away.

Because of you.

Shaking my head, I walk over and take Erica's place to push Trev, squeezing her hand as she passes me. She sends me a sweet smile and wink before she walks ahead of us and out the door.

"Where did your parents go?" I ask as I wheel him down the hallway.

"They went home, begrudgingly. I guess finding out your son lost his memory of the last few years makes you overbearing as hell," he draws with a sarcastic chuckle.

I scoff and shake my head because only Trev would make light of something like this. It doesn't escape my notice as we go that Trevor's head swivels every time Erica takes a turn, his eyes practically burning holes into her ass cheeks. I take a corner sharper than I probably should of, jostling Trevor in the process.

"Fuck," he grumbles as he cradles his casted arm.

"Sorry," I offer coolly as we finally make it out the doors of the hospital. A nurse is there ready to take the wheelchair from us and with a wave, I help Trevor stand up, slipping an arm around his side as I walk them over to my car.

I pull out my keys and hit the unlock button as I open the back passenger door. Trevor slides in carefully before scooting over to the driver's side. I go to shut the door when Erica sneaks in after him, taking the seat next to him as she takes out a wadded up sweatshirt from her bag and places it in her lap before resting his casted arm on it. Trev gives her a sweet smile that makes me fucking nauseous before I slam the door and storm around the car to get into the driver's seat.

It doesn't take us long to get to campus, mainly because I sped the whole way. I couldn't help sneaking glances in the mirror to see what was so fucking funny. They laughed and whispered practically the whole ride and when I would catch a glimpse of them their heads were bent together, secretive smiles on their faces as they laughed like they were having the time of their lives. It was like I was chaperoning a couple of teenagers on their first fucking date, and to be honest, it's kinda bullshit.

We get out of the car and make our way up to the house. Erica and I both watch Trev like a hawk as we go up the stairs, looking for any flicker of recognition but he seems to be scoping the place out, a lot like he did the first time we looked at it. I told Mikey and Slater that Trevor was coming home today and about his memory. The look they gave me was filled with pure pity, and it made my skin fucking crawl. The doc said we had to ease Trevor into his life around here, so I told the guys to make sure the house was empty today and based on how quiet it is as we step through the door, I think they thankfully listened.

Trevor is looking around at the hallway when Slater comes barreling downstairs, Mikey on his heels.

"Trevor man! What the fuck is up?" Slater hollers with a wide smile as he brings him in for a bro hug, careful of his injured arm.

He smiles at him and nods. "Doing alright. What's your name, bro?"

Slater's smile falters as he looks over to Mikey before slapping back on that smile again.

"I'm Slater. Best running back this team has ever seen. You're welcome," he teases.

Trevor lets out a laugh and shakes his head and turns to Mikey.

Mike clears his throat as he nods and fist bumps Trev.

"Mikey. Linebacker."

"I can tell," Trevor says as his eyes flick over Mikey dramatically, causing all of us to laugh.

It eases some of the tension in the room and the hurt that Slater and Mikey are trying to hide. It isn't Trev's fault that he doesn't remember them. They are a year younger than us, so Trev doesn't remember meeting them our sophomore year.

The laughter slowly dies down and an awkward silence falls over the room before Erica speaks.

"Do you want a tour?" She asks.

Trevor looks at her with a smile and a nod.

"You know your way around here?"

She nods and shrugs before she starts walking him through the house. Meanwhile I stay behind, tracking their every movement as Trevor takes every opportunity to lean into her, to touch her. And she isn't stopping him. She isn't pushing him away. I know that he is injured, and we have to ease him into life and all that shit but the caveman in me just sees my girlfriend staying within two steps of a man who had confessed to me that he wanted her more than he wanted to fucking live. Obviously, that hasn't changed much. And I'm fucking pissed.

CHAPTER THIRTY-FIVE

ERICA

"So, that is Slater's room, Mikey's is next to his, Sebastian's is across the hall and this one is yours," I say as I open the door to Trevor's room.

When we step inside, I notice that even though the place looks the exact same as the last time I was in it, nothing else is the same. Everything has changed now. There are clothes strewn out across the floor, his bed rumpled and unmade and a few textbooks stacked on the desk in the corner. Typical Trevor.

"Damn. I need to hire a maid or something," Trevor teases, obviously reading where my clean freak brain is at.

I laugh lightly. "Or you could do this crazy thing called picking up after yourself?"

His eyebrows raise in surprise with a playful smile on his face.

"Ohhh, she's got jokes. Alright, alright. Point taken, killer."

I smile at him and shake my head as I go to continue showing him around, but he catches my hand with his and stops me in place. Cocking my head to the side slightly I turn to Trev who has lost his teasing smile and is now looking at me seriously.

"Little Red," he says so softly it's almost a whisper as he reaches out and hooks his pinky with mine yet again. "What happened to us?"

"Trev," I sigh with a shake of my head. "Not now, please."

"I gotta know," he says as he takes a step forward. "I gotta know what happened and how I can fix us."

"There is nothing to fix, Trev. We are still great friends, best friends. Just nothing more."

"I want more, though," he says as he closes the distance between us, wrapping his arm around my lower back as he does and pulling me into him.

"Erica, I need more with you. I know that you say we have been just friends and all, but I know deep in my soul that I wouldn't have been okay with it. I can hardly be in the same room with you without wanting to take you into my arms and never fucking let you go. The last thing I remember is having an amazing night and promising you and myself that you were my forever. That we were forever. So, what happened?"

My throat begins to constrict as tears well up my eyes at the memory. His words are so raw and honest, so pain filled and determined. It hurts to think about how he is feeling, waking up to this virtually new life and everything he thought he knew has changed. A tiny part of my long ago broken heart begins to heal at his words too, craving to hear why he did what he did two years ago.

"You broke us," I whisper on a ragged exhale.

I glance up to see Trevor wince like he'd been slapped as shame and devastation play across his face. He shakes his head solemnly.

"Why?"

I shrug and try to pull out of his hold but he only clings to me harder when I do, like a child desperate for comfort and so I give it to him.

"You were going to college, and you were worried about the distance between us. You didn't admit it at the time, but I think you wanted to experience the full college experience with no ties, and I get that now. But back then, it damn near destroyed me.

"We stayed in close contact for a few weeks but then our daily calls became weekly and then monthly and then we really only saw each other over break. We needed the breakup to find who we were without each other. You have been my other half since I was ten years old, Trev. I needed to become a whole person and so did you. It was for the best in the end."

"And now?" He asks gently, his face ducking down slightly until his mouth is only a few inches away from mine.

The familiar smell of Trevor, the strong hold of being in his arms and the look of complete devotion and love in his eyes has muddled my brain practically useless. My heart is thundering in my chest as the weight of our past washes over me all the love, heartache, lust, passion. Everything slams into me at once like a tsunami wave. My eyes flick over his face as my head is playing his words over and over in my head, knowing that I need to respond but for some reason, I can't open my mouth. I'm frozen in place just staring at Trev.

"Now, she has to go home," a deep voice rumbles from behind us.

As if a fog has suddenly cleared, I quickly turn around and pull out of Trevor's hold to see a very pissed off Sebastian. His fists are clenched at his side, balled up so tight they look like the bone will start peeking through the skin soon as his near murderous gaze burns a hole in me. Shame fills me instantly. What the hell is wrong with me? If I would have just found Sebastian in his ex's arms like that, memory loss or not, I would be livid too. I didn't mean to, I just got caught up and...shit.

"Now?" Trevor questions, irritation clear in his voice.

"Now," Sebastian grits between clenched teeth, the single word coming out with such finality, I quickly walk out the room and past Sebastian.

I don't stop there, though. Keeping my head down I walk down the stairs and out the front door without so much as a backwards glance. I am practically power walking towards my dorm when a tingling sensation pricks at the back of my neck. A feeling I only ever get when one person is around. Knowing that he is following me, I pick up my pace. I don't want him to look at me with the disgust and anger that I know he will. I have enough of that aimed at myself for the both of us.

Just when I am going around a corner and coming up on the quad, a thick arm bands around my stomach and hauls me back into a hard chest. I let out a short gasp as I am basically drug/carried over to the grassy section of the walkway behind a tree. My back pushes against the bark of the tree before a large body cages me in, one hand cupping my jaw almost too tightly as he tilts my head up to face him.

When I do, I find the normally soft melted brown color gone as a deep black takes its place. His nostrils are flaring steadily like he is trying to control his breathing and his body is visibly shaking.

"What. The. Fuck. Was. That?" He practically growls each word, taking a deep breath with each word.

I open my mouth to speak but nothing comes out. Tears quickly cloud my vision before one spills down my cheek. Sebastian's eyes track the tear, but he makes no move to catch it like he normally would. Something inside of me cracks at that.

"Nothing," I whisper shakily, doing my best to steady my voice. "H-he asked how we broke up and why and I told him. He wanted to know so-"

"So, he could fix it, I fucking heard," Sebastian snaps. "I also heard him ask if you two being split was for the best now and I heard fucking crickets on your fucking end. So, please, Erica. Enlighten me. I'm a little fucking confused to hear that *my* fucking girlfriend isn't sure how to tell another man that she doesn't see herself with him, unless of course she does but is too chicken shit to say it to my fucking face!" He seethes.

A chill runs down me at his words and I know that I visibly pale. He has never spoken to me like this, ever, but it's not the words he is saying that hit me hard. It's the fear in his eyes, the betrayal, the hurt.

"Seb," I whisper brokenly as I reach up a hand and cup his cheek. "I love *you*. I'm *your* girlfriend. You are the *only* man I want to be with, I promise. I'm sorry that I didn't correct him right away, I don't know why I didn't, honestly. This is all a lot, for all of us. But it wasn't right. I have been so focused on being there for Trevor, but I haven't been there for you. I'm so sorry."

He stays quite for several seconds, his eyes watching me steadily as if to detect any hint of deceit or a lie before that vibrating in his body slows.

"I won't be anyone's second choice, Erica. If you want him, you better fucking let me go."

"I don't," I say quickly, shaking my head. "I love Trevor. I always will but not the way I love you, Seb."

We are silent for a few moments as we just stare at each other, hiding behind this tree like it can shield us from the world if we let it.

"Do...do you want to let me go?" I ask dejectedly as my eyes begin to fall to the ground.

"Fuck no," he barks. "But I won't fight for someone who doesn't want me. You have to choose me fully or I have to walk away."

I nod. "I choose you, fully, always."

Sebastian lets out a near feral growl as he dives down and slams his mouth down on mine. Butterflies fill my stomach, and my entire body instantly lights up from his touch. His hands go to my hips before quickly yanking down my jeans until they are at my ankles. I glance around us and see a few people walking through the quad towards the dorms.

"Seb, not here!"

He crouches down at my feet, his hands on my jeans as his eyes pin me into place.

"Step."

"But-"

"Step," he demands.

Flicking another look around us, I quicky step out of my pants and panties as Sebastian quickly slips them off my legs before backing me up against the tree again, palming my ass before lifting me up before pressing his body against me. With one hand, he undoes his pants and frees himself just before he drives into me. My mouth opens on a silent moan, but I don't dare make a noise when I hear a loud group of people walking not twenty feet away.

Sebastian's thrusts are brutal, near punishing, and they have my body buzzing with pleasuring. When I look down, I see that his eyes are pinned on me, his face not showing the amount of pleasure that I know mine do. I realize then that this isn't about having sex or making love or any of that. This is about him claiming me, taking what is undoubtedly his. My pussy spasms at the thought as he drives into me deeper.

"You're mine, Erica. Fucking all mine. No one will ever make you feel like I can. No one can make this pussy tingle or your body ache just right. No one will be able to fuck you until you can't even speak your own name but make you beg for more. That's just me, and I'm all fucking yours."

I arch into his hold as I throw my head back.

"Fuck. Yes, Seb. All of it. All of that. I'm yours. You're mine. Just us."

He lets out an appreciative growl as his pace quickens before he reaches a hand down between us and rubs my clit in a few quick strokes that has me coming so hard I have to slam my hand over my mouth to stop it. Seb follows right behind me, sinking his teeth into my neck harder than ever before as warmth floods me, his dick pulsing and jerking inside of me as he coats every inch of me.

When he pulls his head out of the crook of my neck, he leans his damp forehead against mine, breathing heavily as he does. I still see the doubt and fear heavy in his eyes, and it breaks my heart that I have done anything to make him feel unsure in our relationship. I'm just trying to fix what we broke.

I love Trevor and because of Sebastian and I, his life is now changed forever in one of the most extreme ways. The guilt I feel combined with the sweet words and declarations from Trevor had me a little distracted, I'll admit. But this right here is everything. Sebastian is my everything, and he is right to want me all to himself. He deserves it. I just need to pull back from Trevor to do that and I can. I think.

Chapter Thirty-Six

Trevor

Before I know it, several weeks have gone by. I've been going to my classes, which aren't too hard and helping out at practice with what I can and going to the games. Obviously with my fucked up arm there is only so much I can do, but it's nice to be a part of the team.

I was the starting quarterback so from what Sebastian and Slater said, the team has had some growing pains getting used to the new QB, but he is doing damn good. Unfortunately, there seemed to be some kind of rift in the balance of the team and the season ended earlier than anyone anticipated. No one said it out loud, but I knew that it was partly because of me. The quarterback is the backbone of a team, and when you lose your starter three quarters of the way through a season, it throws everything off.

I'm not sure if I should feel honored that I was such an integral part of such a talented group of guys or like absolute fucking shit because my accident cost a lot for all of us. Some guys won't get the scouting exposure they were hoping for now because of the short season but there is always the NFL Combine to get picked up. Unfortunately for me, it looks like even if I was invited, I couldn't go. Not this year at least. As much as I'd love to play pro ball one day, it's not my main focus. I only have one of those right now.

Erica and I have hung out a lot since I got discharged from the hospital, but it isn't enough for me. I want her every day, every hour, every fucking minute. When she does come over, she usually hangs out in the living room with all of us, and we either watch film or whatever is on tv. She usually stays until dark and every time Sebastian walks her home before I can offer. I thought about walking with them too but thought it looked a little desperate.

I'm not an idiot. It's plain as day that Sebastian wants her, and based on the looks that I have seen her give him, she wants him too. Maybe they are even together, that won't stand in my way, though. I just need to remind her of how amazing our relationship is, or was, whatever. I know she still feels something for me, I can feel it. Like the day she brought me home, I was two seconds away from kissing her and there wasn't a doubt in my mind that she would have let me. Then fucking Sebastian Caldwell walked in and took her away.

Everyone tells me that Sebastian and I were tight as fuck, brothers practically, but honestly, I don't really see it. Yeah, we hit it off when we toured the school together. I also really liked the guy by the end of the summer clinics that we did together, but since I woke up in that hospital bed, I kinda fucking hate the guy.

Maybe it's because he is a constant reminder of a supposed friendship that is now lost, maybe it is because he is so goddamn broody all the time or maybe it's because he is clearly fucking the woman of my fucking dreams. My woman. Yeah, I'm not a fucking fan of the guy.

Today I know for a fact that Sebastian had to go to some meeting with a professor, so I invited Erica over. Getting her alone lately has been a fucking bitch. When the door sounds with a soft knock, my heart picks up and anticipation buzzes through me before I walk up to the door and open it. Erica smiles up at me before coming in for a hug. I waste no time scooping her into my arms and burying my head into her neck before inhaling deeply. She smells the same. She smells like home.

When she begins to wriggle, I reluctantly let her go and take a step back. Her previous smile seems a bit strained now, and I can tell that my overly enthusiastic hug has made her uncomfortable. I'm not really sure why but I'm sure it has something to do with Sebastian fucking Caldwell.

"Come on in, Little Red. You want a water?"

She smiles and nods. "Thanks Trev. What are you up to?"

I walk over to the kitchen and grab a water bottle before handing it to her.

"I was just working on a statistics project that is due next week. Class is fucking brutal."

She wrinkles her nose up and nods. "I know the feeling. Some of my classes literally kill me just to stay awake. Has anything come back yet?" She asks me hesitantly, just like she does anytime my memory is brought up.

I frown and shake my head softly, causing her face to droop and shoulders sag.

"No change."

"I'm so sorry, Trev," she whispers as her eyes trace over me.

I shrug. "Not your fault, Little Red. Shit happens. I'm just trying to look at it like a new opportunity. A second chance, you know."

She nods. "That's a really healthy way to look at it."

I let out a hollow laugh as I nod. "That's what the expensive as fuck counselor my parents hired said too."

"They care," she says with a soft smile and a nod of her head.

"Yeah, they do. C'mon. I was just about to turn on The Exorcist," I say as I start walking towards the living room.

"Fuck THAT! You know I hate scary movies, Trev."

I send her a smirk and a wink before I pick up the remote. I honestly didn't expect her to practically tackle me in the process. We fall backwards, bouncing onto the couch cushion. I do my best to spin us but with only one functional arm it's a little useless and I end up more landing on my back then anything. Erica lands on top of my lap, each leg on either side of me as she reaches for the remote. Her tits press against my face as she does her best to reach for my outstretched hand while my legs lock her down and I'm not fucking mad about it.

She continues wiggling on top of me, inching her way closer to the remote when her pussy rubs against my cock. It was hard the moment I saw Erica but now that she has been rubbing up against my lap, I'm hard as a fucking steel pipe. Instantly, she stills, her eyes flicking down to me where she realizes that she is basically suffocating me with her tits, again, not complaining.

Immediately, she tries to leap up off my lap, but I don't let her. My legs keep hers pinned to me as I drop the remote and use my one good arm to wrap around her waist, pinning her flush against me. I don't miss the barely audible whimper that slips out of her mouth when my cock pushes against her again. She must not have meant to make the noise because her eyes instantly go wide with horror as she holds up a hand to cover her mouth.

"Trevor, let me up. Please."

She goes to push away from me, but I roll my hips, rubbing against her again.

"Do you remember the first time you crawled on top of me, Little Red? I took you to the lookout on the coast in my Camaro. You were wearing that pretty blue dress that made your eyes practically sparkle," I say softly, watching as the look in Erica's eyes shift, like she is lost in the past. God knows I am.

"It was one of our first official dates and when I put the car in drive you were blushing like a tomato. I knew you were nervous, but I knew I had to touch you, to feel you against me so I linked your pinky with mine and gently guided you over to me."

I smirk as I hold her a little closer, lifting my hips up again just enough to brush against her, causing her to let out a shallow shuddering breath.

"You fumbled a little to get over the console but once you fell into my lap it was like you had done it a thousand times," I whisper as I move against her again.

She doesn't make a sound, but I can see she is as wrapped up in this memory as I am. I can see it all. I see the way her nipples strain against her bra, the way her breathing has picked up and not slowed down once since she fell on top of me. She is turned on. She wants me, and I want her more than any fucking thing.

Slowly unwinding my arm from her hips, I trace my fingertips up her side, brushing just the side of her full breasts before drawing a lazy path over her collarbone and up her neck. She doesn't move a muscle as my fingers stop their ascent, my thumb pulling at her full bottom lip gently. Fuck. Why does it feel like I can still taste those lips even though it's been god knows how long since I have actually had them?

Erica swallows roughly as she stays on top of me before she clears her throat and shakes her head, essentially shaking herself out of our little memory cocoon.

"Trevor, you need to let me up," she says a little firmer this time.

My thumb continues tracing over her lips as I cock my head slightly. I'm not ready to give up that easy. She feels this between us, she just needs to let herself.

"Is that what you want, Little Red? What you truly want?" I ask as I roll my hips more subtly this time.

Her body stays plastered to me the entire time and tells me what her mouth won't.

"Trevor–"

Lifting up to keep her pressed against me once more, I cut her off as I speak.

"Little Red, please. Just listen to me, listen to yourself. You still want me. You still love me. I know it. I can fucking feel it. What I don't understand is why you won't let yourself fall? It's okay. I'll catch you, always."

She shakes her head but doesn't say anything.

"No? No, what?" I ask.

"I don't love you, Trevor. Not like that. Not anymore."

I rub against her again, trying to help prove my point.

"Bullshit. You may have yourself convinced but you don't fool me. Now tell me the real reason."

Those beautiful eyes I love so much look down at me with so many warring feelings I don't even know how to read them all.

"I'm attracted to you, Trevor. That's all this is but I am in love with someone else."

I blink at the verbal blow she just served me, and she takes my momentary pause to pull out of my hold, moving to stand and taking several steps away as she does. I lean forward to sit up, my cock harder than it's ever been in its life as I do. I don't bother trying to hide it and she doesn't hide the few glances she does down to my visible bulge before she speaks again.

"I love someone else, Trev. Before your accident, we talked about this, you said you were happy for me. You said that you would support me so that you wouldn't lose me in your life."

I grit my jaw in irritation as I hear her say those fucking words again.

"Well, maybe I was lying. Maybe I wasn't happy for you because I'm sure as shit not right now."

Erica raises a brow and crosses her arms. "Well, that's incredibly selfish of you."

I shake my head and wipe a hand down my face as I stand up and go to stand in front of her. Like a spooked animal though, she back tracks a few steps. I pause in place as I speak.

"That's not what I meant. You know I want your happiness above anything else. I just think you aren't considering all options."

"I have," she assures me.

"Then what is this?" I say, gesturing between us.

Uncertainty fills her eyes before she grimaces and shakes her head.

"Leftover chemistry from an incredible relationship and an even better friendship that spans almost a decade. I had the choice to pick you, Trevor, and I didn't. I chose him."

Her words are like a physical blow, knocking the wind out of me and punching a hole straight through my heart. It doesn't take a genius to know who the fuck she is talking about.

"Sebastian?" I practically spit.

Her eyes widen with horror and a little bit of excitement.

"You remember?" She whispers.

I screw my face up. "Remember? What? No, I see the way he watches you, the way he watches me when I'm near you and the way you are with him. I may have gotten hit in the head, but I'm not fucking stupid."

Disappointment floods her features as she hangs her head.

"I'm sorry, Trev. I don't want to hurt you, but at the end of the day, you and I are best as friends. We just work better like that. Sebastian he, he gives me something that I never knew I was missing but always knew I wanted."

"And what's that?" I ask a little too coldly.

She gives me a sad smile and shrugs. "That little extra. The little extra bit that makes you feel like you've slammed three espressos back to back just when you make eye contact. That little bit that makes his touch light up my entire body like a Christmas tree. The little extra that tells me he would do anything and everything just to see me happy."

"I would too," I defend as my chest begins to squeeze, panic settling inside of me as I watch her face close off from me more and more by the second.

Erica nods but doesn't say anything more. We stand there in a stare off for several long seconds before she turns and leaves without another word. The loud clunk that sounds when the door shuts behind her squeezes my heart before rage fills me. I pick up the closest thing to me, which happens to be an empty beer bottle before I throw it against the wall, shattering it into a million pieces as I do.

Fuck Sebastian Caldwell.

CHAPTER THIRTY-SEVEN

SEBASTIAN

Once I wrap up with Professor Andrews, I send Erica a text before I make my way to her dorm. Now that the season is over, I have a lot more free time and almost every second of that has been spent with Erica. An annoying amount of that time has been spent with Trevor as well.

I don't know what it is, but he seems different. Maybe I don't really remember what he was like when we were first becoming friends or maybe it is all the trauma that goes along with losing your memory but either way things feel off between us. When I try to talk to him, he keeps things short and to the point. There is no lighthearted teasing or casual conversation. It fucking sucks.

Someone walking into the building lets me in, and I head upstairs and to Erica's door. Palmer opens the door after I knock, a surprised smile on her face as she steps to the side.

"Hey Seb."

"Hey," I say as I look around the room. "Where is Erica?"

She walks over to grab her purse as she shrugs. "I don't know. I just stopped by to swap out my clothes. I'm heading back over to Ethan's. I'll see ya," she says as she waves and head out the door.

Furrowing my brows, I glance down at my phone to see that she hasn't read my text yet. Granted, we didn't make any plans for today, but it isn't really needed, it's just become a habit that we spend all of our time together. I take a seat on her bed and scroll through my phone. Five minutes go by, then ten, then twenty before I hear the door handle jiggle.

I sit up as Erica quickly steps inside the room, slamming the door shut before startling when she sees me.

"Seb! What are you doing here? You scared me."

Her breathing is labored, like she ran here from wherever she was. There is also a hint of something that I can't quite pin down. Fear? Panic? I slowly stand as I look down at her.

"I texted you. Everything okay?"

"Oh. Sorry. I haven't checked it."

I shrug. "What were you up to?"

She pauses before she glances at her feet for a moment until her eyes meet mine again.

"I was hanging out with Trevor."

Instantly, I'm put on edge. It isn't necessarily her words, I'm not *that* insecure. There is something in her tone, something hesitant, something uneasy that sends my stomach twisting in knots and pricks against my skin.

"And?" I ask, doing my best to remain calm.

She swallows as she blows out a breath and looks up to me.

"And we talked. He wanted me to give us another chance."

Fuck. I feel a case of de ja vu coming on.

"We were just messing around, fighting over the remote and I fell on his lap. He didn't let me get up and he kinda grinded against me as he asked me to let myself fall for him."

My vision blurs. Despite my best effort to keep my head on, I nearly lose my fucking shit right then and there. Are you fucking kidding me? Brain injury or not, I don't give a fuck. I'm gonna kill the little fuck. Then again, sounds like she didn't put up much of a fight, which is honestly fucking worse.

"What then? Did you fuck him?"

Her eyes shoot open wide as she frantically shakes her head.

"No! Oh my god, no. Sebastian, of course not!"

"Kiss him?"

She shakes her head rapidly once again.

"So, what? I had some shit to take care of and you decided to go hang out with my roommate, my best friend, your ex-boyfriend that doesn't fucking remember that you guys broke up and dry hump a little?"

Tears well up in her eyes as she shakes her head.

"No. It wasn't like that. I told him that I don't love him, not like that. I told him that I loved someone else. He guessed that it was you. Said that he could tell that something was going on between us."

That doesn't surprise me. I haven't exactly tried to be subtle because I'm honestly sick and fucking tired of all the lies and sneaking. It also explains his shitty attitude towards me. I stare at Erica, looking for any trace of deceit but find none. I know that she still loves Trevor, but I believe her, I don't think she is in love with him. I do think that all of this shit has fucked with her head and the more time she spends with Trevor the more muddled her mind becomes.

"If nothing else happened, why tell me? You had to of known how pissed I would be, at him and you."

She flinches at my words but nods as she raises her head.

"Because I love you, Seb. I don't want there to be any secrets between us."

Her words do something to me. I have some shit that I haven't talked to her about, but I wouldn't necessarily call them secrets. Just pieces of my past that I would like to stay in the past. I've tried to open up about it more times than I can count, but it's just not in my nature.

I nod as I stuff my hands in my pockets.

"How did he take all that? About as well as the first time?" I practically sneer.

Shaking her head, she shrugs. "I don't really know. I got out of there fast. I can't do this anymore though, Seb. I love you so fucking much. I want to be with you. It's even harder than before because now Trevor doesn't even remember us being broken up, he doesn't remember that his life was fine before I came to Brighton. The guilt I feel is fucking crushing, and I can't lie that old feelings have been brought up. In the end though, none of them come even close to what we have. As much as it hurts me to say, I just can't be there for him. I need space before I lose the best thing in my life," she says, tears streaming down her face as her sobs take over, her breathing coming in choppy and cut off.

I wait until she is finished before I cross the room and wrap her into my arms. When I do, she falls apart even more, sobbing uncontrollably as she balls her hands up in my sweatshirt and lets out all of the heartache and struggles that she has been feeling over the last several weeks. I know she needs this right now and there isn't a place I'd rather fucking be. I knew shit was going to get complicated from the moment Trevor woke up. But complicated isn't going to keep me away from my woman.

"It's fine, baby. I know it's hard. It's hard for me too. I just have to know that when all of this is over, you'll still be by my side."

"Always," she sniffs as her eyes come up to meet mine.

I cup her wet cheeks softly before I bring my lips down to hers. Gently, I move my lips over hers, not ravaging her mouth like I often do but instead savoring her, treasuring the feel of her lips on mine. When we break apart, I wipe some stray tears away from her face as I give her an encouraging smile.

"Want me to order some food?"

She nods with a sniffle. "Chinese, please."

"You got it," I say as I give her one more peck before pulling out my phone and tapping in our order.

Erica moves over to her closet, taking her shirt off before setting it in her dirty hamper. When she opens the closet door, a painting falls out, before another and then another, and soon the floor is littered with Erica's incredible pieces, all of which are being shoved into the back of a college dorm room closet instead of on display like they deserve.

I cross the room and begin helping her lean them all back up carefully.

"Have you heard back from Alexandra Campo about your portfolio?" I ask.

Erica cringes as she leans a piece up against the wall.

"No."

"No?" I question. "That surprises me. She seemed really excited to see your work."

She shrugs, clearly trying her best not to make eye contact with me.

"Erica."

Her eyes dart up to meet mine, a look of uncertainty in them as she does.

"Did you ever send her your portfolio?"

It looks like she bites the inside of her cheek before shaking her head.

"Why, baby?" I ask with furrowed brows.

"Because I'm terrified! It's everything that I have ever wanted, and she is my idol! What if she says that I'm no good? What if she hates my work? What if-"

"What if she loves them?" I ask gently.

She cocks her head to the side like she hadn't even considered that as an option. She is so fucking incredible, and she doesn't even see it. Everyone else does, though. Every person that shares a room with her feels how amazing she is. *That's our biggest fucking problem.*

"You are always pushing me towards my dreams. We both deserve to have our dreams come true. And I know for a fact that you will never forgive yourself if you don't at least give yourself a shot. I don't want to listen to you complaining for the next fifty years about what if either."

A smile starts to form across her face as her cheeks pink up.

"Fifty years, huh? You seem to be getting a little ahead of yourself there, buddy."

I look at her seriously as I shake my head. "Trust me, I'm not."

She looks surprised at that for a moment before she smiles and lifts her head up until her lips meet mine. Shit. I could kiss this woman for the rest of the days. I fucking plan to, too. First, there is just one problem I need to take care of. Or should I say *person.*

Erica and I spend the day watching movies, eating food and fucking our brains out. Unlike most nights though, I choose not to spend the night. I need to handle some shit at home tonight.

Stepping inside the house, I see Trevor, Mikey and Slater huddled around the kitchen table eating some takeout from Rocco's. All eyes swing up to me as I step inside.

"Sup, man. We didn't think you'd be home," Slater says over a mouthful of food, but my eyes aren't on him. They are on the man that I came here to see and apparently, he expected it because his eyes are on me as well.

"We need to talk," I state, not needing to address who I am talking to.

"I'm good," Trevor says before he takes another bite of his pasta, not taking his eyes off me as he does.

I grit my jaw in irritation, my anger quickly rising inside of me as I take a step closer.

"Please," I grind out between my clenched teeth.

"Nope," Trevor pops as he wipes his mouth with a napkin.

Smacking my fist down on the table so hard all of the trays bounce, I get only a few inches away from Trevor's face.

"Stay the fuck away from Erica! She's my girlfriend, has been for a while. I get that you don't remember breaking up with her, but you fucking did and guess what? You had the time of your fucking life after that.

"You fucked Cynthia Johnson your first day freshman year and proceeded to make your way through every female in our class before broadening your horizons. You fucking loved being single, and you never showed the slightest interest into anything more until the end of this summer when you came back from Grovebury.

"You had her once, and you let her go and you were just fine. Just because you don't remember doesn't mean that changes anything. She isn't yours anymore, Trevor. She's fucking mine!" I bellow.

"Whoa, let's take it down a notch," Slater says as his eyes flick back and forth between Trevor and me, but I could honestly give a fuck what he has to say right now.

"If you ever pull some shit like you did today, injured or not, I'll beat the fucking piss out of you."

"What are you actually mad about, Sebastian? The fact that I had Erica on top of me as I rubbed against her of the fact that she liked it?"

I leap for him, ready to choke the motherfucker to death when Mikey intercepts me, slowly backing me up until my back hits the wall. If the fucker wasn't a comparable size to me, I would have him on his back in a second but unfortunately the asshole is strong.

"Fuck. YOU! I don't know what the fuck your problem is, but I don't give a shit. Just back the hell off. I'm not going to tell you again."

Trevor scoffs as he stands from the table, taking several steps towards me but still leaving space between us. *Smart.*

"I don't know what the fuck you think you have with Erica, but I can guarantee it doesn't have a tenth of the power of what we have. We have been best friends for nearly a decade, and you have known her for how long? You are just a phase. I am the end game. So, if you aren't going to walk away, then you better be ready to fight for her because I'm not going down without a fight."

Without another word, Trevor steps out of the room and heads up the stairs. He is going to put up a fight against me for Erica? I'd like to see him fucking try.

CHAPTER THIRTY-EIGHT

ERICA

I t's the last day before winter break, and I'm currently packing. After I skillfully dodged going home for Thanksgiving, my
mother made it clear that Christmas was mandatory, so I'm bringing Sebastian. She wasn't too happy about a 'stranger intruding on
family time', but when I told her that it wasn't up for debate, she
actually backed down for once in her life, and I couldn't believe
it. I know Sebastian doesn't have any family to go home with and
he probably would rather just stay here and ignore the holidays
altogether, but I want him with me.

Palmer already went home with Ethan early. We have seen each
other here and there, but she has been spending more time at
Ethan's place and I have been spending practically all my time
with Trev and Seb, so we just don't see much of each other
anymore.

Since the day that I told him I needed space from Trevor, we
have been even closer than before, as if that were even possible.
It's not just a spending time closeness, it's an emotional one. One
that I feel inside of me every time we are together. Me trying to
be at Trevor's beck and call since he got hurt was doing serious
damage to our relationship and let's not even talk about the couch
thing.

I don't know what happened to me. I don't know why I acted
the way I did. Call it leftover chemistry, call it simple attraction

or call it guilt filled infatuation. Whatever the case, I will never allow something like that to happen again. It felt so good to have Trevor look at me like he used to, not that he hated me and was insurmountably disgusted in me like he did just before his accident. I've been clinging to it, riding it out hoping that we could just move on past it but then the thought of how selfish that is that he never recovers his memories weighs in, and I can hardly fucking breathe.

Trevor has texted and called a lot and even showed up to my door. All times I have given him the same answer. I need some space. I want to be there for him, especially in this really hard time in his life, but I also need to make sure that mine and my boyfriend's mental health can handle that, and right now, they can't.

A short knock comes on the door before Sebastian steps through the door. I smile as I turn to greet him but pause when I see that he is reading a piece of paper with a heavy look on his face.

"Seb, what's wrong?"

Slowly, his eyes lift to mine, confusion and disbelief filling them as he does.

"I got invited to the Combine in February."

My eyebrows shoot up and I let out a squeal as I leap into his arms. Seb catches me easily as I pepper kisses across his face. Oh my god! This is amazing! Because of the seriously shitty end to the season, none of us were sure if any of the guys would get any NFL scout attention, let alone be picked up for the NFL Combine. It is an invite only try-out basically for all the NFL teams to see what kind of new blood is coming in. A little over three hundred invites are sent out, and my man is one of those three hundred.

"Oh my god, Seb! I am so freaking proud of you! I can't believe it. I mean, I can, but I was worried that people wouldn't have recognized the fucking superstar that you are after that end of the season."

Sebastian laughs before he gently kisses me.

"Thank you, baby. Once we get back, I gotta start training even harder."

I roll my eyes on a laugh. "Like you ever stop."

Sebastian smirks to me before shaking his head and pushing his forehead against mine.

"I wouldn't be here if it wasn't for you, baby."

"Sure, you would. Your talent is what got you here," I smile.

He shakes his head softly again. "You have changed everything. If football doesn't end up working out, I'll be okay. I've got a new dream I'm working on, and it's bigger and better than a career in the NFL."

My heart beats out of rhythm for a second as my stomach does a happy flip.

"Care to share that dream with me?" I ask softly with a soft smile.

He gives me a wink as he slowly sets me down on my feet.

"Trust me, when it comes true, you'll know."

Smirking to myself, I walk over to grab my packed bag before Sebastian takes it from me and tucks me into his side as we lock the room and head out to his car. It's a four hour drive, so we decided to get an early start to avoid traffic. When we step out into the quad, it is extremely silent, peaceful almost. Maybe that's because it's Christmas Eve and everyone that was going to leave campus has already left.

The drive goes by pretty quickly. We talk about the Combine and how Seb is going to prepare in the meantime. I am so fucking proud of him and way too excited for what is to come for him, for the both of us.

When we pull up to my parents' private driveway, I hear Sebastian make a noise in the back of his throat. I turn to see him assessing the property. I know that growing up in foster care he didn't grow up with much money and my parents obnoxiously flaunt their wealth, so it is probably a little uncomfortable for him.

I reach over and grab his hand gently and give him a soft smile. He nods his head and kisses the back of my hand before lacing our fingers together. We drive around the circular driveway before Sebastian pulls off to the side. Sebastian goes to the back and grabs our bags before getting my door. I kiss his cheek before walking up to the house.

I don't bother knocking as I push the door open for us. Once Sebastian is inside behind me, I shut the door and call out to my parents.

"Mom? Dad? We're here!"

My mother walks into the entry way from her study and her eyes immediately snap to Sebastian, completely looking right past me. Her gaze slowly snakes over him, the scrutiny plain across her face. Sebastian is standing still with a polite but small smile on his face.

If he can tell some of the nasty things my mother is probably already thinking, he doesn't give it away. I for one am all too familiar with her looks of disappointment. Based on how she just looked at him, I would say that she isn't impressed. Like I give a shit.

"Good. Please show your guest where he will be staying," she says as she stalks off back to her study.

I roll my eyes before turning to Sebastian. "Fun, isn't she?"

He lets out a tight-lipped chuckle before slinging his arm around me. We walk down the hallway before making a turn to one of the guest rooms. My mother was very explicit that though I have undoubtedly shared a bed with Sebastian before, it won't be happening this weekend. She even made me promise that he would stay downstairs instead of in the guest room across from mine. It's almost like she isn't the same woman that used to let Trevor stay the night when we were dating when I was just 16. Whatever.

Sebastian puts his bag on the guest bed before turning to me with mine still in his hand. He lifts his eyebrow in question, and I smile mischievously before I take his hand and run through the hall and up the stairs to my room. For being such a big guy, he is surprisingly light on his feet and doesn't make too much noise up the mahogany stairs.

When we make it to my room, I drag him inside with me before I shut and lock the door. I grab my bag from him and toss it on the ground before I pull his lips down to mine. He kisses me for a few moments as I lick the seam of his lips before he pulls away.

"Baby, your mom already doesn't like me. I don't need your dad chasing me out of here with a gun."

"My parents are liberal. They don't believe in owning guns," I say as I lean back into him, pushing him against my door.

He kisses me back but pulls away again.

"Come on, sweetheart. I don't want to make a shittier impression than I already supposedly have."

"Sebastian. There is nothing that you can do to get those people down there to like you. They barely tolerate me. The only person you need to worry about liking you is me, and right now, I am not a fan of you pushing me away."

His eyes darken and before I know it, his hands have wrapped around the backs of my thighs, as he lifts and spins me in the air until I am pushed up against my solid door. My legs snake around his waist as his hands firmly hold me up. I feel his rock-hard dick press against my clit with only my panties separating us. I am suddenly so thankful that I opted to wear a dress today.

"This what you want, baby?" He growls as his jeans rub against my lace clad pussy.

I let out a soft moan before I nod. He does the move again as he kisses my neck.

"You want me to fuck you against your door while your parents are downstairs, my little rebel?"

I whimper as his fingers tease the sensitive skin of my thigh. Sebastian lets out a rough chuckle before kissing my lips.

"Alright but try not to make too much noise or I'll find another way to occupy that sweet mouth."

In one quick move, Sebastian pulls my panties to the side and undoes his pants before lining himself up to me. He quickly sinks himself into me and buries his head into my neck as he begins to thrust. I bite back my moans as he rhythmically rubs the perfect spot.

"Seb," I moan as my nails curl into his back.

"Shhh," he whispers as he covers his mouth with mine.

Our tongues fight for dominance as he picks up his pace. The door is making a loud thumping noise with every thrust, but I could honestly give two shits. It's too good and too perfect to stop. One of his hands skates across my thigh before dipping between us and brushing against my clit in perfectly quick strokes. My legs begin to quake with anticipation as his pace quickens and his pressure increases.

He pulls away briefly, and just when I am about to protest, his fingers come together and pinch my clit, sending me falling over the edge as ecstasy crashes down over me. He swears under his breath as he bites down onto my shoulder to muffle his release. I, however, do no such thing, allowing my screams to be heard throughout the whole house.

Our breathing is ragged for a few moments as Sebastian milks every bit of his orgasm before he slowly carries me over to my en suite. He sets me onto the countertop before slowly pulling out of me and moving to get a warm washcloth.

As he cleans us both, he gives me an amused smile. "Well, if your parents didn't like me before, I'd say they are gonna fucking hate me now."

"Too bad, cause I really fucking love you."

Sebastian dives down for one more tender kiss before he helps me off the counter. I straighten my dress and pat down my hair so that it looks just a little less mussed. We both are definitely rocking the freshly fucked look in our eyes though, so even if the whole house didn't just hear us, they will definitely be able to tell.

When we make it downstairs, my mother and father are working on their laptops in the living room while the caterer in busy making our dinner in the kitchen. I'm fairly certain my mother couldn't even make a piece of toast herself, so holiday dinners were definitely not her forte.

She gives me an unimpressed look before her eyes flick back to her screen.

"Oh good. Now that you're finally done, we can eat."

I roll my eyes. "We both know dinner doesn't start until promptly 6PM as usual, mother."

She doesn't respond as her fingers fly over her keyboard. I look to my dad, who seems a little less preoccupied.

"Hi, Dad."

He glances up and does a double take when he sees Sebastian. Guess mom didn't tell him I was bringing someone home. He lives and breathes his job, and I swear he doesn't notice half of the stuff that goes on around him outside of his job.

Standing up, he crosses the room and holds out his hand to Sebastian.

"Daniel Pembrooke," he says formally.

Sebastian shakes his hand while politely nodding his head. "Sebastian Caldwell. It's a pleasure to meet you, sir."

"Caldwell? You are that Tight End at Brighton, right? You were at the hospital with Trevor."

Sebastian's eyes tighten with tension at the mention of Trevor but that is the only indication he gives to his uncomfortability.

"Yes, sir. That's me."

He nods. "I didn't know Erica was bringing anyone home. I'm sure Trevor will enjoy having someone else to talk to."

My eyes widen as they flick over to my mother. "The Michaels are coming over for dinner?"

She huffs out an irritated breath before closing her laptop. "Yes, Erica. Just like they have for the last nine years."

"I don't know if that's such a good idea," I say as I take a step closer to her and cross my arms. "Trevor and I aren't really speaking right now."

My mother shrugs as she sets her laptop to the side and stands up. "That isn't my problem. I am not going to break tradition just because you decided to make a mess of things."

"Excuse me?" I ask. "You don't even-"

I'm cut off by the sound of the doorbell. My mother glides towards the front entry way and I shoot Sebastian a worried look. The tension hasn't quite left his face, but he gives me a reassuring nod and kisses the top of my head as we follow my father into the dining room.

Chapter Thirty-Nine

Erica

The large table is set up for all of us with several festive centerpieces in the middle. Some appetizers are already spread out across the table, and I grab a few for Sebastian and me as we sit down.

When the Michaels step into the room, they all seem to freeze for a moment when they see Sebastian. Trevor's eyes narrow in on him before bouncing over to me. He tries to give me a friendly smile, but it is laced with pain, and it breaks my heart that my best friend is hurting and that I am the cause, but I can't keep living my life for other people's happiness.

"Sebastian, sweetie," Shannon says with a warm but tight smile. "I didn't know you were coming. How have you been?

"Mrs. Michaels, I've been doing good, thank you," he greets with a soft smile.

Shannon walks over to us and hugs us both before placing a kiss on top of my head. Jonathan also comes over and shakes Sebastian's hand and pats me on the back before taking a seat next to my father. Trevor settles in at a seat across from me, and his eyes never once leave mine. I look to my left and see that Sebastian is staring at him intently, no doubt waiting to jump him if he does as much as speak out of line.

"Merry Christmas, Trev," I say softly.

His eyes flare for a second before they soften. "Merry Christmas, Little Red."

I feel Sebastian's hand on my thigh tighten at Trevor's nickname for me and I rub it softly to try to remind him that I am sitting with him, I am his. He looks down at me and nods softly before his grip loosens.

Dinner is served quickly, and it is filled with idle chit chat between my parents and Trevor's. Sebastian, Trevor, and I don't say a word the entire time. It could be worse for sure, but I will be so grateful when we are back in Brighton and away from all of this shit. I must have jinxed myself though because my mother then turns to Sebastian and settles her hands on the table as our plates are cleared, and the caterers bring out dessert.

"So, I understand you grew up in foster care."

My eyes widen, and I look to Sebastian, panicked at how he might react. I never said a thing about that. Hell, the only thing I ever did tell her was his name and that he plays football. Sebastian briefly looks down at me and pats my thigh, seemingly knowing that it wasn't me who shared his past.

"Yes, ma'am."

My mother tilts her head slightly. "That must have been a hard life."

"For some. I think it helped shape me into who I am today."

Leaning forward a little, intrigue glints from her eyes as she asks, "And who might that be?"

"Someone who cares for your daughter very much," he says evenly, unyielding to her intimidation tactics.

She settles back into her seat as she lifts her glass of wine. "Mhmm. Well, in that case, I assume she knows about your troubled past."

The room instantly stills as everyone freezes in their seats. Sebastian tenses and withdraws his hand from my thigh before settling it into his lap. I slowly look to Sebastian out of the corner of my eye and see him stoically watching my mother, giving nothing away.

When I look back, I see that my mother is staring at me with the hint of a victorious grin as she pulls a file folder from seemingly nowhere as she begins to flick through it.

"Yes, that's what I thought. When Erica told me that you two were seeing each other and that you would be coming home for Christmas with her, I had to do my due diligence as a mother," she says as her eyes flick up to meet mine before she continues to read.

"Your little friend grew up in a rundown trailer park in southern California, Sunny Crest Trailer Park or something like that where his mother eventually died of an overdose when he was six years old. After that his sister, who was only sixteen, took custody of him without the authorities knowing and proceeded to raise him until she was gunned down in a strip club eight years later.

"Then, he has a very violent, very appalling record from the age of fourteen to seventeen. I have to say, I am quite disappointed that the admissions board at Brighton would even admit you to begin with, let alone give you a scholarship. They don't need criminals poisoning the student body, corrupting our children," she says as she snaps the folder shut and tosses it on the table as if that was all that there is left to be said.

All of her words hit me like a freight train at once. I had assumed that his upbringing wasn't the greatest, but I didn't know all of that. And I'm sure it isn't even the beginning. My heart aches for the young Sebastian who lost his mother and then his sister. It hurts for who he no doubt had to become for survival.

I lift my shoulders a little higher as I face my mother, my chin raised.

"Well, that sounds all like his story to tell, mother, not yours, and this is certainly not appropriate dinner conversation."

Her eyes narrow towards me before they flick back to him. Sebastian says nothing, his face an impassive blank mask. I have gotten to know him on a much deeper level though in the last few months. I can see it in his eyes. Her words are hurting him, which in turn hurts me. Of course, the fact that he isn't fighting back or arguing with her only irritates her more and pushes her further.

"How despicable can you be? Not only have you stolen a scholarship from someone who would have actually deserved it, but you come in and ruin my daughter's life! Her future! You think that you can give her the life she deserves? You won't be able to take care of yourself. You should have stayed out of things instead of confusing Erica and distracting her from the one person she has always belonged with."

My mouth drops and my eyes widen as I flick my gaze over the entire table, the Michael's look uncomfortable, Trevor especially, but I honestly don't give a fuck. If Trevor is going to be a little bitch and whine to my mother about how I chose Sebastian over him, then fuck him and fuck all of them. I take a deep breath as I steady my voice.

"Mother, Father, I am in love with Sebastian. He is the best thing that has ever happened to me, and he is an incredibly good man. I don't care about whatever bullshit you dug up on him. I know who he is, and it's really unfortunate that you didn't give yourself the same opportunity to get to know him. You are the ones missing out."

The table is silent for a few moments before the sound of Sebastian's chair moving against the floor echoes through the room.

"Thank you for having me. Have a Merry Christmas," he says emotionlessly as he strides out of the room.

"Seb, wait," I say as I throw my napkin onto my plate and rush after him. I pause mid step, reaching across the table and snatch up the file folder before sending my mother the deadliest look I can possibly manifest before I run out into the hall.

When I catch up to Seb, he is already in the spare room grabbing his bag.

"Seb! Stop, please!" I beg.

He turns to face me, his face hard and blank.

"I'm not staying here, Erica. I tried, for you. But I can't-"

"It's okay. I understand. I'm fucking furious with my mother. I want to leave too. Let me just grab my bag, and we will grab a hotel tonight and drive back to Brighton in the morning, okay?"

His jaw ticks as he looks at me seriously.

"Aren't you at least going to ask me about everything that your mother said about me?"

I shake my head as I take a step closer to him and hand him the file. He looks down at it for a moment, his eyes narrowed suspiciously.

"Only if and when you ever want to tell me."

A small amount of tension eases out of his shoulders as he nods, taking the file out of my hands and stuffing it into his bag before wrapping me up into a tight but brief hug. He kisses the side of my head gently as he pulls away.

"Go get your bag. I'm gonna go start the car."

"Okay."

We both make our way out of the room, him going straight out the front door and me turning to head up the stairs. When I open my door, a startled gasp escapes me when I see Trevor sitting on the edge of my bed with his head in his hands.

"What the hell are you doing in here?" I grit as my jaw tightens.

Trevor's head whips up to look at me and what looks like regret is written across his face.

"I'm sorry. I didn't know she was going to do a whole back-ground check on him. My mom called me last week to ask how you were, and I told her the truth. She must have told your mom what I said," he says meekly.

I scoff. "No fucking shit, Trevor! They are the two biggest gossips in town and best friends. Of course, they fucking blabbed. You should have kept your damn mouth shut! What the hell is the matter with you? You don't get what you want so you send my mom after me?"

He shakes his head as he looks up at the ceiling. "None of this is going the way it was supposed to, Little Red. You were always supposed to be mine and I don't know what fucking happened in between knowing that with every fiber of my being and waking up in a hospital and finding out that the love of my life is off fucking my supposed best friend!"

"Look, I'm sorry that you feel like your whole world has changed. To be fair, over the last two years, it has, but you can't expect me to compromise my happiness for other people's. I've been doing that my whole life, Trev and I'm fucking tired.

He stands up, crosses the space between us until he is cradling my jaw.

"You wouldn't have to compromise your happiness, Little Red. I can make you happy. I know I can. I've never been happier in my life than I was when I had you and I know you were too. Please stop pushing me away, pushing us away. You are my other half, Little Red. Like two pieces to the same puzzle."

I shake my head when his thumb comes to brush against my lower lip, gently tugging at it.

"You felt it too. I know you do. The spark that comes from the barest touches. Like all of the feelings that we shared rush to the surface all at once. I know you feel it. Admit it," he whispers.

Swallowing back the mix of tears and shame that I do feel a connection with Trevor, I shake my head and do my best to pull away from his grip.

"I can't, because it isn't true."

He is silent for a moment, his bright blue eyes flicking back and forth between mine before he speaks again.

"Maybe you just need a reminder."

I furrow my brows in confusion. Before I can even ask him what he means by that, he grips my head in his hands almost painfully before slamming his lips on mine. I'm instantly stunned, frozen in the moment. What the fuck is he doing? I put my hand between us and push him away, but he only holds me closer, desperately pushing his lips against me like it is his last chance. Though I will admit the kiss feels nice, familiar, safe, it isn't coming from the only man I want, and I hate to break it to him, but he never really stood a chance against Sebastian Caldwell.

"Seriously?" Sebastian's growls.

Finally, Trevor releases me as I spin on my heel to see a wild eyed Sebastian. His gaze is flicking between Trevor and I almost manically, seemingly not sure who to focus his rage to.

"Seb, it isn't like that," I say as he seemingly chooses his target, storming past me and straight up to Trevor before winding back and decking him so hard across the face that he spins in a full circle before he crumples to the ground.

Normally, I would rush to check on Trevor, but Sebastian is already barging out the room and down the stairs. I chase after him, calling out his name, begging him to look at me, listen to me, anything.

"Seb! Babe, please! Just stop. That wasn't what you think it was! He kissed me."

"Yeah, you looked to be putting up a real fight, again," he snaps as he rounds his car, making his way to his door.

"I was! I tried to get him off me! Come on, you know me! I would never do anything to hurt you, you know that. Just listen to me for a minute.

He tenses, his hand on his door handle as his shoulders rapidly rise and fall like he is doing his best not to lose his shit.

"I knew this would happen," he says lowly.

"What?" I gasp.

He looks over his shoulder only barely as he speaks again.

"I knew this would happen. I saw it coming from a mile away and I got with you anyways."

"Saw what?" I shout desperately.

He punches his door before whirling on me, anger like I have never seen before flaring in his eyes.

"THIS! YOU! HIM! I knew that you two would end up together one day, I knew I was just a place holder, a way to kill some time, maybe stick it to mommy and daddy for a little while until you got bored. For a moment there though, I forgot. I thought maybe we could have a future. I should have taken the dozens of red flags more seriously. Biggest mistake I ever made was walking up to you at that fucking party."

I gasp, my throat suddenly becoming hot and scratchy. "You don't mean that," I whisper as I shake my head.

He lets out a defeated sigh as he looks to the ground before looking up at me.

"Just go, Erica. Go be with him, go to law school, live in a big fucking mansion down the road from your parents and live your perfect life. We don't fit."

He takes a step towards the door and opens it before I begin to panic.

"Please, Seb, I love you."

He doesn't say anything as he shuts the door. The window is down though, and he looks at me hollowly, like he doesn't even recognize me, and I see it in his eyes. I see that he has already given up on us. That there is nothing that I can do now. It's done.

"No. You can't do this to me," I say as I speed walk to keep up with the car. "Please, Seb. Sebastian!" I shout as he drives a little faster and makes his way down the driveway.

I watch as his red taillights disappear into the dark night before I crumble to the ground and fall apart. How could everything go so wrong? How could we be dreaming up a future together one moment and the next he walks away and tells me to move on with someone else?

Because you fucking ruined everything.

I don't know how long I lay in the middle of the driveway, crying my complete heart out. I vaguely register being lifted into strong arms and carried into the house. My tears have finally dried out, and I'm left feeling shocked, numb.

Someone says something to me, but I don't actually hear the words as I stare at the door that we just made love up against a few hours ago. I see a set of legs walk away from my bed and through the door, but I don't bother to look up and see who it was. Instead, I just stare and wonder how I will ever be able to feel anything other than the hurt and searing pain of heartbreak that has enveloped me.

Chapter Forty

Sebastian

It's been a month since I broke up with Erica, and every day hurts more than the fucking last. It damn near broke me to do it but after her mother drug up the ugliest parts of my past and served it for dessert on Christmas Eve, I knew I didn't have a choice. Walking in on her and Trevor just sealed the deal.

I was fooling myself into thinking that a woman like Erica could ever have a future with someone like me. A fuck up, an orphan, a criminal. How did I ever think I stood a fucking chance?

She doesn't know it yet, but one day, she'll thank me. Sooner or later, she would have woken up with me and realized that she wanted more. Probably more than I could ever give her. Maybe Trevor finding out about us the way he did, losing his memory like he did was for the best. She didn't seem all that torn between me and him before, but once he woke up from the hospital, I saw a change. It was small, but it was there. Every time they hung out, I could see it in her eyes. She was starting to fall for him again even if she was resisting because of me. They were practically fated to be together and who am I to fuck with fate's design? They are the real love story here, I'm just the place holder.

I thought that I was taking the hurt out of it this way, getting away before I completely fell for her. Only it was way too fucking late for that. I've never hurt so bad in my entire fucking life. I turned around three times that night on my drive back to Brighton. Each time, I got right back onto the road though, telling myself to stop being a selfish fucking bastard for once and let her go.

When I got back to the house, I drank until I blacked out and then drank some more. I woke up to a pounding on the door and Erica's broken voice, begging me to let her in. I heard her sobs through the door, and it shredded at my already tattered heart to pieces.

She sat on the porch for two hours knocking and shouting and pleading for me to talk to her. I know because I sat on the other side of that door the entire fucking time. I heard every nasty word, every desperate plea and every promise she made if I would only open the door. I didn't though. I couldn't. I knew if I opened the door, it would be all over with. I would wrap her up into my arms and hold on even tighter than before.

Pain was always going to come if I stayed involved, for all three of us no doubt. Erica was the prize and Trevor and I would do anything to have her, anything to keep her. Erica and I were never supposed to be, what we had was an unplanned mistake. But it happened. We collided and it was fucking painful and great and hard and perfect, until it wasn't.

After that day, she never came by again. I half expected her to confront me on campus and chew me out for cutting her off so callously, but she never did. I'd be lying if I said I wasn't slightly disappointed by that. My brain is a cluster fuck every day and all my thoughts are torn between wanting her back in my arms and forcing myself to let her be.

The kiss with Trevor honestly didn't bother me as much as I probably acted. Sure, in the moment, it pissed me off, but it was clearly one sided. But the thing that hung me up is that she didn't push him away, again. His words played into my head in that moment.

"What are you actually mad about, Sebastian? The fact that I had Erica on top of me as I rubbed against her or the fact that she liked it?"

I had to get the fuck out of here. Everything was too much. Her, them, my life being brutally filleted open like a motherfucking spectacle. I knew that it was goodbye for us, and I high tailed it out of there because I didn't want those to be my last memories of her. Unfortunately, instead I have the image burned in my mind of her mascara-streaked face combined with a look of pure devastation. I have been through some shit, and I haven't shed a single tear in over eight years, but damn if I wasn't close that day.

I got back from the Combine two weeks ago. It went really good. Several scouts showed interest in me, and I was in the top five for the fastest 40-yard dash times. I wanted to be excited. I wanted to focus on football and all my dreams that are so close I can practically fucking taste them. But they just remind me of the newest dream that went up in smoke. A dream of a life with a beautiful woman with fiery red hair, aqua eyes and a smile that untwisted my jaded heart.

I can't think about her anymore, though. I can't let myself. Its fucking selfish and downright pure torture. I need to focus on the positives. In less than three months, the school year will be over, and I am currently projected to be a second round pick. Life is good. I'm happy.

Right?

Chapter Forty-One

Erica

I t's been six weeks since Sebastian smashed my heart to pieces in my parent's driveway. It's been six weeks of feeling numb, broken and hollow. I wish I was being dramatic, but I have really never felt so completely lost.

When I woke up the next morning, I was hoping that it was all a bad dream. Unfortunately, when I raced downstairs to the empty guest bedroom, I realized that it was all real and the sharp pain in my chest returned with a vengeance.

I didn't speak to anyone after that. I ran upstairs, grabbed my bag and ordered a ride. A few hundred dollars later and I was standing outside of Sebastian's house. My mother called me about ten times before I blocked her. I was so done with her. If she didn't see that coming after the shit she pulled, then she wasn't nearly as smart as she claimed to be.

I sat outside Sebastian's door screaming and begging for him to talk to me for what felt like hours, but he never did. I honestly wasn't even sure if he was home. His car was out front but maybe he was out with someone. My heart clenched painfully when I thought about the possibility of him being with another girl.

I wanted him to talk to me, to tell me what he was thinking. Hell, I didn't give a damn about the stuff my mom said. As far as I cared, we could never talk about it again, I just wanted him. I wanted him to listen to me about the kiss with Trevor. I wanted him to hold me tight and tell me that he loves me as much as I love him. I wanted him to stay.

But he didn't, and there is only so much humiliating begging one person can do before you have to get up off of the porch, dust your pants off and let go. Well, I did the first two pretty well, the last one I'm still working on.

I have drafted up my portfolio to Alexandra Campo at least a dozen times and deleted the email the same amount of times. I just don't think I have it in me to put myself out there like that, especially not to someone like her. Sebastian was the one who pushed me, the one that made me feel like my work was good enough. Now that he is gone it all feels kinda...empty. Cliché, right?

A few days after I left Sebastian's house, I was sitting holed up in my room when a heavy knock came from my door. Maybe it was Sebastian? Maybe he was there to apologize for walking away? To say he made a mistake?

I rushed to the door only to feel all my hope come crashing down to the ground when I saw it was just Trevor. Anger burned fiercely through my veins before I gripped the edge of the door and slammed it closed. If it wasn't for him and his petty jealousy, none of this would have ever happened.

"Little Red, please," Trevor said softly through the door.

Please? Please! Please fucking what?

I quickly ripped the door back open and punched Trevor in the gut. He bent over for a second, obviously surprised as he wheezed out a breath.

"You are a son of bitch," I spat at him as I balled up my hands at my sides. The idea of hitting him again was pretty fucking tempting when he stood up a little straighter.

"I know. I'm sorry."

"Sorry for what!?" I shouted. "Because the list is pretty fucking long!"

He blew out a breath and nodded. "I know. I fucked up, in a lot of ways. I'm sorry. I just wanted you so fucking bad, I was willing to do anything."

I let out a humorless laugh. "Oh, you did anything, alright. You put your own selfish desires ahead of everyone else and hurt Sebastian and I both. Mission fucking accomplished," I barked with a huff as I spun on my heel and walked over to sit on my bed.

He took a tentative step inside before shutting the door and shaking his head.

"No. I never wanted you to hurt, Erica. I knew that we were a better match. I thought I was preventing you from more hurt. I just...fuck maybe you are right. I'm a fucking son of a bitch."

"And the kiss?" I snapped.

"The kiss was for me. A last ditch effort, I guess. It was selfish and manipulative. All I've ever wanted is the best for you, though. To keep your heart safe-"

"Little late for that," I laughed bitterly.

He looked down at his hands for a moment before he crouched down in front of me and held my face in his hands.

"Are you okay?"

The concern in his words was pouring out as he searched my face. Though, I don't think he had to look long. I had seen myself in the mirror. The heartbreak is plain as day.

"No," I choked out, avoiding eye contact with him as best as I could.

His sighed as he dropped his head down for a few seconds before looking up at me with anguish written across his face.

"I'm so sorry, Erica. I love you so much. I never want to see you in an ounce of pain. Please, forgive me."

"Why should I? You have always been there for me, Trevor. ALWAYS. But not the other night. You were there for yourself. You were hurting and you wanted to hurt us too. Don't deny it."

Trevor opens his mouth to deny it, because I know him way too fucking well, when I cut him off.

"Just...go, Trev. I don't have it in me right now. I cut my parents out of my life, I lost Sebastian and I fucking hate that I lost you too, somewhere along the way you stopped being my best friend."

"No!" He says with a quick shake of his head. "I will always be first and foremost your best friend, Little Red. Always. I'm sorry that I fucked up. If I could take it back, I would."

His eyes were filled with remorse and sincerity. I knew this guy like I knew the back of my hand, I knew he meant it. I just didn't know if he would pull stupid shit like this again, if he did then I was fucking done. But right now, I didn't have it in me to hate Trevor. Not really, at least. I have lost everyone close to me in a matter of one night. Trevor was all I had left.

"If you ever pull any bullshit like the other night, I'm done, Trevor. Best friends or not, a decade of friendship or not. I'm gone."

He swallowed roughly, his eyes rounding as he nodded, obviously understanding the seriousness in my tone.

"I promise. I'm sorry, Little Red. I just-"

I waved him off before sniffing and wiping away a stray tear.

"In the end, he was the one that ended things, the one that blocked my number and won't even speak to me. We could have worked through the shit storm you started but I guess I wasn't worth it-"

"Don't say that," Trevor scolded quickly. "You are worth the world."

I gave him a pathetically sad smile. "I guess not everyone agrees."

Trevor wrapped me up in a hug before I let the dam break and began to sob into his shoulder for what felt like hours. We didn't hardly move all night. Trev ended up staying the night and force fed me Chinese takeout before I cried even more.

We have been spending a lot of time together since that day. He helps take my mind off things and though he insists that I don't smile as much as I should be, I feel better, well kinda. My heart still aches and practically every square inch of this city reminds me of Sebastian, but I don't randomly break down anymore, so that's progress.

Trevor got an invite to the Combine, of course he obviously wasn't cleared to play, and he had been too out of shape to go but just the invite alone is hope that his NFL dreams may not be completely dashed yet.

It's Sunday, and I am finishing up a paper due for my poly sci class tomorrow when the door opens and closes, the smell of Chinese instantly wafting through the small room. I don't take my eyes off my laptop as I continue typing.

"You know, if we keep eating take out every day, I don't think either of us will fit through that door," I say blandly.

Trevor chuckles as he sets down the takeout on the bed and shrugs.

"I don't know. You, me, endless amounts of Chinese food trapped in a bedroom for the rest of our days. Kinda sounds like one of the fantasies I used to jerk it to when I was a teenager."

I scoff and roll my eyes before shoving his shoulder.

"Trev, gross."

He laughs at his joke for a bit, but I don't miss the way it dims when I don't join in on the laughter. It's hard to find much enjoyable these days. I know I'm being dramatic. It was just a breakup, one that followed a high stress and short relationship at that. But when it feels like a piece of your fucking soul is missing, it doesn't feel so dramatic.

Running my eyes over the now perfectly polished paper, I hit save before opening up my email and hitting send. The next thing that flashes across my screen is my drafts, or should I say draft. The one to Alexandra. I got to minimize it before Trevor snaps the laptop out of my hands.

"Is that Alexandra Campo? The girl you used to always go on about? You guys are emailing?" He asks as his eyes look over the screen, quickly opening up my attachment as he does.

"Trev, stop. Give it back."

He bats me away as he stands with my laptop in hand, his brows furrowing before raising in what looks like surprise before he sets the computer down and shakes his head softly.

"Little Red, is that all your work?"

Feeling sort of self-conscious, I fidget under his stare before I nod softly. He looks shell shocked as he shakes his head again.

"Fuck. I knew that you were talented, but you never really let me see you paint. You are fucking amazing. Alexandra is going to mentor you?"

"No," I rush with a shake of my head. "I mean, yes. If she liked my work and I wanted it, but I don't think I do anymore. I don't know. Working on my art with her would be really cool, but I am already maxed out with school."

Trevor's brows crinkle. "But this is like your dream. I know you don't want to be a lawyer, even if your parents pressure you to do so. You at least owe it to yourself to take this opportunity. Even if it turns into nothing, you miss one hundred percent of the passes you don't throw."

I roll my eyes as I reach for my laptop. "You did not seriously just give me a football themed pep talk, did you?"

Trevor shrugs, which causes me to blow out a breath and shake my head. I set my laptop on my bed and close it before turning back to him.

"I'm gonna take a shower. Pick a movie?"

He nods as he moves over to the Chinese food, taking the containers out and spreading them out before his eyes flick from my laptop and then back to me. I know what he is thinking. He thinks I should still submit my portfolio. He is one of the most determined people I have ever met. When he wants something, he goes after it no matter the cost.

Case in point, I guess.

Chapter Forty-Two

Erica

A week or so later Trevor and I are hanging out at my dorm when his phone rings. He answers it quickly and talks to what sounds like one of his friends before hanging up.

"Caleb and Alan are at Rocco's. Want to grab some pizza and beer?"

I shrug before my phone pings with an email. Unlocking my phone and flicking through it, my heart seizes when I see the sender. Alexandra Campo. My eyebrows knit together as I read over her words.

Dear Miss Pembrooke,

I knew that you had talent from the moment I met you, but I wasn't aware you were at this caliber, especially for a self-taught artist. I would be honored to mentor you and have already spoken to the Brighton Museum of Art director, and he has agreed to hold an amateur night showcase where you will highlight your pieces. If you have all of the pieces you sent to me and are willing to potentially part with them, then you will only need to create one more for the event. I hope to hear from you soon.

Sincerely, Alexandra Campo

I'm frozen in place. What. The. Fuck.

Quickly, I scroll down to the bottom of the message where I see that my portfolio has been sent as well as half of what I had written. The second half isn't my words though. They talk about how thrilled I am for the potential to work under someone I have admired for years. I didn't send this! But it's not like Palmer even knows about this and the only other person who has had access to my laptop is...

Slowly, I drag my eyes up to land on Trevor. He is watching me with a casual smile, his hands tucked into his pockets.

"Ready to go?"

"Did you send my portfolio to Alexandra Campo?"

His eyes widen before he lets out a nervous chuckle.

"Umm, maybe. Why? Did she get back to you?"

"Trevor!" I bark. "How could you go behind my back like that?"

He throws his hands up in surrender but holds his ground.

"Because I know you never would have done it. It's your dream, Little Red. You need to go after it."

"That is my decision to make, Trev," I sigh as I massage my temples.

"What's the big deal? Did she reject you? So what? Fuck that bitch. I bet-"

"No," I say as I cut him off. "She loved my work. She organized my pieces to be shown in an event at the art museum."

"What?" He asks with a huge smile.

Despite my lack of belief that I had it in me to smile, I do. It's not a huge one, but it is the most genuine one that I have felt in months. Trevor whoops before he lifts me up into the air and spins me around. His words of praise are quickly drowned out as my own thoughts take over.

Oh my god. Is this actually happening? Am I really going to be in an art show? How could I not, accept, right? I can't believe this is happening.

After the shock had worn off, Trevor had insisted that we go and celebrate so we decided to meet up with his friends. We are sitting in a corner booth while the guys devour the two large pizza's

that they ordered. Despite the heightened lift in my mood, I just
don't have much of an appetite. Tuning out Alan's story about a
threesome he had last night, I stare at the blank wall ahead of us,
thinking about what an amazing opportunity I have in front of me.
For some reason though, it doesn't feel quite right. Trevor slides
his arm around my shoulders and pulls me into his side.

"You okay, Little Red?" He whispers, concern swirling through
his bright blue eyes.

I look up at him willing myself to give him a convincing smile.
Not sure how convincing it is but it is a smile so it will have to do.
Trevor gives me a tentative one in exchange before he kisses my
cheek and focuses back on his friends.

I turn my attention back to the wall when a familiar pair of
caramel colored eyes catches my gaze. I freeze in place and so
does Sebastian. He is halfway up to the counter, but his head is
turned towards me, his body completely still. He almost looks like
a statue, a gorgeous absolutely perfect heart-breaking statue.

*His hair is longer than I remember. Has it really been long
enough for his hair to grow?*

I watch as his eyes flit over me briefly and settle on where
Trevor's arm is around me before he turns away as if he didn't
even see me and grabs a box of pizza. He pays for it quickly before
striding out the door without a backwards glance.

Shit. That hurt really bad.

I have been fortunate enough not to run into Sebastian at all
since the new semester started. At first, I wanted to run into him
but then I wondered what I would even say. He shut me out,
pushed me away and made it clear that he is done with me. So
why would I want to be the desperate ex that can't get over him?
Even if it is true, I don't want him to know that.

It hurts to see that he is clearly not taking it as hard as I am. He
looks good, healthy, happy (As happy as broody Sebastian Cald-

well gets.). Whereas my normally bright eyes are dull, encased with deep dark circles. My lack of appetite has caused me to lose fifteen pounds that I did not have to lose in the first place. It looks like my body is wasting away, and honestly, I feel that way too.

Chapter Forty-Three

Sebastian

Trevor and I have done a good job of staying out of each other's way at the house. I tried to move out, but with only a few months of school left, not a lot of options and even less in my budget, I decided to tough it out. Thankfully, any time Erica has been over I have made myself completely fucking scarce. I think yesterday at Rocco's was the first time that I had actually seen her in a few months, and it hurt more than I could have fucking imagined.

I guessed that they would get together after that night, but some stupid fucking part of me had hoped that she wouldn't give in so easily. Guess me walking away really was for the best. For them, at least.

It's for the best that we stay out of each other's way. Things ended so harshly, so ugly between us, a friendship of any kind will probably never be salvaged, with either of them probably. Something doesn't sit well with me about that, though. I don't like thinking that the last memory Erica will have of me is hearing the one-sided nasty side of my life and then my taillights as I left her behind on the cold ground. It fucking tears me apart.

Glancing over at the folder that has sat untouched on my desk, I walk over to it tentatively like it will jump up and strike me. The vile venom of words inside makes it feel that way. I flick through the various police reports, statements taken, records and paperwork that sums up my broken fucked up childhood. I know she didn't read the file, she just got the cliff notes from her mother, but something in me wants her to know, to know everything. I want her to know what people think is the facts and what actually happened.

Without thinking twice about it, I grab a pad of sticky notes and begin scribbling. The words flow from my pen freely, my handwriting slanted and messy but fuck if I care. These words are fucking impossible to speak let alone write, but she deserves them. She deserves to get the full story, so that maybe when she looks back at our time together, she won't think of me as the villain, the wolf in sheep's clothing. Maybe it will just solidify the thought that has no doubt always been in the back of her head that I was never the right one for her. Either way, I have to do it.

When my hand is sore and the ink is dry, I flick through all of the papers that are now lined with bright yellow notes on the side. Snapping the file shut, I tuck it closely to my side as I head off for my destination. I've done this walk what feels like a thousand times, but it feels like ages since I've actually done it.

As soon as I get to Erica's my hands twitch to knock on the door. Is she home? Or is she out with Trev again? Do they go out a lot or do they stay in? He isn't around at the house much these days, so I can only assume he is spending all his time with her. Would she answer the door if she saw it was me? Or would she slam it in my face? Guess I couldn't fault her either way.

No matter how desperately I want to inhale that sweet subtle peach smell one more time, to feel that silky smooth skin or that thick hair wrapped around my fist, I take the chicken shit way out and slide the file under neath the door before pocketing my hands and quickly heading back to my house.

Maybe she'll read it, maybe she'll toss it. Either way it doesn't matter in the end. This isn't me trying to get her back. This isn't me trying to fix what is clearly broken. This is me setting the record straight. For her and me.

CHAPTER FORTY-FOUR

ERICA

I'm reading over the same sentence over and over again, being no better off than I was twenty minutes ago. Why do I struggle so much these days? I excelled in high school. I was valedictorian with perfect grades and sky high test scores that secured me a place at this school. *That and my last name.* With every day that passes I get less and less motivated to keep moving forward. Honestly, what is the point? I'm not speaking to my parents anymore, despite my mother's various calls threatening that I call her back or she will take away my tuition. *What a threat.*

Being a college dropout goes against everything I was raised to believe in and strive for and yet, the option has never sounded so appetizing. Fuck my mother. Maybe I'll take a gap year and apply for some scholarships, I'll pay for my own education and get a degree in something that I want to study. The only thing holding me back in all of that is Trev. He has been my rock since my life went to complete shit. Maybe I'm just using that excuse as a crutch, though.

A rustling noise sounds from my door before a cream colored file folder slips underneath it and skids across the floor. Furrowing my brows, I set my books to the side as I slide out of bed and walk across the room, picking up the folder as I unlock the door and peek out into the hall. I look both ways but don't see anyone besides a group of girls sitting in the common space who seem way too preoccupied in their own conversation to be the ones to slip something under my door.

Closing the door, I flick open the folder as I sit down on the bed. The furrow in my brows disappears as my eyes slowly widen. The first words that I latch onto are *Sebastian Caldwell*. It's his birth certificate. I flick through the pages and see dozens and dozens of reports, rap sheets and different documents all having to do with Sebastian.

Oh my god. This is the file my mom had. The one that my mom presented at Christmas dinner. The same one I gave back to Sebastian before he drove off with my heart and this file in the front seat of his car. Flicking back to the front, I notice there is a bright yellow sticky note next to his father's name. The name scrawled on the paper is Jimmy Lanahan but the sticky note says differently.

"My mom didn't know who my father was so she put down the first name she could think of and tried to go after him for child support. After a DNA test it was proven he wasn't the father."

Did Sebastian write this? Why would he do that? Not being able to help myself I flip to the next page that is a police report talking about his mother's death. She was only 32. Stephanie Caldwell. The police stated that it was a typical overdose and that the two minors who were found in the residence are being taken in by their uncle. After I scan over the facts, my eyes flit over to the several sticky notes placed on the side of the page.

"My mom was a heroin addict. Ever since I can remember the trailer we lived in was filled with rusty spoons, empty syringes and a smell that all the bleach in the world couldn't get out of my nose. My sister was ten years older than me, so she definitely saw a lot more than I did. She tried to protect me, shield me from it all, but sometimes it wasn't enough. Alexis did everything she could to take care of me, but she was just a kid herself. Mom overdosed

*when I was six. I just got home from school and was trying to show
her my spelling test when I realized she wasn't breathing."*

Six? He was six years old when he lost his mother? And his sister
was only sixteen and with no father. Oh my god. Seb.

*"I don't know how Lex did it, but she somehow got one of the
neighbors to lie and say they were our uncle and that we would
be staying with them. Maybe she was really convincing or maybe
the cops just didn't give a shit because they left it alone. We started
staying with that neighbor in their extra bedroom. Lex dropped out
of school and got a job so that we could pay for our room and food
and all that shit. She quickly realized it wasn't enough to keep us
going, though."*

Flipping to the next page, I find another police report, but
instead of only one or two sticky notes on this one, the entire
report is covered in them.

*"When Lex turned eighteen, she started working at a strip club
downtown. I was only eight at the time, so I didn't really know
what the place was, just that I was never allowed to go there. She
fell in with a bad crowd working there and got mixed up with some
gang shit. When I was fourteen, I got a call from one of her friends
at the club who told me what happened one night.*

*"A regular of Lex's was a part of the Snakeback MC, and when
he found her in a red room with one of the rival MC's, he lost his
shit and shot them both. The club turned into a blood bath and a
huge investigation was launched. That's when the cops caught on
to me and threw me into the system."*

Quickly flipping to the next page, unable to stop if I had to. I
need every bit of information I possibly can get, every word he
wrote just for my eyes. I need it all. The next page is a report on
Sebastian, about the foster house he was sent to live in and the
struggles he faced.

"I was lost for a while. I had no family, no home, no future. I didn't even get to do a funeral for Lex. Fuck if I know what ever happened to her body. I was a minor and didn't have any rights. She was like a mother to me. She gave up her entire life to raise and take care of me, and in the matter of ten minutes, she was just...gone."

The next page is a booking report for a juvenile detention center. Sebastian's name typed boldly across the top.

"I got in with some of the other kids at the group home who were dealing drugs, petty theft, that kind of stupid shit. This was the first time I got caught holding, but it wasn't the last. We were dumb kids and just wanted to make some cash on the side, something to put to the side so that when I turned eighteen, I could get the hell out of that hellhole of a city.

"It took my football coach calling me out on my shit when I was seventeen for me to get my shit together. He told me that I didn't have to be me, that I could be anyone I wanted to be if I worked hard enough for it."

A newspaper clipping of a high school football team winning state is slipped inside, Sebastian's trademark scowl front page with the title of 'Local Superstar takes the Vikings to Victory at State.'

"So, I got my shit together and got a full ride to Brighton, amazingly so, as your mother pointed out."

I cringe at his words as I flip to see the next paper is Sebastian's scholarship offer and acceptance letter to Brighton. How the fuck did my mother get her hands on this?

Shaking my head as I pour over every word over and over again until I have it all practically memorized, my heart aches for Sebastian. For the childhood he never got to live, for the little boy who lost so much so young, for the jaded hurt teenager that his past shaped him to be. It's amazing he isn't dead in a ditch or locked away in prison. For someone to crawl out of life like that and start completely fresh is something, but to turn into a man like him is something extraordinary.

Surprisingly, hurt isn't the only feeling that fills my body. Anger burns bright and hot inside me as I slam the file shut and begin to sob big fat angry tears. How fucking dare he! How could he give this to me, open his entire life up to me with detailed notes, and he couldn't even look me in the fucking eyes as he did it? Does he just enjoy seeing me in pain? Because that is all I have felt since Sebastian Caldwell drove away from me that night. Pain. So much fucking pain.

By now, I am practically hyperventilating as I let out gasps for breath that sound more like a dying animal's last groan. Everything hurts so fucking bad. I don't realize that someone else is in the room before arms are wrapping around me. The feeling is nice, but the smell is all wrong.

"Shhh, Little Red. Shhh. What is going on? Are you hurt?"

I let out another sob as I nod, not having it in me to open my eyes as tears pour from my eyes.

"What happened? Where are you hurt? What can I do?!" Trevor rattles off as his arms hold me tighter.

Taking a balled up fist I pound against my chest, the stupid fucking excruciating organ that is slowly destroying me. Understanding must dawn on Trevor because he blows out a deep breath and leans us back until we are laying down on my bed as he holds me, shushing me like an inconsolable child.

When my tears are nothing but dried streaks against my skin, my eyes red and raw, Trevor speaks.

"You still love him."

I don't have to ask who Trev is talking about. We both know.

I nod, my voice still too hoarse to speak. I feel Trevor shake his head before he turns my chin so that I am facing him.

"Why? Little Red, we were so good. Things were so good between us. I am so good to you. I would never hurt you like he did. It was always supposed to be you and me. When you finally came to Brighton, I fucking told him that and instead of being a good fucking friend he stabbed me in the back and stole my fucking girl-"

Wait.

"What?" I rasp as I sit up slowly.

Trevor's angered expression morphs quickly into a cool shrug.

"What?"

"No, wait," I say as I sit up until I am on my knees. "Trevor, do you remember the beginning of this year? You remember me coming to Brighton?"

"Uh, yeah. Stuff has been coming back to me a little at a time."

My brows furrow as my eyes flick over his face.

"Since when?"

Trevor shrugs, his eyes breaking away as he looks at his feet.

"A week or so."

I stay silent for a few moments, studying him closely, his eyes looking anywhere that isn't my face. Just like when we were kids. He could never lie to my face. Oh my fucking god. My eyes widen, and my stomach drops as I stare at him in disbelief.

"Y-you're lying."

"What?" He snaps defensively before guilt flashes across his face.

OH MY FUCKING GOD.

"Trevor!" I screech as I scramble off the bed. "You son of a bitch! You fucking son of a bitch! You never lost your memory, did you? DID YOU!"

He winces at my screams as he slowly stands up, holding his hands out placatingly.

"Little Red, calm down," he says as he reaches for my pinky.

I slap his hand away as rage like I have never felt before begins to consume me.

"Did you?" I ask, a hard steeliness taking over my voice as I lift my chin a little higher.

His eyes flick over my face frantically, as if he is trying to think about what to say but I don't give him a chance to come up with any bullshit. I wind my hand back and slap him across the face as hard as I can.

"I can't believe you! I genuinely can't! What the fuck is wrong with you! Why would you put me through that, your parents! Sebast-"

I stop myself as realization dawns on me.

"Sebastian," I whisper almost to myself. "You did this because you were mad at Sebastian and me. You wanted to hurt us, to punish us."

"No," Trevor says with a shake of his head. "I wanted to hurt him, but never you. I woke up in that hospital room, and I heard you two declaring your love to each other, how you would make it through this together. Like you both didn't give a fuck how bad I was hurt! The loyalty *he* broke."

"So, you fucking faked amnesia?!" I balk, still completely shell shocked.

He has the good decency to at least look ashamed as he rubs the back of his neck.

"At the time, it seemed like a good idea. I just wanted to put some distance between you two. He had you fooled into thinking he was someone he wasn't. You were this close to being mine before he walked in and fucked everything up. I was just getting my girl back, no matter what it cost."

I scoff as I storm over to the door and thrust it open.

"Well, I hope you enjoyed the last several weeks because it just cost you fucking everything, Trevor."

"Little Red, don't do this. I'm sorry. I didn't want to lie. I just wanted you to see-"

"Oh, I see pretty fucking clearly now. I mean this in the sincerest way possible. Go fuck yourself, Trevor Michaels. Lose my number and get the fuck out of my life."

Hurt and panic flash across his face as he scrambles over to me, his hands quickly reaching out for me, but I quickly bat him away.

"Leave!" I bark in a tone that must have him realizing how serious I am.

Agony takes over his features as his shoulders slump.

"I'm so sorry," he whispers brokenly.

I let out a laugh that lacks any humor as tears begin to drip down my face. Shit, I thought I was all dried up. I guess being lied to and deceived by your best friend is enough to stir up the old waterworks once again.

"No, you aren't. You are a selfish prick who only thinks about what is important to you without considering those around you. I'm serious, Trevor. I'm fucking done. With my parents, this school and you. I. Am. Done."

He hangs his head, solemnly walking out the room without a backwards glance. As soon as he is through the threshold, I slam the door shut, lock it, and slide my back down on it as I begin to sob hysterically all over again.

CHAPTER FORTY-FIVE

ERICA

That day opened my eyes in a lot of ways. I realized that I didn't really know anyone that I thought I did. I knew Sebastian had a hard life, but I had no clue the extent of it. It still bothers me that he didn't have it in him to even tell me these things, but instead write them down and slip them under my door like a coward. I knew that Trevor never gave up when he wanted something, but I had no clue that he would stoop to such a disgusting level to *have* me. I also realized that I didn't even know myself, or at least I wasn't honoring myself. What the fuck was I doing wasting my time in a school I didn't want to be in, studying for a degree I didn't want, surrounded by people that I had no interest in having in my life. I. Was. Done.

So, I packed all my things that night, went to a hotel using my mother's credit card, and the next morning, I let the school know that I would be withdrawing from classes permanently and to give up my dorm. I left a note to Palmer since she was at Ethan's, and I didn't want to delay my leaving. We weren't really that close anyways.

I called Alexandra and asked if she knew of any galleries that were hiring and that I had dropped out of school for personal reasons and want to focus on my art. To my surprise, she seemed thrilled by the news and all too eager to get me set up with a receptionist job at the Brighton Museum of Art. I used what I had in my savings to put first, last and a deposit on a little studio apartment within walking distance of the Museum. The place was about as big as my dorm room back at Brighton U and, it was in desperate need of a paint job and new carpet. It wasn't much but it was mine.

Trevor blew up my phone for the first week that I was gone, begging and pleading for my forgiveness, but I eventually decided to just block him. I have no interest in anything he has to say, not anymore. He fucked up, and I don't know if he will ever earn my forgiveness. He doesn't deserve it.

My mother had her assistant bombard me with phone calls and text messages for a while since I had already blocked her number. They were all demanding why she got notification that three years of tuition was reimbursed to her and to call her immediately. I never did.

"Hold the door!" I shout.

I pick up my pace and try to hurry. Just as I get two steps away, it closes, and I smack the doors as I curse.

"Son of a bitch. What a fucking asshole," I growl as the doors swing back open.

A handsome man that can't be older than twenty five is watching me with an amused smirk, and I blush under his gaze, knowing he just heard me. I give him a sheepish grimace as I step inside and hit my floor before settling back into the corner.

"Sorry," I mutter.

"No, you aren't," the guy says with a confident smile. "You thought that I was refusing to hold the elevator for you. That would be an asshole thing to do."

I laugh lightly, glad that he isn't taking the name calling too personally. The last thing I need is to piss off my new neighbors.

"I am John, by the way. Some people do call me asshole, though, so whatever works for you," he says with a friendly wink.

My laugh is a little louder this time as I nod. "I'm Erica."

"Did you just move in?"

I nod as I watch the elevator numbers light up as we rise through the floors.

"Lucky me," he smiles.

"Yeah?" I ask with an eyebrow raise.

He nods sincerely. "Definitely. Up until you, the most beautiful woman that lives in this building is Mrs. Rothchild, and though she is gorgeous for an 87-year-old, I am afraid she is happily married and has declined all of my attempts to take her out."

I let out a surprised laugh as I shake my head. This guy is a character. His green eyes sparkle as he takes a half of a step closer to me.

"So, how about you?"

"How about me, what?" I ask.

"Are you married?"

"Uh, no. Definitely not," I laugh.

His smile widens as he takes another half step towards me. "Good. Boyfriend?"

I flinch slightly before I shake my head. It isn't like I am upset at the fact that I am single. I have never really minded it, honestly. But the reminder of Sebastian picks at a wound that I am trying desperately to close. Every day gets a little better, but I am just not all the way there, not yet.

John smiles, obviously oblivious to my sudden mood change.

"Well, if you are unattached, then I would love to take you to dinner sometime."

I force a smile as I look up at him. He is tall, seems to be in good shape and handsome in the traditional kind of way. There isn't anything about him that sends a thrill through me, and his eyes don't make me feel like they could strip me bare with just a glance. He is average at best but maybe that isn't a bad thing. I seem to take too long to answer because he shrugs casually with a warm smile.

"It's okay to say no. Offer still stands if you change your mind. I am in 4C. Come by anytime," he says before the doors open and he strides out with a kind smile and a wave.

I wave back before the doors shut to take me one more floor up. I am not sure why I hesitated. I mean, he seems nice, and he didn't give off creeper vibes, which is always a good thing. He could be a potentially good time or maybe even a good boyfriend. Not that I think that I am necessarily ready for anything serious, but we probably could have had fun together. He is nothing like Sebastian which should have been the selling point. Unfortunately, I think that was also his biggest downfall.

The NFL combine was two months ago, and the draft is tonight. From all the talk of the sports outlets and commentators, Seb is anticipated to be a second round pick with both the Seattle Crusaders and the Boston Hawks interested in him. Good for him.

I try not to think about him, more often than not I'm not successful, but when I am, those days hurt a little less. Each day I put myself back together a little bit more and more. I'm surrounded by incredible art all day every day, I am making connections in the art community and I'm currently getting dressed for my first ever art show featuring my work. I'm so nervous I could puke and so excited I could jump to the moon.

Alexandra said I had to come up with one more piece to feature tonight. I was stumped for a while. I sat for days in front of a white canvas in the middle of my apartment, trying desperately to conjure something brilliant, something revolutionary. Quickly, I realized none of that mattered, though. The critics would either like my work or not, and there wasn't a thing I could do about it either way. At the end of the day, it was *my* work, *my* art.

So, I let my brush lead the way. Time blurred as my strokes varied in color, shape and pressure and when I came up for air it was like I was awaking from a daze. I glanced down at the finished piece, and my battered heart panged at the sight.

Two captivating caramel colored eyes stared back at me, the whites shining brightly against the harsh contrast of the pitch black background. The normally guarded look I have come so acquainted with is gone, and in place of it, the eyes ooze every feeling that I would imagine run through the mind of the owner. Pain. Regret. Loss. Longing. Devastation. Defeat.

It's all there, maybe not for everyone to see but for me it's as plain as day. I don't know if I channeled it from memories or if I manifested the look entirely, but it is the most raw and real thing that I have ever painted that brings me happiness as well as a nasty twinge of something else.

I thought about keeping it for myself, a memory, a reminder or maybe something more, but quickly decided against it. I was letting it go. Starting fresh, a brand new life, one that I had never dared dream of but am so blessed to be living. No one ever tells you just how lonely it can be when you finally make it.

The TV flashes with images as the narrators ramble on about the draft picks and announcing the newest members of the teams. I don't know why I'm watching it, tonight of all nights. I guess I'm just curious where he is going to end up, who he is going to be playing for. The name 'Sebastian Caldwell' catches my attention, and I practically scramble over to the screen as I watch with bated breath. I missed the first half of what the narrator said, but I don't miss the last part.

"The Seattle Crusaders have picked Tight End, Sebastian Caldwell from Brighton University."

My heart swells with pride and aches with pain simultaneously.

Guess he's moving to Seattle.

I meant to change the channel right then and there, but my thumb stays frozen over the power button when I see that familiar gait stride across the stage, a humble look on his face as he nods and shakes hands with Coach Stanson before they hold up an emerald green jersey with the number 89 on the back and Caldwell scrawled across the top.

He'll look good in green.

Making eye contact directly with the camera, the look that is spread across his face is what has me gasping for breath and quickly turning the TV off. Instead of joy, happiness, fulfilment and pride, all I saw was confliction with a touch of sadness. It was like he could see straight through the camera and into my tiny apartment, which I know is impossible, but I felt it all the same.

Shaking my head and pushing any and all thoughts of Sebastian Caldwell aside, I blow out a breath as I nod my head and slip on my favorite Dolce & Gabanna black cocktail dress and pair it with a pair of black pumps. I decide to do my hair up into an intricate yet sophisticated updo before I work on my makeup. A pang of something sharp hits my chest when I look at myself all done up.

I haven't worn this dress since that amazing date with Sebastian. The one that caused me to meet Alexandra and opened this huge door for me. The one that ended with Trevor finding out about us. It all went to hell from there. I sigh heavily before I push away the hurt that still swirls inside of me. As I make my way out the door to the museum, I need to help set up and make sure everything goes on without a hitch. Tonight, is a big night, one that I will no doubt remember for the rest of my life.

Chapter Forty-Six

Sebastian

I waited until the last possible minute to catch my flight to Kansas City where the draft was being held. Fuck if I know why, but here I am, last minute packing for my mid afternoon flight with the draft only in a handful of hours. I've heard murmurs that several teams want me, and honestly, I'd be happy to go anywhere. It's always been my dream, and I'm this fucking close. Boston and Seattle. That's what people are saying it's coming down to.

They're both so fucking far.

I don't know what I expected after I gave Erica the essential highlights of my entire life. It's not like anyone in their right mind would read that shit and come running back to them, and I made it more than clear to her that we were done despite her efforts. Of course, she never reached out, I blocked her number because it tore my fucking chest out every time, I had to hit decline on that call in the beginning. Now? Fuck. I think I'd give almost anything to see it. Just one more time.

Trevor hasn't brought her around at all lately, not that I would know if they were here when I am out. We still have yet to say a word to each other. What the fuck is there left to say?

Zipping up my bag, a heavy knock comes from my bedroom door before it opens. I glance up to see Trevor staring at me with a raised brow as his eyes flick over to my bag.

"Headed off to the draft?"

I nod as I sling the bag over my shoulder. We stand toe to toe for several seconds before he lets out a humorless laugh and shakes his head.

"Fuck. Are you even going to ask about her?"

"What the fuck do you want, Trev? Did you come in here to gloat? To rub it in? You got the girl. Congratu-fucking-lations. Now let me fucking move on," I say as I shoulder check him and make my way down the stairs.

"Hey!" He shouts as he follows behind me. "Hey!"

I turn to see him right on my ass as he keeps talking.

"Have you even noticed that she is gone?"

My feet halt in place, stuck to the floor like cement. Gone?

"What do you mean? Where'd she go?"

Trevor crosses his arms across his chest as he lifts his chin in the air.

"Are you asking because you care?"

I give him an incredulous look as I cock my head to the side slightly.

"What kind of fucking question is that? Of course I fucking care. Is she okay?"

Trevor shakes his head and drops his arms before running a hand through his hair.

"I hope so," he says on a soft sigh.

"What's that supposed to mean?" I snap quickly, I don't have time to sit here and decipher his bullshit.

"It means, I don't know. She left, almost two months ago. She dropped out of school, cut off contact with her parents, with me. I found out she is working at the Brighton Museum of Art."

Wow. How the fuck did I not know any of this? She is working at the museum? Does that mean she sent her portfolio in? And she dropped out of school?

"Good for her," I say with a nod, doing my best to keep my tone even.

Trevor's eyes narrow. "Is that really all you have to say about that?"

I shrug. "I don't know what else there is to say, Trev. I got a flight to catch," I say as I turn on my heel and reach for the door, pulling it open a few inches before he speaks again.

"I fucked up!" He blurts.

I pause.

"I-I'm sorry. Looking back, it was a fucking asshole thing to do. I was just so pissed. You fucking betrayed me, you broke my trust, the loyalty we shared as friends...I just. I wanted her and I was willing to do anything to steal her back."

Slowly, I turn my head to meet his eyes. He looks fucking scared shitless before he puts the look down and blows out a breath.

"I faked it, all of it. The amnesia. I didn't forget. I woke up in the hospital and remembered it all. I also heard you and Erica professing your love for each other and I-Fuck. I don't know. I lost my mind."

What?

Slamming the door shut with a loud bang, I drop my bag off my shoulder as I spin to face him.

"I'm sorry, Seb. I fucked up. It was a shitty thing to do, to everyone. I'll never be able to forgive myself, and I don't blame you if you don't forgive me either."

"You *faked* it? All of it?"

Trevor swallows as his shoulders slump forward. I don't even have time to think, my body reacts out of instinct. I close the distance between us in a flash and Trevor is underneath me, pinned to the wood floor as I beat the fucking piss out of him.

"You FAKED it!" I roar as my fist crushes against his nose, sending blood spraying across the floor.

"I'm sorry!" He shouts in between hits but I'm too fucking gone to give a shit.

"Whoa whoa whoa!" Slater shouts before I feel two pairs of hands grabbing at me before yanking me off Trevor, but I'm not done with him. I go to charge him again as Slater tries to sit him up but Mikey the ogre blocks my path and pins me to the wall. I thrash like a rabid animal as he does, desperate to make Trevor feel even a tenth of the amount of pain that I have felt over these months.

"Seb!" Slater snaps. "Calm the fuck down and talk to us!"

"He LIED! He ruined fucking EVERYTHING!" I snarl.

Slater and Mikey share a look before facing Trevor. His bloodied face fills with shame as he nods.

"I didn't forget the last two years. I just wanted Erica back," he says softly.

Slater puffs out his cheeks and blows out a deep breath as he puts his hands on his hips and takes a step back, clearly stepping out of this conversation.

Mikey looks at me for a second once my thrashing settles.

"You chill?"

I huff out a rough breath and give him a curt nod before he lets me go. I shake out my arms as I glare at Trevor like I could fucking kill him with my eyes. I fucking wish I could.

"Look, I know I fucked up," Trevor says. "I hurt you, both of you, and I fucking hate myself for it."

"Does Erica know?" I ask.

Trevor nods. "She figured it out just before she dropped out of school. I haven't heard from her since."

"But you didn't think that maybe I needed to hear this information?"

"Would it have changed things?"

"Fuck yes it would!" I shout.

"Like what?"

"Like what?" I ask incredulously. "I would have gone to her, fought for her, for us. You got in between us and fucked everything to hell."

"So? You are the one that walked away from her. I didn't make you do that."

"Trev, man. Shut the fuck up," Slater says with a shake of his head.

"No. This douchebag needs to pull his head out of his ass. I'm not stopping you from going and getting her. You've had months. She's been gone for months, and you didn't even realize it. What's up with that?"

My brows crash together as my jaw clenches, but I don't say anything. Mainly because he's kinda right and I fucking hate him for it.

Trevor reaches behind and grabs a flyer and what looks like a ticket before he tentatively takes a few steps towards me and hands them to me.

"She is in love with you, or at least, she was when she cut me out. So, what are you going to do about it?" He says as he holds out the papers to me.

My eyes flick down and quickly read across it. Erica is in an art show, tonight. And the ticket is an admission to it. I flick my eyes up to him again as I stare at him.

Trevor blows out a breath and laughs.

"I never thought I'd have to convince someone to go after the woman I love. Look, I didn't see it before, but I do now. She didn't look at me the way she looked at you, ever. What we had was special, but with you...she was different. Over these last few months, I've watched her light go out slowly, and I'm shit scared that it's going to snuff out altogether one day. So, I'm stepping aside. I'm letting you have this one chance, this one time. Go after our girl, Seb, and don't fucking let go this time."

Chapter Forty-Seven

Erica

I am a nervous wreck from the moment I get to the museum. You would think that having basically my biggest dreams come true would make me happy and excited, but instead, I just feel nervous and sick. What if they hate my work? What if nothing sells? What if-.

Stop.

I take a deep breath as I drink a glass of champagne in a corner of the gallery and remember what Sebastian told me when I felt this way about sending my work to Alexandra.

What if she loves them?

What if they love my work? What if my pieces do sell? What if my dream is no longer a dream but a reality?

My little self-pep talk gives me the courage I need to float around the room and eavesdrop on what people are saying. I take a deep breath with each group that I come by, waiting for the nasty words of my own insecurities to come spilling out of their mouths, but instead, I have only heard praises.

Who is she? Why haven't I seen her work before? The balance is exceptional. The subject matter moves me in a way that I haven't felt in a long time.

I try to contain my goofy smile and maintain a sense of composure, but I'm too excited! People like my work! They really like it.

I'm practically bouncing on my heels when Alexandra comes up behind me and places a soft hand on my shoulder.

"I am hearing good things, Erica," she smiles.

"Really?"

"Really," she nods. "Especially Caramel Delight. It has already been purchased."

"Wow! That's amazing."

She smiles and squeezes my shoulder, whispering conspiringly.

"It was my favorite."

I glance across the room at the painting of two deep, expressive caramel eyes as a sad smile touches my lips.

Mine too.

As the night winds down, my smile doesn't leave my face. I speak with several people who all praise me and ask when more work will be available. I am blown away at the overwhelming support and admiration that I am currently drowning in. I never would have imagined my life could be this amazing.

I turn on my heel to go talk with Alexandra and freeze as I see a giant of a man in what I recognize as a custom sized black suit with a black shirt and a black tie. *Of course, he is wearing all black.* He is holding a dozen roses in his large hands as he stares at me with a soft look.

"Hi," Sebastian says gently.

I have to physically swallow over the lump that has suddenly formed in my throat before I respond.

"What are you doing here?"

Ignoring my question, he steps forward and hands me the roses.

"These are for you. I don't know if flowers are a dumb thing to give someone for their first art show, but I saw them, and I just...I don't know."

I take them from him and smile softly. His hand brushes against mine, and the familiar burst of electricity rushes through my body.

I want to lean into the touch, to beg him to never let me go. But instead, I take a small step away as I keep my pleasant smile in place.

"Thank you. They are beautiful."

We stand there silently for a few moments just staring at each other as if we are both trying to re-commit the other to memory.

"How'd you get here? Weren't you just in Kansas City?"

"A plane," he says flatly.

I nod. "Well, congratulations. Looks like you are going to need an umbrella where you are heading."

He gives me a sad smile and nods. "Thank you. It's an amazing opportunity."

I cock my head to the side as I take him in. This is everything that he has ever worked for, shouldn't he be more, I don't know, excited? He stands there for a few more seconds before he curses under his breath and shakes his head. Sebastian eats up the space between us until I am wrapped up in his arms. Before I can tell him to stop or back away, he is speaking.

"I'm so fucking sorry. I should have never driven away that night, I should have stayed. I should have fought for you, for us, for our future. I fucking hate myself for walking away. I didn't think I stood a chance. I thought I was standing in the way of your happiness. I thought Trevor-"

"Trevor is a fucking liar," I snap a little too loudly before I glance around quickly before looking up at Sebastian again.

"I know," he says with a slight tick to his jaw. "He told me. This morning. He also told me about the show."

"He did?" I ask incredulously.

Sebastian nods as his thumbs gently caress my cheeks.

"Is that why you are here?" I ask.

He shakes his head. "I'm here because I can't fucking live without you, Erica. I miss you so fucking much, it's killing me. I need you, and I hope to fucking god that you need me too."

"Sebastian," I say softly. I don't know what I planned on saying after that to be honest. Maybe I just wanted to remember what it felt like to say his name on my lips.

"I love you, Erica. So much. You bring out the good in me, you make me want to strive to be better. You *see* me. And I see you. I know that you may not feel the same way anymore, but I can promise, no one will ever love you the way that I do. I can't promise that I'm not going to fuck up again, I'm a man, it's pretty much ingrained in my DNA. But I can promise that I won't walk away, I can promise to stand by your side through anything and I can promise to love you every fucking second of every goddamn day."

My heart is racing at his declaration, and more than anything, all I want to do is to jump into his arms, kiss him and never stop. I try to talk myself down. To remind myself that we might not last, that he might choose to walk away again someday. That not all love stories end in happily ever after.

"Sebastian, you're moving to Seattle," I sigh, my head currently winning the duel against my heart.

"Come with me," he whispers urgently as he takes my hand into his.

I shake my head. "You want me to uproot my life now that I am finally on my own two feet with a job I love and my own place just to follow your new career?"

He bites the inside of his cheek for a moment before he gives me a firm nod.

"You're right. That's not fair for me to ask that of you. I'll quit and stay here with you."

"You'll what?" I shout with wide eyes.

He doesn't answer me though as he pulls his phone out from his pocket instead.

"What are you doing?" I ask warily.

"Calling Coach Stanson to let him know," he says simply.

I practically attack him to get the phone out of his hand before I smack his shoulder. I tuck it protectively to my chest as I take a step backwards and give him a look that lets him know I think he is absolutely certifiable.

"Are you fucking crazy? You just had all your dreams come true not five hours ago, and you're going to throw them all away at the drop of a hat? For me?"

His face softens as he takes another step closer to me and cups my face with his large hand.

"My dreams don't matter if you aren't in them, Erica. The NFL was my dream when I was a kid. You're my dream as a man. I'll do anything to be with you. I'll beg and plead. I'll call Coach right now and tell him I have to withdraw so that I can stay here with you. Whatever you want. Just tell me what you want, baby."

All of my protests die on my tongue as I look up into those swirling pools of caramel. They are practically begging me to answer him. I'm fairly certain that I could tell him I wanted all of the stars in the sky, and he would find some way to get me every last one.

"Don't quit, dummy," I say simply.

He shakes his head. "I won't go without you."

I look around at the beautiful art gallery, adorned with all of my paintings. I look around at the people happily chatting and buzzing around the room and I even watch in the corner as some of my paintings are being packaged for those that have purchased them. I am finally establishing a life for myself. A life I have only dreamed of. It's all within reach. I can't just uproot my entire life for a man. The answer should be easy, right? It's just one little word.

"I don't have an umbrella, and I hear it rains like nine months out of the year up there."

Sebastian lips twitch with the start of a smirk as he nods. "I'll buy you one for every day of the year."

"And I'd have to see if there were any galleries hiring. I now know for sure that this is what I want to do with my life."

"I'll help make some calls."

"And-"

I don't get to finish my last condition before Sebastian cradles my face and crushes his lips to mine. His lips alone cause my body to light on fire and spin my world around. Everywhere his fingers touch, electricity hums its way through my body. He is pouring so much tender passion into this that I swear I could fly away.

When we break apart, he smiles down at me softly as he brushes his thumb against my now swollen lips.

"You are everything to me."

"Everything?" I ask on a soft whisper.

A flash of determination and promise sparks in his eyes as he nods.

"Everything."

I can't help it, I let out a smile, one that practically cracks my face.

"Can we start over?" I ask. "Forget all the bullshit we went through and go back to the beginning?"

Seb nods, a soft smile on his face as he cups my cheek.

"Yeah. You know where the closest washing machine is?"

EPILOGUE

ERICA

5 Months Later

The roaring of the crowd in the stadium is deafening, even if I am in the plush player's box. The crowd is going wild with the anticipation of the first pre-season game that is about to begin. The stadium is a sea of Crusader green, and I am currently a mix of excitement and nerves.

Sebastian and I moved to Seattle two weeks after my art show. I told Alexandra that night, and instead of being insulted that I was turning my back on her and the amazing opportunity she handed me, she smiled, hugged me, and then whispered into my ear, "I'd follow that man anywhere too."

That night I sold five pieces which was really shocking for someone as unknown as me. I like to say that it was because Alexandra put her seal of approval on me, Sebastian said it was because I am just that talented. I think he is just a kiss ass, though.

I was completely taken by surprise when just before we left, Sebastian took my hand and walked to the back of the room where he accepted a packaged piece of mine and paid for it. When I asked him which one he bought, he just smiled softly and I instantly knew that he was the one that bought Caramel Delight.

Sebastian stayed at my apartment with me that night, and we spent the entire night making up properly. The next morning we packed up my apartment, gave my two weeks notice to my building manager, which thankfully was all that was required to get out of my lease, and then we were off to do the same at Sebastian's house.

When I walked through the door, Slater whooped before picking me up and giving me a slobbery cheek kiss. Sebastian quickly yanked me out of his arms, and I kid you not, growled at him.

"Well, I'm glad this dipshit got his head out of his ass and went after you. I was only a few days from swooping in and taking you for myself," Slater teased with a wink.

I smiled slyly at him as I faked intrigue.

"Really? Hmm. Maybe I need to think about this a little more," I said as I took a few steps towards Slater.

Sebastian snarled as he yanked me into his side before placing a possessive kiss against my lips. Slater hooted with amusement, and I certainly didn't mind either. We were interrupted by a knock on the door before someone stepped inside with a box in their hands.

"Trevor," I said as I tried to step out of Sebastian's arms, but the move was futile.

Instead of seeing anger or hurt across Trevor's face, he gave me a small smile.

"Hey, Little Red. How are you?"

I gave him a stiff nod.

"I'm good. You?"

His smile got a little bigger. "Really good."

Without another word he set his box onto the ground and walked towards me but I hold my hand up, stopping him short before he can actually touch me. I'm not ready for that. I don't know if I ever will be. The taste of betrayal is still sharp and bitter on my tongue.

Trevor's smile slowly faded as he nodded his acceptance.

"I'm so fucking sorry. I don't want to lose you forever, but I get it. I'm really happy for you. I want you to have the best of everything, and Sebastian is the best man I know. I know that he will always take good care of you."

"Thanks," I said with a short nod and a tight smile.

"I love you, Little Red," he said softly, almost to himself but I knew he wanted me to hear it because his eyes were focused on me intently.

I've never not said it back to him. Ever. But I guess there is a first time for everything because instead I just gave him another short nod. There was an awkwardness to us now. One that has never been there before. It's a gap between us a mile wide and painfully deep. I don't know if friendships can ever come back from what we went through. I hope so, maybe, one day.

Since Slater and Mikey were sophomores this year, they weren't eligible for the draft. Trev didn't make the draft either, so they will all be back at Brighton next year to get their shot. They all ribbed Sebastian about not forgetting them when he becomes the best tight end in the league, I could tell they were being partially serious, but they will figure it out just like I did. When Sebastian Caldwell loves you, it's for life.

We hopped on a plane a few weeks later and what do you know, it was raining when we landed in Seattle. I officially had to say goodbye to sunny weather and hello to rain.

Sebastian bought a house before we even made it up to Washington and it was the first place we went to when we landed. I was completely shocked. I don't know why, but I was assuming we would be moving into some apartment or condo since the city is so urban, but he found and incredible house, no, a mansion, up on a hill that overlooks the city.

The place has everything that you could ever imagine with an incredible view. I wasn't the only one that was surprised. Sebastian bought it basically online and had yet to see it in person. He said as long as it had room for a gym, a bathroom, a bedroom and a kitchen then it was good enough. When we stepped inside, I had to forcibly close his mouth several times which was so fucking adorable.

I found a job at a local gallery, thanks to a very good phone call from Alexandra to the art director. It's a great fit because there is a lot of flexibility in it so I can travel to most if not all of Sebastian's games with him during the season.

As if we didn't have enough change in our lives in such a short amount of time, we were living in Seattle for barely a month when Sebastian came home with a big fat Harry Winston engagement ring. He proposed to me at home in bed one night because he said he couldn't wait one more minute.

Of course, I said yes, and we are currently planning for a wedding in March when his official free time will begin before the next season. After Sebastian's incessant pushing, I did call my parents. Since they didn't have my new number, they didn't have a way to reach me and were actually happy to hear from me.

My mother seemed very remorseful and had realized all of the ways that she could have handled, well, everything better. I told them that we were engaged and living in Seattle, and she said that they were happy for us. They are planning to come and visit one of these days, but honestly, I'm not holding my breath.

The crowd in the stadium begins to roar as the teams take the field, and I know that I'm bugging some of the players' wives with my excited squeals and clapping but I don't care. My *fiancée* is about to start in an NFL game. That sentence alone feels completely unreal.

Even though it is just a pre-season game, I know that Sebastian is a little nervous. I told him this morning to come out here and take care of business, just like he always does. He smiled and kissed me before he was off and now that the time is here, I'm the one that is nervous.

Nerves and butterflies flutter through my stomach as I watch that green jersey number 89 jog out onto the field.

He's my everything.

THANK YOU

Thank you for reading The Loyalties We Break! I loved these characters so much and I am so happy to announce that this isn't the last you will see of all of these characters!

The Walls We Break is the next book up in The Alphaletes Series, which will be coming out early 2023!

The Walls We Break was actually written before this one and was intended to be the first book of the series but after it was written I just knew that Sebastian and Erica's story needed to be told. Throughout the series you will see a few more characters that you got to know in The Loyalties We Break and who knows, maybe some of them will even get their own story!

Reviews are huge for Indie Authors like me so if you have the time to leave one, I would so appreciate it!

Other books by Katelyn Taylor:

Mariano Men Series:
Inevitable – A second chance mafia romance
Undeniable – A single dad mafia romance
Untouchable – A friends to lover's romance

Stand Alone:

<u>Jagged Harts</u> – An enemies to lovers MMA romance

To keep up with the latest releases, giveaways and more make sure to follow me @katelyntaylorauthor!

<u>Instagram</u>

<u>Tiktok</u>

<u>Facebook</u>

ACKNOWLEDGMENTS

First off, as always, I want to thank my readers from the bottom of my heart. I adore you all and appreciate every single one of you. You taking the time to support indie authors like me means the world and pushes me to bring you better and better stories! To my alpha, Skarlet, you deserve more praise than I can give you. From the minute you made the mistake/decision to be my alpha you have been my damn rock. We have gone through this book until our eyes were raw, we have talked about it until our throats were hoarse and we have thought about ways to make this book what it is today until we were too damn tired to think about anything else. Thank you for being there for me throughout all the craziness. You are the best book step-mother there is!

To my betas, Alisha, Andrea and Lara Jean, thank you so much! You girls are everything! You took my book to new heights with your ideas, opinions and feedback. I appreciate the time and effort you dedicated to making this book a success. Thank you so much for listening to my constant yammering, asking my ridiculously random questions and overall being the best support system! I wouldn't be anything without you ladies!

To my street and ARC team, you all are incredible! Every single one of you made such a difference in the success of this book's release! Thank you for taking the time to read and provide your feedback for my work. It means everything to me, and I am so thankful for all of you who have shared and spread the word about this book as well as my others. Talking with you all about this book has been the highlight of this release for me. I am so happy that you love these characters as much as I do. You all make the difference!